THE HELLBURNER
OF
SOVI

A NOVEL

R. E. Van Rossum

Self-Published by R. E. Van Rossum

This is a work of fiction. Names, characters, places, and incidents are products of the author's imagination. Any resemblance to actual persons, living or dead, events, or locales is entirely coincidental.

ISBN: 979-8-218-92892-6

PRINTED IN THE UNITED STATES OF AMERICA

Cover design by Andrew Day
Book design by R. E. Van Rossum

First Paperback Edition

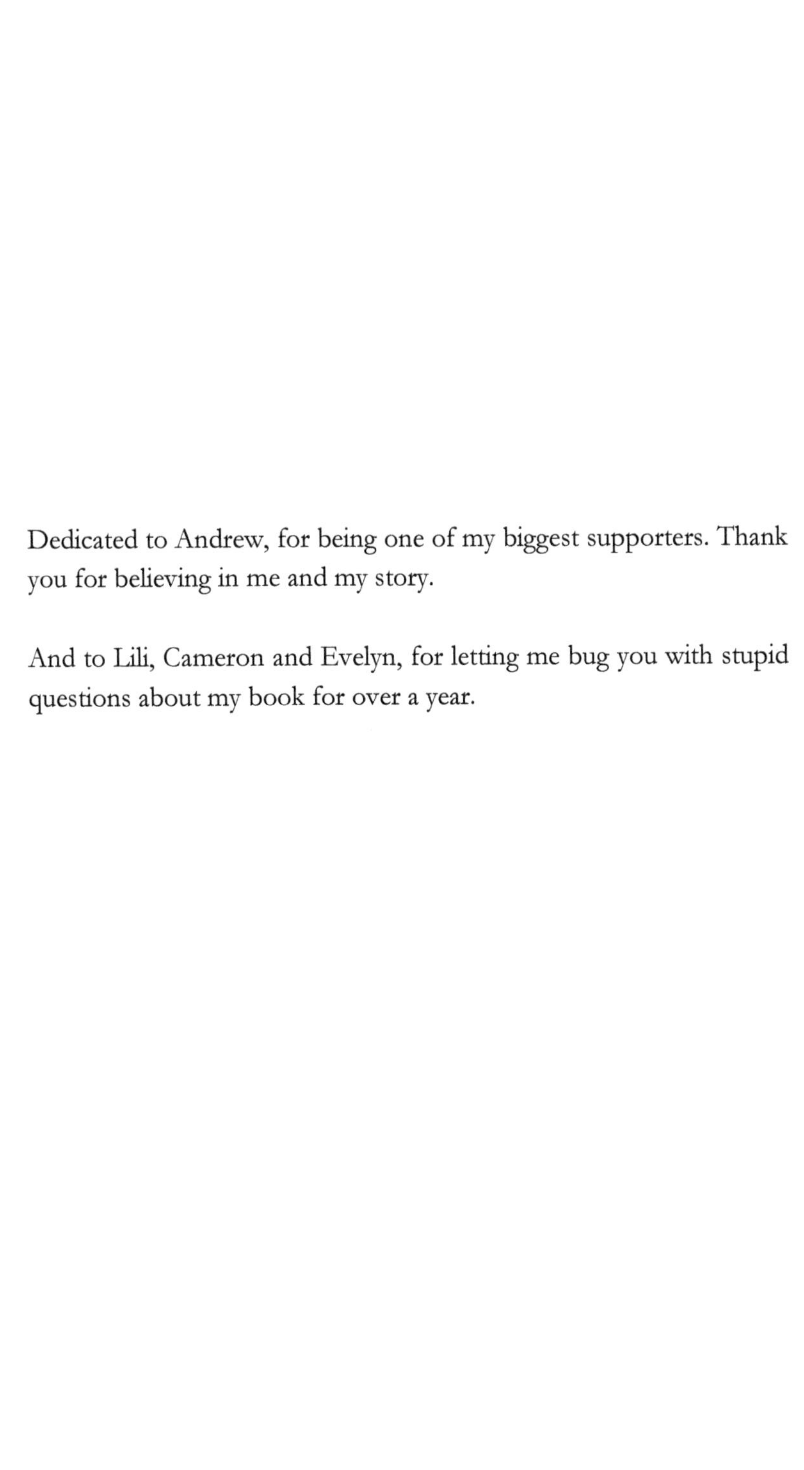

Dedicated to Andrew, for being one of my biggest supporters. Thank you for believing in me and my story.

And to Lili, Cameron and Evelyn, for letting me bug you with stupid questions about my book for over a year.

CONTENTS

Citadelle
Sovi
Vanstead
Aerithos
Selenia
Ra'Sehara
the Chain
Islands

Vyena
Archeandria
Corte

I

PART ONE

ONE

SEAS THE DAY

JESPER

The sailor took a deep breath as he walked down the gangplank, a smug grin on his face as he observed the place he thought he'd never see again. Old memories bubbled to the surface as he inhaled the salty smell of Dobriand Harbor and Archeandria's capital city that stretched out for miles just beyond that. He had been here countless times, and yet the looming towers and sails that graced the horizon never failed to amaze him. It was almost as if he was rediscovering the city every time he stepped off his ship. The familiar sounds of creaking wood and conversation rang in his ears warmly, beckoning the young sailor to join in. And he obliged all too quickly.

"Happy to be back, Jesper?"

Jesper glanced back as his crewmate came down the gangplank. His friend, Ari, grinned at him eagerly, his bright eyes shining gold in the late afternoon sun. Jesper smiled and nodded to Ari, then quickly tucked the tips of his ears under his hair – the thought of anyone else figuring out what he was making his heart race.

"Let's just stop for a quick drink, make the trade, and then get out of here."

The two men walked together into the crowded port, disappearing among the people. So many people swarmed Dobriand Harbor that it was nearly impossible to walk a few paces without bumping into someone. Jesper followed closely behind Ari, pushing through the crowds to get to their favorite spot at the edge of the port: The Southern Cross Tavern.

Being jostled around by the throng of people irritated Jesper to no end; the hundreds of unfamiliar bodies slamming into him threatened to burn through his already short fuse. His skin crawled with unease, like it was warning him to get out before he started a fight. Or worse, someone managed to find out his secret.

And almost as if he predicted it, Jesper collided shoulders with a passing deckhand, the deckhand sending him crashing into Ari. That was all he needed. Something within him snapped, and he wheeled on his heels to yell at the deckhand.

"Hey! Watch where you're going!"

The deckhand stopped suddenly and turned to face Jesper. He growled frustratedly and moved to close the distance between them, towering over the younger man with a menacing glare. Clearly, he wasn't happy to be bothered. "Yeah? And what are you going to do about it?"

Jesper's hand subconsciously moved to the gun that rested on his hip, hidden under the flaps of his jacket. He could feel his fingers twitch over the handle, wanting desperately to satisfy the itch that nagged at him. "Why don't you make a move and find out?"

But even as the words left his mouth, Jesper winced in regret. He knew he shouldn't be saying things like that, not with how intense the naval patrols were getting these days. And the last thing he needed was the attention of any authorities in his direction. Especially right before the meeting.

The deckhand seemed to genuinely contemplate it, his massive muscles rippling with a tension he tried to suppress. Jesper figured the guy had never even considered the possibility that someone else might dare to fight back. But after a moment, the deckhand grunted and walked away, mumbling about 'kids these days not having any respect.'

Snorting to himself in satisfying victory, Jesper turned around to continue to the tavern, almost immediately bumping into another person in front of him. He glanced back to apologize as the person walked by, stopping when he saw who he had bumped into. Removing his hat, he humbly bent down and picked up the small bag that the young lady had dropped at his feet.

"Sorry, ma'am. I didn't see you there."

"It is all right," she replied, smiling gently. Whoever the young lady was, she was brilliant and warm in the afternoon sun, unlike anything he had ever seen before. He was used to the rough and tumble of sailors, not whatever angelic creature was standing before him in that moment. There was something so different about her. Different from the likes of the women he had been raised around, or like the local townswomen who offered pleasure and rest to weary travelers.

What did it hurt to play a little anyway? This was an opportunity he never got out at sea, and there was certainly no shame in being slightly nicer and more charming to a pretty stranger, right?

Handing her the bag, Jesper said, "Here you go. I believe this belongs to you."

"Thank you, sir." He smiled back at the young lady, fingering the hat in his hands. But his attention was averted when he heard his name called by Ari from somewhere in the crowd.

"Jesper! C'mon!"

"I'll be right there!" Jesper began to turn around again to face the young lady. "Sorry about that. That was just my –"

But she was gone.

"– friend."

Jesper frustratedly stuffed his hat back on top of his mass of dark hair and walked away, already mentally preparing how he'd make Ari regret ruining the moment. Ari was waiting for Jesper by the tavern door, rocking back and forth on his heels impatiently. But when he saw his crewmate approach, his face lit up in a huge grin. It was a face that Jesper could never stay mad at for long.

"What took you so long?"

"I got distracted for a moment. Just talking with someone."

Ari raised his eyebrows in genuine shock. "You? Talking to someone? That's a surprise."

"I talk to people," Jesper insisted.

"If you're arguing with them, yes."

"Well, I wasn't arguing. I was having a normal conversation. Like a normal person."

"What a surprise. But we don't have enough time for you to make small talk. You know it won't go over very well if we show up late tonight, and we *have* to get this deal done," Ari argued as they walked into the tavern together, the door's bell announcing their entrance.

"No need to remind me," Jesper snapped. "I'm aware."

* * *

"Jesper, my boy! It is good to see that you're still alive!" the tavernkeeper roared from his spot behind the counter. Jesper chuckled as the tavernkeeper set down his pitcher of beer and rushed to hug him. The warm embrace was something that Jesper would constantly shy away from – there wasn't much he hated more than people invading his personal space – but the tavernkeeper was always so insistent that there was no way to escape.

"It's good to see you too, Nigel. How's business?"

"Oh, you know. It comes and goes in waves. Used to be bursting at the seams in here. Brutal now, though, with the new tax."

"Taxes," Jesper muttered, his nose crinkling in disgust. "You know, that's one of the reasons that I avoid cities. That and all the people."

Nigel laughed. "Everywhere except here, it seems." Jesper couldn't argue with him there. The tavernkeeper walked back behind the counter and grabbed a large glass from the rack that hung against the wall. "What can I get for you today?"

"I'll have the usual."

"I'll do one of those, too!" Ari called from across the room, quickly sitting himself down with a group of men playing cards, a hefty amount of money already on the table. Pulling out one of the wooden stools at the bar top, Jesper watched Nigel make their drinks – two whiskeys that were mixed with hot water and sugar – with impressive speed.

"Just passin' through?" a voice asked beside him. Jesper glanced over to see a rugged young man sitting to his left, the wide-brimmed hat on his head tilted down far enough to cover most of his face. From what Jesper could see, the man looked to be in his early thirties – if Jesper had to take a guess – and his voice was thickly accented in a relaxed, sing-songy kind of way, like he had grown up in the countryside. The man had a smirk tugging at the corners of his mouth, smug and oozing with self-confidence, a small toothpick sticking out from between his lips.

"Who's asking?"

"Just makin' conversation, s'all," the man chuckled, putting his hands up in mock surrender. Jesper narrowed his eyes at him, unable to discern who the man was or what he really wanted.

"Yeah, you could say I'm passing through. And you?"

The man shrugged nonchalantly. "Got nowhere particular to be." He paused for a moment, his gaze resting on Jesper's hat on the counter. "You got yourself a ship?"

"Yeah? What's it to you?"

"She a fast ship?"

Jesper snorted. She was a fast ship, all right. The man took a giant swig of his drink, downing the amber liquid in one go and then roughly placing the glass back on the bar top.

"A word of advice," he drawled. "The Navy's started patrollin' the waters just south of Dobriand Harbor. Hidin' out in the bays along the coast. Crackin' down real hard on … your sort."

"My sort?"

"The, ah … not-so-legal sort."

Jesper couldn't keep a small eyebrow flash of amusement from his face. Whoever this man was, he certainly had an eye for Jesper's line of work. He wouldn't be surprised if the man was in the same business, judging by how quick he was to pick up on Jesper's profession. Jesper let his eyes fall to the glass in front of him on the bar, fidgeting with one of the rings on his fingers. Something about the guy didn't sit entirely right with him. And Jesper rarely allowed anyone to know more about him than he knew about them.

When he looked up a moment later to ask who he was, the man was gone, his empty glass the only sign that anyone had been sitting there in the first place. Jesper hadn't even heard him leave.

Turning over his shoulder, Jesper glanced around the room for the man, his search coming up short as his eyes eventually landed on the door. He couldn't keep the worry from rising in his chest that maybe the guy had bolted to notify the Navy. But, then again, the man's appearance and mannerisms said otherwise. Countryfolk almost never sided with the Navy.

In an attempt to push the worry to the back of his thoughts, Jesper shifted his attention to Ari's poker game, watching the pool of money on the table continue to grow. Jesper used to be notorious for jumping into games whenever he got the chance. But after losing so much money in one sitting that he slept on the streets for a week, Ari wouldn't let him play again. Jesper had claimed that game to be a once-in-a-lifetime stroke of misfortune and would ride that to his grave, but Ari wouldn't hear it. Something or another about being stupid with his earnings. Ari, on the other hand, usually fared quite well in every game he played, but never had Jesper been able to convince him to share the winnings.

Jesper let his gaze slide back to the door as the bell rang merrily for customers coming and going, hoping to spot someone interesting enough to entertain him. Old ship builder? Boring. Port administrator? Absolutely not. But, only a short while later, he was shocked to see the red head of the girl he had bumped into earlier coming in through the door. *What is she doing here?* She made a beeline for a table occupied by a couple of wealthy, clearly out-of-place young men, greeting them with hugs and handshakes.

"Hey, Nigel. Who is that redhead lady over there? She doesn't exactly look like a sailor. Or her friends, for that matter."

"No, certainly not. She's an aristocrat from the inner city, the daughter of a powerful lord. Rumor has it she's engaged to some other stuck-up aristocrat. I try to keep my distance from that folk. They're not the nicest lot by any means, that bunch."

"Engagement?" Jesper wanted to barf. He had given up on the idea of love a long time ago. Just the thought of it threatened to make him sick.

Jesper opened his mouth to continue talking, but he stopped when he saw the girl walking up to the counter to order a drink. He waited a moment for her to approach before turning his head to look at her. "Fancy seeing you here."

"Oh!" she exclaimed, putting a hand over her mouth in surprise. *She sure is a jumpy little thing.* "What are you doing here?"

"What kind of greeting is that? And really, I should be the one asking you that question."

"I am sorry, I did not mean it like that! And I am so very sorry for running into you in the port. That was my fault."

"Eh, no big deal." Jesper waved her off. He took another drink before saying, "The name's Jesper."

"Do you have a last name, Jesper?"

"Why do you want to know?" he joked.

The young lady chuckled to herself and then shrugged. "It did not hurt to ask."

Jesper paused a moment, studying her. "Well, if you must know, it's Jesper Pleiades Kelsey," he finally replied, adding a little bow for emphasis. The young lady just laughed at him. *Good.* She didn't seem to recognize the name.

"What kind of name is that?"

"Don't judge. My parents were weird." Jesper rolled his eyes. "Do you have a name I could refer to you by?"

"Karyna Marfont. It is a pleasure to formally meet you. After practically running you over."

"Can I get you something, Miss Marfont?" Jesper asked, gesturing to Nigel, who was serving a couple at the other end of the counter.

Karyna smiled respectfully but refused his offer. "That is very nice of you, but I am all right. My fiancé would not appreciate me accepting drinks from other men."

"Fiancé, huh? What's he doing letting a pretty girl like you hang out in a place like this?"

"Well, it definitely took some convincing on my part," Karyna giggled, her cheeks flushing when he called her pretty. "And besides, I needed to get out and just breathe for a bit."

Jesper nodded. "Oh, believe me, I get the feeling. But please, let me buy you something. Your fiancé don't gotta know."

Taking a few gold coins from her pocket, Karyna slid them across the bar top to Nigel. "One Scotch, please."

Jesper couldn't help but scoff at her. She was definitely headstrong; he had to give her that. "So, Miss Marfont –"

"Karyna, please."

"Karyna," Jesper corrected himself. "What *is* a girl like you doing down here in a tavern at the edge of the port?"

Karyna just shrugged. "What is a sailor like you doing docked at a port?"

"Fair enough. We're restocking before heading out again," he lied, the words coming as smoothly from his mouth as if he had told the truth. Well, it was part truth. He just was neglecting to mention the whole under-the-table deal that was going down that night.

"And I am just meeting a few friends here for some drinks. I convinced them to go on a little adventure with me."

"This is your idea of an adventure?" Jesper questioned. *Oh, please.* "If you think the tavern is an adventure, then you really have no idea what else is out there, do you?"

"How should I?" She seemed almost offended, like he should have known better. Crossing her arms over her chest, Karyna frowned at him. "So, what is it like, then?"

"I'm sorry?"

"Sailing," she clarified quickly. "Being so far from civilization, with the wind blowing through your hair and the sun on your face. What is it like?"

Jesper shrugged, trying to find the best way to properly describe the feeling that had been giving him life for as long as he could remember. "Well, it's the most incredible thing you'll ever know. But it's not something you can really put into words. You just have to … experience it, I guess."

Karyna frowned, and the glow in her eyes faded ever so slightly. "Oh. I understand."

Jesper studied Karyna's face before moving his eyes to the drink in his hand. Running a hand through his hair, he downed the rest of his drink and said, "But, trust me. It's truly amazing. I mean … it *is* my life, so I feel like that has to count for something."

Karyna nodded, her brow furrowing in disappointment. "I believe you."

"You know, if you wanted to experience it yourself … I'd be willing to make you an offer."

"An offer?"

"You could come with us to the islands. It'll be about a two month voyage, and then you could hitch a ride with someone else right back. Or go anywhere else, for that matter." He couldn't recall ever having invited someone to join his crew on a trip, and certainly not an aristocrat. But Jesper couldn't shake the feeling that she seemed caged, almost. Her eyes looked weary. Maybe even desperate. It was too familiar.

"I … I could not." Karyna paused before the realization crossed her face. "It is nothing against you, though! I do not mean it like that at all! You are a wonderful person, I am sure; I promise it is not because of you! It is just that my father would kill me."

"You think I'm wonderful?"

"Well, no – I mean – I did not –"

"It's all right; I understand." Jesper accepted her answer, dropping the teasing that she clearly didn't pick up on. "My offer still stands, though. After we finish restocking, we'll leave in two days."

"Thank you for the proposal. But what about your captain? I am sure he would not appreciate stowaways."

"I'll take care of that," Jesper said, shrugging nonchalantly. "I'll put in a good word for you with the boss. I'm sure he'll like you."

"Okay, thank you. I appreciate it."

"Yeah. If you decide to come, it's the Fortuyna, Dock 13. We'll leave at noon, with or without you."

Karyna laughed softly and nodded to herself. "I will keep that in mind." Jesper snorted in response, amused by how quickly Karyna was entertained by any given comment. He opened his mouth to reply, but the sound didn't leave his mouth before Nigel slid down the counter to where Jesper and Karyna sat.

"Here's your Scotch, ma'am. My apologies for the wait."

"It was not a problem at all. Thank you, sir," Karyna replied, smiling warmly. She turned to Jesper with the drink in her hands and said, "I should really get going. My friends are waiting for me."

Jesper stood from his stool as she moved to leave. "Oh, yeah, sure."

And then she was gone, and Jesper was left alone again standing by the bar. He slid back into his seat with a long sigh, feeling suddenly very awkward by himself. The room seemed almost darker and colder without Karyna's warm smile, but Jesper tried to drown the feelings with his glass of whiskey. It didn't take long for Ari to come rushing up next to him and steal Jesper's glass away before he could have too much. Jesper hated when Ari did that, acting like his mother. Ari had a habit of caring too much about what Jesper did with himself, which – to be fair – wasn't always the healthiest or safest of choices. And it pissed Jesper off.

Ari glared disappointingly at Jesper before lowering his voice to ask, "What are you doing?"

"Drinking too much."

"Jes, you know that's going to kill you one day, right?"

"Shut up," he muttered. "And give me my drink back."

Ari ignored Jesper's muttering entirely, switching the subject. "Who was that pretty lady you were flirting with?"

"I wasn't flirting, Ari."

"Oh, right. My bad," Ari scoffed. "I forgot about your whole 'love is disgusting, I have commitment issues' thing. If I were you, though, I wouldn't let an opportunity like that pass."

"She might be joining us when we launch in a few days."

Ari raised his eyebrows. "Really?"

"*Might.*"

"Why'd you invite her, though? I thought you didn't like most people."

"Emphasis on the word 'most.' Plus, everyone else on the crew is boring by now. I need something a little new, you know? To keep me from losing my mind."

"I'm not boring," Ari huffed. "Neither is Gen." Jesper grabbed his discarded glass and took another swing of his drink in annoyance.

"Besides you and Gen."

"I don't understand you sometimes."

Jesper chuckled as a smile spread across his friend's face. "Is that why you've stuck around all these years?"

"It is definitely one of the perks."

Jesper sighed deeply before slowly putting his hat back on. He was in no way anxious to get back to the grind after being spoiled with a moment's rest. But he couldn't keep procrastinating forever, as much as he wanted to. "Let's get out of here. We've got a brig to command."

Together, the two sailors rose from their seats at the bar and started towards the door, swerving around the tables and swaying people. One of the people in particular caught his eye, a wealthy young man who couldn't have been more than 25 or 26 who was walking up to Jesper. He was undoubtedly one of those people who thought the world revolved around him, and he seemed very set on telling Jesper that. Jesper watched as the young man, who had been with Karyna, approached him, and he groaned internally at the inevitable interaction.

"Excuse me, were you the one being friendly with Karyna?" the man snapped, coming between Jesper and the all-too-appealing door. *Just great.* Jesper had places to be; there wasn't time for this.

"Depends on who's asking," Jesper quipped. "You know what? I don't really care. Miss Marfont and I were just talking. Can I go now?"

Karyna's friend almost scoffed at Jesper, which infuriated the sailor greatly. "Just talking? Is that so?"

"Eugene, leave him alone," Karyna begged, approaching the two men hastily upon seeing the tension start to rise. "He was not doing anything."

"Oh, believe me, he was."

"Yeah, and what did I do?" Jesper growled. Eugene took a step toward Jesper in aggression.

"Listen here, smart-mouth. You stay away from my fiancée, you understand?"

"Your fiancée, huh? Bit jealous that you're not getting all her attention, wouldn't you say?"

Eugene's face turned bright red and his jaw dropped. "I am not jealous."

"Well, I would agree with you, but then we'd both be wrong."

And before Jesper had time to think, he found a bony fist meeting his left cheek. The punch was weak and harmless, but all the same, Jesper couldn't keep his anger hidden any longer. He retaliated with more force, sending his fist flying straight into Eugene's nose. There was a satisfying crack and a wimpy yelp as blood started pouring from Eugene's nose and his legs gave out from under him. A graceless jumble of limbs floundered around on the floor of the tavern, and any dignity that Eugene might have had previously was now destroyed. The whole tavern was now in an uproar, laughing hysterically at the spectacle. Jesper held back a smirk as he watched Eugene cower on the floor, clutching his broken nose and crying like a little baby.

"Whoops," Jesper snickered.

Karyna seemed almost reluctant to rush to her fiancé's side in the hopes of comforting the whimpering man. Jesper could tell that Eugene was beyond outraged with him, but what did Jesper care anyway. It wasn't like he had exactly the best reputation in the first place. With a grin on his face, Jesper tossed a coin to Nigel and walked to the door. "Here's for your troubles. Sorry for the mess on the floor, Nigel."

"Thanks, son."

"Any time. I'll see you around. Ari, let's go." A brief wave of disgust passed over Jesper as he glanced at Karyna and her pitiful fiancé, thinking back to that time when he tried to chase the same wealth and privilege. Perhaps not with the same lifestyle, but even being comparable to the kind of person Karyna's fiancé was scared Jesper.

Ari raised his eyebrows and shrugged as they walked out the tavern door and into the bustling street. "Well, that went well. Your new friend seemed to really enjoy how you broke her fiancé's nose."

"Shut up."

"Real smooth, too. She'll totally want to travel with us now that you've assaulted the groom-to-be. I should be taking notes: 'How to pick up a chick 101.'"

"Ari," Jesper warned. He could only handle so much of Ari pushing his buttons.

"Yeah, I'll stop talking now," Ari muttered, falling into step next to Jesper. They walked in silence for a few minutes, basking in the sights and smells of the port, before Ari spoke up again. "So … when are you going to tell her?"

"She'll find out eventually."

"You were planning on telling her the truth, right?"

Glancing at Ari from out of the corner of his eye, Jesper sighed and nodded hesitantly. "I will, I promise."

"Right, of course. Why should I have any reason to doubt a compulsive liar?"

"You're mad at me for keeping secrets," Jesper replied, repressing the urge to glance over at his friend. He instead kept his eyes trained on the road ahead of them, silently fighting to control his mind from replaying old memories he wanted to forget. Memories littered with pain and anger and blood. So much blood.

"What gave you that idea?"

"Look, don't take it personally. I keep secrets from everyone, not just you."

"You shouldn't need to keep secrets, Jes."

"'Course I do. It adds a little excitement," he joked to lighten the mood, playfully bumping Ari in the shoulder. "Am I a sinner or a saint? You might never know."

"I'd wager on the first." Ari chuckled softly at him. "And your past –"

"I know what I did in my past. Don't throw it in my face," Jesper snapped suddenly, his demeanor shifting. His past was the last thing he wanted to be talking about.

"Sorry. I didn't mean –"

"No, don't apologize. Just drop it."

"Sure thing."

And so they walked side by side down the crowded streets of Citadelle, Jesper eternally grateful that Ari was willing to drop the conversation. Ari had been around Jesper for long enough now that he should be able to trust his friend without knowing absolutely everything. Because Jesper certainly wasn't going to talk about it. No one needed to know the full extent of his story. And no one ever would.

Leaning in towards Ari, Jesper dropped his voice low to ask, "Do you have the stuff for the trade tonight?"

"Yeah, of course. Why?"

"'Cause we're going now."

"Now?" Ari questioned, a frown tugging at the corners of his lips. "Why? It'll be at least another half hour until sunset."

"We agreed to meet all the way on the northernmost point of the port. It'll take some time to get there." Jesper sidestepped around a pair of merchant sailors walking by, snatching one of the men's coin purses as he passed. The movement was seamless and unnoticeable, and the two merchants continued walking away like nothing had happened. Jesper couldn't help but smile to himself, the twitching urge in his hands to pickpocket curbed slightly. He had grown up into this life; it wasn't his fault if his fingers managed to pick up a few shillings here and a couple valuables there.

If Ari noticed, he didn't mention the stolen purse at all. "Fine. Let's just go, then. Lead the way, Jes."

* * *

In the fading light, the shadows of the alleyway loomed like bottomless pools of darkness. Jesper scanned the narrow path, his eyes flickering over the various crates and heaps of garbage that littered the ground. *Only one exit.* "C'mon. Let's make this quick."

Ari nodded at his side before following Jesper into the alley. About halfway into the alley, Jesper stopped suddenly, his mind firing off warning signs. There was obviously no one here, despite what they had agreed upon originally.

"You're late."

Jesper whipped around at the sound of the gravelly voice, his only exit now blocked. His hand moved to his pistol like it always did when he sensed danger, though he knew if a shootout happened, he and Ari would be vastly outnumbered. "Dregor! How wonderful to see you!"

"You're late."

Were those the only words he knew how to say? Pasting a charming grin on his face, Jesper spread his arms wide in greeting to the smuggler. "Only by a minute! Look, we just got caught up by those officers by the outpost; you know how it goes. The Navy's always tightening the noose."

Dregor only grunted, his gaze turning colder. "Do you have what you promised me?"

"Yeah, yeah, of course." Jesper looked to Ari, who pulled a small cloth bag from his jacket pocket and held it out. "The opium, just as we promised."

One of Dregor's slimy, wiry men stepped forward and snatched the bag from Ari's hand, immediately opening it to check the contents. He sniffed the brown powder, giving a nod of approval to his boss as soon as he recognized the pungent smell.

"And the other thing?"

"The – the other thing …?" Jesper thought for a moment, his eyes widening when he remembered the other request. "Wait, you were being serious?"

"I don't joke."

"Well … so, about that."

Dregor's face didn't move, and that scared Jesper more than anything else. Of course Jesper didn't have what he had asked for; the request had seemed foolish at the time. "You don't have it."

Jesper put his hands up, trying to defend himself. "No, I don't … but, listen! I can make it up to you!"

"You made me come out all this way, risk my business, and you only have half of what I requested?"

Jesper cursed under his breath, his nerves spiking as the air between them began to crackle. He wasn't one to get anxious in these types of situations, but Dregor's reputation preceded him. And not in a good way.

"Give me a month, and I can –"

"You are no man of honor," Dregor interrupted, his voice still even and cold. "Not even worth the spit it takes to insult your name. And here I thought you were an infamous man."

Jesper snapped, his chest going hot with fury. Who was this man to think he could speak like that? *He has no idea who I am.*

Without thinking, Jesper ducked down and ran full speed at Dregor, slamming into the man's torso and taking him to the ground. Jesper could feel his sides and face being pummeled beneath Dregor's fists, but it didn't matter. With the burlier man under him, Jesper began throwing punch after punch. It wasn't until Ari was pulling him off Dregor that Jesper cared to look at the damage he had caused, his knuckles stinging and bruised. The smuggler was breathing just as heavily as Jesper was, and his nose bled profusely.

"You're dead, Kelsey. You hear me?"

"Oh, I'm so scared," Jesper shot back, cradling his throbbing ribs. He was tempted to send his fist flying again, just to prove a point, but it was at that moment that an unassuming naval lieutenant just going about his rounds stumbled upon them.

"What's going on here? Everything all right?"

Jesper immediately dropped his gaze to the cobblestone beneath his feet, picking up his hat that had fallen in the fight and placing it low on his head. "Of course, sir. No problems here."

The lieutenant took a moment to scan the scene before him, undoubtedly noting the bloodied faces of the men in the alleyway. But then he nodded and clasped his hands behind his back. Clearly, he wasn't paid enough to deal with this sort of issue. "Very well. Finish your conversation quickly and get out of here. We don't allow people back in these alleys at this hour."

And then he left, and Jesper breathed a deep sigh of relief. He wasn't exactly in the mood to deal with the consequences of being caught in a contraband trade tonight. Dregor seemed to be thinking the same, his anger temporarily pacified as he turned to face Jesper again. His cold demeanor had returned.

"I feel fit to withdraw from my end of the bargain. You didn't follow through on yours."

"I gave you half. I at least deserve half of what I asked for." Jesper crossed his arms over his chest as the smuggler exchanged muttered words with one of his men for a moment.

"Fine. Half." Dregor tossed a rusty key to Jesper; the key to the cellar where Dregor often stored his illegal goods away from prying eyes. "And you've lost yourself a business partner."

"Nice going," Ari mumbled beside Jesper. Tightening his fists at his sides, Jesper grimaced, internally kicking himself for losing control of the situation in the first place. He had never liked Dregor to begin with, but he certainly made a good smuggler and a good ally. As good as someone could be in a business like this.

But he would take what he could get, even if that meant walking away with only half of the trade and one less smuggler to deal with. At least Dregor had decided against pounding Jesper within an inch of his life.

"Fair enough. But you'll regret it, Dregor. You know I'm one of the best in the business."

Dregor scoffed at him and shook his head. "I'm starting to think that perhaps the stories I've heard about you maybe are true. It's not every day that I get attacked by the other party during a trade."

Jesper's breath caught in his throat. The stories about him were still circulating, seven years later? Suddenly, Jesper felt much less safe than he had a minute ago. "I don't know what you're talking about."

"Sure you do, Kelsey. Everyone's got skeletons in their closet, so to speak. But I'm willing to bet yours are quite literal. And from what I've heard, it's not just a few."

"Those are just stories."

"Every story has some ounce of truth to it. Even the ones as dark as yours."

TWO

REAL GONE

KARYNA

He's going to kill me, she thought as she slid out the back door. Guilt and fear pounded in her gut, threatening to keep her tied down to her life-long home as they had too many times before. So many "what-if's" ran through her head, but she took a deep breath and pushed the thoughts to the back of her mind. She couldn't go back. She wouldn't.

"Karyna. Where are you going?"

"Eugene!" Karyna whipped her head around to see her fiancé standing in the open doorway, looking extremely upset at her unannounced departure. She quickly hid the bag she was carrying behind her back, forcing a fake smile on her face. "I did not see you there!"

"You did not answer my question. Where are you going?"

"Oh, right!" She fumbled for an excuse. "I was just, uh, going to take a walk to the ocean. You do know how much I love the ocean." Karyna could see Eugene eyeing the bag she so desperately tried to hide, his frown growing deeper with each passing second.

"And what are you doing with that bag?"

"I was going to pick up some goods at the port. For Mother. For tonight's dinner," she lied quite horribly. Stepping out the front door of the house, Eugene closed the distance between himself and Karyna. She resisted the urge to take a step backward, instead firmly planting her feet on the road. Eugene narrowed his eyes at her, clearly doubting her story.

"Well, you should not go into that part of the city by yourself. That is where all the dangerous men congregate and prey on unsuspecting passersby."

"Dangerous men?" Karyna breathed, swallowing slowly.

"Thieves, vandals, *pirates*," Eugene elaborated, coming uncomfortably close to Karyna's face. He was obviously trying to intimidate her, and it was working perfectly. But she couldn't let him know that. "To them, you would be the perfect target."

"Eugene, stop it. I know what you are trying to do, and it is not going to work."

"What are you talking about?"

"You are trying to scare me out of going. But I am going." She attempted to remain unwavering in her decision, despite how much Eugene was frightening her.

"Karyna, darling, it is just a few goods," Eugene crooned, his tone suddenly switching from anger to a concerned sweetness. He always did that when he was trying to convince her of something. "I can always have one of my servants run the errands later. We do not spend near enough time together as we should."

"No. I want to go. I need to get out of the house for a bit. You know how it gets when the whole family is around; everyone constantly arguing with each other."

Eugene sighed at her, and his shoulders seemed to sag slightly in defeat. "Then at least let me accompany you."

"No!" Karyna exclaimed a little too quickly. "I mean … I am all right. I promise. I will be back by supper."

"You are not even hearing me right now! Just stop!" Karyna flinched at Eugene's sudden outburst. Taking a deep breath, Eugene attempted to calm himself again and put on a face of compassion once more. "I am sorry, Karyna. I did not mean to – my sincerest apologies."

She wanted to believe in the sincerity of his apology. But his outbursts happened too often to be accidental at this point. "I have to go …"

Karyna turned to leave again, but she stopped when Eugene grabbed her arm. He clutched her tightly, his fingernails practically digging into her skin. His whole body looked tense with desperation, like he was willing to do whatever it took to keep her at home. It was the same look that her parents gave her any time she wanted to go out and explore. The same look that all of her friends gave her when she proposed a little trip to the tavern in the port.

"Maybe you did not hear me clearly. Let me accompany you."

"Eugene," Karyna said, lowering her voice into a warning as strong as she could muster. "Let go of me."

Her fiancé hesitated a moment but reluctantly let go and took a step backward. He seemed to have given up, and while his defeat broke her a bit, Karyna took the opportunity to walk away. Shockingly, Eugene didn't follow her. He didn't pursue her. He didn't even call out to her to make her come back. And that hurt more than anything else. Maybe it was for the best that she was leaving, then.

* * *

She felt her stomach sink with each step she took towards the port, each step carrying her further and further away from her old life. It was utterly terrifying, the idea of leaving everything behind to chase some childhood dream. But, at the same time, it was completely freeing.

Karyna recalled what Jesper had said back in the tavern two days ago: *It's the most incredible thing you'll ever know. It's not something you can really put into words.*

How she longed to experience just that. To see the world. To not be tied down to anyone or anything. It was all she had been dreaming about since before she could remember. Every waking hour, something inside her screamed to leave everything behind and just disappear. Part of her believed her family wouldn't even care. Not really, anyway.

She had always stuffed those urges away into the deepest parts of her mind, trying to focus on the endless responsibilities she had to fulfill at the request of her family. But in just a matter of seconds, a stranger in the tavern had made her more eager than ever. A dream that was impossible to ignore.

The pit inside her stomach grew, to the point where she could have sworn she was going to vomit right there on the road. *Count your steps. Focus on the rhythm of your feet.* Karyna began to listen to the sound of her footsteps on the gravel path, the repetitive thudding. But every time she reached ten, she would lose control and her mind started to wander.

Her mind first went to Eugene's anger and sadness. Then to the lies she threw right in Eugene's face. Then to her excitement about finally being able to see the world for its true beauty for the first time in her life. Then to Jesper.

Something about the young man put her off slightly, something she couldn't quite put a finger on. Something almost … not human. Perhaps it was the accent, thick with the charisma of the southernmost reaches of Ra'Sehara. She hadn't expected to hear it so far from home. Or perhaps it was the fiery glint in his eyes, or the long scar that ran from his eyebrow down his cheek, or maybe it was the menacing pistol and sword that hung at his side. And his effortlessly charming grin, and his golden skin, and that dark hair that fell around his face in long, windswept locks to his jaw. *No.*

Stop it, she scolded herself. What was she thinking? She was scared of him, terrified even. Whatever it was made her skin crawl, a feeling she couldn't push away. But her need to leave was stronger than her fear, and she had committed to following through.

Focus on the path laid out before you. Focus on the sound of the waves getting louder and louder. Focus on anything other than the anxiety you feel. It was the only thing keeping her going. Until she arrived at the port.

A wave of adrenaline shocked her senses as she walked into Dobriand Harbor, her heart beating a mile a minute. She was really doing this. It hadn't truly dawned on her until that point that she was running away, that she was committing the first act of rebellion in her life. Who knew it could be so thrilling? Every ounce of guilt she had carried completely vanished, and the argument with Eugene was forgotten.

As she approached the docks, Karyna sucked in a breath at the sight of all the sails gracing the sky as far as the eye could see. It was like she had entered a white city, each billowing building marked with a unique flag and its own story to proclaim. She hadn't even made it out to sea yet, much less step one foot onto the deck of a ship. And here she was, already falling in love with a life on the ocean.

Dock 13. *That is what he said, right?* Karyna could only hope that she remembered the right number. Walking down the rows of docks, she was bombarded with the overwhelming smell of salt and old wood. Endless seagulls squawked overhead, and various seamen engaged in adamant conversation, carrying crates of food and goods to go across the ocean.

Jesper's friend that had been in the tavern with him that day stood at the end of Dock 13 in front of a magnificent-looking ship. He seemed preoccupied with another crew member, conversing with grand gestures and loud laughter. They evidently knew each other quite well, the closeness between them making Karyna slightly uncomfortable and rude for interrupting their conversation. Nevertheless, she approached the two sailors, internally wishing that she was instead greeted by the familiar face of Jesper.

"Excuse me? Sorry to interrupt –"

"Hey! You're the one who was talking to Jesper in the tavern, right?" Jesper's friend didn't even wait for a response before saying, "I'm Ari, the quartermaster. This here's Deacon, our cartographer."

"It is a pleasure to meet you both," Karyna replied, shaking both of their hands. "Is Jesper here?"

"Yeah, he's right this way. Follow me." Ari led Deacon and Karyna up the gangplank, making a very obvious point to show off the beauty of the ship as they walked. "Welcome aboard the Fortuyna! One of the fastest ships on the Seven Seas, if I do say so myself!"

"Is that so?"

Deacon nodded proudly. "Sure is. And she's seen more battles than we can count."

"Is that supposed to be a good thing?" Karyna muttered under her breath. Ari and Deacon didn't seem to notice.

"And there's Jesper." Ari pointed upward to the main sail, Karyna's eyes straining against the bright sunlight to see where Ari was pointing. Once her eyes adjusted, she noticed Jesper standing effortlessly on one of the beams that the sail was tied to. He looked to be checking the ropes that held down the sail to the mast, before glancing down at the deck and spotting the newly-boarded crew members. Jesper grabbed a loose-hanging rope that was attached to the mast, and after giving the rope a good tug, he jumped off the beam and swung down towards the deck. The long coattails of his leather jacket billowed out behind him as he flew down, looking like a bird dancing on the clouds.

"Likes to make a big entrance as usual," Ari mused. Deacon snickered at him.

"You can't blame him, though."

They both fell silent when Jesper landed swiftly on the deck and made his way over to where they stood. His hair fell gracefully around his face and in front of his eyes, prompting him to push back some of the strands with a hand. A large grin spread across his face as his gaze landed on Karyna standing with his crewmates.

"You made it!" Jesper exclaimed, extending his arms out wide in a warm greeting. He seemed surprised that she was actually there.

"Your offer was too tempting to pass up."

"Fair enough. I'm surprised you didn't stay back. Honestly, I wouldn't have blamed you, either. You seem like you got lucky with a good life. You rolled the dice well."

"Yes, right. You have no idea," Karyna murmured to herself, finding it ironic how dreadful her life really was despite how perfect it looked from the outside.

"Well, now that you're here, welcome aboard the Fortuyna." Elegantly, Jesper dipped into a bow and kissed her hand. Karyna couldn't keep a slight blush from coloring her cheeks. He was definitely charming, but part of her was curious if this was all an act he was putting on for her. There certainly weren't any other women onboard, as far as she could tell.

"Thank you. Is the captain around, that I might introduce myself?"

Karyna heard Ari and Deacon snickering beside her, and she bit her lip nervously. Had she said something wrong? Jesper, on the other hand, flat out ignored her question.

"How about I show you around the ship? It takes a lot of people to get this vessel up and running smoothly, and it would probably be in your best interest to get to know them so you're not lost in the chaos."

"What about the captain?"

"Don't worry about that," he shot back, his charismatic front cracking a bit. So it was an act. Karyna wanted to protest further. She, by no means, desired to get in trouble with the captain for being invited aboard by a crew member she hardly knew. But her thoughts were interrupted when she focused her attention on an approaching man, who walked up behind Jesper and stopped abruptly.

"Captain, we are ready to leave upon your command. Do we have a heading?"

Jesper closed his eyes and released a long sigh, clenching his jaw like he was upset at the interruption. Or perhaps for his cover being blown. Karyna frowned, a sharp pang of panic hitting her senses. *This was a mistake.* Maybe Eugene had been right about the whole pirates and thieves thing after all.

"Set the course for New Haven Port in Sovi, Ozias. We'll leave immediately."

"Of course. Your hat, Captain." The man behind Jesper, Ozias, held out a three-cornered hat, and Jesper snatched it frustratedly and set it on his head in one swift motion.

"Oh, and when we leave port, head as far north as possible. I have a feeling there might be some … obstacles we'd want to avoid to the south."

Ozias nodded curtly and stepped away towards the helm. Karyna's mind was running a million miles a minute, screaming at her to turn back. Furrowing her brow, she opened her mouth to question Jesper, but he quickly put up a hand to stop her.

"Yes, I am the captain."

"But –"

"I didn't tell you because that would jeopardize my crew's work and safety. Especially if you chose not to come with us. You have no idea how much the Navy is itching to destroy our line of business," Jesper explained, as if he was defending himself. But it wasn't like Karyna was willing to hide her growing anger and dwindling patience.

"Your line of business? Which is what, exactly?"

Jesper didn't answer immediately, and Karyna could practically see the gears turning inside his head as he attempted to find the right words to say. Whatever it was that he really did for a living, he clearly wasn't too keen on sharing.

"We, uh … I transport various substances to the ports in Sovi."

"Various substances … like?" Part of her didn't want to know the answer. But he ignored her question, shooting back,

"So what if I am? Doesn't matter to you."

"So you are a pirate," Karyna snapped at him, her hands starting to tremble at her sides. She had been so stupid to think she could run off and do something by herself for once.

"That's a harsh title. I prefer 'smuggler.' Or maybe 'export specialist.'"

Karyna let out a snort, half a scoff and half a huff of anger. "Export specialist? Absolutely not!" She turned quickly on her heels and walked away, trying to put as much distance between herself and this man as possible. Karyna felt an anxious churning in her gut; there was no way she would sail under the command of a smuggler, or pirate … or whatever he wanted to be called.

But then a rough hand caught her arm. He wasn't going to let her leave. He had never planned on letting her leave. "Look, I like you, Miss Marfont. But I can't exactly let you leave and go tell your friends what you've seen. I have an entire crew to protect here."

"You are mental if you think I would willingly sail across the ocean with the likes of you!"

A darkness clouded his eyes as he stared at her. "And what were you expecting? No upright citizen or merchant is going to take you."

"And why not?" Karyna shot back, ripping her arm out of his grasp.

"You're bad luck. There's this huge superstition about women on ships. Causing them to sink. No one else would dare take you."

"So what makes you so *generous*, then?"

"I don't believe in superstition." He said it like it was so simple. But she knew there had to be more to it than that. "I'll make you a deal, though. You accompany me to Sovi. From there, you can take any ship you want. The island is full of ports, and people there are much more willing to take you anywhere in the world you want to go."

"Why would they take me there and not here?"

"Seamen over there are less irrational." *And more dangerous.* She knew the rumors surrounding that country, how it had been borne of convicts and exiles. "No offense or anything, but you folk here are so … skittish all the time."

"Why should I trust you?"

"Regardless of what you may or may not think of me, I don't intend on harming you. I'm just trying to give you an out, just as I always wanted as a kid."

"How noble of you," Karyna mocked, the sarcasm thick in her voice. But at the same time, part of her wanted to believe him. Either he was being downright honest, or he was the most convincing liar she had ever met.

"So, do we have a deal?"

"And what if I say no?"

"You'll have made things much harder for the both of us." He paused, his mossy-colored eyes scanning her face. And as much as she attempted to keep her emotions from her face, she couldn't stop the fear from invading her expression. But it seemed like he couldn't care less. "I'll show you to your quarters, and I'll make sure my men know to leave you alone."

She took a minute to look around, her heart rate spiking again. The deck of the ship had been transformed into a whirlwind of chaos, every man scrambling about to launch the ship from the dock. As much as she had tried to convince herself earlier that she could do this, Karyna wasn't anywhere near prepared. So much could go wrong. After all, the handsome stranger she had met in the tavern had turned out to be a pirate captain, and he was most definitely smuggling illegal substances on the very vessel she was being forced to travel on. What if they got caught? What if the men onboard were less than gentlemanly towards her? *What if I am making the biggest mistake of my life?*

But it wasn't like she had much of a choice in the matter anymore. The captain wasn't going to let her walk away from this; she could only hope that he wouldn't try anything.

"Shall we?" Jesper gestured to an open trapdoor with a set of stairs leading down, presumably towards the sleeping quarters. Taking a deep breath to steel her flaming anxieties, Karyna nodded once. She allowed Jesper to lead the way, stopping at the top of the stairs to look back to the beautiful city she called home. Hopefully, she would see it again someday soon.

THREE

STRANGER DANGER

KARYNA

"I trust you've settled okay?" Jesper didn't wait for a reply before turning on his heel and walking out of the cramped space in the hull reserved for sleeping hammocks. Karyna scowled at him, grumbling to herself about how long these couple months would be. And what happened to that charisma he brandished when they first met? "You coming?"

Karyna suppressed a groan and paused to reign in her frustration before walking out the door to face Jesper again. So much for manners. "What now?"

"C'mon. We're going to the galley."

"What's so important in the galley?"

"Poker." And that was the only answer she got – like that explained anything at all. It seemed he felt too entitled to elaborate, as if no one had ever dared question him before.

Silently, she let Jesper lead her back up on deck and then down more stairs into the galley, where a large group of crew members had already gathered around a table towards the back of the room. Most of the faces Karyna didn't recognize and didn't care to remember. Every one of those unfamiliar faces, though, seemed quite interested as to who she was. Karyna had an itching, suspicious feeling that despite what Jesper had said, several of the men in the room really didn't like the idea of having a woman on board, their mouths turning downward into deep scowls and their eyes boring into the back of her head.

The only person who showed any ounce of excitement to see her was Ari, the quartermaster waving warmly to her from his spot at the table with Ozias and Deacon. Jesper quickly crossed the small room to join them, sliding onto the bench across from Ari, and Karyna shuffled into the standing room behind Jesper to peer over his shoulder at the game.

After some sort of payment to start the game from both Deacon and Jesper, Ozias shuffled the bent and stained playing cards in his hands before passing two cards out to each player. Already, Karyna was lost in the rules and plays. She would never admit it out loud, but she had absolutely no idea what was going on. Eugene had played poker, once, but he told her that gambling was immoral and not a gentleman's game. He refused to teach her.

The betting continued in rounds for some time, with Jesper occasionally tapping the table with his knuckles to signal something to Ozias, until they reached the final round of the game. Deacon had forfeited his cards in the second round, or as Ari had graciously explained, folding. By this point, the pile of gold coins in the center had grown immensely, and Karyna could only guess that it was all of their earnings there on the table. And both pirates were eyeing it with a hungry stare.

"You're awfully confident, aren't you?" Jesper asked after they had both bet everything they had left, his grin not fading. Ari smiled right back at him.

"Not necessarily. But I know you're bluffing."

"Me? Bluffing? I would never."

"Go on, then. Flip over your cards."

"All right. I will." Reaching out, Jesper flipped over his two cards. Ari took a moment to let his gaze rest on the cards before beaming wildly and showing his own. The men standing behind him began clapping him on the back and congratulating his victory, the exuberant cheers growing to fill the hollow space of the room and spilling out into the early evening air.

Leaning down slightly, Karyna asked the captain, "How much did you put on the table?"

"A lot."

"How much is a lot?"

"Probably around two thousand shillings."

"Two thousand?" Karyna hissed, utterly shocked at the amount of money that Jesper was willing to just throw away over a game of poker. *How could anyone be that stupid?* "You are insane!"

"Yeah. I've heard that once or twice." He was so nonchalant about it, and she felt a wave of annoyance rise in her chest. Jesper just shrugged and rose from the table, not even sparing one last glance at the gleaming pile of gold that Ari had claimed. "Follow me. I have someone to introduce you to who I think you'll like."

"How do you even come by that much money?" Karyna pressed as she jogged to keep up with Jesper's long strides. "Surely smuggling cannot pay *that* well."

"What would you know about smuggling?"

"Well, I mean –" He got her there. She really didn't know a single thing about smuggling other than what her father's books said about the unlucky few who had the misfortune of getting caught.

"It's earned wealth. From over the years. I used to get pretty lucky back in the day, and I saved most of it."

"Lucky? Doing what?"

"Different jobs. I was all over the place." Wonderful. He was back to his frustratingly vague replies.

"Like …?"

At that, there was no response. Jesper didn't even acknowledge her as he walked, keeping his focus solely in front of him. They crossed the length of the deck again, back down the stairs that led to the expansive hull and sleeping quarters. Below the main deck, the endless waves seemed amplified by the enclosed space. The entire ship groaned like a dying animal, every wooden beam bending to their breaking point. Very little light filtered in through the small windows on either side of the hull, and Karyna had to blink several times to adjust her eyes to the darkness. Candles hung from ancient metal rungs, lighting a path that ran straight to the back of the ship.

"This way," Jesper directed sharply, striding down the hall. They eventually came to a narrow corridor at the far end of the hull, and Karyna could faintly hear the sounds of metal on wood. As they approached, the sounds grew louder, and with it, her curiosity.

Putting a hand on the door, Jesper pushed the door open and knocked. The person in the room had her back to them, and it didn't seem to Karyna that the girl had heard them enter at all.

"How's it going down here?" Jesper called, raising his voice to be heard above the clanging of nails being driven into the wooden body of the ship. Without stopping her work or turning around, the girl snapped,

"You need something?"

Jesper sure did know how to pick them. "Hello to you, too," Jesper chuckled dryly, leaning against the door frame. He didn't seem phased or deterred at all by the girl's short reply. "I have someone for you to meet. Gen, this is Kie. Kie, Gen."

Karyna frowned. "Actually, it is Karyna."

"That's what I said."

It was at this point that Karyna realized Gen had stopped working. The girl stood before Karyna, her deep blue eyes piercing through Karyna's skin. Karyna fidgeted nervously, feeling as if Gen could somehow see into the darkest corners of her mind with how intense the girl stared at her.

Then Gen suddenly broke into a smile, and she outstretched her hand in a formal greeting. Karyna was taken aback by the girl's sudden change of demeanor, but she moved to take her hand all the same. Gen's hand was rough and calloused, dirt and grime covering every inch of her. The girl was quick to notice Karyna's observation, and she wiped her hand on her pants in an attempt to rid it of the dirt.

"Sorry about that," she muttered. "Nice to meet you, Kie."

"Gen's our carpenter," Jesper explained. "Finest on the Seven Seas, too."

"Is that so?" Karyna raised an eyebrow at Gen, but the carpenter snorted and shook her head.

"Don't listen to him. The captain is prone to exaggerations from time to time."

"I see."

"We will leave you to your work." Jesper leaned out the doorway, a silent request for Karyna to follow along. Gen nodded once, raising a hand to rub the side of her nose and leaving behind a dark dirt smear.

Karyna gestured to the location of the mark on her own face. "Oh, you got –"

"Are you coming?" Jesper called from down the hall, his voice anything but forgiving of Karyna's lack of haste. It was evident that he wasn't going to wait around for anyone at all. Gen snorted as she resumed her work on the hull, telling Karyna,

"You'd better hurry along. The captain's quite the impatient person. It was nice meeting you, Kie."

"A pleasure to meet you, too."

* * *

It wasn't until later that afternoon that Karyna realized just how far from home they already were. The thin strip of land that had lingered on the horizon had disappeared, and Karyna could no longer ignore the pit of dread welling up inside her. Now, it was just her and a handsome but dangerous pirate captain and the open ocean.

"You're probably hungry." Jesper stated it almost like he was commanding it of her. There was no room for argument; she *would* be hungry.

"Sure, I suppose."

"Don't worry, Mr. Colbert is an excellent cook."

Jesper gestured to the large metal trapdoor that led down to the galley, where a rich, warm smell wafted up through the holes in the trap door cover. But as he was mentioning it, Karyna could feel an aching hunger gnawing at her stomach. When was the last time she had eaten anything?

Propping the door open, Jesper bounded into the cramped space with an eagerness that Karyna had never seen out of him before. The ship's cook stood in the middle of the room with a pile of dirty pots and pans in his big arms, an old rag draped over his shoulder that had once resembled the color white. He was turned towards the kitchen, which was attached to the eating area by a saloon door, but he was quick to face the captain upon hearing his heavy footsteps.

"Hey, Jesper!"

"What are you cooking down here?"

"Why don't you go take a look?"

A sly smile stretched across Jesper's face. Taking off his hat and setting it down, he leaned over the counter. "Can I?"

"Sure, help yourself."

And with that, Jesper disappeared into the kitchen, leaving Karyna behind with the cook. Chuckling to himself, Mr. Colbert moved his attention to the young lady in front of him.

"I don't believe we've met before. And you might be?"

"Karyna. Karyna Marfont. Jesper invited me to accompany you all to Sovi when he visited the port's tavern."

"What made you decide to come, if you don't mind my asking?"

"Well … I suppose I needed to get away. And when I got here, I really could not leave, so …" She didn't want to tell him that she had been forced to stay against her will; not with Jesper just an earshot away from their conversation in the kitchen area. Mr. Colbert nodded like he understood what she was getting at, the both of them falling silent and listening to the various banging and crashing sounds coming from behind the closed door. "I have been told that you are a splendid cook," Karyna commented, offering him a warm smile. At the compliment, Mr. Colbert's ears flushed a bright red, and he desperately held back a pleased grin.

"Well, I don't like to brag, but I try my best to please the crew with the food I make. And I do whip up a mean salmagundi."

"I am sure. Jesper spoke highly of you."

Mr. Colbert's apparent shock spread across his face, his eyes widening in bewilderment. "He did?"

"You are surprised?"

"The captain isn't necessarily one to compliment others," the cook explained. "Likes to keep his opinions to himself mostly. Unless he gets downright angry."

"What happens when he is angry?" Karyna asked hesitantly, her voice almost a whisper. The more she was learning about Jesper, the more nervous she was becoming. What exactly had she gotten herself into?

"Oh, you feel it, all right. It hangs in the air around him like a black fog. Best to let him be. He gets unpredictable, that one, and you never know when or who he'll lash out at."

Whatever it was that had made Jesper so bitter and angry, it was clearly big enough to have stuck with him and terrifying enough to want to avoid. Karyna bit her bottom lip nervously in the silence that followed, a hundred questions rushing through her head. And she couldn't stop them from coming out.

"Has anyone ever made him that angry before?"

"Yes. One person."

"What happened to them?"

"She suddenly disappeared one day, and no one knows what became of her. The captain still refuses to speak of her."

"Is she … dead?"

Mr. Colbert hesitated slightly but finally replied, "No, I don't think so. If she was dead, I believe the captain's soul would finally be at rest."

"But he is not satisfied, is he?"

"No. Poor kid; he's got so much of his life yet to live, and he will be forever consumed by what happened all those years ago."

"What *did* happen?"

"No one knows, except for himself and his quartermaster, I believe."

"Ari? What does Ari have to do with any of this?"

But the conversation was cut short when the kitchen door slammed open and out came an irritated Jesper, clutching the ear of a young boy and dragging him in front of Mr. Colbert. The boy was maybe 14 or 15 at most, his dark hair sitting in a curly pile onto of his head and his black eyes darting back and forth in panic. He was abnormally lean for his age, and Karyna's mind immediately pictured the numerous orphan boys throughout Dobriand Harbor who looked just like he did.

Jesper refused to ease his grip on the boy's ear, despite the boy's whines of pain and protest. "What are you doing down here? And eating my men's food?"

"I'm sorry, mister! You can't turn me in, please! I'll leave, I swear! You won't even know I was here!"

Jesper lowered his voice and brought his face close to the boy, making the boy cower in fear. "I'm only going to ask once more: What were you doing in my kitchen?"

"I was hiding from the navy officer, sir."

"Navy officer?"

"He was chasing me, sir."

"You know this vessel has cast off, yes?" Jesper asked. The boy nodded timidly. "And you understand that I don't tolerate stowaways on my ship?" He nodded again. "Then we're on the same page." Once more, the boy nodded and refrained from speaking. Next to Karyna, Mr. Colbert frowned as he stared down at the boy.

"What's going on?"

"I found this stowaway in your kitchen, Mr. Colbert," Jesper explained, visibly attempting to smother his frustration. He finally dropped his hold on the boy's ear, and the boy released a hesitant breath of relief. "Eating all our dried meats."

Karyna bit her bottom lip before asking the boy, "Why are you hiding from the Navy?"

"They want to put me behind bars."

"What did you do?" Jesper hissed.

"Nothing, sir, except take a little food to survive. I was hungry."

Karyna felt her heart ache with sadness and pity for the boy; she had assumed right about who he was. But she still frowned and scolded, "You cannot just steal food."

"Sure you can, if it's survival." Jesper's demeanor shifted suddenly, and he was quick to jump to the boy's defense. Karyna didn't doubt that it was purely because Jesper was a thief himself.

"Well, what are you going to do with him?"

Jesper took a step back to get a good look at the boy, narrowing his eyes as he tried to decide what to do. Eventually, he asked,

"Do you have a name, kid?"

"Newt, sir."

"Well, *Newt*, first of all, stop calling me 'sir.' I hate it. It's *Captain* to you. And secondly, I'm going to give you two choices. You can either spend the remainder of the trip in one of the very spacious cells we have, or you can be my cabin boy and run all my errands for me."

Newt didn't even need to ponder his options before giving an answer. "Cabin boy sounds all right."

Jesper nodded in response, smiling slightly to himself. "Wonderful. Your time starts now."

"What do I do?"

"I'll bring you up to Ari, my quartermaster. He will show you the ropes, but then, you're on your own."

The captain turned swiftly on his heels and marched up the stairs, Newt following behind with a sad sort of look on his face. Apparently, the tour of the ship had been abandoned all together, and Karyna was left standing once more with Mr. Colbert.

"It seems that we are alone once again."

"It does seem that way," Karyna replied, turning her attention back to the cook. Gesturing to where Jesper had just left, Mr. Colbert said,

"That one likes to leave you behind, doesn't he?"

"Yes, it seems that he most certainly does."

"He'll grow on you, don't worry. He's a little rough around the edges, but he cares a lot. He's just not very good about showing it."

* * *

For the rest of the day, Jesper managed to keep himself occupied and away from Karyna. So she busied herself with exploring all the hidden nooks and crannies of the spacious ship. She tried just sitting on one of the barrels along the railing of the ship and watching as the clouds rolled by, but she had long since abandoned that endeavor as soon as she started letting her thoughts wander back to home. Mulling over her current situation was proving to be a horrible decision for her anxiety; it was much easier to keep herself distracted by roaming the ship's cabins.

And when the sun set over the rolling ocean, Karyna was blown away by a beauty she had never seen before. The sky lit up in vibrant oranges and pinks, painting the fluffy clouds in a kaleidoscope of colors. Looking directly at the sun was a risky move, but Karyna couldn't keep her eyes away. The sun shone like a gold coin in the firelight, glinting with a warmth and intensity that Karyna had never seen in the city before. It was like everything out here was magnified, more brilliant than she thought possible.

Even after the sun disappeared below the watery horizon, the stars that appeared shined and sparkled brilliantly. Every constellation was perfectly mapped out in the heavens, a replica ten times the scale of the charts Karyna had studied from a young age.

"The stars are beautiful, aren't they?" Jesper asked, walking up from behind Karyna. She glanced back at him before turning back to look at the countless stars that dotted the night sky. His voice was surprisingly more gentle than it had been earlier that day.

"Breathtaking."

Jesper came up beside her, pointing to a cluster of stars in the sky. "You see those stars over there? That's the Cirripedia constellation. And the brightest star, over on the top right, that's Cataryna."

"That one there?"

"Yup. It's where you get your name. Cataryna is one of the stars that we use for navigation. It always rises at exactly true east and sets at true west, and when it's at its highest point in the sky, it sits right over Sovi on the horizon."

Karyna nodded quietly to herself, mentally taking note of everything he was explaining to her. How her books had failed to inform her of how Cataryna was a navigational star for sailors baffled her; how much else about the world was she missing?

"And at the beginning of the new year, Cataryna will come to align perfectly with the star Shéaspar in the heavens, marking the beginning of St. Elyor's."

"Oh, I studied that holiday in my classes!" Karyna exclaimed, getting extremely excited that she actually knew what Jesper was talking about for once. "But my family never celebrated it."

"Why not?"

"My family despises anything … not normal. Anyone Gifted, anyone not human, they are looked down on by my family." She hated having to admit such beliefs. The further she could distance herself from the ideals of her family, the better.

Jesper didn't seem to enjoy hearing that as much as she didn't enjoy telling him. Quite hesitantly, he asked her, "And do you share those sentiments?"

"Me? Oh, no! Certainly not."

"Good." Releasing a sigh of relief, Jesper chuckled, leaning down to rest on the railing. "You know, you picked a good night to come out here. Sometimes, when the weather's real bad, and the clouds are hanging pretty low, you can't see the stars at all."

"It would make for amazing sunsets though, I am sure."

"Oh, yes."

"Back home, I always used to love looking out over the city and watching the sunset light up the whole sky in bright colors. But this – this tops it all."

"I'm guessing you don't get out much?"

"Not really," Karyna admitted. "Eugene always liked having me around to keep him company. And he is not much of an outdoors person."

"He sounds like an awful person."

"You do not even know anything about him!"

"Oh, believe me, I've heard quite enough." Jesper fidgeted with the rings on his fingers, and Karyna studied him for a minute before letting her eyes rest on the tattoo that circled his bicep, now uncovered by the absence of his jacket. The black ink was intertwined in a way that reminded Karyna of waves on the ocean.

"That tattoo on your arm. Where did you get it?"

"Oh, this old thing? I got it years ago, back when I joined the Brethren Court. It was supposed to represent strength and protection, you know, when people actually believed that inking their skin protected them from misfortunes." He chuckled to himself like the whole idea of it was stupid. "Besides, most pirates have some sort of tattoo. You kinda look pathetic and spineless if you don't."

"Is that so?"

"Sure is."

"Well, what about Ari? I do not see any tattoos on him."

"He does, believe me. He has a compass on his chest, so you can't really see it."

"Ah, I see." She smiled, bringing her gaze back to the starry sky. "I hope I do not have to get one."

"Naw, you'll be fine. Unless you want to become a pirate, that is."

"Right," Karyna replied, unable to stop her face from crinkling up in disgust. That was never going to happen if she had anything to say about it. "I think I will pass, thank you."

"When we get to the port in Sovi, I wouldn't tell any of the sailors that you're from the city."

"Why not?"

"Men from the sea don't exactly take well to city folks. There's this … stereotype that everyone from the city is haughty and pretentious."

Karyna frowned. "But we are not like that at all! I mean, I suppose some people are, but not me."

"And you'll likely become an easy target."

"For what? Stealing?"

Jesper paused a moment, his eyes flickering over to her. "Not necessarily … just, for your own safety, maybe don't mention the city."

"Okay."

"Great." Jesper turned his attention once more to the horizon that stretched out before them, and Karyna took the chance to glance at Jesper again.

Typically, she was one to pride herself in her abilities to decipher other's emotions, but for whatever reason, Jesper was impossible to read. His face seemed neutral, almost peaceful, but Karyna was wise enough to know that he was most definitely deep in thought.

A gentle breeze danced on the air, pushing against the hair that almost shielded Jesper's face completely from her. And in a split second, Karyna noticed something that made her heart skip a beat. She had to be dreaming. Or seeing things wrong.

Jesper seemed to sense her shock, his eyes darting to meet hers again, though he remained otherwise motionless.

"Your ears …"

"You can't tell a living soul, or I swear, you will wish you were dead," he snapped, his voice low and threatening.

"But I thought the elves died out centuries ago –"

"Slaughtered by men. We didn't just 'die out.' Get that distinction through your head."

"You are an elf –"

"*Half*-elf, yes."

"… How are you still alive?"

"We're not all extinct. Not yet. Those of us that are left, we do what we can to survive. Hiding. Running."

"Are you going to kill me?"

Jesper turned suddenly, the utter shock evident in his demeanor. "What?"

"Is that why you wanted me to come and forced me to stay? So that you could lure me away and kill me?"

"Why would you think that?"

"The stories I was told as a child … elves would torment men, giving them bad dreams and causing illness, and then eventually kill them."

A smirk tugged at Jesper's mouth, but Karyna couldn't figure out for the life of her what was so amusing. "And that's what you think I am going to do to you."

"Yes?"

"Well, it seems there is quite a lot you don't know about my people, then."

A sharp pang of embarrassment slammed into Karyna's chest. "You must think me ignorant and stupid."

"Most humans are, yes."

"I am not like that, I swear."

"And I am not like the stories say."

In humiliation, Karyna's eyes fell away from Jesper's gaze. He had proved his point, very effectively at that.

"I just … I have so many questions. I cannot believe elves are real."

"Maybe another time," Jesper replied shortly, his jaw tightening as a long sigh escaped out through his nose. "That's much too depressing a topic for such a beautiful night."

Karyna wanted desperately to push for answers, but she knew it would be in vain. Jesper seemed set on moving from that conversation, his demeanor noticeably more tense than before. She tried her best to do as he wished, but her mind was absolutely reeling. She was standing next to what quite possibly remained of the elves, pureblood or not, and she was completely terrified. Jesper's race was supposed to be extinct, their forces subdued in the Great Purge. But if the elves were still around, did that mean that other creatures like dragons and mermaids existed? And what of the legends of the Gifted? Were they real too?

Reaching under his shirt, Jesper pulled out a brass compass that hung around his neck. He popped the top open and glanced at the needle before nodding, satisfied with the direction in which they were headed.

"That is a gorgeous compass."

"Thank you." He held out the compass for Karyna to see, and she found herself in awe of the intricate engravings along the top and sides. "It used to be my father's, back when he worked as a deckhand at the port. Right before he died, he gifted it to me."

Karyna felt a twang of guilt and pity. She shouldn't have brought up such a touchy subject. Sometimes she forgot that not everyone was as fortunate as she was to have a family. "I am sorry."

"You don't need to apologize. It's been years, and my crew is my family now."

"You really care about all of them, don't you?"

"Of course. It's my job to protect them and look out for them."

"And even if it was not?"

"That doesn't matter." After a moment, Jesper rose from his position against the rail and patted the wood lightly with a hand before turning to leave. "Well, I've got to get some rest. We have a busy day tomorrow, so I suggest you do the same."

"All right. Thank you."

Jesper just shrugged and grunted in acknowledgment. Then he turned and began walking away down the stairs to his cabin. But at about halfway, he stopped and looked back up at her. "Oh! And one more thing."

"Yes?"

"Don't freak out if you hear little noises in the sleeping quarters. Sometimes rats get onto the ship from the port. They shouldn't bother you, though." Karyna's eyes widened in nervousness, making Jesper laugh heartily. "I'm joking, I'm joking. They're only in the cargo hold."

That didn't do much to ease Karyna's worries, but Jesper was already walking away again, laughing to himself. It was going to be a long night.

FOUR

INTERESTING CONCEPT, POOR EXECUTION

ARI

The few days at port had been dreadfully long and horribly boring, and despite Ari's constant begging, the captain had refused to leave even slightly early. But they were finally taking off, and Ari couldn't hold back the excitement he felt of the sea breeze blowing through his hair. He could never get enough of the ocean. A handful of days on land was too long, and to think, that had been his entire life only a few years ago. He could barely remember the countryside life he had led with his family before he found Jesper half-dead on the beach that one morning.

Secretly, it scared him that he struggled to remember the names of his siblings and mother. After all, his siblings had only been infants and toddlers when he had left, some of them not even born before he was gone. So he had taken to repeating their names over and over again in his head when he was running errands for Jesper. *Sabien, Kerani, Leo, Parisa. And the youngest … what was his name again?* Momentary panic flooded Ari's senses as he scrambled to think of the name. *Kaj.*

It had been so long since he had last seen them. He knew that they still lived in his childhood home right off the shore of Vyena, so it wasn't like he couldn't visit them. But it was hard to find the time to travel out there, and there was no way that Jesper would go out of his way to take Ari home. And as far as Ari was concerned, his loyalties lay with his captain.

"Earth to Ari. You done daydreaming over there?" Jesper asked. "We got a crew to take care of, remember?"

"Right. Sorry, Cap'n."

"I just wanted to make sure that you didn't lean too far over the rail. I'm not in the mood to deal with a man overboard just yet."

It was at this point that Ari realized just how far he was leaning over the edge of the ship. Apparently, he was a little too eager to be back on the ocean.

"What are you talking about?" Ari joked. "A man overboard always adds a little excitement."

"That's true, but if it was you falling in, it would be me who'd have to jump in to get you."

"Jesper, you're literally the cap'n. If you have an issue with jumping into the water, then we have a major problem."

Jesper laughed and bumped Ari in the shoulder playfully. "Oh, shut up."

"I think you might have to reconsider your career choice. You could always be a shipbuilder in the yard."

"Yeah, right. I'd be bored before the week is up."

"Tavernkeeper?"

"In your dreams."

Ari wanted to continue their banter, but they were swiftly interrupted by Deacon, who was perched in the crow's nest high above the deck.

"Captain, there's a ship on the horizon! Two o'clock!"

"Who is it?"

"Navy, Captain."

"How far off?"

"About twelve miles! It would take them at least three hours to catch up to us in this wind if we didn't raise our sails."

"Well, what are you waiting for?" Jesper yelled as he peeled his eyes away from the ship that was moving dangerously fast toward them, pacing quickly down to the main deck from the helm to stand beside Karyna. "Put us into the wind! The faster you move, the faster we get away!"

Ari hardly had a moment to question why Deacon was up there in the first place instead of Nyssa, the usual lookout, before he had to start yelling at the deck hands to get them moving. Most of the men were just as eager to pick up speed, and the whole deck of the Fortuyna was thrown into a whirlwind of frantic sailors. Remaining close to the wheel of the ship, Ari glanced to Jesper, who stood below him on the deck and simply observed his surroundings.

But despite the chaos that ensued around them, Jesper refused to show his panic. Ari knew that, in reality, the captain was internally freaking out, but on the outside, his face was stone cold. He could tell that Jesper was deep in thought, trying to plan his next move. And Ari figured it was worth picking Jesper's brain, regardless of his responsibilities to maintain control over the scrambling crew.

Ari bounded down the stairs from the helm, momentarily losing sight of Jesper and Karyna. But as soon as he emerged from the crowd of crew members, he realized that Jesper had disappeared. Karyna stood by herself on the deck, looking slightly terrified and completely out of place.

"Hey! Kie!" Ari approached Karyna, and her face lit up upon seeing him. "Where'd the cap'n go?"

She simply pointed towards Jesper's cabin, and Ari could faintly see a light flickering from the small window. Of course he had retreated to his cabin. Jesper was always one to disappear in times of distress.

Ari didn't hesitate to stride over to Jesper's cabin and walk right in without knocking. As soon as the door opened, Jesper shot up from his seat at his table and glared at Ari.

"What did I tell you about knocking?" Jesper snapped.

"That's a good question. Maybe you should refresh my memory."

"What is it?"

"I want to know what your plan is."

"You assume I have one."

"What are you talking about? You always do," Ari protested, chuckling nervously. But Jesper exploded in anger and fear, his voice rising to a threatening volume.

"I don't know, okay? I don't know why the Navy's after us! I don't know how to avoid them! I don't know what to do!"

"And that's why we figure it out *together*!" Ari matched Jesper's volume, trying desperately to keep his captain's hope alive. "How do you expect to know all the answers if you didn't even get a full education as a child?"

"But I'm supposed to!"

"You're supposed to what? Have all the answers?"

"Yes!" Jesper roared. "I'm the captain! The crew looks up to me! I'm supposed to protect them! How can I do that if I don't even know why the Navy is coming after us?"

Ari suddenly stopped short, confusion clouding his mind. "Why *is* the Navy coming after us?"

Jesper placed his hat on the table and ran a shaky hand through his hair to push it out of his face. He started tapping his knuckles on the table, his old habit that he had picked up from poker years ago. His stress was finally starting to show, and part of Ari couldn't help but feel somewhat relieved. Jesper was gradually opening up to him.

"What do I do, Ari?"

"Well, right now we're fine, right? I mean, the Fortuyna is the fastest ship on the seas. So –"

"So we get to Sovi, and then we disappear."

"Exactly!" Ari snapped his fingers and pointed at Jesper excitedly. "So now –" Ari grabbed the hat and placed it back on Jesper's head "– how do you put it?" He brushed off the front of Jesper's leather jacket. "Right. You have a brig to command, my cap'n."

Jesper gave Ari a small smile before clearing his throat and stepping back out onto the deck of the ship. The crew seemed to sense his commanding presence, and they immediately stopped racing about the deck to wait for a new order. It was almost supernatural, the silence that hovered over the crew. They clearly respected Jesper, and for good reason, too. He took care of them, something that was often hard to find in the smuggling business.

And now they were looking to him for what to do next. Ari could tell that they were scared. Scared of the vessel that was chasing after them. The crew wanted answers. So they waited for Jesper's advice, hoping beyond hope that he could find a way to get them out of their terrifying situation.

But before Jesper even had the chance to begin addressing his crew, Ari noticed a sudden movement out of the corner of his eye, and turning his head, realized that it was Karyna storming up to him and Jesper. She had an angry glint in her eyes, and Ari found himself holding his breath in anticipation. There was no way this would end well. "What did you do?"

"I didn't do anything!" Jesper exclaimed, his face betraying his utter shock at the fact that he was being yelled at. He was used to people just accepting his command quietly and obediently.

"Well, you are clearly lying because the Navy is chasing after us!"

"I don't know why they're after us, okay?"

"Are there illegal substances on this vessel?" Karyna suddenly asked, reigning in her fury.

"What?"

"Are you carrying drugs?" she asked again, enunciating each syllable.

"Yes!"

"Oh, no, I cannot get caught!" she exclaimed, her eyes wide and frantic. She looked like a caged animal. "I have never done anything wrong in my life! I cannot start now! My life would be ruined if I was caught by the Navy!"

"Hey!" Jesper exclaimed. He grabbed Karyna by the shoulders to gain her attention. "We're not going to get caught!"

"You do not know that!"

"Yes! I do! And besides, it'll be a fun little adventure."

Karyna shook her head fiercely. "No! This is certainly not my idea of a 'fun little adventure!'"

"What do you think an adventure is? A walk in the park? It's supposed to be dangerous! We're supposed to take risks!"

"Well, I did not sign up for this!"

"Then you're clearly on the wrong ship, woman!" Jesper made wild gestures at her, his patience obviously wearing thin. Karyna gawked at him for a second, completely in shock, before yelling back,

"You think I do not know that?"

"Good! Just making myself crystal clear!"

"Oh, believe me, you are!" Their faces were practically touching, but neither dared be the first to back down. It was so silent among the rest of the crew that Ari could hear his heart racing inside his chest, and he resisted the urge to cover his chest with his hand in an attempt to muffle the pumping.

Jesper and Karyna had miraculously stopped screaming at each other, and Ari didn't realize that he was relishing the quiet until Jesper broke the silence once again.

"Ari, get her out of here. I can't think when I'm being yelled at."

"Me yelling at you?" Karyna screeched. "What do you think you are doing to me?"

"Ari!" Jesper yelled over Karyna, his voice almost turning to a whine. Ari released a long groan before stepping towards Karyna, lamenting his forced involvement in the escalating argument. He knew enough not to be surprised by Jesper's demands, but, nevertheless, he couldn't help feeling slightly bitter toward his captain.

"C'mon, let's get you down into the hull. Don't make this any harder than it has to be."

Gently grabbing Karyna's arm, Ari began to lead her away from Jesper. But Karyna, still seething, wouldn't let Ari's job be easy. She leaned in toward him and hissed, "Why do you let him walk over you like that? You do not need to listen to him."

"He's my cap'n. I obey him out of respect."

"Yeah, well, he is not my captain." When Ari made no reply, Karyna ripped her arm from his grasp and snapped, "Take your hands off of me."

Ari obliged, and surprisingly, Karyna willingly made her way away from the bottom of the stairs of the helm. Risking a quick glance behind him, Ari saw Jesper still standing by the stairs with Ozias at his side. The captain's face had relaxed back into its usual composed expression, and Ari took that as an improvement from the yelling match that had occurred just seconds ago. Karyna, on the other hand, refused to let go of her frustration. Every movement she made was abrupt and sharp, fueled by her anger towards Jesper. And, of course, she was the one that Ari had to deal with. How Jesper had managed to find such an unbearable companion was beyond him.

Still not exchanging words, Ari helped Karyna open the hatch to go down into the hull. They descended the steps, Karyna only slightly ahead of Ari, and began to make their way around the corner to the room where Gen was working. But just before he disappeared down the hall, Ari could feel a pair of eyes burrowing a hole into the back of his head. He turned around and met gazes with Deacon, who remained at the top of the stairs. Deacon seemed to offer a silent apology; his brow furrowed with pity for Ari's miserable task. Ari returned the gesture with a small smile, eternally grateful for Deacon's sympathy. There were few crewmates on the Fortuyna that Ari felt particularly close with, Deacon being one of them.

When Ari turned around again, Karyna was nowhere in sight. He assumed she must have found Gen's workspace, so he resolved to retreating back up the stairs. There weren't many places to go down in the hull, so as long as Karyna wasn't getting into trouble, she would be fine. Gen would take care of her and calm her down. The carpenter was exceptionally good at that sort of thing.

"Gave up on her?" Deacon asked, chuckling.

"She's with Gen. She'll be just fine."

"You never saw her go into the room, did you?"

Ari bumped his friend in the shoulder playfully, shushing him as they walked away from the hatch door. "The cap'n doesn't need to know that!"

"All right. I'll add that to my already endless list of favors you owe me for keeping your secrets."

"Since when do you keep track of anything besides the ocean?"

"Since I met you."

* * *

The crew had returned to their normal bustle, preparing the ship to take full wind. Nyssa was back in the crow's nest, and Newt had his hands full with loose lines and the most confused expression on his face. Jesper had moved to the helm with Ozias, and they consulted one of Deacon's various maps as they huddled close together. Ari knew that Jesper was simply buying time until he returned from escorting Karyna, but Ari was in no rush to deal with Jesper's irritation. He had no doubt that Jesper was still secretly fuming from the argument, and even one misspoken word or misstep would land him in the path of Jesper's fury.

"Is the cap'n still upset?"

"If you're worried about getting yelled at, don't worry. You'll be all right. The captain likes you, if you haven't noticed by now."

"I know," Ari muttered. "I just don't want –"

"Ari! There you are," Jesper called from the helm, gesturing for Ari to join him. "Come here. I need your opinion on where we should land."

Deacon nudged Ari, and Ari reluctantly obliged, moving to the helm. If Jesper noticed Ari's unwillingness, he ignored it. He had returned his focus to the map in front of him, occasionally glancing at the navy ship on the horizon through his telescope. Clenching his fists, Ari ascended the stairs and stopped behind Jesper, remaining silent.

"What do you need?"

"Like I said, come look at this. Where do you think we should land?"

Ari glanced at the map, only half paying attention to ports Jesper had marked. He quickly pointed to a bay on the coast of the mapped island and stated, "Well, Pressons Landing is always a safe option. Clary could help get the officers off our tails."

"No, not Clary." Jesper was quick to dismiss Ari's suggestion. "You know I haven't seen her in ages."

"But you asked for my opinion."

"Not that one," he muttered, not taking his eye away from the telescope. Ari huffed and suppressed a retort, instead choosing to keep Jesper's temperament as calm as possible.

"What do you think is best, Cap'n?"

"I was thinking Emden Harbor. It's secluded enough to keep the ship in the bay for a period of time until we can leave again. And the dockmaster, Fenix, is good people."

"But that harbor is on the far side of the island. It'll add at least a few more days to the journey."

"If we don't get caught, then it's worth the extra couple days."

"Your call," Ari said, shrugging nonchalantly. He knew that when it came down to it, Jesper would always have the final say. And he had learned to trust Jesper's judgment. Jesper was fast on his feet and brilliant when it came to street smarts. It was like watching a king lead his people, the way Jesper commanded his ship. Confidence and courage radiated off of the captain, and Ari couldn't tell if those sentiments were superficial or not. That was another thing about Jesper. He was good at acting. Almost too good. Every day, it was a mystery as to whether Jesper would reveal his true emotions to Ari or not. Ari would have thought that seven years of being the best of friends would change that, but, at this point, the idea of Jesper actually opening up to Ari seemed like a pipe dream.

"Ozias, set our heading for Emden Harbor. Keep ahead of the Navy as much as possible. We don't need another skirmish with them now."

Ozias nodded and moved behind the wheel, Ari and Jesper watching him work. Ari waited for Jesper to move back to reading Deacon's maps before he asked, "You nervous?"

"About what?"

"It's been seven years since you had a skirmish with the Navy, Jes. And I think I'm understating it when I say that your last encounter wasn't pleasant."

"For both of our sakes, let's hope that encounter remains the last," Jesper said, standing up straight and resting his right hand on the hilt of his sword. His eyes scanned the horizon before them, only glancing over when Ari spoke.

"I can't even remember the last time we had to fight anybody. I think I'm a little rusty."

"Try not to worry about it too much. Keep a smile on your face, too," Jesper muttered, demonstrating with his own cheeky grin. "The crew can sense when we're worried. Doesn't help with morale."

"Right, yeah. A smile." Ari found the notion a lot easier said than done. When faced with the very real possibility of death, smiling wasn't the first thing that came to Ari's mind.

"I'm sure you can manage. It's not too difficult."

"Easy for you to say."

Ari could tell that Jesper wanted to make a snarky reply, but, for reasons unknown, the conversation was dropped. Picking up the discarded telescope, Ari tried to distract himself by staring intently at the horizon. But the silence was killing him. Ari dropped the telescope from his eye and looked to Jesper.

"So, you're telling me that if you had to fight the Navy, you wouldn't even be a little nervous?"

"I never said that."

"You don't seem nervous anymore."

"Yeah. I'm just good at faking it. And if I was fighting the Navy, no, I wouldn't be nervous. Because I could beat them all," Jesper said with a smirk. Ari returned the boast with a look of disbelief.

"No, you couldn't." Taking the telescope, Ari pointed to Jesper with the instrument. "*You* don't even know how to deal with a lady from the cities."

"Get that out of my face."

"It's in my hand, not your face. There's a difference."

"Just move it," Jesper muttered, pushing the telescope away forcefully. For a minute, Ari was worried that he had upset his captain. He couldn't tell if the tension he felt was a trick his mind was playing on him or not. At least, not until Jesper started chuckling.

"You're right. I don't know the first thing about women."

Ari laughed. "But the Navy you could defeat single-handedly."

"Right."

It felt good to laugh with Jesper for a moment in time. Instances like this were always bookended with trouble, and Ari was by no means looking forward to what lay ahead. They couldn't run forever, no matter how much Jesper wanted to believe that. So, it was a countdown. A countdown till the next sign of trouble. The calm before the storm.

FIVE

I REGRET EVERYTHING

JESPER

Jesper had gone to bed that night relatively satisfied with his day's work. Sure, he had had some rough spots – the new cabin boy and the Navy chasing their tail, to name a few – but he still felt somewhat relaxed as he slipped into bed. Something about having his own cabin and a real bed instead of a hammock was so comforting. It was surreally quiet that night, as if the whole world was holding its breath for a coming storm. And the storm coming was bigger than Jesper was prepared for. *Way* bigger. And just when everything seems to be going the way you want, life decides to throw a curveball.

"Jesper!" Ari burst into the cabin late that morning, as per usual, jolting Jesper awake. Jesper sat up quickly in his bed, still half asleep and reeling from his latest nightmare.

"What?"

"You've got to get out here right now! We have a problem."

Jesper groaned and fell backward onto his bed, squeezing his eyes shut like it would block out the entire world. "Don't we always have a problem?"

"A big problem. Get dressed, too."

And just like that, Ari was gone again. Part of Jesper believed that it had all been a dream, but then again, Ari had never sounded so anxious in his life. For Ari to be that nervous, something had to be truly wrong. So, Jesper jumped up and dressed fully as fast as he possibly could before racing out of the room. And no sooner than he had stepped foot outside of the doorway, he stopped short and stared. The sails, every single one of them, had been slashed from top to bottom. They were catching no wind. *They were catching no wind.*

Jesper bolted up to the front helm, scanning the horizon for the navy ship that was following them. It didn't take him hardly two seconds to spot the ship in the lingering wisps of morning fog that still hovered over the surface of the water. Now, instead of being twelve miles away, it was more like two. Jesper rounded on Ari, his anger untamable at this point.

"Where was the crew who was supposed to keep watch last night? Were they not doing their jobs? Are they blind?" he roared at Ari.

"I don't know. They should have been keeping watch. Nyssa Lovelle was in charge if you want to check with her."

"Go find her. And find me the cabin boy as well."

Nodding, Ari sprinted down the stairs and away into the hull of the ship. Jesper took a deep breath and ran a shaky hand through his mass of wavy locks to calm himself. It would be significantly more difficult to get out of this one now.

He walked over to the ship's wheel and took over for Ozias, hoping that taking control of the ship would help steel his nerves. They were within firing range of the Navy's cannons, which was never an ideal circumstance. Of course, he had skirted around many encounters with the Navy before, but never had it been this close. Too close.

Within a couple minutes, Ari had returned with the crew's lookout and cabin boy. Both of the crew members seemed to sense that they were in trouble, neither daring to look Jesper in the eye. Clearing his throat, Jesper waited until Nyssa peered up at him before addressing her. He chose to speak calmly but sternly, hoping that his reigned-in anger would prompt Nyssa to open up to him honestly.

"I'm going to give you one chance to tell me the truth. What happened last night?"

"You mean with the sails?"

"No, I don't see anything wrong with the sails. I don't know what you're talking about," he replied sarcastically. But, realizing that Nyssa didn't pick up that he wasn't being serious, Jesper exclaimed, "Yes, the sails!"

"I don't know, Captain."

"What do you mean you don't know?"

"I never saw anything," Nyssa explained. "I did fall asleep for a little, but it wasn't long."

"You fell asleep. When you were on watch." Jesper huffed and fought back a laugh of frustration. This day was not off to a good start, and with each passing minute, Jesper was getting more irritated. Nyssa didn't seem to want to elaborate, so Jesper chose to move to Newt, who fidgeted nervously as he stared at the approaching navy ship. Jesper pushed up the sleeves of his shirt and folded his arms over his chest. "Did you do this?"

"Me?" Newt whipped his head back to look at Jesper, a wave of shock passing over his face. "No! I swear I didn't!"

"How do I know you're not lying?"

Jesper was almost certain that Newt couldn't have anything to back him up. After all, it was the boy's first day on the job, and it didn't seem to be any coincidence that the sails were destroyed that night. If anyone on the ship was guilty, it had to be Newt. He had no alibi. But, apparently, Karyna didn't agree with that.

"He is telling the truth! He was with Gen and myself the whole night." Karyna and Gen bounded up the stairs, coming at just the right moment to Newt's aid. Jesper took a pause to study Karyna's face, finally settling on the notion that she wasn't lying. And Jesper's judge of character was rarely wrong.

"Then who destroyed my sails?" The following silence was palpable, and Jesper had to suck in a deep breath to repress his fury. "No one. No one at all?"

Not a single person dared respond. In a huff of frustration, Jesper stormed off, pushing past Karyna and Gen without a second thought. He needed space. And time to think properly. Because everyone was being way too bothersome.

Jesper slammed the door behind him, eternally grateful for the blissful quiet and solitude that the cabin provided. It was now that he could finally breathe again, if only for a brief moment. And a brief moment it was.

"Captain?"

"Gen," Jesper groaned, not rising from his chair or lifting his head from his hands to look at her.

"Sorry to bother you."

"Is there something wrong?"

Gen snorted. "Why do you always assume there is something wrong?"

"Because no one ever comes in just to make small talk with me."

"Fair point."

"So, what's wrong?" Jesper pressed, taking a moment to rub his temple before looking to Gen. The carpenter pursed her lips together before shrugging nonchalantly, her arms crossed over her chest.

"Oh. Nothing. I was just hoping you knew what to do. Since, you know, everyone's kind of waiting for your instruction."

"I'm working on it."

"Yeah. Right." Nodding, Gen moved to leave. But something made her hesitate. "One question. Why'd you go through all the trouble to bring her along? It's an awfully suspicious coincidence that we're being pursued right after you invite a landsider from the cities onboard. And if she's the reason we're being pursued by the Navy, are you really willing to face off against the Navy just because you wanted to bring some pretty girl to the islands?"

"I needed the change, you know?" Jesper said quickly, his eyes dropping to the table. But Gen apparently wasn't willing to accept that answer.

"No. Why did you *really* bring her along?"

Jesper hesitated. He hadn't signed up for a conversation like this. And how much could he really trust Gen? But when he glanced back up, Gen was looking at him with such genuine curiosity.

"Back in the tavern, Kie told me about how she wanted to explore the world but she couldn't escape her old life. And I just … that was my childhood, too."

"You were also raised incredibly rich and were stifled by your parents?"

"No, not quite like that," Jesper quipped. "But, growing up, I wanted to escape my old life, too. And I couldn't. I wanted so badly for someone to come and pull me out, so I figured I could be that someone for Kie. If that makes any sense."

"She must be extremely grateful to you for that."

Jesper pressed his lips together before admitting, "She … doesn't know."

"You should tell her."

"Maybe in another life."

"Why would that be so hard to do?"

"Later, Gen," Jesper shot back, trying in vain to shut down the conversation.

"But –"

"Jesper!" Ari burst through the door, his eyes wide as saucers. Jesper attempted to repress an annoyed sigh.

"Why does no one know how to knock?"

"Cap'n, I think we've got bigger things to worry about right now," Ari argued.

"Like what?"

"Come see for yourself."

Bolting out the door after Ari, Jesper gawked at the ship that glided along beside them. The white sails alone were double the size of the Fortuyna, flapping elegantly in the ocean breeze. Everything about the vessel was pristine, from the flag down to the sailors themselves, all embroidered with gold and shimmering in the noon day sun.

Growing up, that had been all Jesper ever wanted. As a child, he would read stories of legendary naval officers and their glorious victories in battle. And for a kid with nothing, the glory of serving in the Navy was the dream of a lifetime.

Standing on that deck, staring at the beauty and extravagance of the ship, Jesper couldn't help but feel a sense of awe and, at the same time, utter worthlessness. How was it that some people could have such glamor when people like him couldn't even come close to half of that?

"Oh, whoa."

He could only muster out so much. Ari, on the other hand, was less preoccupied with the splendor of the ship and more worried about their bigger issue: being arrested by the Navy. "Jesper, they're going to board. What should we do?"

"Oh, right. Yes." Jesper pinched the bridge of his nose, trying to fully bring his attention to the current problem at hand. His crew was looking to him to protect them, and he couldn't let them down. "Have the crew return to their posts and stand down. I'm not losing any men today. Kie, I want you and Newt to follow me down into the kitchen. You'll hide there until I come back to get you."

"But –"

"No, don't argue with me. Trust me. I'll handle this."

Karyna seemed deeply troubled by this command, but she reluctantly obeyed when Jesper grabbed her hand and pulled her towards the stairs. Newt followed closely behind, the three of them hurriedly descending into the dining hall. Mr. Colbert stood behind the kitchen counter, wiping off the tabletop absentmindedly. He clearly had no idea what was going on.

"Captain? What's the matter?"

"We're being boarded by the Navy. Stay down here with Karyna and the cabin boy –"

"It's Newt, sir."

"Not now," Jesper snapped before turning back to address Mr. Colbert. "I'm going to hide them in the kitchen's storage space. If any lieutenants come down here, you don't know that either of them are hiding in the kitchen, you understand?"

"Of course, Captain."

"Jesper, wait –"

"Karyna, get in the closet. Now."

Gently, Jesper guided Karyna and Newt into the tiny storage space. Karyna's eyes betrayed her concern and worry, but Jesper knew there was nothing more he could do for her than try his best to protect her. He owed her that much.

"I promise that no harm will come to you, okay? Everything will be all right," he promised. Breaking eye contact with Karyna, Jesper slammed the door shut and bolted the lock, apparently much to the surprise of Karyna on the other side.

"Jesper? Jesper, unlock the door. Please!" When he didn't respond or obey her pleas, Karyna started banging on the door. "Jesper! Open the door! Please open the door! Jesper!"

She sounded like she was two seconds from breaking down into tears, her voice laced with desperation and fear. But he couldn't open the door. It was for her own good.

Pocketing the key, Jesper turned to return to the deck. Mr. Colbert looked extremely upset at Karyna's distress. Jesper sighed deeply and told the cook, "Trust me, it's for their safety. I'll come get them once this is all over."

The cook could only nod in response. Then Jesper left, his heart unsettlingly hurt at Karyna's cries. But her voice eventually grew quiet as he walked away, and he pushed the feelings down. He had bigger things to focus on, bigger problems to solve.

* * *

"Ari, quick, hand me your scarf," Jesper insisted once he reached the helm, holding his hand out. Ari complied immediately, untying the worn brown scarf from his belt and handing it over. His eyes still fixed on the navy ship, Jesper hurriedly tied the scarf around his head, making sure that the fabric properly covered his pointy ears. If he was coming face to face with an officer of the law, Jesper didn't need them knowing who – what – he was.

The navy vessel was close enough for the sailors to throw ropes over and tether the two ships together. Nothing could be done now but stand and watch as the sailors prepared to board the Fortuyna. With a sinking sensation in his stomach, Jesper squared his shoulders and approached the plank where the naval officer was crossing. No one could know that, internally, Jesper was panicking and scrambling to find a way out of the situation. Every thump of the officer's boots on the wooden plank twisted Jesper's stomach into a tighter knot, only stopping when the officer stood before him on the deck of his ship.

"Well, well, well. What have we here?" The officer took a moment to look around, his eyes lingering on the shredded sails. A commander, by the looks of it. He had a smug grin that made Jesper want to punch him in his perfect face, but Jesper simply crossed his arms over his chest and frowned.

"What do you want?"

"I received an anonymous tip that there was contraband being smuggled onboard. So, I thought I'd stop by and take a look."

"How very kind of you."

Jesper glared at the commander as he walked around the ship, inspecting everything within his arm's reach. None of the crew members dared to breathe as the commander's eyes passed over them, as if releasing a breath would somehow reveal their darkest secrets. The commander didn't walk more than ten steps before stopping and turning to face Jesper. He seemed satisfied with what he had seen, coming back to where Jesper stood near the gangplank and placing his hands behind his back.

"All right, I've seen enough. You're coming with us."

Two of the commander's lieutenants approached from behind Jesper and grabbed his arms harshly. In surprise, Jesper whipped his head around to glance at the lieutenants and tried to rip his arms from their grasp. Their hold was iron strong, making it nearly impossible for Jesper to get out. Jesper could feel his stomach drop and his heart rate begin to race. *This isn't good.*

Ari seemed to sense Jesper's panic, and he moved to attack the lieutenants. But the commander was quicker. No sooner had Ari taken a step forward when the commander whipped out his gun and pointed it at Ari's head. Ari froze, surrendering from his mission of rescuing his captain.

"No one move, and no one gets hurt. Understand?" the commander asked coldly, prompting Ari to nod in reluctant obedience. Seeing the gun aimed at Ari disrupted Jesper's panic, and his demeanor shifted to fury with the flip of a switch.

"Touch my crew," he growled, "and I will tear you apart with my bare hands. I swear to that with my life."

The navy commander turned his smug face on Jesper, forgetting entirely about Ari. In one swift movement, the commander strode over to Jesper and sent his fist flying into Jesper's gut. Jesper doubled over, groaning in pain and gasping for air. The wind was knocked from his lungs, and he felt as if he had been shocked to his very core. A sharp, searing pain spread from his stomach to his chest, burning with an intensity that almost brought tears to his eyes. The only thing keeping him on his feet was the grasp the lieutenants had on his arms.

Leaning down to whisper in his ear, the commander hissed, "I can do whatever I want."

Jesper kept his head down and his face hidden by a curtain of hair, staring at the wooden planks beneath his feet rather than the punchable face of the commander. But when he dared glance at the man leaning over him, Jesper noticed that the commander's eyes were fixed not on his own, but on the compass that hung around his neck.

It was barely visible, tucked away under his shirt, but the sunlight reflecting off the gold surface beckoned the commander. And the commander couldn't help but reach out and pull down on the compass, snapping the chain that held it around Jesper's neck.

"Hey! Give that back!"

"Now this is priceless. Where would someone like you come across this beauty?"

"It was my father's!" Jesper rasped, fighting furiously against the lieutenants holding him down. "That compass belongs to me! Give it back!"

"You know what? I think I'm actually going to keep it. It'll sell quite well in the city."

"You can't do that!" Jesper watched in desperation as the commander pocketed the compass, knowing that there was nothing he could do. "By all means, take what you came here for, and get off my ship. But give me back the compass."

"Oh, don't worry, you'll be coming with me."

"You can't arrest me!" Jesper roared. "You have no proof of anything."

"I suppose you're right. Men, search the ship!"

On request, the commander's sailors spread out around the ship in search of illegal substances, harassing the crew and upturning anything they could get their hands on. Their bright uniform jackets littered the deck, making Jesper's crimson shirt stand out blatantly against the sea of blue. The commander watched them work for a minute before turning back to Jesper.

"You know, it's quite a pity, the state of your vessel. You should really take better care of it."

Jesper knew he was referring to the sails. "We were sabotaged. By your anonymous informant, no doubt."

"Sabotaged?" The commander feigned surprise. "Well, who is your mole?"

"I don't know."

"Why don't you come out, darling, and show our friend here?" As he spoke, Nyssa stepped forward, the corners of her mouth tugging upward into a sly smile. She didn't hesitate to walk up to the commander and wrap an arm around him, planting a kiss on his cheek.

"It's good to see you too, dear."

"Surprise!" the commander exclaimed as Jesper's eyes widened in shock and disbelief. Nyssa, of all people, was working with the Navy? She had joined the Fortuyna's crew almost a year ago, and never once had she shown any loyalties outside of the crew. But that didn't stop Jesper from internally kicking himself for not seeing it earlier.

"You're dead, Nyssa. You hear me?"

"Oh, I'm shaking in my boots right now."

Neither Nyssa nor the commander seemed even slightly fazed by Jesper's threats. "Well, now that we have everything cleared up, let's wrap this up and head home. What do you think?"

"I think that sounds like a wonderful idea, Phineas." The commander, Phineas, squeezed Nyssa tightly and softened his gaze, as if he had forgotten where he was or what he was here to do. Then he glanced at Jesper, a hand still wrapped around Nyssa's waist.

"Isn't she just extraordinary? A Shadowjumper, too!"

"Oh, stop, Phineas," Nyssa giggled. "You flatter me too much."

A Shadowjumper? Jesper had never actually met someone Gifted before. "You're … Gifted?"

"How else did you think I could do this so easily?" Nyssa scoffed, gesturing to the ripped sails. Phineas squeezed her tighter before bragging,

"What? You thought the Gifted were just stories? The world's a lot bigger than you think, pirate."

"You have no idea," Jesper muttered under his breath, the comment going thankfully unnoticed by Phineas.

Eventually, Phineas's sailors had returned empty-handed and somewhat dejected. They were visibly hesitant to report the unfortunate news to their commander, only one of them speaking up after working up the courage. "Commander Prescott."

"Yes?" Phineas wouldn't even turn his head to look at his subordinate.

"There is nothing on board, sir."

"You checked every inch of this vessel? And found *nothing*?"

"Yes, sir."

Phineas was furious with the report and apparent lack of contraband onboard. Stomping over to where Jesper stood, Phineas grabbed the captain by his shirtfront threateningly and pulled him so close that Jesper could feel Phineas's breath on his face. "You may have bested me this time, but I swear to it that I will catch you red-handed."

"I would like to see you try." Jesper couldn't keep a smile from spreading across his face. Phineas knew that Jesper was carrying illegal drugs and weapons, but without proof, there was nothing he could do. And Jesper enjoyed that a little too much.

Phineas threw Jesper down, Jesper's knees buckling and sending him crashing to the deck. His work was done, so, without another word, Phineas took his men and crossed to his own vessel. The crew was left in silence, disheveled and in complete disarray from Phineas's search.

* * *

No one moved until the navy ship had moved away from them, everyone in shock from what had just happened. Jesper released a painful sigh of relief as the navy ship glided away, grateful that he hadn't lost the life of a crew member. In all honesty, he had expected Phineas to kill at least one of his men.

"Jes, are you okay?"

Ari rushed to Jesper's side suddenly, trying to help pick Jesper up. But Jesper gently pushed his friend away, the throbbing pain in his stomach too intense to stand. Besides, he didn't want to burden Ari with his insignificant problems.

"I'm fine, I'm fine. Go check the cellar in the kitchen. Make sure Karyna is all right."

"Jesper, no. You're my priority, not Karyna."

"Ari. Go," Jesper commanded. "I'm fine."

Reaching into the pocket of his pants, Jesper pulled out the key to the cellar and slipped it into Ari's hand. Reluctantly, Ari obeyed and left Jesper's side. Deacon was quick to replace Ari's absence, offering Jesper a hand without uttering a word. This time, Jesper obliged and took the cartographer's hand, groaning as he came to his feet. He still couldn't stand fully straight, but it was better that the crew saw him on his feet than not at all.

"I'm sorry, Captain."

Jesper just sighed and shook his head, dismissing the apology. There was nothing to be sorry for. Not now. He wasn't going to let Phineas get away with trashing the ship and then leaving.

"Jesper!"

Karyna bounded up the stairs to the helm, Newt and Ari close behind her. Her eyes were wide with panic as she ran up to him, clearly confused about what had just happened. She seemed to study Jesper a moment before lifting her hand and smacking him across the cheek, her hand making a crisp slap as it met his face. The silence that followed was deafening, and the throbbing in his cheek was completely fogging up Jesper's ability to retaliate. He couldn't even process what had happened, his mouth parted slightly with shock.

"You promised we would not get caught!" Karyna protested.

"I know."

"What did they want?"

Jesper frowned to himself, his mind lingering on the abnormal weightlessness around his neck in the absence of his father's compass. "It was just a tip from a source. Someone knew we were smuggling."

"Who?"

"Not sure," Jesper huffed, not caring to tell her who had really tipped off the Navy. She didn't need to know he had messed up.

"I cannot believe you are still alive after pulling a stunt like that."

"Yeah, well, I'm just as disappointed as you are, but we don't always get what we want, do we?" he replied sarcastically. Karyna snorted and lowered her head, her ginger-colored hair hiding a small smile that had begun to tug at the corners of her mouth. Jesper allowed himself to smile slightly, trying to push away the sudden guilt he felt burrowing a hole in his chest. "We have to follow them."

"We … what?"

"They took something from me." Jesper wanted desperately for Karyna to understand him. But he knew that she would never comprehend why he would risk his life for a compass. "I need to get it back."

"Do you really need to, or are you just telling yourself that?"

"I'm sorry. I need to."

There was another moment of silence as Karyna became lost deep in her thoughts. Then she nodded, swallowing in nervousness. "Okay."

"Ari, have the men repair the sails as quickly as possible and then make headway for Emden Harbor."

SIX

BLOOD IN THE WATER

ISA

She couldn't close her eyes. Not without seeing his compelling hazel eyes staring back at her. She wanted to scream at him to leave her alone, but no matter how much she tried, he never disappeared. He was always there, taunting her, threatening her. Yelling at her, blaming her for the deaths of a million innocent lives. Lives he himself had taken. *I wasn't the only one*, she wanted to shriek. *You can't blame me for having ambition and wanting nothing more than to be seen.*

In a sudden fit of anger, she threw back the sheets and slipped out of the bed. She swore that she would go mad if she laid there for even one minute longer. Walking from the dark room, she rubbed her face in anxiety and exhaustion. It had been too long since she last had a decent night's sleep, so long that she couldn't even recall the last time she had slept peacefully. She just needed time to think, time to figure out what to do. Because she couldn't keep living like this. It was tearing her apart.

"What's wrong, love?"

She whipped around in surprise to see the figure of a man standing in the door frame to the kitchen, illuminated by the silver moonlight streaming in through the window. The man who she told herself she loved.

"Nothing. I'm fine," she reassured him. "I just can't sleep."

The man stepped toward her to wrap her in his arms, but she backed away. He frowned at her recoil, worry lines creasing his forehead. "Something is troubling you. Did you have another nightmare? Do you want to talk about it?"

"No."

"You can't keep pushing me away like this."

"Just … just give me a minute, Gyles."

"All right."

They had been together long enough for Gyles to recognize when she needed space, and tonight, she needed it more desperately than ever. She felt like she couldn't breathe, like she was drowning in an overwhelming wave of worries, of lost hopes and dreams. But she had to get through it alone; she had come to realize that years ago. No one could help her but herself.

After spending a long while pacing back and forth around the room, she walked into the kitchen where Gyles sat reading and pulled up a chair next to him. She wasn't surprised that he was still at her place, reading at such a dreadful hour in the morning, as he often liked to spend the night close by to comfort her when she woke from yet another nightmare. He was used to this routine. So, without saying anything, he moved his chair closer to hers and wrapped his arms around her. But, in the suffocating silence, despite the comfort that Gyles's embrace should have brought her and had in the years past, she couldn't get rid of the pit growing inside of her. Her restlessness and dissatisfaction were only intensifying with every passing minute.

"Do you ever wish that you could do anything you wanted?" she blurted out, unable to keep the question to herself any longer. For a moment, she thought that he hadn't heard her until he replied,

"What?"

"Imagine you had all the riches and all the power in the world right at your fingertips. Wouldn't that be incredible?"

"Love, you can already do anything you want," he murmured.

"No, I can't."

"Why not?"

"There is one person who is in my way."

"Then you stop them first." He made it sound so easy. But he didn't understand. He would never understand that the one person on the entire planet who could stop her was … untouchable. She loathed this person with her whole being, but at the same time, he was her heart's deepest desire. It was all so confusing, and she knew that she would never gain the world without him on her side. Because she knew everything about him. Even down to the most absurd, tiniest details.

She knew that he was left-handed, that he had a habit of tapping surfaces with his knuckles when he was nervous, that he had the most amazing memory when it came to storytelling but couldn't remember where he had placed his pants the night before. He could speak sarcasm so fluently that people couldn't tell whether he was serious or joking, and had a million random, useless facts stored away in the back of his mind.

"It's not that simple. I can't stop him."

"Why not?"

When she didn't respond, Gyles lifted his head to look at her. He had always been a little too good at reading her face, and tonight was no different.

"Do you love him? Is that why?"

"Love?" she scoffed, trying to ignore the tugging in her heart. Gyles knew, as much as she wanted to hide it. "Love is not the right word for how I feel about him."

"Then what?"

"I wish I had an answer, same as you."

The room fell into silence once again, the couple sitting together in a never-ending embrace as their chests rose and fell in sync. She was suddenly much more awake than she had been a minute ago, and her mind raced with a million thoughts. As long as that one person was still alive, still haunting her night and day, she would live in the shadows and in the alleys her whole life. She couldn't live that way.

"I need to go."

Springing upward, she jumped out of her chair and scrambled around in the darkness to her bedroom to find her boots and jacket.

Gyles also got up and followed her, upset that she had once again left him.

"Go where? Isa?"

"There's something I need to do."

"Now?"

"Yes, now."

"But it's three in the morning."

"I can't sleep."

"Maybe I can help," he offered, but the nagging questions were bothering her more than they were helping. In an instant, she snapped, and the weight she had silently carried on her shoulders was thrown off.

"No! You can't help me, okay? I killed everyone he ever loved, and until I make things right, I'm not going to be able to sleep! And we had built a good life together; he just doesn't realize what he's missing! So let me go!"

Gyles tilted his head at her, trying to make sense of the slew of information she had just dumped on him. "Who are you talking about?"

"No one that concerns you."

Gyles was used to Isa pushing things away and ignoring problems, but apparently, this issue was too big to cast aside. So, of course, he had to keep pushing her. "Isa, who are you talking about? Who did you kill?"

"No one! Now leave me alone!"

What a lie. She had killed more people than she could count on her fingers, but that wasn't the problem troubling her. It never had bothered her. *Her* actions were justified. But she knew that one person didn't believe that. He believed that every misfortune that ever befell him was her fault. He probably believed that all the evil in the world came from her existence. But she needed to make him see that she wasn't to blame for all his problems. She needed to make him see that he needed her.

"I didn't do anything wrong!" Isa cried out, unable to stop the words from slipping out of her mouth.

"What are you talking about?" Gyles yelled at her, getting even more frustrated with her cryptic answers. He watched as Isa angrily stuffed her belongings into the small sack in her hand and double-checked that all of her various weapons were strapped in the places they needed to be.

Without another word, Isa turned on her heels and made her way toward the door, not speaking to Gyles. He didn't deserve to know the truth. And she didn't owe him anything. But Gyles wasn't so easily deterred. He quickly placed himself right in front of the door to prevent her from leaving, his large frame effortlessly taking up the whole doorway.

"Gyles, move out of my way."

"You know I can't do that."

"Gyles, move!" she roared, trying desperately to push him out of the way. He wouldn't budge. Not until he had answers, anyway. "Move!"

Grabbing her shoulders to stop her from trying to shove him, Gyles calmly asked once more, "Who are you talking about? Isa."

"Someone I used to work with, okay?"

"What about them?"

"I need to find him."

"Why?"

"I just do!"

"Isa –"

"I don't have to tell you anything!" she shrieked, trying and failing desperately to overpower Gyles.

"No, you're right. You don't. But please. Just talk to me. I'm right here. Tell me what's going on."

"I … I can't."

"Why?" He just couldn't understand. And he never would; Isa knew that. There was too much to explain, and even then, he would have to see things from her perspective. And that was impossible.

"All you need to know is that he is the reason why I can't sleep at night, so I'm going to find him and end this madness, okay?"

Gyles's hands dropped from her shoulders as a sort of realization washed over him. The loud, booming voice that usually dominated the room diminished to an almost voiceless whisper as he asked, "You're not coming back, are you?"

"Try not to take it too personally."

"If you're leaving me, I at least deserve to know why."

"Don't make me do that," Isa hissed, her eyes narrowing to slits as she glared at him in the darkness. He simply nodded and removed his body from the doorway.

"I'm sorry for whatever pain this person has caused you, and I'm sorry that I wasn't enough to fix it."

"It wasn't that you weren't enough. It is that he is too much."

She ignored the pang of shame that struck her heart and the invisible weights that made her shoulders droop. Isa could no longer ignore that invisible pull – that strong reckoning – that would inevitably lead her back to the person who haunted her day and night. She had to keep going, to confront the one problem that she needed to fix. Her future – her legacy depended on it. Because if she couldn't fix that one problem that kept her awake at night, she would be forfeiting the destiny she deserved. No one would know who she was, and no one would care. The mere thought of that was terrifying. And there was no way she was going to sit back and just let that happen. Not when she had the power to change that.

* * *

The frigid night air smacked her in the face as she stepped outside, and she gasped in shock at the cold, her breath coming out in a white cloud. All around her, the thick darkness hovered heavily, almost to the point where Isa could swear she felt the darkness crawling on her skin. The cobblestone streets that were usually swarming with people and bright colors were empty and dull. Sometimes, even the most beautiful of places turned foreboding during the night.

One of the only signs of life for miles around was an old man sitting at a small table at the docks, a handheld lantern as his only source of light. Perhaps he was Isa's ticket out of here.

"Excuse me, sir? I need a ride to get out of this town."

"You're not going to find one at this hour of the night."

"But I need to leave. Now."

"Look, lady," the man said, the impatience in his voice quite plain. "I manage what ships come in and out of the harbor. I don't sail them."

"Are you absolutely positive that there is no brig leaving right now?"

"I'm sure."

As the older man spoke, someone else walked up behind Isa, and she could have sworn for a second that her reflexes would cost him a limb. "I can take her. You need a lift, ma'am?"

"I do, in fact." She reigned herself in, calming her nerves with a deep breath. "Where are you headed?"

"New Haven Port in Sovi. We've got some cargo to drop off."

"Wonderful. That is perfect." It was just the place to start looking for the solution to her problem.

"All right. Follow me this way."

Isa quickly fell in step beside the sailor, almost too eager to get away from the grouchy man who was clearly having a bad morning. "Thank you so much. Do you have a name I might refer to you by?"

"Just call me Ricky. That's what all my friends call me. No need for any of the 'sir' nonsense."

"Right. Of course."

"Might I ask why you are looking for a ride so early in the morning?"

"I'm looking for someone."

"Oh?"

"I've had some late nights," Isa admitted, her glassy eyes dropped to the street beneath her feet.

"Who are you looking for?"

"An old friend. You remind me of him, actually. You two look very similar." Too similar, in fact. It was almost scary, if Isa ever got scared of anything. At least, that's what she would tell herself.

"I hope in a good way," Ricky chuckled, glancing at her with his stormy green eyes as he led her down the docks. His strides were long and swift, and Isa had to practically jog to keep up with him.

"Yes, right. Of course."

"How do you know where to look for your friend?"

"I know him. Probably better than he knows himself, really."

Ricky nodded, clearly impressed with her boasted intimacy with her friend. No doubt he didn't have such a relationship with anyone. "You two were that close, huh?"

"You have no idea."

"Might I be of any help in your search?"

"You already are, believe me."

"Well, if you ever need anything else, I'm always willing to help out." He paused, coming to a halt before a small, well-worn ship. Isa had to physically restrain herself from showing the disgust she felt at having to travel in such a tiny vessel. Surely the thing couldn't even withstand a storm. "Okay, here's the ship. It's not much, but it'll get you where you need to go. We'll cast off in a little, so feel free to make yourself comfortable in the meantime."

Then Ricky walked off, leaving Isa alone on the docks in the cold night air. She was all by herself once more, and she tried to tell herself that it was fine. There was no reason to be concerned. Except she was. It was a nagging at the back of her mind, like something was going to jump out of the darkness and drag her into the shadows. Something that she couldn't stop, couldn't fight. No matter how hard she tried.

II

PART TWO

SEVEN

LET'S DISAPPOINT EACH OTHER

KARYNA

The darkness was thick enough to cut with a knife and seep through the fabric of her salty, stiff clothing with an icy chill. Karyna strained to see ahead of her, barely able to see the hand in front of her face. Above her, the moon and stars had disappeared, and the thick clouds that hovered over the water blocked out any light. The darkness didn't scare her anymore; she had come to recognize the rhythm of the ship's groaning and the shuffling of the crewmates as they worked. Even the shifting of the wooden floorboards now felt like second nature, and her sea legs were steady and sure beneath her as she moved about the deck.

It had been about half an hour since Jesper ordered the crew to extinguish the lights, but one minute felt like an eternity. She couldn't understand why they had to travel the last leg in complete darkness, but Jesper wasn't answering her questions. No one was. Why was it that they all understood Jesper's commands? Or maybe it wasn't that they understood, rather that they just blindly followed his orders. The entire crew seemed to trust Jesper with their lives, and Karyna supposed that the reason she didn't feel the same was because she had only seen glimpses of the man Jesper was underneath the rough exterior; small wavers when his walls would come down and she noticed the real person he was. And she was slowly beginning to understand who he was. Well, only a bit. Two months stuck onboard with the same people who weren't too keen on showing much of themselves could only do so much. Despite the setbacks, perhaps Karyna was enjoying getting to know Jesper a bit more than she was willing to admit. But Jesper was nevertheless hiding things. She could feel it.

In a way, she was taking a leap of faith just as blindly as the crew was. She was the one who had originally decided to travel the world on a whim, leaving the only home she ever knew with no intention of returning. Maybe *she* was the one acting foolishly.

Karyna gasped as she was pulled from her thoughts by a leather-wrapped hand grabbing her arm and pulling her backward, sending her crashing into someone's chest. The person she ran into grunted slightly before chuckling and whispering,

"You lose your balance?"

"Don't scare me, Jesper!" She shoved Jesper in the chest jokingly, despite still not being able to see him. Her heart was racing a million miles a minute, and she took a deep breath to steady herself. Jesper only laughed harder at her, clearly amused with her distress.

"My apologies."

"What did you want?"

"I wanted to talk to you," he said, keeping his voice hushed. Karyna could feel the heat of his body close to hers, and it was somewhat comforting against the cool night air.

"You could have just asked me to come over here."

"You don't know where 'here' is."

"Fair point … but still!"

She heard the soft rustling of fabric and the creak of the wood deck as Jesper shifted on his feet. Karyna could just picture the smirk on his face that she had grown accustomed to over the last few months as he teased her. "What I wanted to tell you was that we're coming into the harbor now. After we finish docking, I want you to stay close to me when we go into town. This town isn't exactly safe."

"Then why are we docking here?"

"Because it's hidden and tucked away. The ship's not going to be disturbed out here."

"And that's important … why?"

"Because we're pirates." Jesper stated it like it was an obvious fact, forgetting how much Karyna disliked being reminded that they were thieves of the sea. Her playful mood was quickly soured, and she huffed in irritation before asking,

"Meaning?"

"Meaning we're not wanted. Anywhere, really."

"I see."

The heat of Jesper's body suddenly disappeared, and she could hear receding footsteps thudding on the deck. His voice barely cut through the dense fog as he briefly talked to who Karyna could only assume to be Gen for a minute before more footsteps followed. He shouted commands at the crew from somewhere above her, undoubtedly now standing at the helm. A chaotic shuffling ensued around her, all of the crew members scrambling in the darkness to find their posts.

Only a few moments later, another wave of heat brushed against her side. Karyna knew immediately by the voice that it was Gen. "What are you doing just standing here?"

"It's not my fault that I don't know where to go!" Karyna laughed. Gen snorted in amusement, which usually meant that she was about to follow up with a sarcastic comment.

"The captain's a huge help, isn't he?"

"There's no need to blame Jesper."

Karyna could hear the fabric of Gen's blouse shift as she moved, like she was shrugging to herself. "Nevermind that. The captain's another conversation entirely." Gen grabbed Karyna's hand and gently tugged her forward. "C'mon. Let's get you out of the way."

Stepping somewhat gingerly to avoid tripping over anything in the darkness, Karyna let the carpenter lead her away from the center of the deck. She could tell they had made it to the stairs to the helm when Gen placed Karyna's hand on the stair railing to ground her. Then Gen put something small and metal in Karyna's other hand, the metal cold and slightly damp against her palm.

"Here. Drink this. It'll help with the nerves."

"I'm fine, Gen. Really," Karyna insisted, realizing that the metal thing had to be a flask of alcohol. Likely rum. Jesper's crew seemed to be quite fond of the stuff, Gen in particular. "I don't really want a drink right now."

"You seem tense. Losing your bearings in the dark tends to do that to someone who isn't used to sailing. The rum will help."

"I'm not tense." It was partly true. While she had grown quite accustomed to how the ship and its crew operated, there was still a part of her that held strong to her roots. To the feeling of unmoving soil beneath her feet, to the constant stimulation of city noise, to the soft light that radiated from the buildings even on the darkest nights.

"You're tense. Drink."

Reluctantly, Karyna held the flask to her lips and let the sweet, burny liquid run into her mouth. She coughed as the tingling sensation hit her throat, and Gen clapped her on the back as she laughed heartily.

"Easy there, Princess. You okay?"

"Yeah," Karyna coughed. "Just swallowed wrong."

Gen just continued to laugh at Karyna's side, clearly entertained by the coughing fit. And once Karyna had settled down, Gen took the flask back and sighed deeply. "You're somethin' else, that's for sure."

"What's that supposed to mean?"

"Nothing! We're just very different people, that's all."

Karyna frowned, momentarily forgetting that Gen couldn't see her reaction. "And that's bad how?"

"Never said it was bad. I like it, actually," Gen replied, her voice more lighthearted than her usual tone. "Keeps things exciting."

"Thanks, I guess …?"

Gen didn't say anything else after that, but she wouldn't leave Karyna's side for the rest of the trip into shore. And the chorus of sounds around them didn't stop until the ship had stopped moving and was securely tied to the dock.

Jesper returned to her side, this time with a small lantern in his hand. He held the light out in front of him, pushing back the darkness by just a couple feet. Karyna squinted to see through the darkness as Jesper led the way down the gangplank, pointing out various spots for her to watch her step. Besides Ari, the rest of the crew didn't follow, most likely to keep watch over the ship under Gen's care.

"Welcome to the magnificent Emden Harbor. Follow me this way."

There wasn't much of anything "magnificent" about the harbor from what Karyna could see. The docks and shack were worn down with age and rough weather, and the few ships that docked there were nothing to boast about. A single lantern above the door of the shack was the only sign of life for as far as the eye could see. Karyna couldn't help but swallow the lump in her throat as she looked around. If the dockmaster was anything like the harbor he inhabited, Karyna had a logical reason to be worried.

Her face must have been betraying her anxiousness, as Jesper tried his best to ease her worries before knocking on the door of the shack. His face was abnormally soft in the light of the lantern as he smiled at her. "Don't worry. I've known Fenix for years. We're in good hands."

"When was the last time you actually talked to Fenix?" she heard Ari whisper to Jesper. Jesper's reply, on the other hand, was too quiet to make out.

Reaching out, Jesper knocked three times on the door of the shack and then stepped back to stand between Ari and Karyna. They waited patiently on the doorstep, hoping that Fenix would still come to the door in the dead of night. Karyna felt slightly guilty for waking the dockmaster up at such an ungodly hour, but if he was a friend of Jesper's, then surely he wouldn't mind the disturbance. She sighed loudly as they waited, earning a quick glance from Jesper. But just as soon as his eyes landed on her, they were on the closed door again.

"He'll come. Just give him a minute."

One minute turned into two, and two into ten. And Fenix still didn't come to the door. Karyna looked to Jesper questioningly, noticing his slight frown and frustrated demeanor. Stepping forward, Jesper raised a hand to knock on the door, pausing when the doorknob turned and swung open.

An older man with greying hair and frown lines towered over them in the doorway, clearly not happy to see them. He seemed worn down, as if life had dealt him the hardest cards and he had been forced to live through every single one. Karyna couldn't even begin to imagine what horrors he had faced in his lifetime.

"What do you want?"

"Good to see you too, old friend," Jesper replied, putting on his most charming grin. *That charisma.* Jesper was so good at pulling that mask out for any given occasion and wearing it like it was second nature. Maybe that was why she had such a difficult time growing to trust him. Fenix didn't seem to like the charm either, and he frowned even deeper at the trio standing before him.

"Friend, eh? Did someone hit you in the head a little too hard?"

Jesper's grin faded ever so slightly at Fenix's hostility. "What are you talking about?"

"You're a little backstabber, that's what. And I don't take too kindly to traitors and liars."

"Oh, c'mon! That was years ago! And I made it up to you!"

"Clearly not," Ari muttered under his breath, and Karyna choked to hold back a laugh. Jesper wasn't picking up on the fact that Fenix didn't want them there. Or, if Jesper had noticed that, he wasn't letting it stop him.

"Get off of my doorstep and go dock someplace else."

"Look, I would if we could. But we have nowhere else to go."

Fenix narrowed his eyes at Jesper. "Yes, you do."

"No, no! I'm not going there. You know how much she hates me! I'd be dead before I walk two steps."

"Good. One less nuisance for me to deal with."

"Give us three days," Jesper begged. Fenix simply crossed his arms over his chest and said,

"No."

"Five shillings."

"Ten."

"Fine."

"Deal."

No sooner than Fenix had made the offer, Jesper's money was in his outstretched hand and the deal had been made. Karyna blinked a few times, unsure that the deal had even occurred in the first place. It was struck and settled in a matter of seconds, and it had all happened so quickly that she didn't even see Jesper's hand move to his pocket to grab the small bag of shillings. He now held a gold key that had a blood red ribbon tied to the top.

"What's that do?" Karyna asked, reaching out to touch the key in Jesper's hand. Without replying, Jesper quickly closed his fingers around the key and moved it out of Karyna's reach. She glared at him in annoyance as he followed Fenix inside the shack, leaving her standing with Ari on the doorstep.

"Ladies first."

Ari dramatically gestured towards the open door, bowing his head and urging her to go inside. Nodding in gratitude, Karyna stepped through the door and into the shack, pleasantly surprised at how the building seemed bigger on the inside than on the outside. Still, there wasn't much to it, but it was better than nothing. Better than what she thought the inside was going to look like.

"Our room is up here."

Karyna looked up to see Jesper standing at the top of the stairs, waiting impatiently for her and Ari. She followed him to their room, which was an uncomfortably small size.

"One room?"

"All the other rooms were full. What was I supposed to do?" Jesper exclaimed, exasperated. "Look, I'll sleep on the floor, you and Ari can take the two beds."

"I don't want you sleeping on the floor."

"You would rather we share a bed?"

Karyna paled, horrified at the suggestion. "No!"

"That's what I thought."

After taking a moment to survey the room they would be staying in, Karyna frowned and asked, "Where does the rest of the crew stay?"

"On the ship. They take care of it while we get a well-deserved break."

"Is that fair?"

"There's not enough room, first of all. And most of my men don't even have enough to pay for themselves." It made sense, but Karyna couldn't help feeling slightly guilty at the treatment she was receiving, especially when she wasn't even a part of the crew. But now they were at the island, and now, all she needed was a new ship and she could go anywhere she wanted.

* * *

After settling down in the shack that Fenix called home and waiting it out for the night, Jesper offered to take Karyna to the large town closest to Emden Harbor. When Karyna nodded in agreement, Jesper's typically smug expression faltered ever so slightly, but he seemed to push it away and focus instead on putting a few things in order back on the ship before they headed for town.

"Ari, you and Newt are in charge of the ship until I get back. No funny business, you understand?"

"C'mon, Cap'n. Would you expect anything less?" Ari asked cheekily. Jesper then turned to Newt, who stood stiffly at Ari's side.

"Cabin boy, keep Ari in line, you hear?"

"Yes, sir. And it's Newt, sir."

"Right, of course. And stop with the whole 'sir' thing. You address me as Captain."

"Yes, sir. Sorry. Captain."

"I'll only be gone for a few hours. When I come back, I better not see or hear of any goofing off."

"I hear you loud and clear, Cap'n."

As they walked away, Karyna couldn't help but frown. "You're really leaving the ship in the hands of Ari and Newt? I don't know if that's the smartest idea."

"Oh, don't worry. I'm not," Jesper reassured her, a sly glint in his eyes. "I just tell Ari that so he can feel important and good about himself. But Gen knows that she's really the one in charge."

"I take it you've done this before."

"Really? What makes you think that?"

Karyna rolled her eyes at him before returning her focus to the path ahead of them. "Very funny."

"C'mon. The town's down this road. Let's find you a ride out of here."

They walked silently side by side down the road, Karyna desperately scouring her brain for something to talk about. Anything.

"So … can I ask you a few questions?"

"I'm assuming this is about my people, yes?"

"How'd you know?"

"I figured the questions would come sooner or later. Ask away."

Karyna paused for a minute, trying to figure out the best way to word what she wanted to ask. "What happened in the Great Purge? You said that your people were killed and you didn't just die off."

"You really don't know?" Karyna just shook her head, slightly embarrassed. "Well, what men don't put in their stories was that the elves were originally looked upon with disdain and were used as slaves for men. They felt we were inferior to them. But as the elves grew in number, the men became scared that we would revolt and take over, so we were hunted down and slaughtered in our own homes because man thought we were weird and different and dangerous."

"So, if you don't mind my asking, how is it that you are alive?"

"Some of the elves, my ancestors, managed to hide and wait out the Purge. We've lived in the shadows ever since."

"If elves are real, does that mean dragons are, too?"

"No, they are just myth."

"What about the Gifted? Are they a myth?" Karyna questioned, her curiosity piqued.

"Well, I met someone that claimed to be a Shadowjumper."

"If I was Gifted, I would love to be a Lightweaver."

"I don't think that's how it works," Jesper chuckled, clearly teasing her lightly. "You don't get to choose."

"I know. But it would be cool. Imagine being able to bend beams of light at your will."

"I'd wager that the Lightweavers have a lot more to worry about than just playing with rays of sun."

"Or what about a Glassblower?" Karyna continued, barely hearing a word of Jesper's halfhearted objection. "I have heard they can craft the most intricate stained glass windows from a handful of sand."

"Does everything you know come from the pages of a book?"

She frowned before muttering a small lie. "Not everything …"

"I bet your books only tell you that the Alchemists deceive and poison and not about how they assisted the High Kings in the Golden Age. Or that the Peacemakers are only capable of understanding and inflicting bodily harm, not how they can also save lives."

"And how is it that you know all this?"

"My parents told me stories," Jesper said simply, like the answer was obvious. "Tales that were passed down through the generations."

"How are those any better than the books I read?"

"Because my parents' stories are stories of *life*." He leaned slightly closer to Karyna as they walked, emphasizing his point with a sharp glint in his eyes. "Your books are just ink on paper written by a bunch of old geezers who haven't stepped one foot outside their front door."

"That is not true!"

Jesper didn't respond to that. And once again the quiet hung over them, the pair each lost in their own thoughts. If anything, the answers Jesper had given her only produced more questions rather than satisfied her curiosity. But they had also given Karyna a newfound respect for Jesper. The more time she spent with him, the more she realized that he was more than just a thief. And there was perhaps a great deal more that Karyna didn't know about the young man.

"And here we are. The town of Corsair."

Corsair was a busy town, where every person had somewhere to be or something to do, but it was friendly all the same. And the *people*. Karyna never felt so out of place in her entire life. Every single person, from the babies to the elders, had a sort of ruggedness about them that seemed present in all aspects of their lives. Their clothing was bare and dull, as if they lived in a colorless world. The faces of the people in the town reflected the same tough nature, undoubtedly from their daily work on the sea. After all, they were a port town. Karyna was certain that many of the people here relied on the ocean to survive. And Jesper didn't seem to be much different from the townspeople.

Karyna walked beside Jesper as he wandered down the streets, and she stopped every once in a while to admire the craftsmanship of the local artisans. But Jesper's mind seemed to be elsewhere, his gaze darting about the busy marketplace and watching everything except the wares of the vendors. At one point, he paused completely, his eyes locked on something – or someone – across the square.

"Is everything all right?"

Almost having to tear his gaze away, Jesper turned back to look at her. "Uh, what? Oh, it's nothing."

"What were you looking at?"

"I just thought I saw someone familiar. See that guy over there with the gambler hat and the sandy hair and the blue vest? Right by the flower stand." Jesper pointed across the way, and Karyna attempted to follow his finger to where he was looking. But there was no one who met his description, despite how sure Jesper sounded of who he saw.

"I don't see anyone …"

"Never mind," Jesper huffed, waving it off and turning on his heel to face the vendor they stood in front of. Frowning in confusion, Karyna faced the vendor with him, forcing down a small wave of concern that was growing in her stomach. *Surely if it was someone to be worried about, Jesper would have said something.*

Returning her focus to the vendor, Karyna took a moment to scan the intricate weapons laid out on the table before them. One of the daggers in particular caught her eye, and she resisted the sudden urge to reach out and feel its cold metal beneath her fingers just to know it was real.

"Jesper, look at the detail on this one. It's beautiful."

"It is." Jesper's voice was uncharacteristically soft, and when Karyna glanced up to read his expression, his gaze was firmly locked on her instead of the dagger display. He didn't care to spare the weapons a single glance.

"Stop looking at me like that," Karyna giggled somewhat awkwardly, unsure what to make of Jesper's piercing look.

"Like what?"

"Like that!"

Jesper raised his eyebrows, finally breaking eye contact with her. "I don't know what you're talking about. I wasn't looking at you any particular way."

Karyna tried to laugh it off and shifted her focus back to the daggers, telling herself that she was just overthinking things. Of course

Jesper wouldn't look at her any other way. *He must think me daft. Just pretend you didn't say anything at all.*

The older woman selling the weapons moved to stand in front of Karyna, holding up the dagger that Karyna's eyes were fixed on to the sunlight. She slowly turned the dagger in her hands, the light reflecting from the gold detailing and minuscule rubies. In the center of the handle, a woman lined in gold posed regally with a sword in her hand.

"This dagger tells the story of the legendary Celia 'The Siren' Knottley," the woman explained. "She was one of the most feared pirates to sail the Seven Seas until her supposed death hundreds of years ago. Some say that Celia is still out there, luring sailors to their deaths with a siren song. The bravest of them all, she was, and the most cunning, too. It is a fine dagger for a fine lady."

"Thank you." Karyna couldn't help but blush slightly. Her eyes were transfixed on the dagger until Jesper spoke up.

"How much is it?" he asked the woman.

"Twenty-six shillings."

"I'll take it."

Surprise rattled Karyna as she gawked at Jesper. Had he heard the price incorrectly? The dagger was expensive, and she knew that Jesper wasn't one to throw away his money on a dagger that was more beauty than harm. Much less buy something like that for someone like her. "What? But Jesper –"

"I'll take it."

Jesper had made his decision, and there was no stopping him now. Somehow, he managed to pull out more money from the depths of his jacket, as if the pockets had a magical ability to keep supplying endless amounts of money. How he came across such a vast amount of money baffled Karyna, because there was no way that smuggling contraband was worth hundreds of shillings.

She watched as Jesper calmly handed over the money in exchange for the dagger, much more calmly than the exchange between him and Fenix earlier that day. He looked almost happy to be giving away his money, which was something that seemed so out of character for Jesper.

"Thank you," Karyna breathed, running a hand over the dagger's handle.

"Not a problem. It's a beautiful dagger."

"You know, you're not too bad."

"Oh?"

"For a pirate, I mean," she quickly clarified. Jesper seemed to repress a small smile at that. Like her comments were amusing to him somehow.

"Right. So you've met worse pirates, then?"

"I've … never met other pirates, actually."

"Then who's to say we're not all good men?"

He had a point. "Well, the stories –"

"– are false."

"Hey, there he is!" Karyna looked up from the bladesmith's table to see two naval lieutenants pointing at them from across the town square. They began running over to where Karyna and Jesper stood, so she grabbed Jesper and turned him to face the oncoming lieutenants.

"I think we have to go."

"Say less." Wheeling around, Jesper and Karyna sprinted from the square, desperately dodging various townsfolk and artisan stands. Jesper glanced over his shoulder to see the lieutenants gradually getting closer, so he pushed Karyna forward to pick up the pace. "Go, go, go!"

Jesper directed her to a small alley that cut through to a different street, both of them flying through the corner with impressive speed. Karyna could feel her feet slipping out from under her, but Jesper managed to hold her up while still running as fast as his legs could carry him.

Once they reached the busy street, Jesper slowed down to a brisk walk to blend in with the crowd. Karyna followed his lead, using the brief moment to catch her breath. She couldn't help but admire Jesper's ability to think so quickly on his feet, but she couldn't see how slowing down would help them get away from the navy lieutenants. It seemed counterintuitive, but surely Jesper knew what he was doing.

"Jesper, what are we doing?" Karyna hissed lowly as they strode down the street, weaving in between people. "Aren't we supposed to be outrunning the officers?"

"You trust me, don't you?"

"I suppose, but I don't see how –"

"If we run, we'll be easy to spot. Just keep walking normally. Don't look back."

Karyna obliged and tried desperately to keep up with Jesper's long strides, her eyes fixed ahead of her. But the further they walked, the more tempting it was to glance over her shoulder. Giving in to the desire, Karyna snuck a small glance behind her, spotting the two sailors coming out from the alley. They skidded to a halt as they noticed just how busy the street was, their eyes frantically scanning the heads of the crowd. Karyna knew they would spot her red hair immediately.

"Jesper, we need to go. Now."

Jesper turned to look back, almost instantly making eye contact with the sailors. The sailors broke out into a sprint, practically plowing over the people in their way to get through. Jesper muttered a curse under his breath in frustration before firmly grabbing Karyna's arm and pulling her into a run again.

As soon as the docks of the harbor came into view, Jesper suddenly turned sharply and dragged Karyna into a large building. Karyna had failed to see the sign out front, but she quickly recognized it as a furniture store, judging by how many intricate wooden pieces littered the rooms. *Why a furniture store?* She didn't have the faintest idea.

Jesper beelined for a freestanding wardrobe in the far back corner of the store that was partially covered in an old sheet. One of the doors to the wardrobe was just barely hanging on and sat crookedly in the frame, but Jesper didn't hesitate to throw open the door and shove Karyna inside. He quickly followed suit, closing the door behind him as best as he could.

The space inside the wardrobe was significantly smaller than Karyna had initially thought, and once she and Jesper had shuffled around to find the most comfortable position, Karyna realized just how close they were standing to each other. Their faces were only inches from each other, and her heart skipped a beat every time Jesper's warm breath fanned her face. They were close. Extremely close.

He smelled of salt from the sea, sharp and clean, and the lingering warmth of old leather from his weathered jacket. The smoky smell of rum tainted his breath, and there was something else that Karyna didn't recognize. It was sweet and peppery – the remnants of foreign spices. She wanted to inhale deeply, to commit his scent to memory; her skin crawling with the unexplainable sudden desire to draw him closer still.

Pull yourself together, Karyna! What are you thinking?

She struggled to find the words to say, her cheeks heating up dangerously to a vibrant shade of red. In the small space, Karyna took the moment to study Jesper, her gaze not escaping his notice. Jesper grinned at her, his hazel eyes sparkling with good-natured humor.

"Like what you see?" He smirked, making Karyna fight the urge to melt into the floor.

"Oh, shut up."

"C'mon, Marfont. You don't have to lie to me."

"I'm not!" she hissed, trying to desperately ignore how flustered Jesper was capable of making her. And he enjoyed it, too.

A small chuckle escaped his lips. "You look cute when you're blushing like that."

She wanted to retaliate, but Jesper put a finger up to his mouth to signal silence, averting his piercing gaze to the cracked door. The naval lieutenants were walking through the store, peering in every crevice for any sign of the fugitives.

Karyna's breath caught in her throat. If the lieutenants found them, they were dead. They had nowhere else to run. But, after what felt like ages of waiting in that horribly cramped space, the lieutenants seemed to give up their search. She could feel the tension in Jesper's body release as soon as the lieutenants left the store, a sigh of relief fanning her face before he pushed the door open and stepped out of the wardrobe.

"Okay, we're all clear. Let's go before they decide to come back."

She didn't need to be told twice. Anything to get out of that miserable wardrobe.

As soon as the lieutenants were long gone down the street, Jesper stepped out of the store and started dragging her back into the sea of townspeople. He seemed to be leading her back in the direction of Fenix's harbor, when he suddenly grabbed her arm and pulled her behind a stack of wine barrels, peering intently over the lid of the top barrel.

"What are you –"

"Shh!" Jesper put a hand over her mouth to stop her, and Karyna angrily pushed the hand away.

"Don't shush me!"

"Look."

Slowly rising on her knees, Karyna glanced over the barrels to see where Jesper was looking. She followed his gaze to the closest dock, where a group of navy sailors stood on the gangplank of a magnificent vessel. The vessel far bested any of the other ships in the port, its sails so white that Karyna had to avert her eyes for fear of being blinded.

"Who are those people?"

"They were the sailors who boarded my ship and ransacked it for 'illegal contraband.' One of them stole a compass from me."

"They're searching for you, aren't they?" she whispered, watching as the sailors began talking with the two lieutenants that had chased them through the streets. The lieutenants were making wild gestures and pointing in all different directions, clearly attempting to explain how they had just lost one of the most wanted pirates on the seas.

"Their commander is practically begging for an excuse to lock me up."

"Well, we can't let that happen. Let's just lay low and not draw a lot of attention to ourselves, and we should be fine."

"I'll be right back." Jesper jumped up and began striding over confidently to where the navy vessel was docked. Karyna was quick to grab him and pull him back behind the barrels.

"Jesper! What do you think you're doing?"

"I'm going to get my compass back."

"Sneaking in and out of a heavily guarded naval ship without getting caught is impossible! It can't be done."

Jesper leaned in towards Karyna, a mischievous grin growing on his face. "Just because it's never been done before doesn't make it impossible."

"You'll never make it out of there alive. Besides, an old compass isn't worth risking your life for!"

"What makes you think I care?" Jesper asked, his demeanor suddenly going tense and cold. Karyna frowned dejectedly and averted her eyes to the ground beneath her feet.

"You should."

"And why's that?"

"Because I care."

"Oh, wonderful!" Jesper hissed sarcastically, his voice rising. "I'm glad we've got that all cleared up! Now, can I go, or are you just going to stand there and waste my time?"

Karyna stayed silent for a moment, not wanting to anger Jesper more than she already had. But something inside her craved answers.

"Why are you so reckless?" she blurted.

"Why am I reckless? Why am I reckless," Jesper scoffed. "Oh, I'll tell you why. Because none of it matters, that's why! In case it hasn't occurred to you yet, I'm not the hero! I'm not some knight in shining armor! I don't get a happy ending! There's no golden standard I need to live up to, no one expecting better of me, and you certainly shouldn't either! The only people you need to be concerned about are the men out there whose lives are worth ten, even a hundred of my own, and I've killed three times that number! You don't know me, Kie, so don't even pretend to try."

The words didn't register at first. She felt like she had been punched in the gut. For a minute, she couldn't even find the words to say. So, she settled for whispering, "You … what?"

"I didn't – I mean, you weren't supposed to hear that." Jesper's fiery demeanor quickly disappeared, being replaced with stress and remorse. He ran a shaky hand through his hair, and his body seemed to curl in on itself.

"How many people?"

"Well … it's hard to say."

"It's hard to say?" Karyna was in complete disbelief. She paused, trying to make sense of the millions of questions that were hurdling around in her brain. Her thoughts were a mess; she couldn't reconcile the bright and mischievous smile of the handsome captain with the killer he claimed to have been. "Who knows about this?"

"Just Ari."

She couldn't help but let out a sharp, humorless laugh in anger before repeating back what Jesper just told her. "Just Ari."

"I've changed. I swear."

She wanted to believe him. Part of her *did* believe him.

"That's what every murderer says."

At the word "murderer," Jesper flinched ever so slightly. "I'm not a murderer."

The denial was so simple. Like it would just fix everything. But Karyna's fear was creeping in alongside the anger, cold and harsh, the more she looked at him. Nothing about this was simple anymore. What if he had never slipped up and accidentally told her the truth? And if he could hide something like this so easily, what else was he withholding?

She feared what he had done. And what he was still capable of doing. But the memories flooding to the front of her mind of Jesper's laugh and his charming jokes and how eager he was to keep peace between the men on his ship. Things weren't adding up.

"No matter what you are or aren't, you're not getting on that ship," she snapped at him. "No one can."

"Watch me."

Karyna pressed her lips together, hard. He was back to being the Jesper she was familiar with. It scared her, knowing what she knew now. "If you want that compass, you're not going to get it by hopping on a heavily-guarded ship and just taking it back."

"Says who?"

"Your conscience, for starters."

"Oh, you mean that little voice inside your head that tells you if you're doing stupid things or not? Yeah, I don't have one of those," Jesper joked, shrugging nonchalantly. Karyna sighed at him.

"Well, that explains a lot."

"What's that supposed to mean?"

"Jesper, the amount of stupid decisions you've made since I've known you I can't count on just one hand." Upon his incredulous look, Karyna quipped, "Do you want me to start listing them? How about the fist fight with my fiancé the first day we met, smuggling illegal contraband, that game of poker against Ari, not to mention your cheekiness to the navy commander that Ari told me about or the countless other instances that Gen mentioned. Shall I continue?"

"No," Jesper mumbled.

"Good, because I don't enjoy pointing out your stupidity."

"Yeah? Well, I don't enjoy your … meanness."

"That's the best you could come up with?"

"Shut up." Dropping the clearly unfavorable conversation, Jesper turned his attention back to the docked ship. She could see the gears turning inside his head as he scanned every inch of the scene laid out before them. Karyna was concentrating equally as hard, but for a different reason. She was busy trying to justify what she had just learned, everything that Jesper had dumped on her. Her mind was absolutely reeling, trying desperately to make sense of what Jesper said and failing miserably.

But before a word could even leave her lips, he was already gone. And there was nothing she could do about it, either. Trying to stop him would only get her into trouble as well, so she figured it would probably be better to just let Jesper do his thing. Whatever it was that he was doing.

She watched as Jesper drew as close as he could to the gangplank of the ship before tipping his hat down to cover his face and turning so his back stayed to the naval sailors. In one swift motion, he grabbed a stack of crates to hold in front of his face and slipped around the sailors and up the gangplank, going completely unnoticed by the sailors. Their eyes met briefly before Jesper disappeared behind the rail of the vessel, his mischievous wink confusing Karyna even more than she had been a minute before. What exactly he was planning to do or how he was going to accomplish it, she hadn't the faintest clue.

In a huff, Karyna sat down on the street, her back against the stack of barrels she hid behind. How long would it take for Jesper to come back out again? Or maybe the better question was: how long would it take for Jesper to get caught?

EIGHT

TOO MUCH CONFIDENCE AND TOO LITTLE SENSE

JESPER

Not long. Not long at all. He screamed at himself internally to go faster. It wouldn't be long before another sailor came down the hall; that was just his luck. Besides the fact that he was horrible at timing things properly in the first place. Perhaps he should have realized that long before putting his plan into action, but there was no time to turn back. That was how his life worked, just an endless cycle of rash decisions and temporary regret. The consequences would have to be dealt with later, no matter how big they ended up being or how lousy they were. This time was no different than all the others.

Jesper slid down the long corridor in the hull of the enormous ship, every instinct in him firing warnings through his mind. There was nowhere to hide. It was as if the ship had been designed specifically to catch unwanted trespassers in a maze of endless halls. He shouldn't be there. It was an extremely stupid idea. Even *he* could recognize that, and that was saying something. And just as he pushed the thoughts away, Jesper heard the harsh sound of footsteps on wood. Someone was coming around the corner in front of him.

Jesper froze for a split second before turning on his heels and speeding back down the hall. But he screeched to a halt when Nyssa came around the corner and appeared in front of him. *There was nowhere to hide.*

A sharp laugh pierced the air, followed by an all-too-familiar voice. Jesper's heart sank. "Well, look who's back for round two! You just couldn't get enough of me, could you?"

"Commander Prescott! How wonderful to see you!" Slowly turning around, Jesper plastered a mocking smile on his face and stared Phineas down shamelessly. "I hate to break it to you, but you can't get rid of me that easily."

"I'm sure we can arrange something."

"I'll gladly call the Admiral myself," Nyssa sneered behind Jesper. Jesper's heart sank further down. He couldn't get arrested; not now. Jesper was this close to getting his compass back. So, if he couldn't escape the sailors, he would talk his way out. It had worked for Jesper before, and it could work again.

"That won't be necessary."

"Oh?"

"I'm just here to claim what you took from me," Jesper explained. "After that, I'll be out of your perfectly manicured hair for good."

"The compass, I'm assuming?"

Jesper contemplated fabricating a lie for a brief moment but settled on telling the truth. "Yes."

Phineas scoffed. "What moron risks his life for a compass?" Nyssa joined in on the mocking, her sounds of amusement turning to unrestrained laughter. Jesper refrained from letting his anger get the better of him, instead clenching his jaw and hissing through his teeth,

"Don't you have better things to be doing?"

"Oh, yes. There is a never-ending list of tasks I must complete, but I'm enjoying this. Aren't you, Nyssa?"

The sailor behind Jesper nodded vigorously. "Very much so."

"Of course you are," Jesper muttered under his breath. He shifted uncomfortably on his feet as Phineas studied him. Phineas squinted at him, as if staring intensely at Jesper would suddenly answer all his unspoken questions.

"Your face seems familiar. Have I arrested you before?"

"You *did* raid my ship and try to arrest me without any evidence. And you stole my property."

"No, no," Phineas said dismissively, waving his hand as if to brush off the stupidity of Jesper's reply. "Before that."

"I don't think so. I'm sure I would remember having to tolerate a dimwitted fool."

Phineas's jaw dropped as utter shock and rage clouded his mind. "Do you think you're funny?"

"You know you love me." Jesper flashed his most charming grin at Phineas, enraging the sailor even further.

"Bold words coming from a dead man."

"I've been called worse by better."

"Why, you little –" Suddenly, Phineas lunged at Jesper, his fists clearly intended for Jesper's face. Jesper was quick to dodge the punches, but Phineas managed to grab Jesper by his jacket and slam him against the wall, making Jesper release a small grunt as the air was forced from his lungs. In a flare of frustration, Jesper retaliated, kicking Phineas as hard as he could in the stomach and twisting away from his grasp. Just as soon as he had escaped Phineas, Jesper crashed into Nyssa, who was all too ready to catch him. She didn't hesitate to send her fist flying into Jesper's nose, and he felt his eyes water as blood poured from his nose.

Grabbing the blade of Nyssa's outstretched sword with a leather-wrapped hand, Jesper swiftly thrust the hilt of the sword into her stomach and pulled it away as soon as she doubled over; instantly, he brought his foot up off the wood beams of the floor, jamming it hard into Nyssa's throat. She made a squawk of alarm and pain as she recoiled from the kick.

Out of the corner of his eye, Jesper could see Phineas preparing to jump back into the fight. And when Phineas lunged at him once more, he was ready. Jesper turned and immediately found a hold on Phineas's forearm, pushing it downward. Then he suddenly pulled

Phineas's arm up behind his back, twisting his arm in the highest arc it could possibly go. Finally releasing his arm, Jesper rammed his heel into Phineas's back, forcing him to fall onto the floor, his limbs sprawled wildly.

Jesper turned to survey his work before reaching up to feel his damaged nose. Blood was everywhere, but his nose wasn't broken, so he considered it a job well done. His eyes still watered like crazy, and he quickly wiped away the tears from his cheeks. Giving a nod of approval to himself, Jesper began to make his way back down the hall once more in search of his compass.

"Wait!" Phineas called, rising to his feet and cradling his twisted arm. "Let me make you an offer!"

Jesper paused a moment, contemplating what Phineas possibly had to offer him. There didn't seem to be much on the table that Phineas could use to bargain, but the idea still intrigued him. Deals were his weak spot. "I'm listening …"

"Look, there is no way you are going to find the compass without getting caught by another officer. You can't get to it on your own. But I can get it back for you."

"What are you talking about?" Nyssa hissed next to Phineas, her voice a mere whisper from being kicked in the throat. Phineas shushed her with a firm glance before facing Jesper again. Jesper frowned.

"What's the catch?"

"I need your help."

"With …?"

"Acquiring a vessel."

A sly smirk grew as Jesper eyed the sailor before him. "You've resorted to stealing now, huh? Does Daddy know you're being a bad boy?"

"No. And he doesn't need to know." Jesper repressed a snort of amusement as he watched Phineas's uncomfortable frustration, the way he bristled like his feathers were being ruffled. Clearly he had never stepped out of line before. Nyssa bumped her lover in the shoulder, her disapproval evident.

"Phineas! If your father found out –"

"So, let me get this straight. You want me to steal a ship and hope that no one finds out?"

"It's not stealing!" Phineas argued. "The vessel is rightfully mine."

"Is it really, or do you just believe that because you feel entitled?"

"No! The vessel belongs to me by birthright. The Admiral took it from me and I want it back."

"And you're asking me to do this … why?"

Phineas rolled his eyes at Jesper, as if Jesper was expected to understand why he was being asked to do this. "You clearly make a decent thief, and I need someone who is willing to navigate highly perilous situations to retrieve the vessel."

"English please."

"I need someone expendable."

"And there it is," Jesper muttered, nodding to himself.

"Oh, shut up and take my offer already! I get my vessel, you get your … *compass*, and I'll discharge you without a word to anyone else. Deal?"

Jesper stared hard at Phineas, keeping his face stone cold and void of emotion. Then his eyes moved to Nyssa, trying to read her expression. Discerning nothing, he shifted his gaze back to Phineas. He couldn't tell whether Phineas's offer was meant to be a set-up or not, and it threw Jesper for a loop. Clenching his jaw tightly, he went through all the possible scenarios in his mind before coming to a hesitant conclusion.

"What did you decide?"

"Get me my compass," Jesper replied. "And you've got yourself a ship. Where is the vessel docked?"

"New Haven Port. It's docked over with the other navy vessels."

"Oh, wonderful. That makes stealing the ship so easy."

"Don't worry. I'm certain you'll be fine."

"Right," Jesper scoffed. "Like you care."

Jesper rolled his eyes at Phineas in annoyance. Of course he would pretend to care about what happened to Jesper. The tragedy of a criminal actually being arrested or killed. *How awful.* That's why Jesper was partially convinced that Phineas was playing him, that there was some trap set up to catch Jesper in the act and put him behind bars. Jesper was at least smart enough to know not to trust Phineas. Too much could go wrong within the deal, too much could be hidden in between the lines in fine print. But he needed that compass. And he was willing to do whatever it took to get his father's compass back. It was all he had left of his father, and he wasn't about to let some arrogant, pigheaded commander pawn off the compass for a few shillings.

So he was going to do it. Whatever it took. He kept having to remind himself. *Whatever it takes.*

Jesper allowed a smirk to spread across his face before walking away down the hall. Phineas called after him, but he didn't stop this time. He could hear Phineas huff in frustration before rounding the corner of the hallway. Pausing, Jesper silently did a small dance of celebration. He was going to get his compass back. Sure, it came with strings attached, but he was getting it back all the same, *and* he could avoid killing anyone for it. All he needed to do was tolerate the unbearable navy commander for a short while and steal a vessel from right under the nose of the Admiral. Easier said than done.

* * *

Taking a deep breath, Jesper attempted to calm his mind and steel his nerves. This was going to take an insane amount of planning, and executing that plan would be a whole other story. Not to mention that he had to do this completely alone. So much for flying under the radar. One wrong move, one misstep, and his perfectly crafted life would be thrown to the dogs. He couldn't give that up, for the sake of Ari and his crew.

"Excuse me, sir!" Jesper was wretched from his thoughts, and he internally kicked himself for allowing himself to get so lost in his mind as he wandered down the halls. "I don't believe you are allowed to be here."

Glancing over his shoulder, he watched as an older gentleman wearing a lieutenant's badge began striding over to him. *Just great.* In a split second, Jesper pondered his choices. Either wait for the lieutenant and risk getting taken in, or make a run for it and risk getting taken in. Neither option was ideal.

"Did you hear me, sir?"

Jesper took off. He figured that he would stand a better chance by running than confronting the lieutenant face to face. Each move Jesper made was copied by the lieutenant as he tried to keep up, the two darting through the halls in an all-out chase. No matter what Jesper did, he couldn't shake the lieutenant. And a small worry crept into his mind as he began mounting the stairs to the deck. How was he going to escape unnoticed off the ship?

Once he reached the top deck, Jesper slowed to a stride and made a beeline for the first officer he saw. Jesper wiped the blood from his nose furiously to avoid being questioned about it. He took a deep breath to calm himself and slow his heart rate. "Officer, can you help me?"

"What are you doing aboard this ship, sir?"

"I'm part of the loading crew. You know, bringing the crates down to the hull. And as I was walking back from stocking up your storeroom, I was chased by one of your men." The officer frowned, crease lines appearing on his pale forehead. "I'm sure he meant no harm, but it spooked me a bit, if you know what I mean."

"Thank you for bringing this to my attention. I will see to it at once."

"Thank you, sir." The officer nodded and turned to leave, but Jesper wasn't finished yet. "Oh, and one more thing, if you don't mind."

"Yes?"

"Would it bother you to accompany me off of this magnificent vessel? I'm sure you'd understand, I'm a little jumpy."

"Yes, of course. Follow me this way. Let's make it quick; I have things to attend to."

Smiling to himself, Jesper eagerly followed the officer down the gangplank to the dock. Luckily, the two sailors that were searching for him earlier had disappeared.

"Thank you for your help, sir."

"Of course. Now, be on your way."

"Yes, right." He didn't need to be told twice to leave. As he walked away, his eyes met Kie's, who was still hiding behind the barrels. Even from as far away as he was, it was extremely easy to see the confusion and surprise on her face. When he reached the barrels, Kie stood up and started to walk at his side.

"What happened? How did you –"

"Never underestimate a pirate. We are capable of a great many things."

"Clearly." The word was flat and sharp. With Jesper back at her side, Kie's unease didn't seem to let up at all, her shoulders still tense and stiff. "You got the compass?"

"Not yet."

"What was the purpose of that stupid decision, then?"

"I made a deal. I'm going to get the compass back."

Kie clearly didn't understand what he meant by that. "A deal? With someone in the Navy?" Jesper nodded. "I thought you hated them and they hated you?"

"That hasn't changed. We just made a temporary pact. I'm sure it won't last very long."

"Right …" she muttered, her lips pressing into a thin line. "So, what now?"

"Now, I have some work to do."

"What kind of work?"

"Work that's going to take some serious thought and planning," Jesper said. He didn't have the energy to explain everything, and he was exceedingly grateful when Kie chose to simply nod, though the movement felt strained and rigid, like she was forcing herself to let it go.

Jesper found his thoughts wandering again as he walked down the street with Kie, his worries and aggravation over the extensive planning that was going to have to go into executing a theft. From the Admiral. In a heavily guarded area. With the reluctant help of a naval commander.

What could possibly go wrong?

"What can I do to help?" Kie asked suddenly in a quiet voice, and Jesper refocused his attention on her. Since when was she eager to help?

"Nothing. This is something I need to do alone."

"You never need to do anything alone. Let me help you." Jesper felt her hand brush against his before jerkingly pulling away, but Kie's face showed no indication that she had done anything at all.

"Thank you, Kie. Really. But I really do have to do this by myself. I'll be fine."

Kie fell silent then, her arms remaining crossed tightly over her chest and her shoulders tense as they walked side by side. The silence between them felt charged, like she was holding something back. Jesper could tell she was uneasy, and he wanted to convince himself that it was just the new town and the Navy chasing them that was worrying her. But he knew that was a lie. He knew she was really unsettled by *him*. By what he had accidentally admitted to her.

Jesper clenched his jaw and sighed deeply, not letting Kie's quick glances at him go completely unnoticed. The trust they had begun to build up over the last couple months was slipping, and he could feel it. And what he was about to do next wasn't going to help, either.

"You're going to hate me for this, but you're going to need to go back to the ship by yourself."

Kie stopped walking to turn and look him in the eye, her gaze sharp and wary. "By myself? Where are you going?"

"I need to meet someone a couple towns over in a bit. I'll be back soon, though. I promise."

"You promise," she echoed, like the words sounded wrong coming from him. "So you just expect me to trust that you're leaving to just … *meet* someone?"

Jesper sighed, feeling his confidence deflate like water leaking from a ripped waterskin. He had no idea what else he could possibly do to make her understand. "That's not – I don't live that life anymore, Kie."

"Can I believe you? Even when you're telling me to leave?"

"It's just … I need to keep you safe, okay? Please?"

She clearly wasn't reassured in the slightest, her fingers curling into fists as her sides. But she eventually nodded with a great deal of hesitation and said, "Okay."

"Thank you."

"Just don't make me regret trusting you."

"Of course. I won't."

As Kie turned away to head back to the Fortuyna, Jesper took a moment to squeeze his eyes shut in frustration. Then he shoved the bitterness at himself to the back of his mind and focused on the task laid out before him. If, by some miracle, he could pull off a feat this big, life could return to normal. And he could be with his crew again. That was all he needed to push himself forward. It was the fuel that kept him going.

It was time to get to work.

NINE

AN OFFER I SHOULD HAVE DEFINITELY REFUSED

JESPER

"You showed up." Phineas jumped up from his seat on a crate of eggs as Jesper approached, his face betraying the shock he felt. "Four hours late, but …"

"Don't sound so surprised."

"You really want that compass, don't you?"

"So what's your plan?"

"My what?"

"You know, if it was your job to steal this ship, we would both be dead," Jesper quipped as he scanned the docks. His stomach twisted into knots at the vast number of sailors wandering around the ship. This was by no means going to be easy.

"But it's not."

"Yeah. I come prepared."

"Okay … so, are you going to tell me what the plan is here?" Phineas asked shortly. Jesper rubbed his face in regret before muttering,

"I can't believe I'm saying this … punch me."

"What?"

"Punch me. In the face."

"Why?"

"It needs to look like I put up a fight against you and lost."

Phineas raised his eyebrows in surprise and confusion. "Wait. You're being serious?"

"Yes."

"Okay, sorry. I just couldn't tell if it was you or me saying that. I mean, when I look at you, I always hear that."

"Just do it."

Without hesitation, Phineas balled up his fist and sent it flying at Jesper's nose. Jesper wasn't prepared in the least for the punch, and he stumbled backward onto his knees. His eyes immediately started watering, and he clutched his bloody nose delicately.

"Ow!"

"You asked me to do it!"

"I know I did! But did you really have to punch that hard?"

"Sorry," Phineas said, shrugging unapologetically.

"No, you're not. You enjoyed that a bit too much."

"Perhaps you're right. And I'd happily do it again," Phineas quipped. Rising to his feet, Jesper handed Phineas a pair of shackles begrudgingly, much to Phineas's unspoken astonishment. "What am I supposed to do with these?"

"Put them on me."

"What?" Phineas watched with wide eyes as Jesper turned around and put his hands behind his back.

"Arrest me." When Phineas hesitated and said nothing, Jesper looked over his shoulder and glared at the commander. "C'mon, I haven't got all day. Let's make this quick. Just do it before I change my mind."

Phineas silently obeyed, making sure that the shackles locked shut before stepping back and letting Jesper turn around again. Jesper swallowed a growing lump of anxieties in his throat, extremely uncomfortable with the situation he had thrown himself into. He had spent so many years avoiding this very situation, and to willingly put himself in such a position felt so wrong.

"What now?"

"Now, you take me onto that ship and pray that we aren't stopped by one of your sailor friends."

"*That's* your plan?"

"Yes?"

"That's the worst plan I've ever heard," Phineas stated plainly, clearly not impressed with Jesper's proposal. Jesper rolled his eyes and asked,

"Well, do you have a better idea?"

Jesper took the following silence as a no. He scanned the docks once more before signaling Phineas to lead him down to the ship, who grumbled something to himself and scowled deeply before complying. Realistically, their odds of successfully making it onto the vessel and stealing it were extremely low. But Jesper liked those odds.

Phineas grabbed roughly onto Jesper's arm, guiding him down towards the docks. Jesper could feel his heart practically leaping out of his chest, so he sighed deeply and closed his eyes for a brief moment to calm himself. This wasn't going to work.

"Commander, where are you taking this prisoner?"

Phineas came to a halt, his grip on Jesper's arm tightening uncomfortably. Jesper kept his eyes to the floor, hoping that his dark mass of hair would hide his face from the officers. Phineas had to come up with a good lie, and fast, and Jesper couldn't help him with this one.

"I was instructed by the Admiral to detain him on this vessel until further notice. May I pass?"

"Of course. Our apologies, sir."

Phineas didn't need to be told twice to continue onward. They passed up the gangplank together, Jesper fighting to hold back a relieved grin. Leaning towards Phineas as they walked, he whispered, "Good one. I thought you couldn't lie."

"I can," Phineas hissed back. "I just don't like doing it."

"Well, bravo for stretching yourself."

"Stop talking."

They made their way to the helm, constantly keeping watch for any unwanted company. Just as they reached the stairs, Phineas paused for a brief second before shoving Jesper under the stairs without warning. Jesper pitched forward, barely managing to stay upright without the support of his hands to catch his fall. He turned on his heels and was about to jump out, until he heard the booming voice of an older man.

"Phineas! What are you doing here?"

Jesper shifted to peer through the cracks in the steps, watching as Phineas straightened up formally when a man with neat grey hair and piercing blue eyes walked up to him.

"Father! I, uh, wasn't expecting you to be here."

"Why shouldn't I be here? This *is* my vessel. I am the one who wasn't expecting to see *you* here."

Phineas's father owned the vessel? But then that would make him … the Admiral? Jesper's mind was suddenly reeling, his knees growing weak from under him. He was going to be stealing a ship … from the Admiral of the Navy. For the Admiral's son.

"Right, of course. My apologies," Phineas replied meekly.

"You never did answer my question, son."

"Oh, right. Um … well, you see …"

"Well?"

"I must have received incorrect orders. I was told that my presence was required on this vessel. Must have been intended for someone else. Or perhaps for a different vessel."

"No matter," the Admiral replied, brushing it off. "But now that you're here, I can go attend to the absent lieutenants in New Haven Port. They supposedly ran off after someone and never returned to their posts." Jesper squeezed his eyes shut and mentally kicked himself. The Admiral was obviously talking about the lieutenants who had chased after him and Kie. So much for laying low.

"Yes, of course. Do you want me to remain here?"

"Just finish inspecting the vessel, and then you are free to go back to your post."

"Yes, sir." The Admiral turned to leave, but paused and turned back again.

"Oh, and one more thing."

"Yes?"

"I thought you should know: there have been rumored sightings of a dangerous convict around the area."

"Oh?"

"You've heard of the Hellburner of Sovi, have you not?" Phineas could only nod in reply. From Jesper's spot beneath the staircase, he could see the Admiral pull a folded paper from his pocket, handing it to Phineas. And when Phineas unfolded the paper, there was Jesper's face, staring back at Phineas menacingly. "If you see this man, bring him in immediately. He should not be allowed to roam the streets with the threat that he poses."

"Yes, sir."

"That's all."

* * *

Phineas waited until his father was long gone before harshly pulling Jesper out from under the stairs. His movements were sharp and angry, and Jesper attempted to push away the growing fear inside of him. Phineas could easily toss out the deal and arrest Jesper if he wanted to. Jesper had already done half of the work himself. Jesper wouldn't even be able to fight back against Phineas if he chose to do so.

He was whipped around and shoved against the rail of the stairs, Phineas's elbow pressing painfully into his back. Jesper panicked for a moment before realizing that Phineas was unlocking the shackles on Jesper's wrists.

"Get me this vessel, and then I'm turning you in."

Jesper turned around after his hands were unbound, facing a furious Phineas. "You made a promise!"

"You're a murderer!" Whipping out his sword, Phineas pressed the blade to Jesper's throat, breathing hard. "You didn't tell me you were a wanted murderer!"

"And you didn't tell me the Admiral was your father, but here we are stealing a ship together!"

"It's not stealing, it's *my* ship!" Phineas roared, pressing the sword harder against Jesper. Jesper resisted the urge to lash out, instead taking a deep breath and suppressing his emotions.

"Well, we're going to get caught on *your* ship if you don't drop the sword and let me take the wheel."

Phineas chose to ignore Jesper's warning. "Why didn't you tell me?"

"I'm sorry?"

"Why didn't you tell me that you are a murderer?"

"I'm sorry, were you expecting me to introduce myself as a wanted convict and a murderer when we met?" Jesper asked incredulously, dumbfounded at such a ridiculous question. "'Hello, nice to meet you! My name is Captain Jesper Kelsey, the Hellburner of Sovi!'"

"You were the one who killed my mother!" Phineas yelled in Jesper's face, unable to restrain his intense anger.

"Well, my apologies. What do you want me to do, bring her back from the dead?"

"Do you remember?"

"I'm sorry?"

"Do you remember her?"

The question caught Jesper off guard, and he sucked in a breath as the world dimmed for a moment. Phineas's mother's face immediately came to his mind, her terrified eyes burning a hole through Jesper's soul. He had tried for years to make her go away, to make them all go away. Nothing he could do would ever bring back the lives he had taken.

"I remember all of them."

"You're a monster," Phineas hissed, his eyes brimming with unshed tears. Clenching his jaw in bitter resignation, Jesper replied,

"I know. I hear that one a lot. It keeps me awake at night."

"I should kill you right now."

"You need me. You're not going to kill me. And don't go backing out of your deal, either. You made a promise."

"Keeping you alive was *never* part of the deal."

"Perhaps not. But kill me, and you are also a dead man." Jesper knew that, without his help, Phineas would never leave with the ship as his own. Even as they spoke, the sailors who previously stood on the dock began making their way towards the gangplank to investigate the yelling. "Do you want to get caught or not?"

Phineas glanced over his shoulder at the approaching sailors, his face paling slightly at the sight. After a minute of just staring at the sailors and not moving, Phineas lowered his sword and stepped away from Jesper. Jesper took the gesture as a sign to jump into action in an attempt to save themselves with the little time they had left.

He raced up the stairs to the helm, yelling at Phineas to release the lines. Once he reached the wheel, Jesper directed the ship to the mouth of the bay and whispered a silent prayer.

"Push the gangplank away and open the sails when I say so!"

"Why?"

"Just do it!" Phineas obeyed, hurriedly moving to the rail of the deck and using all of his strength to shove the plank away. When the plank dropped away and the sailors on the dock began firing their muskets at the ship, Jesper yelled, "Now!" Phineas tugged on the lines that loosely held the sails up and the sails fluttered open, immediately catching the strong wind and rocketing the ship forward. "You might want to duck!"

Slipping his pistol out from its holster under his jacket, Jesper fired back at the sailors as musket balls whizzed past him. Phineas had ducked to hide behind the rail, progressively getting angrier as each musket ball punctured the hull of the ship.

"Stop firing at my ship!" he roared, as if that would stop the sailors from sending bullets hurling at them. Jesper continued dodging bullets as he steered the vessel out of the bay, some of the bullets coming so close to his face that he could practically feel them. It wasn't until the ship had safely made it out of the port that Jesper could breathe properly again, his chest heaving with adrenaline. But, as he inhaled, a sharp pain stabbed his left side. *Something is wrong.*

"Oh my gosh," Phineas gasped elatedly, adrenaline coursing through his system. Jesper watched Phineas regain his composure before bursting into a fit of laughter. Jesper could only offer a small smile in response, attempting desperately to mask his pain. He could feel a warm stickiness seeping through his clothing. *Blood.*

"I told you I could save us from getting caught."

"Yeah, right. I would have done the same thing."

"Sure …" Jesper said, mocking Phineas's confidence. Then the laughing died down, and the two sailors were left silently – and quite awkwardly – staring at each other. Phineas was the first to break eye contact, glancing at the wooden planks beneath his feet before muttering,

"Thank you."

"Yeah, whatever." Jesper shrugged off the gratitude. "Now, I want my compass back."

Nodding, Phineas approached with the compass in his hands. He gently handed it to Jesper, still refusing to make eye contact. "Here. This belongs to you."

"You're … letting me go."

"I'm choosing not to become someone else today. I'll drop you off at a different harbor, but then I don't want to see your face again, you understand?"

"Of course." Jesper didn't want to question what had prompted Phineas's change in attitude. "And if you do?"

"I won't hesitate." There was no kindness in Phineas's eyes. He was completely serious.

"I get it. Don't worry, I'll stay far away."

Jesper was willing to take anything, as long as the deal was still upheld. The commander was preoccupied with manning the ship as Jesper stood on the deck and put a hand to his side to assess the damage. He didn't have to see the wound to know that it was big. And deep. And exceedingly painful. Every breath was like torture, each inhale sending daggers into his side.

"So, now that you have the ship, what are you going to do?" Phineas looked up as Jesper spoke, his face contorted with a range of emotions.

"That's a good question. I hadn't really thought about it that far yet."

"Really?"

"If I'm completely honest, I didn't even think we'd get the vessel," Phineas replied flatly.

"Yeah?" Jesper replied, his hand subconsciously gripping the rail of the ship harder in an attempt to bear the pain. "Well, don't waste it. I risked a lot for your stupid ship. So please, for the love of all things good in this world, use it well."

"You're giving me advice?" Phineas scoffed, his disbelief evident. Jesper raised his eyebrows at the commander.

"You have a problem with that?"

"No. You just don't strike me as a wise person."

"Yeah, I surprise people a lot."

"Consider me surprised."

Jesper couldn't help but let a sly smile break out and let out a small laugh. He regretted it instantly as another sharp stab of pain flooded his senses. "Did you just *agree* with me?"

"No," Phineas shot back all too quickly.

"Yes, you did!"

"Are you always this unbearable?"

"I don't know," Jesper replied, shrugging casually. He tried desperately to hide his growing agony, instead favoring smug disinterest. "Does being remarkably thick just come naturally to you, or do you really have to try?"

"You can't take anything seriously, can you?"

"Serious conversations make me uncomfortable. So I try to subtly avoid them."

"And how's that going for you?"

"Ask me again in a couple minutes." Phineas snorted in response. He took a moment to study Jesper, his eyes moving over the pirate's figure. Scoffing, he commented,

"You know, you're not as impressive as I thought you'd be."

"And somehow I still manage to be the talk of the town."

"You've got quite the mouth on you. It'll get you into a great deal of trouble someday."

"Oh, believe me, it already has."

With that, Jesper returned his attention to the shifting shoreline of the island spread out before him. The conversation was dropped, the sailors opting for a blessed silence that hovered over the ship. Turning so his back faced Phineas, Jesper pressed a hand to his side again, hissing in repressed pain. The bleeding was getting worse. *Way* worse. The thought occurred to him that he was losing an unhealthy amount of blood, a giant wave of dizziness slamming into him in confirmation. Jesper's legs suddenly gave out from under him, but he managed to catch the railing before he hit the ground.

"Are you okay?"

"Yeah. Just peachy."

Phineas ran down from the wheel to Jesper, placing a hand on the pirate's shoulder. "What's wrong?" Jesper simply pulled his hand away from his side to reveal the red staining his palm. Phineas stared at the blood a moment before slowly straightening up again, his expression falling emotionless. "You're bleeding."

"I'll be fine," Jesper grunted through clenched teeth. "Just get me to the harbor."

"And just leave you there?"

"You wanted me dead, didn't you? Well, today's your lucky day."

Phineas shook his head. "No, I'm not about to add another death to my consciousness. It's my fault that you were shot. You'll live long enough to at least make it off this ship."

"How comforting," Jesper muttered to himself.

Keeping one hand pressed to his wound and one hand on the rail for balance, Jesper remained standing there for the rest of the short trip. He knew that moving even the slightest would send him crashing to the deck, and he certainly didn't want to rely on Phineas. Of all people, why did he have to be with the Admiral's son when he got injured?

"We're docked. C'mon, let's move."

"Yeah, sure," Jesper grunted, relenting as Phineas threw Jesper's right arm over his shoulders and began helping him down the plank. As they stepped together into Gocaster Harbor and the adrenaline started to wear off, Jesper's vision began to blur.

TEN

A NOT SO ANGELIC GUARDIAN ANGEL

KARYNA

When Karyna returned from the town without Jesper at her side, she could tell that Ari was internally panicking. His composure remained collected, but he proceeded to immediately bombard Karyna with a million questions. Ari absolutely had to know what Jesper was doing, because he automatically assumed that Jesper was undoubtedly getting himself into a heap of trouble. Which didn't seem too far from the truth, if Karyna had to guess. But it was almost as if Ari felt responsible for Jesper's poor decision making and the resulting consequences. Karyna couldn't help but feel somewhat bad for Ari's irritated desperation.

"Kie, where is Jesper?" Ari paced back and forth in front of Karyna, his boots thudding rhythmically into the cobblestone street.

"Like I already told you, he'll be back. Just give him a bit."

"A bit? Kie, it's been almost six hours since you've returned and Jesper's still missing! I've waited more than a bit! Now, tell me what's going on!"

"He just had to do something, that's all."

"What did he have to do?"

"Grab something."

"Where?"

"On the island."

"With whom?"

"I don't know. He didn't say."

"Gee, you're just so full of information, aren't you?" Karyna chose not to reply. "And what about you? Jesper took you to town to find a new sailor to leave port with."

"Look, I don't know, okay? Stop asking so many questions!"

"I wouldn't ask so many questions if you would just give me an answer!" he yelled after her as she stormed away from him towards the docked ship. She strode to the end of the dock and stopped, fuming as she stared out over the quiet bay. Why did Ari have to be so infuriating sometimes? It wasn't her fault that she didn't know exactly what Jesper was doing with whom. And it certainly wasn't her fault that Ari wanted to play some giant game of cat and mouse with Jesper and constantly have to rein him back in.

"You okay?" Karyna whirled around as a hand touched her arm but let out a sigh of relief when she realized it was just Gen.

"I'll be all right," Karyna huffed, crossing her arms over her chest. "I just don't understand why Ari is getting mad at me for no reason. What did I do?"

"He's frustrated at Jesper, that's all. It's not you. He just so happens to be taking it out on you."

"It's not my fault. Jesper just ran off, said he needed to do something. It wasn't like I was going to be able to stop him," Karyna insisted. Gen nodded in understanding, her deep blue eyes boring into Karyna's.

"Did he tell you what he was doing?"

"No! He only said that he was going to meet someone in a different town, I think. That's it!"

"I believe you. I just hope he's not getting himself into more trouble."

"Would you be surprised if he was?"

Gen let a smile tug at the corners of her mouth. "Not in the least."

"Gen …" Karyna hesitated, internally debating whether or not to ask the question that was nagging at her. "Can I ask you something?"

"Of course. What's up?"

"Do you trust your captain?"

Gen frowned slightly to herself but answered immediately, crossing her arms over her chest. "Yes, I do. Why do you ask?"

"What do you know about his past?"

"Not much," Gen admitted. "Though most people don't, either. The captain doesn't like to talk about that stuff often. I do know that he was a high-profile criminal before he left that life behind; for what reasons I'm not sure. And he used to be really rich. Amassed a lot of wealth. Don't know where it all went."

"And you don't care that you don't know?"

"There comes a point where you just have to trust that his intentions are good. In the five years I've served under his command, he's only ever put his crew first."

Something wasn't sitting right with Karyna. Jesper at least seemed to be telling the truth about only Ari knowing what happened, but Gen deserved to know too. "But –"

Gen's gaze then shifted towards the sound of boots marching over on the wooden planks of the dock. Of course Ari had to intrude when he was least wanted.

"Kie, Gen. I'm going into town. I need to find Jesper."

"I'm coming with you, then." Karyna wasn't just going to let Ari go all by himself. Jesper's disappearance was just as much Karyna's responsibility as it was Ari's. Or, at least, so she felt.

"No, you're not. You stay here with the ship."

"I was the last one with Jesper. You need my help if you want to find him."

Ari's eyes darted from Karyna to Gen, as if he wanted the carpenter to back him up. But Gen instead shrugged and stated, "Sounds reasonable enough to me."

"And you're fine handling the ship by yourself until we get back?" Ari asked, his voice thick with a sudden and unexplainable worry.

"Really? That's a question you have to ask? I'll be fine. Don't worry about me."

"Okay, okay. Just … promise."

"I promise. Go find our captain."

Nodding, Ari turned to walk away. He motioned for Karyna to follow, muttering, "C'mon. Let's go."

* * *

As they walked towards the nearest town, neither of them spoke a word. Karyna could practically touch the tension in the air between them, but she wasn't going to be the first to break. Ari was the one who needed to apologize for getting mad at her. But that didn't seem to be the concern at the forefront of his mind.

"Did Jesper tell you anything about where he was going to be?" Ari huffed, not daring to look in Karyna's direction.

"A few towns over was all he told me."

"We can work with that."

Karyna frowned to herself, questioning how Ari planned on finding Jesper given he had so little to go off of. "But aren't there a lot of towns 'a few towns over?'"

"Well, technically, yes. But only really one that Jesper would actually go to."

"Where?"

"Gocaster Harbor."

"Gocaster Harbor? What's in Gocaster Harbor?"

"A lot of taverns, fancy ships, and concentrated wealth perfect for stealing."

That definitely sounded like him; there was no doubt about that. At least, from what Karyna could tell. And she trusted Ari's judgment; after all, Jesper and Ari had known each other for – how long was it? She hadn't thought to ask that question before. It occurred to Karyna that she really didn't know anything about either of them, and yet, somehow, she had learned to trust them. Well, perhaps not completely. But enough.

"How long have you known Jesper?"

"Quite a few years now."

"How'd you meet?" Karyna asked. Ari didn't respond as fast as he had to the previous question, perhaps trying to think of the best way to word what he wanted to say. But then he seemingly gave up, continuing to walk on in silence. "Well?"

"What's it matter to you?"

"I was just curious, that's all."

"Let's just say, he kinda showed up one day and needed my help."

"With what?"

Ari paused before simply stating, "Staying alive."

"Sorry? I don't follow."

"Jes, uh … he was in an accident of sorts. And I found him on the beach by my house. He … recovered at my house for a while. That's how we met." Karyna wanted to interrogate him further, but she wasn't given the chance to speak before Ari quickly changed the subject. "Ah, here we are. This is Gocaster Harbor. The hunt for our cap'n begins."

The streets of the harbor town felt a lot more dead than Karyna had been expecting. Only a few people here and there littered the roadsides, and most of the commotion came from inside numerous dimly lit buildings, of which Karyna could only assume to be taverns. Ari was right about one thing for certain: the visible wealth of the town was astronomical. Even more extravagant than the vast fortresses and capitol buildings of her home city, Gocaster Harbor was seemingly lined with gold and precious stones and crime looked to be nonexistent. For a town that relied on fishermen, traders, and merchants as a source of income, it was extraordinarily well put together.

Karyna had to shake herself awake. She was supposed to be looking for Jesper, not ogling at the sights of the town. How foolish she must have looked, but luckily for her, Ari appeared not to be paying her any attention. Good for him for actually doing what they came to do. Drawing her eyes away from Ari, she began peering inside of the windows that they passed. From what she could tell, no sign of Jesper yet. And time was certainly not on their side. The sun was setting much too fast for her liking.

Walking among the streets started to feel like somewhat of a lost cause. Jesper was nowhere to be found. And the sun was starting to dip below the horizon line. Just when Karyna began losing hope, she noticed two figures coming towards her and Ari. One of them looked injured, the way he trudged forward, so surely that couldn't be Jesper. But as they came closer, the doubt in Karyna's mind was erased. That was most definitely Jesper. And he looked horrible. His typically tan, warm skin had begun to take on a grey sheen. Sweat dripped from his temples, and his long hair clung to his face. And despite the agony he must have felt, a smile spread across his face the moment he saw them. Karyna was fairly sure that Jesper would have run over to meet them if he didn't have to rely on what looked like a naval commander at his side to keep him upright.

"Jesper!" Karyna yelled, breaking into a run for the two men in front of her. A terrible, strange panic shot through her at Jesper's horrendous state, but it was all too quickly replaced with white hot fury.

As soon as she was within arm's reach of Jesper and the commander, Karyna let her fist fly directly into the commander's jaw. He grunted in pain, ducking from under Jesper's arm to cradle his cheek. Without the commander's support, Jesper collapsed, Ari just barely managing to catch him before the ground rushed up to meet him. But

Karyna didn't care. This commander was the reason Jesper was hurt. She was sure of it.

"Kie!" Ari scolded, but she wasn't paying attention. She wheeled on the commander, roaring at him,

"What did you do?"

"I didn't do anything!" the commander protested, backing away from Karyna's grasp. "I swear!"

"Jesper's injured! What did you do to him?"

"We were stealing a vessel together, and he got caught in the crossfire! I didn't shoot him, I promise!"

"Where were you taking him? A prison cell?" she roared, basking in the commander's fear. His face betrayed confusion and intimidation, but Karyna wasn't going to fall for his lies.

"What? No! I was taking him to a doctor."

"And you expect me to believe you?"

"Yes?" Karyna raised her fist to strike again, forcing the commander to step back once more. "Don't – don't punch me again. Please."

Tempting. But Ari wouldn't let Karyna get away with another punch. The sheer desperation in his voice alone was enough to make her anger turn back into panic. She didn't even know why she was so scared on Jesper's behalf. "Kie! I need your help! Jesper's bleeding out."

"Let me," the commander offered, putting Jesper's arm back over his shoulders. Ari did the same. "As far as I'm aware, the doctor's just down the road here."

Practically dragging Jesper with them, the commander directed them to the doctor's office. Even as they approached, Karyna could have guessed that no one had lived in the building for years. The place was completely in shambles, but the naval commander seemed convinced the town's doctor still resided there. Karyna pounded furiously on the door, but no one answered. The building was empty.

"No one's home."

"No, no!" Ari shouted. "What are we supposed to do now?"

"I don't know," the commander mumbled. This ignited a fire within Ari, and he began yelling furiously at the commander.

"There's no other doctor in this town? There has to be!"

"Well, we can't just stand around and do nothing! We have to keep looking," Karyna protested, pulling Ari's arm to guide him away from the doorstep.

"Where else are we supposed to look?" Ari yelled. In desperation, Karyna yelled back at him.

"I don't know, okay?"

Guiding them away from the old house, the naval commander said calmly and coldly, "The best we can do is keep looking in town for someone that can help us."

So that's exactly what they proceeded to do. Karyna's mind was whirling with thoughts that just kept getting worse and worse, thoughts like the reality that if they couldn't find someone in time, Jesper would die.

The streets were fairly empty, and while the local taverns and such were bursting with people, the commander quickly shot down the idea of rushing in and asking any of them for help. That, he explained, would only result in terrifying a roomful of rich people and getting kicked out.

Karyna continued to spiral, her anxiety turning into fear, which was turning into dread. And just when the thought occurred to her that there was nothing more they could do, she spotted the dark figure of a man running towards them from down the street.

The man slowed as he approached them, his chest heaving like he had just run a long distance. Once he came up to them, he bent over and put his hands on his knees to catch his breath. Karyna studied him, her eyes resting on his hat, then to the dirty blond hair that stuck out from beneath the brim of the hat, and then to his worn blue vest. *It can't be the person Jesper saw in the marketplace a few days ago …*

Ari shot Karyna a skeptical glance. "Um, I'm sorry –"

The man put up a finger, a moment later straightening up again and flashing a brilliant smile. "I know we ain't been properly introduced yet, but I'm here to help."

"I'm sorry?" Ari repeated.

"I'm your friend's savin' grace, his knight in shinin' armor, his guardian angel, his … I'm runnin' outta more analogies. Anyways –" he waved a hand dismissively, "I know a lady who can get y'all housed for the night. Town doctor's dead – how ironic – which means you'll be patchin' him up yourselves."

But Ari wasn't relenting. "Who did you say you were again?"

"What's it matter who he is?" Karyna exclaimed, coming between Ari and the man. "He wants to help us, and Jesper needs it."

"You don't understand, Kie. Who this guy is *does* matter. What if he's working with the Navy or something?"

The commander winced slightly at the comment but chose not to butt in. Between them, Jesper raised his head just barely and muttered, "Just follow what the guy says already."

"But, Jes –"

"Ari, it's okay."

The man in front of them was still trying to catch his breath, reaching up to adjust the hat on his head as he waited for them to stop arguing amongst themselves. "Now, I don't mean to interrupt, but could we move this along a bit?"

"Yes, of course," Karyna agreed.

"I do hope one of y'all knows well enough to patch him up."

What a request. How would any of them be expected to know how to do that? And as she glanced at the faces of Ari and the naval commander, she realized that the extent of their knowledge was likely wrapping the wound in a rag and calling it a day. She was just as clueless. But then again, growing up, she had been taught how to bandage wounds. And how to stitch. Granted, it was stitching on fabric, not on skin. But that was close enough, right? They didn't seem to have any other options. And Jesper didn't have the time.

"I … I can do it."

Ari and the commander stopped short, Ari's face scrunching up in confusion and shock. "You can?"

"I had some training back at home. Just the basics, but I did learn how to stitch. I think … I can do it." Barely clinging to consciousness, Jesper slurred some sort of agreement.

"What do you need?" the commander asked. Thinking for a moment, Karyna began to list a few things off on her fingers.

"A table to lay him down on, a needle and thread, um … rags, water."

"Done."

* * *

The "housing" that the man led them to was an old inn not too far from the docks that stuck out like a sore thumb from the surrounding luxury. It was a quaint little place and the old lady who owned it was nice enough to let them in, no questions asked. And as the commander ran off supposedly to retrieve the items Karyna had asked for, the owner showed them to a small room. The man didn't follow them back to the room for whatever reason, remaining in the front parlor with a smirk still plastered across his face.

The dimly lit room was quite bare, save for the table in the center of the room and a few lanterns. Never had Karyna worked in such conditions, but this would have to do. The commander had collected the items in his arms, and he placed them all on the floor by the table before going to close the door behind Jesper and Ari. Jesper was looking even worse, causing Karyna's anxiety to spike. She didn't have long to get the job done, and she had never done this before.

"Jesper, you're going to need to take your jacket and shirt off. Unless it would be easier for me to cut the shirt down the front."

"Hey, I like this shirt, okay?" Jesper whined with all the strength left in him. "No – no cutting." So, slowly and painfully, Jesper proceeded to slide off his jacket and shirt. With a bit of help from Ari, of course. Every movement sent a cry of pain echoing through the room, and Karyna found herself silently wishing for this torment to just be over.

"Ari, –" Karyna glanced at the commander, "you –"

"Phineas."

"*Phineas*; you both will have to hold him down on the table. This is going to hurt. A lot."

"Just get it over with," Jesper muttered as he let Karyna and Ari excruciatingly drag him up onto the table and lay down. He stared up at the ceiling, his brow furrowed in agony as he shifted slightly to find the most comfortable position. Karyna couldn't help but trace the scars that decorated Jesper's chest with her eyes, then to his tattoo. His compass hung once more around his neck, the seemingly justifiable reward for almost losing his life. Once he was situated, Ari and Phineas each put a hand on Jesper's shoulders and one hand on his arms to keep him down. Jesper clutched their arms in return, his knuckles white with apprehension and pain. Karyna looked to the two men holding Jesper down for confirmation before noticing the expression on Phineas's face. His eyes were locked on Jesper's ears, now no longer hidden by his hair. Phineas had turned sheet white and his breathing seemed shallow. He was panicking.

"Phineas, we don't have time for this. You need to focus."

"I'm part elf. What are you going to do about it?" Jesper managed to say through gritted teeth.

"I can't – I can't be doing this."

Karyna was in no mood to deal with Phineas backing out now. "Hold him down. *Now.*" He reluctantly obeyed, but he still seemed almost afraid to be touching Jesper, like Jesper's skin would burn Phineas's hands.

"Okay …" she breathed, picking up her dagger and muttering to herself, "You can do this."

Even just looking at the bullet wound was a feat, and Karyna felt her stomach twist itself into knots. There was so much blood. She inhaled slowly, gripping her dagger tighter. She could do this. *No pressure.*

Sticking the tip of the dagger into the wound produced the most horrible, gut-wrenching screams she had ever heard in her life. Nothing could have prepared her for this. But the bullet had to come out.

Everything was red. She had never hated a color more than she did in that moment. And it was all his. Her whole being hoped that this was all a terrible nightmare that she would eventually wake up from. His screams and messy slew of curses filled the room, but Karyna pushed forward. She couldn't stop now. Tears stung her eyes and blurred her vision, so she wiped them away with the back of her hand before going back in again. Something about the procedure felt natural to her, too good to be true. It was as if she had grown up doing this her whole life and her fingers had tapped into muscle memory. But that, of course, was impossible.

And then it happened. It started first as a weird, tingling feeling on her fingertips where her hands touched Jesper, like when she would come in from the cold as a child and warm her numb fingers by the fire. Then it was tugging, pulling painfully from deeper inside her. Karyna's breath hitched as a wave of nausea slammed into her, threatening to send her crashing to the floor. Her energy was draining – siphoning out through her fingertips into Jesper.

Jesper's screams faltered into erratic gasps, his eyelids fluttering wildly as he struggled to hold onto consciousness. His body was trembling, and whatever Karyna was doing, it was helping. It wasn't like she could stop anyway. She didn't even know what she was doing in the first place.

What is happening to me? Pushing the thoughts away, Karyna refocused on the wound. She was so close to reaching the bullet. It was right there. Just a little deeper, just one more moment of torment.

The bullet fell to the tabletop and the knife dropped from her bloody hands. Her whole world was spinning, and she swore she was about five seconds from hurling. Leaning over, Karyna squeezed her eyes shut and began taking deep breaths to force down the nausea. After a minute, she felt a soft hand on her back and could faintly hear Ari's voice.

"Are you okay?"

"Yeah, yeah."

"Deep breaths. You did it."

Nodding, Karyna chose to keep her head between her knees until the queasiness subsided. When she stood up again, her gaze met Phineas and Ari, who both looked equally concerned for her. So she attempted to muster up a faint smile.

"I'm okay. Really."

"Me as well. Thanks for asking," Jesper slurred weakly, his chest heaving with exhaustion. How he had managed to stay awake was beyond her, but she remembered the tingling, the warmth, the pull of energy bleeding out from her hands. Maybe that's why she was feeling so queasy? *But I'm not Gifted …*

Jesper still clung desperately to Ari and Phineas's arms, stubbornly refusing to let his eyes close or his consciousness slip away. Ari let a chuckle escape his lips.

"Welcome back, Jes."

"Are we finally done?"

A pang of guilt struck Karyna. He wanted the pain to be over. But she wasn't done. "Not quite yet. I still have to clean the wound and stitch it up."

Groaning, Jesper's eyes wandered back to the ceiling. Karyna quickly grabbed the bowl of water and a small rag, wishing just as deeply as Jesper to finish the process as fast as possible. The skin around the bullet wound was stained red from the blood, and no matter how hard she scrubbed, the stain would not disappear. Eventually, she just had to give up because of Jesper's anguish.

And now came the hardest part. The part Karyna tried to convince herself she could do. But really, she had absolutely no idea what she was doing. Fabric was nothing like skin. But perhaps it would somehow come just as naturally as the first part did.

Exhaling slowly, she made the first stitch with clenched teeth, being extra careful to pinch the skin together properly. Jesper hissed in pain, his face contorted into a grimace with each insertion of the needle. She had to be so precise, so steady and careful. One mistake, and Jesper would get an infection and die within the week. But, as a huge relief to Karyna, it didn't take many stitches to close the wound.

"Okay. I'm done."

"How do you feel, Jes?" Ari asked, the concern evident in his voice.

"Terrific."

"Great. Blondie and I will go out and talk to the owner of this place. We'll see if that guy was telling the truth about her having any rooms left for us to stay the night."

"It's Phineas," Phineas quipped. Ari just rolled his eyes.

"Whatever."

Jesper nodded weakly and grunted out a reply. "Yeah, sure."

"We'll be right back."

After the door closed behind them, Karyna turned her attention back to the wounded captain. Jesper was pushing himself to sit up, gasping in pain as he did so. Karyna allowed herself to take yet another deep breath to calm her nerves, praying that the stitches would hold. They had to.

"Thank you."

"Yeah … I just hope that the stitches don't rip open."

"I'll be fine," Jesper reassured. He paused briefly, taking a moment to study her before asking, "Hey, uh, what was that back there?"

"What do you mean?"

"Oh, c'mon. Don't act like you don't know what I'm talking about."

Karyna shook her head aggressively. "I don't."

"Are you a Peacemaker?"

"What?" she stuttered, her brain kicking into overdrive. No – no, she couldn't be. "No! Of course not!"

"Right …" For some reason, he was making it exceptionally difficult for Karyna to find the right words to say. The only thing she could muster out was,

"Uh, here. Let me bandage the wound. Protect it for a bit." Anything to distract from the conversation.

Grabbing the pile of cloth from the floor, Karyna began to wrap the fabric around Jesper's torso. Jesper said nothing as she worked, but she could feel his gaze boring into the top of her head. She ignored how close to his bare chest she was and how she could feel the heat radiating from his body. Karyna desperately attempted to smother the redness that was making its way to her cheeks. *Not now*, she scolded herself. Now was not the time for this.

Once the makeshift bandage was tied properly around Jesper, Karyna felt the need to risk a glance upward, to read Jesper's face. *He is probably still in a great deal of pain.* Biggest mistake of her life. Tilting her head up, Karyna found herself staring into the most gorgeous hazel eyes she had ever seen. Had they always been so vibrant? Perhaps she had just never thought to really look before and had instead focused on his scar. His gentle breath on her face reminded her that she had to release the breath she was holding, the sensation sending shivers down her spine. They were close. Too close. But Jesper didn't seem to mind. The smug smirk tugging at his lips told otherwise.

"Thank you, love."

Karyna's lips parted to reply, but no sound came out. She was utterly speechless. Was his voice always that smooth?

"So apparently, that guy got us two rooms for the night. Fully paid for it and everything." Karyna jumped away from Jesper as fast as she could, Phineas and Ari coming back into the room not a second later. Luckily, they didn't seem to notice the awkward tension in the small room. All the same, Karyna's heart pounded in her chest as she scrambled to find a response to Phineas's comment.

"Oh, uh …"

"No, it's all right." Jesper apparently didn't have the same issue. "We can head back now."

Ari frowned and crossed his arms over his chest. "Jes, you really need to stay and get your strength back. Don't worry, the ship will be fine until tomorrow morning."

"Ari's right, Jesper," Karyna added. "We'll stay the night. Thank you, Phineas."

"Yeah … right."

"No, I'm serious. Thank you for helping us. Jesper's alive because of you."

Phineas sighed in disbelief and frustration, rubbing his face with a hand. "This is bad. This is really, really bad. I saved his life. I can't believe I just did that."

"I'm right here, you know," Jesper muttered through gritted teeth, delicately rubbing the bandaged wound.

"It's my duty to continue the work of my ancestors, not do the exact opposite!"

"It's your duty to ensure the genocide of an entire race of people?"

"No, I didn't …" Phineas sputtered, dumbstruck. "I never said that!"

Jesper scoffed in disbelief. "It's the same thing!"

"I wasn't supposed to save your life, okay?"

"Says who?"

"I don't know, my people?"

"Your people directly told you, 'Phineas, make sure that on this specific day, when Jesper is shot in the side while stealing a ship with an exceptionally intolerant oaf, you best not help save his life, because lord knows what will happen years down the line when that decision comes back to haunt you.'"

Phineas groaned, and Karyna hid an inescapable laugh with a small cough. "You know, I liked you a lot better when you weren't talking."

Jesper shot the commander a scornful smile before diverting his attention back to the makeshift bandage around his torso. Then he pointed to the pile of clothes in the corner of the room and looked at Ari.

"Can you grab my shirt? I can feel Blondie staring, and I wouldn't want to ruin his willpower."

"Ha-ha, real funny, Kelsey," Phineas quipped. Jesper just rolled his eyes in response and told Ari,

"Just get the shirt."

Ari obeyed quickly, grabbing the discarded shirt and handing it to Jesper. The process of putting it back on over his head was slow and painful, but Karyna could tell that Jesper was grateful for any warmth and cover the shirt provided.

The tension in the room was so thick that Karyna felt she was swimming in it, and she cleared her throat to break the silence.

"I wanted to ask you, Phineas, why *did* you help us?"

"Well, your captain helped me out with a job, so I figured I'd return the favor." Phineas seemed content with avoiding any further explanation. "The guy only bought two rooms, so we'll have to share. I guess you and Jesper take one room, and I'll share the other with … Sorry, I never did catch your name."

"It's Ari."

"Right. Ari."

"Works for me," Jesper shrugged nonchalantly. Unable to ignore her hesitancy, Karyna frowned at the captain.

"Jesper …"

"What? Would you rather share a room with Ari or Phineas?" She shook her head vigorously. "I didn't think so. And besides, I need you to keep watch on my injury if need be, Miss Peacemaker," Jesper insisted, winking at Karyna and flashing a grin.

"Jesper, don't. I'm not – I'm not Gifted." Karyna tried to dismiss the notion, wanting to believe that Jesper was just teasing her.

Her, a Peacemaker? The healers who could just as easily inflict fatal pain as they could repair injuries – who were feared for being unpredictable, dangerous even? It didn't sound like her at all. Besides, she couldn't be Gifted. Especially not after she had spent her entire life being taught that believing in anything supernatural was dangerous. It wasn't unbeknownst to Karyna that her family was traditional in every sense of the word; she couldn't even begin to imagine how they would react if they discovered their own daughter was against every conviction they held just by existing.

"What would be so wrong with that?" Jesper questioned. "You just performed surgery and stitched me up perfectly without ever having done it before. Doesn't that seem a little – oh, I don't know – abnormal?"

"You don't know anything about me."

"My apologies," Jesper said, throwing his hands up in surrender. "But we still have to share a room together for the night."

"Fine."

"Fine."

It was, in fact, not fine. Not only had she never shared a room with Jesper before, she had also never shared a room with another person, period. Not even her fiancé. It was wrong. But she assured herself that it would be all right. It wasn't like they had any other choices. Just one night, and then they could all forget that any of this ever happened.

Jesper clung to Karyna as she led him to the room they were to share together, his footsteps unsteady and irregular as he fought to keep himself upright.

"Hold on. We're almost there."

When they reached the room, Jesper made a beeline for the closest place to rest within his sight. The wooden chair stood facing a small table near the door, and Jesper wasted no time in pulling it away from the table and sinking into it. Karyna didn't doubt that if he had stayed standing any longer, his legs would have given out from beneath him again.

Jesper collapsed into the chair, sighing as his body finally released all the stress it had been holding. He let his head fall back to gaze at the ceiling for a moment before closing his eyes, his hair falling gracefully away from his face. She could tell that he was exhausted.

Karyna bit her lip, not wanting to disturb Jesper's momentary peace. "Perhaps I should take a look at the bandage once more to make sure it's held properly before we head to bed."

"Do as you must," Jesper huffed, not opening his eyes or moving in the slightest. Reluctantly, Karyna knelt down beside Jesper and gently lifted the bottom of his shirt to check the makeshift wrapping around his torso. It seemed to be holding quite well, and she couldn't help but feel an ounce of pride in herself for her work.

"Okay, it looks good. We should probably get some rest before tomorrow."

When he didn't respond, Karyna moved to the bed, pulling back the thin cover and situating the pillows. "Kie?" She looked up from her task, finding Jesper's piercing gaze directed on her now.

"Yes?"

"Thank you. I can see how hard it was for you to, uh, get the bullet out and everything."

"Of course. I couldn't let you die." The answer to her was so simple. There was nothing else to it. But, apparently, Jesper didn't see it that way.

"But that's just it. You could've."

"What are you talking about?"

"You don't owe it to me to save me. You have a family, a fiancé, a life to return to."

Karyna couldn't understand where this was coming from. Wasn't he just grateful a moment ago for her actions? "You deserve to live just as much as anyone else."

"You don't know that."

"Don't I? What don't I know?"

"Nothing," Jesper muttered quickly, his eyes darting away from her. It seemed as though he had suddenly realized what he had said and was trying to take it back. But Karyna wasn't going to let it slide so easily.

"No, tell me."

"No."

"I don't understand –"

"It's none of your business," Jesper snapped fiercely. Karyna was taken aback by the anger.

"This is about the whole killing people thing, isn't it?"

"You have no idea what you're talking about," he growled. What Mr. Colbert had told her about Jesper's anger that first day on the Fortuyna floated back to the front of Karyna's memory; did she really want to instigate Jesper even further? Especially when they had to share a room together for the night?

"Wait, do you believe that you dying would make up for all the lives that you took? It doesn't work like that, genius!"

"I suggest you stop talking before I have to force you to stop."

Taking a quivering breath to steel her nerves, Karyna held the gaze of the most terrifying man she had ever known and conjured up a confidence and poise she didn't know she had. "Is that so? Make me, then."

Make me? What was she thinking? Jesper seemed just as baffled as Karyna felt, his eyes wide with shock. It was as if he had absolutely no idea how to react, the usual charisma and bravado that made his voice smooth and his smile brighter suddenly disappearing like the life was being sucked from him. The man was completely speechless. That was new.

"I'm sorry! I didn't mean –"

"I need to step out for a bit of fresh air," Jesper quickly blurted out as he cleared his throat, rising to his feet with a painful slowness. Karyna frowned in response.

"You're injured, Jesper. You can't just go take a walk in the middle of the night."

"Don't wait up for me" was Jesper's only reply, and then he was gone. Again. He had a habit of doing that. And it was beginning to get incredibly annoying.

Karyna attempted to push away the pit growing in her stomach as she prepared herself for bed. *Should I listen to Jesper and just go to bed, or should I stay up and wait for him? What if something happens to him, and there's no one to help him?*

She sat down on one side of the bed, gently brushing her hands through her hair as the never-ending thoughts in her head grew louder and louder. Every so often, the image of Jesper's eyes gazing down at her and the grin on his face would resurface, and Karyna would feel her cheeks heating up.

Why was this happening to her? Why was she feeling like this? This, whatever it was, never happened with Eugene. With Eugene, things were simple. They had their whole life planned out ahead of them; Karyna knew where she would be and what she would be doing when she was eighty years old.

But with Jesper, that wasn't the case. She couldn't even predict what she would be doing the next day. It was thrilling, in a way. And it had been the life that she had dreamed about since she was a young child.

Karyna slipped under the thin cover, the day's exhaustion beginning to catch up to her. She had settled on remaining awake until Jesper returned, just to make sure he was safe and well. But the faint waves in the distance were sounding more and more relaxing and her eyelids were growing increasingly heavy.

I shouldn't be sleeping. I need to wait for Jesper, she scolded herself. But as the minutes passed by, Karyna knew that staying up would become impossible. She could only hope that Jesper would be responsible enough to get himself back all in one piece.

ELEVEN

JUST WHEN EVERYTHING SEEMED TO BE GOING RIGHT, IT WASN'T

ARI

The next morning, Kie and Jesper both emerged from their room looking somewhat disheveled. Kie had slight bags under her eyes and a rat's nest of red hair on her head, and Jesper was looking exceptionally pale. Ari raised his eyebrows at them, biting back a smile from spreading across his face.

"How did you two sleep last night?"

Frowning deeply, Jesper murmured something under his breath that Ari couldn't catch before shuffling past in the hallway and muttering to Ari, "We didn't do anything, if that's what you're trying to get at."

Ari raised his eyebrows and nodded his head ever so slightly, not wanting to incite Jesper's irritation by saying, "If you say so." He chose instead to keep his mouth shut and let Jesper walk away. Kie stayed standing in front of the door, rubbing her face in exhaustion. It seemed to Ari that she was somewhat relieved to see Jesper go.

"Rough night?"

"How do you deal with him all the time?" Kie suddenly blurted out, her voice laced with anger.

"Meaning?"

"He's completely insufferable! One minute he's thanking me for saving his life, and the next he's upset that I saved his life because he thinks his life isn't worth saving. I don't understand!"

"Yeah, Jes is a master of mood swings. Don't worry, though. You learn to keep up with him," Ari assured her, putting his hand on her shoulder to comfort her. But Kie wouldn't have it.

"I don't want to learn to keep up with him!"

Sighing, Ari let his arm drop. There was no use in trying to reason with her if she didn't even want to listen to what he had to say to begin with. "I know Jesper didn't keep his end of the bargain by finding you a new ship to sail with, but I could get you to one of the bigger port towns to find one. With a more … stable cap'n, that is."

"That's not – I didn't mean it like that."

"So you're sticking around then?"

Kie paused to think, a storm of conflict raging in her eyes. But then she nodded slowly. "That's the plan. As much as I can't stand Jesper, you all are my friends now."

A small smile began to tug at the corners of Ari's mouth. "Well, your company is greatly appreciated, whether Jesper admits it or not."

"Jesper is lucky to have found a friend like you. I can't even imagine the things you two must have gone through together."

"You have no idea," Ari snorted.

"Do I get to know what you mean by that?"

"That's a story for another time, perhaps."

"I thought that's what you were going to say."

"Sorry to disappoint."

"No, it's okay. I'll get it out of you eventually."

"You seem so confident about that."

"Oh, I am."

"I can't wait to see you try." It wasn't happening; Ari was sure of that. Perhaps contrary to popular belief, he had the ability to keep a tight lip. Every once in a while.

Kie had retreated back into the room, and she stood in front of the tiniest circular mirror, running her hands through her knotted hair. Ari remained in the doorway, feeling somewhat too uncomfortable to enter the room that Kie and Jesper had shared for the night. When Kie refused to acknowledge his presence, Ari cleared his throat loudly.

"It's probably about time we headed back to the Fortuyna. The crew's definitely getting restless waiting for us."

"You just want to get back as soon as possible to see Gen."

"What? No – what are you talking about?" Ari quickly turned away from Kie's knowing gaze, his cheeks hot and his words spilling from his mouth in a flustered jumble. She clearly had no idea what she was saying.

"Right, of course," Kie chuckled to herself. "Silly me. I don't know what I was saying."

And then she was on the move again, pushing past Ari in the doorway and proceeding down the hall after Jesper. Scoffing in disbelief, Ari shook his head before following Kie to the front of the small building. The old lady who owned the place sat at the counter by the front door, talking in low voices with Phineas.

When Kie and Ari approached, Phineas straightened to his full height and smoothed out the chest of his uniform. "You're leaving, I take it?"

"We're not exactly on vacation."

"If I let you go, promise you won't make me regret it." Ari could only nod. He feared that if he spoke the words aloud, he and Jesper would end up breaking that promise sometime in the future.

"Where's Jesper?"

"Right outside," Phineas replied, motioning with his head towards the window. Ari could make out Jesper's figure standing outside, slightly curled in on itself and waiting patiently. Or, as patiently as Jesper could. "He refused to stay inside any longer."

"Thank you for your help."

Phineas accepted Ari's outstretched hand, shaking it firmly. "It wasn't like I had much of a say in the matter."

"But it is a thank you all the same," Kie responded. She also took a moment to shake Phineas's hand. "Whatever happened to that man that brought us here in the first place?"

The old woman shuffled forward at the question, interjecting herself into the conversation. "He left in the night after the handsome one returned. Had to make sure your friend was all right."

Ari could only assume she meant Jesper as the "handsome one." Kie handed the older woman a few shillings and spoke with her for a few minutes before Ari was rushing them out the door. They had places to be, things to do. And Ari wasn't eager to wait around and found out how long Phineas could keep a promise before he changed his mind on letting them go.

Jesper said nothing to Ari or Kie as he threw his arms over their shoulders to hold himself up as they walked away. There was a sort of tense reluctance in his body, as if requiring help to make it back to the ship was too much for his ego to allow. Jesper's strides were slow and calculated, his side clearly still aching, but he uttered not a sound.

But by the time they had made it back to Fenix's little shack in the harbor, Jesper had fought through the pain enough to walk on his own. Ari figured it was more a pride thing than a recovery of sorts, Jesper not wanting to seem weak in front of his men. But he didn't want to question it at all.

They slipped into Fenix's house to retrieve their belongings, Kie breaking away from the group to go let Gen know they had returned. As soon as the door to their singular room closed behind them, Jesper began stripping off his bloody clothes as fast as his aching body would allow and throwing them into heaps on the floor. Ari simply watched from the side, his arms crossed over his chest, exasperated. So much for keeping the room decently clean.

And it was when Jesper was half naked that there came a pounding on the door. Without waiting for a reply, Gen opened the door and stepped inside with Kie right behind her to find a somewhat disheveled and very injured Jesper staring at her with his shirt off and his boots strewn across the floor, and a slightly annoyed and exhausted Ari.

"Sorry to bother you, Captain, but –"

"What are you doing?" Jesper hissed, attempting to cover his scarred chest with his arms. His face flushed red with shock and embarrassment.

"Sorry, I just heard that you all had come back. And I had some news to deliver."

"Close the door! Quickly!"

"Sorry." Gen hurriedly obeyed Jesper's command and slammed the door shut as Jesper grabbed his shirt off the table. "Where were you? All of you?"

"Sorry?"

"What were you *doing*? And why is Jesper all bloody?"

"Getting this." Jesper held out the compass that had been stolen from him before slipping it around his neck. Ari rolled his eyes at his friend, irritated at the lack of rationality that Jesper possessed. Clearly, Gen felt the same way.

"You're insane."

"I'm assertive. I get things done."

"Never said you weren't. You're still insane, though." Jesper frowned at Gen but shrugged the insult off and continued to dress himself, though not without his fair share of grimaces and winces in pain. He seemed to regain his composure before asking,

"What's wrong?"

"What do you mean?"

"Your face is doing that weird thing you do when you're concerned about something," Jesper stated bluntly. "Something's wrong. And you didn't come in here just to ask me where I was. You don't care about me that much."

"Wrong?" Gen scoffed. "Nothing's wrong …" She trailed off, swallowing nervously when Jesper glared at her. "Okay, maybe not wrong … you're just not going to be happy with what I have to tell you."

"Spit it out already."

"You have a guest here to see you waiting outside on the deck of the Fortuyna."

Jesper stopped buttoning his shirt to frown at Gen. "Who?"

"A young woman. Um, fair hair. Ridiculously wealthy clothes. Smug expression."

"Isa," Jesper muttered, and in that murmur, Ari could feel all the hatred in the world coming from Jesper's mouth.

"She used to be your quartermaster, wasn't she?"

"Only in name. Ruled like a tyrant, though, and didn't let anything get in her way. Not even me." Jesper moved in sharp motions, snatching his boots and stuffing them on his feet. He had completely forgotten about his half-unbuttoned shirt and the jacket that hung on his chair, instead grabbing the sword that hid in its sheath. "That little worm. I'm going to kill her for showing her face on my ship."

"Jesper!" Kie cautioned. "Maybe think before you –"

"No, Kie!" Jesper wheeled on her, coming only inches from Kie's face. "She took everything from me! She dies! Today!"

As though his pain was completely forgotten, Jesper suddenly stormed over to the door, threw it open, and thundered over to the docked ship with massive strides. Ari shared a glance with Gen, registering the worry in her eyes before the three of them dashed out the door after Jesper. It was Ari's job to calm Jesper down to the best of his ability, but if he couldn't, he at least wanted to see what would go down. Because he knew that Jesper certainly wouldn't resolve this quietly.

"What's going on? Who is Isa?" Kie asked, practically running to keep up with Ari and Gen. "What's she doing here?"

"I don't know," Ari huffed, his eyes still trained on Jesper's figure ahead of him.

After a minute, Kie leaned in towards Ari and pressed, "Why has no one ever talked about her before? Is she bad?"

"You and I have very different definitions of 'bad,'" Ari mused. "By my definition, probably."

"And by mine?"

"Definitely." Kie nodded, seemingly satisfied. But once the realization hit her, Kie furrowed her brow.

"I thought you said you didn't know anything about her."

"Put it this way: everyone has their dark secret, right? Well, for Jes, it's her," Ari explained. "And no one withholds something as forcefully as Jesper does unless it's really, *really* bad."

"Well, there has to be someone here who knows something about her. Anything. *You* have to know something."

Ari leaned towards Kie slightly and muttered with a hint of amusement, "That's just it. Not a single person on this ship sailed under Jesper and Isa. Their past is a complete mystery to everyone. All that anyone knows right now are just rumors, speculations."

"Okay … so Jesper just got a new crew. Captains can do that, right?"

"Of course," Gen piped up, striding alongside them. "It happens all the time. Every run, a captain can pick up a new crew if they want."

"Right. But not Jesper," Ari shot back. He didn't need Kie thinking that Jesper was one of *those* people. Sure, Jesper might struggle with commitment issues, but he wasn't completely disloyal and distrustful. "He's not too fond of the whole meeting new people thing."

"She could have done it for him," Kie offered, shrugging. Ari raised his eyebrows at her in disbelief.

"Your optimism is sickening."

"Okay, well, what do you think, wise guy?"

"I think they were all killed. No man left alive."

Kie laughed at him, playfully shoving him in the arm with the belief that he was joking. But when she realized that Ari and Gen weren't laughing with her and hardly even smiling, she stopped. "You're not joking."

"No, I'm not. It happens from time to time. A secret leaks out that the cap'n doesn't want going around because it could damage a reputation or get him caught, so the crew is killed off so the cap'n doesn't have to deal with any loose ends. To keep the reputation intact."

"You're saying Jesper –"

"No, not Jesper!" Ari exclaimed before quickly lowering his voice again. He hadn't meant to get that loud, and he certainly didn't need Jesper knowing they were talking about him. Regarding the one topic he hated most in the world. "He would never. I'm saying, *she* probably would."

"So you're telling me that this mysterious lady singlehandedly killed an entire crew, disappeared for years, and now randomly shows up out of the blue for who knows what reason?"

"Pretty much."

"Does she have a death wish?"

"Seems like it."

* * *

All too soon, they had arrived at the ship to find a young woman with pale skin, hair so blonde it looked almost white, and cold grey eyes, who stood on the deck with a smug grin on her face. A large mass of crew members had crowded around the woman to get a good look at her, but not a single person dared to approach her, so she remained alone, surrounded by the murmurs of every crew member.

An air of confidence hung about her, and despite her undeniable beauty, there was something incredibly intimidating about her. But Jesper didn't seem to care in the slightest. He strode right up to her, seething with an anger so fierce that it was practically tangible.

"Why, you little –"

"What a pleasure to see you too! I see that you haven't changed at all." The woman seemed completely unfazed by Jesper's anger, refusing to even take a step away from him.

"What makes you think you have the right to be here?"

"Last I checked, there wasn't a rule for who can or can't be on a ship."

"Yeah, well, I say you get off," Jesper spat. "Now. Captain's orders."

"You can't tell me what to do. I'm my own captain now. I can do whatever I want."

"Get off. Before I kill you." His voice had dropped to a mere whisper, and it was even more deadly than his yell. Ari bounced on his heels as he watched the encounter, anxious to step in and stop Jesper from killing the woman in front of him. But, at the same time, he knew that if he tried to step in, it would be *him* that would be dead in a matter of minutes.

"You have a lot of big talk, but we both know that you're not going to even *touch* that sword." As she spoke, Jesper moved his hand to the hilt of his sword, clutching the handle with an iron fist.

"Watch me."

"Did you forget everything that happened a few years ago? You don't remember how close we were? How I knew more about you than you knew about yourself?"

"Did you come here just to gloat in my face?" Jesper hissed. The woman grinned back at him.

"I simply dropped by to say hi, since I heard that you happened to be in the area."

"Don't lie."

"Look, I know you hate me –"

"That is putting it mildly," Jesper mumbled, not taking his eyes off of her.

"– but it does you no good to show such hostility in front of your crew. People like us have a reputation to uphold. And being inhospitable towards guests won't help your case."

"You wouldn't know of such things. Besides, *you* are not my guest, and I can treat you however I want. Especially after what you did."

What has she done? Ari had barely half a guess. The woman let the corners of her mouth slide upward as she let loose a small laugh. "Oh? Is that so?"

"Get out of my sight, Isa. Or I kill you."

She took a moment to glance around at her enthralled audience before sighing and turning back to Jesper. Isa seemed tired of Jesper's anger, rolling her eyes at him with a silent annoyance.

"Are you done pushing me away?"

"Don't raise your voice at me."

"I'm not," Isa said, completely calm in her demeanor. She wasn't raising her voice in the slightest. "Besides, you're not my superior."

"I always was. But you never understood that. You were *always* second place."

"We were equals!"

"You were second! And no matter how much you ignore it or try to be first, you will never win."

Isa seemed to be in physical pain, Jesper's words cutting deep into her. A twang of pity struck Ari's heart, but he shook it away. Surely Jesper had a good reason to be angry with her.

"And now is certainly not the time to start trying to be my equal. Don't even try."

"I don't need to try," Isa hissed. "I've always been better than you."

Jesper sighed and rubbed his face with a hand, his anger fading to an irritation. "If you're really wanting to pick this fight right now, can we at least do it in private?"

"Why? Cause you're scared that you'll lose this fight? Cause you're scared I'll reveal all your deep, dark secrets?"

"My cabin. Right now."

"Aren't you going to introduce me to your friends first?"

TWELVE

WORDS TO LIVE BY

ISA

"Aren't you going to introduce me to your friends first? They seem like such lovely people; I'd love to meet them."

"Stop talking."

Jesper harshly grabbed Isa's arm and yanked her towards his cabin, throwing the door open and dragging her inside. His grip was iron strong around her arm, but she knew that protesting would do nothing to help her. So she decided to play it cool, hoping that her calm demeanor would ease his anger instead of inflaming it. The door to the cabin slammed shut behind them, and Isa resisted the urge to flinch as the booming noise made the whole room shake.

"So … I take it that means I don't get to meet your new friends?"

"No, absolutely not. Trust me, I'm sparing them from an unpleasant encounter," Jesper quipped, rolling his eyes at her. His grip on her arm loosened ever so slightly, and Isa used the opportunity to pull herself away. Jesper didn't retaliate, and Isa pasted a snarky grin on her face as she said,

"Your charm never ceases, does it?"

"I know I'm charming. It's one of my best features; you don't need to turn it into an insult," Jesper insisted, his fingers drumming absentmindedly on the gun holster at his side. Pursing her lips, Isa replied,

"You see, but my ability to turn compliments into insults is one of *my* best features."

"I can't tell if you're brave or incredibly stupid, but I can't imagine for the life of me why you would have the idea that you'd be walking away with your life coming here."

"I would like to think it's bravery."

"Of course you would. That's why I really think it's the latter." Jesper took a moment to study her, the eyes that haunted her staring at her with such intensity. She fought back a shiver that ran up her spine as her nightmares resurfaced, and she took a deep breath to calm herself. Jesper watched all of this with a keen eye, only then choosing to speak again. "So, why are you here? What could you possibly want?"

"I wanted to see you." She laced her voice with a fake sweetness, hoping to get in his good graces. But Jesper wasn't buying it.

"No, you don't. You hate me. You stole everything and chained me to the table and then left!"

"I'm being serious, Jesper," she insisted. "I don't hate you."

"I'm not falling for that again."

"I'm not lying! I really came to see you."

"Stop!" Jesper yelled before taking a deep breath to repress his anger. "Just … stop – stop lying to me. I'm sick and tired of all your lies."

"I'm not!"

"You clearly are! I know you well enough to know that you wouldn't risk your life just to come and say hi. That's idiocy."

"You're one to talk. You were worse," Isa countered, bringing to mind the countless times that Jesper had acted on impulse all for temporary satisfaction. He was *so* much worse, and he knew it, too.

"That is a horrible comparison to make. I clearly don't count."

"Why not?"

"Because I don't have a conscience," Jesper stated matter-of-factually as he folded his arms over his chest. Isa repressed the urge to laugh in his face, instead raising her eyebrows as if to say, *Is that so?*

"Sure you have a conscience. It's just hidden deep in the dark recesses of your mind somewhere."

"I thought we'd established the opposite."

"No. We'd established that you *have* one, you just don't use it ever."

Jesper's face conveyed an expression that vaguely resembled disgust and bewilderment. "Why are you being so nice to me all of a sudden?"

"Like I said, I just wanted to drop by and see you. It's been so long since we last saw each other, and we didn't exactly part on good terms. How long has it been? Seven years, give or take?"

"Your friendliness is extremely concerning and somewhat unnerving. I don't like it. Please yell at me or something. I would even take a good slap to the face at this point."

"I'm past that, Jesper."

"No, you're not. You're not fooling anyone."

"Yes, I am. I've grown up, survived the trials of life. The experiences I've encountered have made me old," Isa explained, puffing her chest out ever so slightly and holding her nose high. But Jesper was quick to shoot down her boastful confidence.

"Stop being so absurd and stop talking like that. Do us both a favor and speak in English, please."

"I was …"

But Jesper wasn't finished. "And you being 'old' or whatever? That's the most ridiculous thing I've ever heard. You're about as far from being mature as I've ever seen."

"But I just got here."

"Exactly. And I've seen enough to last me a lifetime. So leave." When she made no move to leave the room, Jesper walked up to her and pointed to the closed door. "You see that door? I want you on the other side of it!" Spinning her around, Jesper pushed Isa towards the door despite her attempts to resist him. "Bye!"

"You can't just push me out!"

"Yes, I can, and I am."

"No!"

"Get! Out!" Jesper made one last effort to shove her out the door, but Isa spun out of the way and turned so that Jesper's back was now to the door.

"You can't tell me what to do! As much as you want to, you can't control me! I won't let you dictate my life anymore! Not even in my dreams!"

Jesper froze in that moment, as if paralyzed under a spell. "What are you talking about? You dream about me?"

That's what he chose to take away from what she said? "I dream about killing you," Isa hissed, ignoring the fact that she was very much lying. But she couldn't let him know what she really saw when she dreamed. "I dream about making you stop."

A smirk tugged at Jesper's lips as the realization began to dawn on him. "You can't stop thinking about me. All these years, and you can't get me out of your head." Smugly, he tapped her forehead with his finger, and Isa angrily swatted his hand away. "You love me."

"I hate you!"

"And yet, you dream about me." Jesper paused and then asked, "Is it like a daily thing?"

"No!"

"Just curious. I'm flattered, though. Didn't know you thought about me like that."

"You shouldn't be flattered," she spat, the charming, sweet-girl act dissipating like sand slipping through her fingers. "You haunt my nightmares, yelling at me. Controlling me."

"I could say the same about you." Jesper paused and seemed to replay the conversation in his head. "And since when have I controlled you? If anything, *you* were the dictator. I was captain, and yet, you were the one calling all the shots and strutted around with your chest puffed out like you owned the place."

"We ruled side by side."

"There was never a 'we!'"

But Isa could have sworn that there was. They had done everything together. It was always Jesper *and* Isa, not just Isa. Sure, it might have been that Jesper was the face of their legend and Isa was the one behind the scenes, pulling the strings, but that was beside the point.

"Fine!" Isa snapped suddenly, her voice rising rapidly before dipping again, trying desperately to keep her cool. "You want honesty? You want the truth about why I'm here? The real reason why I'm here is because I want our old life back!" The words began to tumble out, too fast to control. "I'm bored, and I'm sick and tired of just sitting around when we could be out there having the time of our lives! Do you have any idea how hard it is to be stuck on land, working a minimum wage job and having to rely on someone else to provide for you? To pretend to be in love?" It was almost as if she had rendered Jesper speechless, the seconds that followed thick with deadly quiet. He refused to open his mouth, instead contorting his face into a scowl. "Why is your face doing that?"

"Doing what?"

"That," she crooned, smiling and tilting her head at Jesper. "Looking so stupid."

"And you said you were more mature now."

"I am."

"You think calling me names is mature?"

"Well, insulting you is the one exception that brings me much pleasure."

"I can tell."

Something fiery and ugly flashed in her eyes, and she felt her hands curl into white-knuckled fists. *This isn't how this is supposed to go.* He had completely disregarded her offer. The gut-wrenching feeling of disappointment flooded her senses. In the days leading up to this moment, she had strategically mapped out exactly what she was going to say, and how she was going to act. But nothing was going according to plan. Everything was going completely off the rails. Not even the words she wanted to say were escaping her lips.

"Why are you like this?" she suddenly blurted. Then she froze. She was ruining the moment; she could feel it.

"I'm sorry?"

"Why are you so shut away from the rest of the world? Why do you refuse the pleasures offered to you in favor of pain and suffering? Why don't you care about me?"

"Why don't I care about you?" Jesper scoffed. "Oh, I don't know … maybe it's because you took everything from me, so you get nothing in return! It's none of your business why I choose to be the way I am. Besides, what makes you think I would come with you in the first place?"

"I don't know," she answered honestly. "But I loved the life we had together. And I know you did as well."

"Don't speak of love. You know nothing of it."

"You're wrong." And he couldn't have been further from the truth. The truth was that she loved deeply but was too afraid to show it. She loved passionately but thought that it would scare others off. She loved with her whole heart but didn't want her heart to get broken. But, of course, no one knew that. Sometimes, not even she knew that. It was like, every day, she was rediscovering who she was. Every day, new doors were opened, and new fears emerged. The fears that haunted her draped her like a thick blanket, and there was nothing she could do to shake the blanket off. It was exhausting and constantly draining, but there was no way to get rid of it.

"Honestly, I don't care. I just need you to leave. Your face is getting on my nerves. And believe me, you don't want to see me when I'm really angry."

"Aren't you already angry?"

"Oh, I'm always angry. But this is me being somewhat reasonable, given the situation you've put me in."

It wasn't like she hadn't seen Jesper angry before. After all, they had practically lived and breathed together before the incident. Isa knew Jesper better than anyone else. But, then again, she had never been on the receiving end of his unbridled rage. And she wasn't so sure that she wanted to.

"Remember your favorite spot by the waterfall? As the sun was setting, the golden light would hit the water just right and dance on the rocks. The water was perfectly cool, but not too frigid. And it was so far from the cities, so we could just sit with our feet in the water and listen to the birds sing without being disturbed. Do you remember that?"

"I do."

"I could take you back there again. When was the last time you visited the waterfall?"

"It's been years. Why?"

Isa studied his face, noting the hint of sadness and weariness in his eyes. Just the mention of the waterfall brought a sudden light to his demeanor. "You miss it, don't you?"

"Of course I miss it. What does this have to do with anything, though?"

"You look weary, Jesper. You need a break from this life you're living." *Be sweet, be charming, be everything he wants.* Anything to get Jesper to agree with her.

"I'm fine," Jesper said shortly. "Sure, I might be a little tired, but that's the way I've always been. That's no excuse to run from my problems. I've put all the pieces back together and rebuilt my life ever since you came through, and I'm satisfied with what I've created. I don't need anything more."

"And yet, even as you say it, you know you speak lies."

"You act as though you know my inner thoughts. Well, I hate to break it to you, but you don't know everything about me."

"Oh, but I do. I can read you like an open book."

"It's been seven years. I've changed since then," Jesper insisted, shifting his weight from foot to foot.

"What makes you think I haven't been following you this entire time?"

"You missed me, so you couldn't have been following me. Not for seven years."

"You doubt my abilities, Jesper."

"You're bluffing."

"Really? Am I?"

"You have to be."

Isa bit back a bitter laugh and grinned at him. She *did* know everything about him. More than he apparently realized. And of course she was bluffing. Up until this point, Isa had no idea where he had been. But she liked putting Jesper on edge a little, making him think that she was more impressive and capable than she really was. It was how she kept control of the situation, how she always kept the upper hand. Of course, *he* didn't know that, but she wasn't planning on telling him any time soon.

As he spoke, she walked over and found a seat at the table in the center of the cabin. Jesper's eyes followed her every movement, constantly wary of what she might do next. It wasn't until she had sat down and called him over that he moved.

"Come sit down with me. We have much to catch up on."

THIRTEEN

ERROR: FRIENDS NOT FOUND

JESPER

"I'm not sitting down. I'm not listening to a word you have to say. You killed my entire crew!"

Isa suddenly leapt up from her seat and slammed Jesper into the wall, her knife just inches from his throat. She was seething with anger, and Jesper was partially convinced that she was two seconds away from finishing the job right then and there. He had to bite back a grunt of pain as his back hit the wall, the impact sending a sharp pang up his side. So much for the kind act she had been putting up.

"And I kept you alive, didn't I? When I locked you in that room, you were protected from most of the destruction. You're still breathing because of me, so I would shut my mouth and sit down if I were you. Or I can gut you alive right now if you'd prefer."

Jesper didn't need to be told twice. He lifted his hands up in surrender and released a sigh as the blade came away from his throat. To save his own skin, he didn't hesitate to start making his way to the table in the center of the room. "Okay, okay, I'm sitting."

"Yeah, you do that," Isa snapped sarcastically, and Jesper wheeled around in an instant to point a finger in her face.

"Shut up, or I'll take it back. I'll ignore you out of spite."

"You would enjoy that, wouldn't you?"

"You know I would. I would do it with a smile on my face."

"Do it, and I'll kill you."

"You know, you keep making that threat but not actually doing it," Jesper said nonchalantly, sinking into his chair with a groan and throwing his feet up on the table. "I'm starting to think that you don't have the guts to follow through with it. And I'm beginning to doubt your level of commitment."

"Don't test me, Jesper."

"I don't understand why you're still mad at me. I'm sitting, just like you asked."

"Fine."

"Fine." Isa huffed and slid herself into a chair across from Jesper somewhat more dramatically than usual. Which was saying a lot, considering that she was a top-tier drama queen. Always had been. Clearly not much had changed.

But, despite this, Isa was still quite persistent in catching up with Jesper, hoping for something resembling a heart-warming reunion. Of course, this wasn't how that conversation turned out. Isa's definition of "catching up" was more of an insult battle than anything else. Jesper's patience was wearing thin, but he managed to keep his cool as he recounted what had happened in the seven years since Isa left. Surprisingly enough, she seemed genuinely interested in his life, despite having betrayed him all those years ago. But, as soon as he had finished, Isa returned to her irritating mockery.

"I pity you," Isa sneered, leaning over the table towards Jesper. Jesper peered at her from over the toes of his boots, trying to keep his conflicting emotions hidden.

"You pity me? Why?"

"Because, someday, you're going to die a pathetic and lonely death."

"So will you," Jesper quipped. "Everyone does. And your death will be even more wretched than mine."

"Lies do not become you, Jesper."

"What are you talking about?"

"I will not die, my friend." Isa sat back in her chair, pleased with herself. She grinned cunningly at Jesper, playing with a strand of her fair hair and staring down Jesper with an unnerving glare. Jesper chuckled nervously at her, struggling to comprehend what she had told him.

"What?"

"Yes, you heard me right. I. Won't. Die. I'll live forever."

"Are you drunk?" Jesper burst out, and Isa seemed taken aback by the question. He found it hard to tell whether she was feigning surprise or not.

"Who, me? Never." The sarcasm was thick in her voice. "Why do you ask?"

Jesper took his feet off the table to stand and walk closer to Isa. She had to be lying. Everyone knew that immortality was impossible. So, either Isa was drunk, or she was an insanely good actor. "Because there is no such thing as living forever. The Fountain of Youth doesn't exist."

"I never said anything about the Fountain of Youth. Those are just stories," she stated plainly, as if the answer was right in front of his eyes and he was just too stupid to see it. "Of course the Fountain of Youth doesn't exist." Jesper frowned, furrowing his brow in frustration and confusion.

"Then what?"

"So you're curious."

"Not at all," Jesper lied. There was no way he was giving Isa the pleasure of knowing that he was indeed curious about her idea of "living forever." He couldn't imagine for the life of him what she so confidently believed in that had the ability to shield her from death. There was nothing on the face of the planet that could do such a thing, and they both knew that. "I simply want to hear how idiotic your idea is. It will bring me great joy."

"Just admit that you're curious."

"I'm not." But Isa was still skeptical.

"A little bit."

"No."

"Just a smidge of curiosity?"

"No," Jesper said more firmly, despite the fact that he was very much lying.

Isa hesitated, seeming to retreat into her thoughts before saying, "Well, in that case, I don't think I'll tell you."

"So you admit that you are bluffing, then, if you cannot give me an answer?"

"I'm not bluffing. But I'll make you an offer."

"I'm not interested in any of your offers. I stopped trusting you a long time ago."

"I cannot tell you my secret to immortality –" Isa completely ignored Jesper's refusal of her offer – "but I can show you."

"I'm listening …"

"Come with me, Jesper, and I will make you live forever. Neither of us will die."

"What's the catch?"

"What makes you think there's a catch?"

"There is *always* a catch."

Isa's bell-like laughter rang out through the room, making Jesper feel slightly nauseous. "You really think so little of me. I swear to you on my life that there's no catch."

"Well, you swearing on your life isn't much of a guarantee, now is it?"

"Fine, then. I swear on the life of my dead mother. There is no catch."

But, of course, there had to be. There was no way that Isa's offer didn't come with strings attached. They were attached all right, but they were hidden. Really well hidden. Jesper scrambled in his mind to search for a loophole, some freak incident that would put him in an undesirable position. Perhaps it was a setup, or some enticement to lead him into the hands of the Navy. His mind ran through a thousand possible scenarios, all of them plausible but none of them quite right.

Isa could sense his hesitation, the doubt that still lingered. "Look, you come with me, and I will promise you all the happiness in the world. Everything can go back to the way it was before. We'll be rich and famous, and you'll have more adrenaline in a day than you've had in the past seven years." She was trying to persuade him, and she was doing quite brilliantly, too. Isa knew exactly what to say. "Just think, Jesper. All of the jewels and freedom and adventure that you could ever wish for. No more boredom. No more scrounging for scraps. No more being the rats of society."

"We became rats the moment we chose the life of piracy. We can't escape that."

"Says who?" Isa cocked her head, sliding down further in her chair. "People worshiped us when we were famous. They feared us."

"Fear is different than respect."

"It produces the same results, though."

"I would beg to differ."

Isa's mouth twitched. Frowning and crinkling her nose in disgust, she asked, "Wouldn't you always?"

"What's that supposed to mean?"

"You always disagree with me, even if you know that deep down, I'm right."

"You make all these claims with no proof of anything."

Isa sighed and dropped her head. Jesper could tell that she was just as fed up with him as he was with her. There really was no point in arguing. It would never get them anywhere. They were both much too stubborn for that.

"Look, Isa. Please just leave. I'm too tired for this. I'm already trying to deal with the Navy chasing my tail, and it doesn't help that the dockmaster hates my guts."

"The Navy?" Something about that made her perk up. "Don't I remember hearing you say that your brothers were in the Navy?"

"Yeah. What does that have to do with anything?"

"Nothing," she shrugged, back to being nonchalant. "I was just wondering."

Nodding, Jesper slumped back down into his chair across from Isa. The conversation had already taken a toll on his injured and weary body. But she just wasn't leaving. No matter how many times he told her to go. Perhaps the only way to get her to leave the room was to hear out what she had to say.

"So, if I came with you, I'd get rich and famous. I get that. But what about the immortality?"

"That comes with it. Trust me."

"That's a stupid thing to say; 'course I don't trust you," Jesper snorted. "And what of my crew?"

"Oh, I'm sure they'll be fine," she replied quickly. A bit too quickly. "In fact, they'd be more than fine."

"I'm sorry?" He felt the muscles in his back go tense, straightening up like his body was subconsciously preparing for a battle he didn't even know was coming.

"Please, Jesper. Don't act like you don't know what I'm talking about. People under your command die."

"That's not true –"

"Of course it is. I'm just stating the facts. And I know you've had a good, long run with your crew here, but how much longer do you wager you have until everything goes south again?"

Jesper frowned, unable to keep the pounding of the cannons and the yelling of his crewmates from his thoughts. Everything going south? It was her fault everything went south; it had to have been her who tipped off the Navy before disappearing. It was her fault for abandoning them all to die. But he also couldn't keep that lingering doubt from seeping in that he was the bad luck. Surely there was something different he could have done to save everyone.

"Has anyone ever told you that you're too young to be this cynical?"

"You're trying to change the conversation." Of course he was … but she wasn't supposed to know that. Jesper let out a nervous laugh as Isa rolled her eyes at him. "Look, I want to help you out."

"How is any of this helping me out?"

"We both know, if you stick around much longer, something bad is going to happen, and everyone on this vessel that you care about is going to die."

"You don't know that." Jesper couldn't stop the slightest of trembling from his voice.

"I sure do. History repeats itself, my friend."

"So … what you're saying is that if I don't want my friends to die, I have to come with you."

"Good job!" Isa crooned mockingly, like she was congratulating a small child. "You're starting to catch on!"

"Would any of this be your doing by any chance?"

"I would never kill your friends!"

"Yeah, right," Jesper mumbled under his breath. He wouldn't put it past Isa at all to take out his entire crew just to get him to go with her. And that thought scared him.

"And that quartermaster of yours would make quite the captain, would he not?"

Jesper couldn't disagree, and yet, he wanted to. He so very badly wanted to. It wasn't that he didn't trust Ari to take over for him, but more that he didn't want to put Ari in that position. Jesper knew what it was like to be stabbed in the back and left behind in favor of temporary pleasures. Ari didn't deserve that same painful fate.

"I can't do that to Ari, or to my crew."

"Oh, c'mon! Really, Jesper? You're going to let a few insignificant people hinder you from living out your dreams? I'm disappointed, really. I expected more from you, Jesper. Just picture the rewards, the fame, the thousands of people bowing at your feet."

"I hate people."

"Everyone except me, right? You love me."

"I hate you."

"Okay … forget the people, then. But, besides that. This – this mindless, futile life you've constructed is not what you were born to do. You were made for so much more, and you know it, too. You're not going to get anywhere by hiding in the shadows. Believe me, I know. I've been doing the same thing myself for the past seven years. It's pointless and a complete waste of time."

"What was stopping you? Your cowardice?" Jesper mocked. Isa ignored the ridicule.

"You."

"Me?" He could hardly believe what he had heard. *Me, stopping her?* It didn't make sense to him, because he knew her. She didn't fear him, didn't give him the time of day. But, perhaps, there were things he didn't know about her.

"And what's stopping you, Jesper?"

He didn't want to answer that question. The answer would be way too complicated. And would reveal way too many secrets that he didn't want her knowing.

"Nothing," he said flatly. "I'm not hiding from anyone."

Isa's smile was thin and unsettling. "And yet, here you are. Running from the Navy."

"Funny how I recall you doing the same exact thing when the Navy caught us off the coast of Vyena," Jesper pointed out. "You certainly didn't stick around long enough to help me out." Isa nodded once slowly. Something like frustration crossed her face.

"I came back."

"That doesn't excuse what you did! You were the one who ratted us out; I know it was you!"

"You don't have any proof of anything."

Jesper scoffed at her. "Yeah? Well, real convenient for you, then, to just lock me in the cabin and run away with all our valuables."

"I didn't do it, I swear."

Jesper let his eyes drop to the rings on his hands, and he absentmindedly began fidgeting with them in the hopes they would distract him from his unwanted guest. He could feel Isa's stare boring into the top of his head, and it was only getting more uncomfortable.

"You keep emptying your cup, Jesper," Isa said softly. "And pretty soon, it's going to run out."

"What?"

"Just as much as you pour into others, you need to be poured into."

"Stop speaking in riddles. It makes no sense." He had absolutely no idea what Isa was talking about. But she seemed to be quite amused by his confusion, the corners of her mouth tugging upward into a smirk. The sign of sarcastic mockery that she had picked up from him.

"Sometimes I forget that you are uneducated."

"Uneducated, and somehow still smarter than you."

Isa waved a hand at him dismissively. "What I was trying to say was that you need to let others take care of you like you take care of your crew. Because you are growing tired. I can see it. In your eyes, in the way you carry yourself."

"Is that so? And how do you propose I do that?"

"The trip we took to the waterfall always seemed to help."

"You think that you are the solution to my problems?" Jesper scoffed, the idea sounding too absurd. She had to have been joking. There was no way that she actually believed she could solve all his problems. The problems *she* had created. *She* was the problem.

"Just as you are the solution to mine."

"Absolutely not."

"The way I see it, there aren't any disadvantages to coming with me. You get money, you get fame, you protect your friends from dying, and you get to have a much-needed break from your exhausting life. Live hard, die young, am I right?"

"Don't use my motto against me."

"It works, though, doesn't it?"

He couldn't disagree with her. But how was it that she knew exactly what he was going through? How did she possibly know that Jesper was practically, silently, falling apart at the seams?

His head was throbbing, threatening to burst with all the conflicting thoughts that clashed together. But the one thought that seared a hole into the deepest part of his chest: being the reason that Ari gets hurt. That Gen and Deacon get hurt. That *Kie* gets hurt.

He would never be able to forgive himself if that happened. And he couldn't help but internally relent and acknowledge that Isa was partly right. He did have a bad track record for putting his loved ones in harm's way. *What would happen if I simply removed myself from the equation?*

"Okay, all right! I'll do it!" Jesper yelled over his thoughts, trying to silence them. Isa shrunk back slightly into her chair, a brief look of confusion crossing her face. "I – I'll go with you … I just – I can't lose anyone again."

"You're making the right decision," Isa purred, her voice sickly sweet. Jesper could feel his heart rate spike suddenly, and he threw a finger in her face accusingly.

"Don't! Don't give me that …"

"Give you what?" She was faking innocence; it was like gears grinding together inside his chest whenever she tried to deceive him like that. It drove him absolutely insane.

"I'm not doing this for you, Isa."

"Oh, I'm sure not. I never expected you to."

"Good, because I'm not," Jesper spat back at her, his hands balled into white-knuckled fists in his lap. Isa, on the other hand, stayed completely calm. She was very good at that sort of thing.

"I know."

"Good."

"Good." Once again, Isa's dark smile made Jesper's stomach twist into knots. She slowly rose to her feet, her body seamlessly straightening with a snakelike motion. Everything about her was eerie, slightly off. She had this otherworldly air about her that hung in the cabin like the cover of fog. But then she reached out a hand and beckoned him, and the aura around her changed. It shifted suddenly to that of an angel or a heavenly creature. Her smile was radiant, and the hand that was outstretched to him seemed enticing and warm.

"Walk with me, my friend. We must tell your friends the news, and then we will make way. We have so much to do."

The news.

FOURTEEN

DEAD MEN TELL NO TALES

ARI

He felt like he couldn't breathe, and his heart pounded so quickly that he feared it would explode. After all this time, he had trusted Jesper. Trusted his captain with his life. And never in a million years had he expected this to happen. It wasn't supposed to happen.

"What are you talking about?" Ari asked, his head buzzing and his body numb with shock. He paced back and forth in the small captain's cabin, his nervous energy too much to let him sit still. Jesper sat draped casually in his chair at the table, fidgeting with the rings on his fingers like he always did when he was anxious but didn't want to show it.

"I'm leaving for a bit, that's all."

"That's all? How long is 'a bit?'"

"I promise I'll be back soon. In the meantime, you can captain the ship in my place. I know you've always wanted to have your own crew and ship. Now's your chance, in my absence."

"I don't want to captain the ship!" Ari shouted, causing Jesper to glance up at him with surprise. "And I don't believe you! I can't trust you! The last promise you made me was that you were leaving your old life behind for good and putting our crew first!"

"You can trust me!" Jesper insisted. "You can –"

"No, Jesper! Are you even listening to me right now?"

"I am, I swear!"

"No, you're not! You're such a liar! And to think, that after all this time, I was willing to do anything for you! I was willing to lay down my life for you!"

Jesper seemed stunned by Ari's criticism, and he rose from his seat. When he spoke again, his voice was unusually soft. "I would do the same for you. You know that, Ari. You're my family, my brother."

Yes, Ari knew that Jesper would do anything for him, but that wasn't what he was doing. Jesper was going to abandon his crew, his friends, to pursue his own desires and dreams. He was being selfish, and if he couldn't see that himself, there wasn't really any point in trying.

"I can't do this with you. Not here. Not now."

"Ari …"

"If you're going to go, just leave. Get out of my sight!"

"Don't be like that," Jesper whispered, his nonchalant and tough demeanor completely gone. Ari sighed, pinching the bridge of his nose and watching as Jesper began to move towards the door to the cabin. And as Jesper reached for the door handle, Ari realized that he wasn't done. Not yet. There were still thoughts that he had to get off of his chest before Jesper ran off with his enemy.

"You know, I left my family, the only home I ever knew, to follow you. I hardly even remember my siblings' names anymore! Do you know how much that scares me every day? I try to recite their names in my head every morning when I wake up, and I panic when I trip up on one of the names. But I do it because I'm devoted, I'm committed to you. I made that promise years ago! And now – now you choose money and power over your friends. Over me!"

Jesper whipped around, his desperation evident in his face. "I'm not in it for the money! I don't care about all that! Look at me, Ari! Do you really think that I would betray my friends, my family, for money?" Conflicted, Ari gave no response. He couldn't even look Jesper in the eye. "Look. Isa says –"

"I thought you would have learned by now not to believe anything Isa says. Don't you remember what happened seven years ago?"

"She says that she has unlocked the secret to immortality. Immortality, Ari!"

"That doesn't exist! I know you're not that stupid," Ari argued, shaking his head. Jesper ignored Ari's retort in favor of defending himself.

"And on top of that, you have to have noticed by now that I don't belong here. This isn't what I was born to do!"

"And what is it that you are born to do, exactly?"

"I …" Jesper struggled to explain his answer, finding himself at a loss for words. Ari bit back a quip and chose to remain silent, trying to stay patient as he waited for Jesper to come up with a response. "I don't really know," he finally admitted. "All I know is that I was made for more. I feel … I feel like I'm trapped in this cage, and I need to get out. Every night, I dream of freedom, and adventure, and this life isn't it! I can't be stuck making boring brandy runs for the rest of my life!"

"I cannot discount your dreams, Jesper. But have you ever considered that your dreams might not be realistic? Sure, that was your life in the past, but times change. Maybe you'd be more content with what life has already given you instead of always reaching for more if you just took a moment to look around at the life we've created together."

"Who are you trying to convince here? Me, or yourself?"

"How could you do this to me?" Ari asked, his voice cracking in despair. Jesper wasn't listening to a word he said, and lord forbid he actually allow himself to be convinced by what Ari was saying. "After everything we've been through together, you're just going to pick up and leave?"

"I'm not doing anything to you! Why do you always have to play the victim?"

"Yes, you are! You are betraying me, that's what you're doing!"

"Betraying you, huh?" Jesper yelled in Ari's face. "If this is what you consider betrayal, then I'm afraid you'll have a difficult life, my friend!"

"What's that supposed to mean?"

"I am simply pursuing something different, and you think I am personally offending you? Please! I have suffered a thousand pains more excruciating than you can even begin to comprehend! Every hour, waking and sleeping, my mind is constantly fixed on the countless tortures I have endured! I have had just a glimpse of what hand life deals to us, so this – what I am 'doing to you' – is nothing compared to the grand scheme of things!"

"Don't you dare lecture me on the tortures of life!" Ari roared, wildly gesturing out of pure rage. He had stopped thinking clearly, stopped choosing his words carefully. In part, the next words that came from his mouth didn't match up with the thoughts in his head. "I don't care what you've endured! I don't care about your stupid life philosophy! That gives you no right to stab me in the back and then go and pretend like it never happened!"

"I am doing no such thing!"

"Stop lying to me! I swear, lie to my face one more time and I'm going to break your jaw!" Ari screamed, completely serious in his threats. But Jesper didn't seem to entirely believe him.

"I'm not lying to you!"

And without hesitation, Ari sent his white-knuckled fist straight into Jesper's jaw, fueling the punch with all of the intensity of his consuming fury. The punch easily found its target, hitting Jesper's jaw with a loud thud and sending Jesper crashing to the ground. Ari stood over Jesper as he watched his friend cradle and massage his jaw, remorseless and numb with anger. Jesper deserved it. He deserved it all.

"Like I said, stop lying."

Slowly, Jesper rose to his feet once more, still cradling his injured jaw. Instead of the hardened and confident captain that Ari was used to seeing, he saw a meek and pitiful young man standing before him. In Jesper's eyes, Ari could see the vulnerable kid he found half-dead on the beach all those years ago. Ari couldn't help but feel a slight twang of guilt shock his system, but he quickly pushed it away.

"Ow," Jesper whined. "That hurt."

"My sincerest apologies," Ari replied sarcastically. Jesper glared at him.

"Shut up."

"At least I can keep a promise."

Jesper flinched and averted his eyes, dropping his hand from his jaw. "I hope that someday, you'll understand why I'm doing this."

"I will never understand. You are *destroying* yourself, Jesper. You really don't think I've noticed all the times that you make absurd bets on games you can't win, drink your pain away, and don't tell anyone what is really going on? You hole up inside yourself and think that it will somehow solve all of your problems. Well, guess what, that's not how it works. And it's backfiring on you. All of your mistakes and your past are catching up to you."

"How do you know?" Jesper asked, crinkling his nose in disgust. Raising his eyebrows, Ari replied as calm as humanly possible,

"If you can't see it as clearly as I can, then you are blind."

"Now you're just insulting me. I see what this is. You're starting to sound like Isa. Always with the insults. Grow up, Ari."

"And you are not listening to me, either. You are deaf as well as blind."

"Insulting me isn't going to help you win this argument."

"I'm not trying to win anything. I am simply telling you what you are." Ari stood confidently before Jesper, trying his hardest to prove that he was the better man in this fight.

"And what am I?"

"A half-wit, backstabbing lunatic who can't recognize betrayal when it's staring him right in the face."

"Oh, thank you," Jesper muttered. "I really appreciate that compliment."

"Look me in the face and tell me I'm wrong." Jesper's eyes slowly found their way to Ari's, his gaze racked with guilt. He didn't open his mouth to argue. "You won't. Because you can't. You know I'm right."

"Despite what you might believe, I do still care about you, and the crew. A lot. Probably more than you realize."

"Then why are you putting yourself and your desires above that of your crew?"

Jesper hesitated, and Ari could tell that he was conflicted. Between making up another outrageous excuse and telling Ari the truth. "Because … because I don't deserve this life, the blessings I've been given. Not after what I've done. And I can't be the reason that you all are put in danger again."

He just didn't get it. Jesper wasn't understanding that his past didn't matter. He was just going to throw away everything they had worked to build together because deep down he believed he was only ever meant to be the bad guy. "That doesn't mean you should go and ruin everything."

"It means that I go back to being the person I was raised to be."

"Which is what exactly?"

"The villain of the story." The statement slammed Ari in the chest, the wind being knocked from his lungs. *Is that really who Jesper believes he is?*

"Who told you that? Who forced you to believe that you're the villain? Isa?" At the name, Jesper's eyes shot up to meet Ari's gaze. The sure-fire sign that Ari had guessed right. And it ripped a hole right in Ari's heart. "Because it's not true at all. You're not the villain of this story, Jesper. Not of any story."

"You're wrong. We both know you're lying. I'll never be the hero. I take lives, not protect them. I destroy things, not fix them or right the wrongs of this world."

"Let me help you fix that problem, then. Just because it isn't like that now doesn't mean it can't be changed."

"I don't need your help."

"Fine!" Ari spat. "You go deal with your own problems and shut yourself away from the rest of the world! Go ahead and break every promise you've ever made to me!"

"You know what? I will! You wouldn't care anyway!"

Shaking his head, Ari stepped away from his old friend. He just couldn't take it anymore. "I used to disagree with you. But I don't think I can this time."

"You do that! Go wallow in your own self-pity and loneliness. I'll be out there, enjoying myself and having an amazing time – and not having to deal with *you*!"

Jesper poked Ari in the chest accusingly. Ari's anger flared, and he swatted Jesper's finger away. "Stay out of my face, Kelsey. I'm warning you."

"And you stay out of my way, Cadwell."

"Don't let me stop you, then."

Ari gestured for the door and stepped to the side, lowering his gaze from Jesper. Jesper silently obeyed, all too eager to get out of the stifling room. He risked one more glance at Ari, and seeing his restrained anger, Jesper nodded to himself and walked around Ari to the door. He didn't hesitate to open the door and leave Ari alone in the cabin, Ari's guilt more overwhelming than it had been a minute before.

After waiting a moment to collect himself and repress his anger, Ari followed Jesper out the door, watching as Jesper walked over to where Isa stood on the deck. He could see Kie looking on as well from the corner of his eye, looking utterly distraught and entirely confused about the situation. Jesper had refused to tell her anything at all or even say goodbye, and Kie was left helplessly in the dark without any idea of why Jesper was suddenly leaving.

Once Jesper reached Isa, he stopped beside her and muttered, "Let's get out of here."

"As you wish, my captain. You've made the right choice, believe me."

"Are we leaving?" Jesper asked impatiently. Isa nodded in reply.

"Right. Sorry."

Ari remained quiet as Jesper and Isa headed for the gangplank. He felt as though he had been pounded into the wooden boards beneath his feet, weighed down by the overwhelming hopelessness and heartbreak growing in his chest. *What if Jesper never comes back?*

And just like that, the person who was the closest thing that Ari actively had to a brother was gone, and Ari had no idea if he would ever come back or not. Part of Ari wanted desperately to believe that Jesper would someday return, but seeing Jesper's pure joy at being free and alive again, Ari highly doubted it. Keeping promises wasn't exactly Jesper's strong suit, nor was putting the needs of others above himself. And when offered the opportunity to have adventure once again, Jesper would always jump in headfirst. After all, who would want to give up such a treasure for a tiresome life already lived?

FIFTEEN

SIBLING RIVALRIES

JESPER

Nearly a month had slipped by since Jesper had last stepped foot aboard the Fortuyna, and while the passing time had softened much of the aching pain of his old bullet wound, he still couldn't shake the chilling discomfort and unease that followed him around. Isa had been nothing but sweet and sentimental in the moments they spent together, too similar to what life looked like more than seven years ago. And as if the world wished to echo her unnatural beauty and charm, Sovi's towns were beginning to transform.

The port town of Pressons Landing was bustling with life, foreigners and locals alike. Everyone was preparing for one of the biggest holidays of the year, the Festival of the Summertide. Banners of bright colors were strung from house to house, and flowers that matched in vibrancy were in full bloom. A tall maypole stood at the center of the town square, its ribbons blowing in the cool ocean breeze. The festivities of the holiday weren't starting for another whole week, but it was as if the holiday was already in full swing. All the sights and sounds and smells overwhelmed Jesper with their intensity, and he had to stop and inhale deeply to take it all in. Fresh bread from the bakery, flowers in the windowsills of every house, the lilting music of the bard. It was all so merry, so warm and welcoming. Jesper could hardly remember the last time he had genuinely smiled. His life was always burdened with pain and anger and suffering, never joy or cheerfulness. But this, this moment, made him feel more alive than he had ever been. His body was somehow lighter, somehow quicker. And he loved every second of it.

"You seem happier than usual."

"That's because I am," Jesper replied, not looking in Isa's direction. He couldn't let his perfect mood get spoiled by her, not now.

"I didn't know you enjoyed the holidays so much."

"I didn't either."

Isa snorted to herself before asking, "When was the last time you came here?"

"It's been a long time."

"Really," she muttered. "I couldn't tell."

They continued walking through the streets together, Jesper admiring almost everything he saw. He was welcomed by everyone that he accidentally bumped into, even a few small children that were running about with colorful streamers in their hands. It was extremely odd to Jesper, being greeted and appreciated by each person he met. Usually, it was the other way around. Most of the time, people were trying to kill him rather than give him free food and shake his hand.

The children he had bumped into were especially taken to him, clinging to him as he tried to follow Isa through the streets. One of the kids managed to climb onto his back and sat on his shoulders, overjoyed with the ability to see over the heads of the crowds. The kid grabbed Jesper's hat and set it on his own head, clinging to Jesper's dark mass of hair and grinning like it was the best day of his life. In one hand, Jesper held a ribbon given to him by a little girl, and in the other, he held the hand of a young boy.

"Over there! Look!"

The boy on Jesper's shoulders pointed towards the town square, where a crowd of people had gathered. Wanting to get a better view, Jesper directed the children to an opening in the crowd to see what was going on. An upbeat folk dance had captured the attention of the crowd, prompting some of the townspeople to even join in. The dancers twirled in circles, their feet moving in an intricate style to the tune of the bard's jig. And at the center was a young girl who looked to be about Jesper's age, and he couldn't seem to take his eyes off her. Pure joy radiated from her, and the setting sunlight hit her golden hair at just the right angle so it looked as though she was glowing.

"Come dance!" the children begged, pulling Jesper towards the circle of dancers.

"Oh, no. I don't dance."

"Come on!"

The two children grabbing at his hands managed to drag him to the front of the crowd, where they got a front row view of the incredible spectacle. Jesper was barely two feet from the circle of dancers, but the children wanted to be even closer. They wanted to be *in* the dance.

"Let's dance!" they screamed, tugging even harder on Jesper's arms. But despite their consistent begging, Jesper refused to give in. Not one chance existed in a million that he would be convinced to dance.

Looking out over the heads of the dancers, Jesper's eyes darted around frantically, trying to relocate the beautiful dancer. After a moment, he spotted the gold head of the girl coming towards him through the group of dancers. And when she emerged from the dancers, Jesper couldn't help but stare.

Her pale blush-colored dress flared out around her like a blooming rose, bedazzled with the shimmering dewdrops of morning. The jewels she wore on her head framed her face perfectly, resting on top of her wavy hair. She had the most striking teal eyes that were sad and refined, like she had seen all the horrors of the world, and yet, she held an air of innocence and purity that glistened as white as the fresh snow on a bright winter's morning.

"Come dance with me," she beckoned, reaching out a hand to take his. The boy on Jesper's shoulders climbed down, putting the hat back on Jesper's head. As soon as the boy's feet hit the ground, he began helping the other children push Jesper toward the dancers. "The children insist."

"Oh, I don't really think –"

Before he could even finish his sentence, the girl grasped his hand and pulled him into the dance circle. She led him in an intricate twirl, spinning around and around until he was dizzy. But he didn't care. His heart raced with adrenaline to the beat of the music, pounding in his chest and in his ears. He could only fall deeper into the trance of the girl's eyes and hope he didn't trip on anyone's feet.

But just as soon as the dance had started, the music ended, and the dancers bowed to their partners in respect. Still partially in a daze, Jesper bowed to the girl, his gaze not leaving her face. He was almost scared to look away, half-believing that she would vanish into thin air if she didn't remain under his watchful eye.

"What's your name?"

"Selene."

"That's beautiful. What does it mean?"

"Why does it matter what my name means?" she asked, peering at him from under her hooded lashes. "A name is just a name."

Jesper shook his head. "That's not true. I believe every name has a special meaning, a unique purpose."

"Well, in that case," Selene purred, "it means moon goddess."

"Very fitting."

"You think?" Jesper could only nod. He had completely forgotten about Isa and his real reason for being in town. "Well, thank you, –"

"Jesper. Captain Jesper Kelsey." He bowed his head, adding a flourish of his hat. Selene giggled at him, returning the gesture with a small curtsy.

"The pleasure is all mine, Captain."

Jesper extended an arm for Selene to take, asking, "Walk with me?"

"Of course."

Selene took his arm, and they began to stroll the square together, talking in hushed voices and giggling like little school children. No one seemed to pay the couple any attention, and Jesper took the moment to relish in the undisturbed pleasure. He could hardly remember the last time that he was allowed to relax fully and not have to constantly be looking over his shoulder. It was like the town was so removed and tucked away from the rest of the world that they had no idea who he really was. How wonderful it felt.

* * *

"Jesper! What are you doing?"

"Isa!" Jesper turned quickly to see a furious Isa striding over to where he stood with Selene. He had completely forgotten about her. Apparently, Selene was just as disappointed to see Isa, her disgust showing in her voice.

"Do you know her?"

He sighed frustratedly, letting his head fall back and his eyes close for a beat. Of course Isa had to ruin the moment. "Unfortunately, yes."

"Jesper, we were supposed to be running errands, remember?" Isa hissed. "Stop flirting with the townspeople!"

"I wasn't flirting!"

"Yes, you were! Believe me, Jesper, I know you. And you were most definitely flirting with her. Come on, let's go."

Jesper shot a quick glance of apology to Selene before stepping away and following Isa down the street. He could tell that Isa was mad at him, her pale hands sheet white from being clenched so tightly and her shoulders tense with frustration. She withheld from speaking to him, and Jesper debated as to whether or not to break the silence between them. He finally settled on keeping the silence, until Isa chose to speak to him first.

"Why did you do that?"

"I'm sorry?"

"Why were you flirting with that stranger like that?" she spat, still refusing to look at him as they trudged ahead. Her hand tightened around the strap of the bag on her back subconsciously.

"What's it matter to you?"

"It doesn't." Her response was terse and thick with emotion, but it was easy to tell that she did indeed care and wanted an answer from him.

Jesper scoffed to himself and rolled his eyes. "Look, Isa … if it's any consolation to you, I couldn't help it, okay? It's just been so long since I've been out around town, and –"

"Can it, Jesper. You don't need to defend yourself against me."

Jesper breathed a silent sigh of relief. He was struggling to understand within himself that it was somehow easier to flirt with complete strangers than people he knew, and that he had so many pent-up emotions that he didn't know what to do with. On any given day, he would blame Isa for all the problems he faced, but today, he found it significantly harder to put on his usual detached mask that he always wore to keep people at arm's length. For what reason, he couldn't quite put his finger on it.

"Where are we going, anyway?"

"Really? You don't recognize it? Has it really been that long?"

And as she spoke, Jesper immediately recognized where they were. The lightly trodden path that led away from the town, the hovering fog, the hidden building that no doubt was waiting for them at the end of the path. He had walked this road a million times; he knew it like the back of his hand.

Jesper walked as if in a daze, each step heavy with anticipation. Each step closer to *her*. What would she think of him? Was it even possible, after all these years, that she could tolerate him? Even before he had run away from his old life, she could hardly stand him.

"Why'd you bring me here, Isa?"

"What are you worried about? It'll be a nice little reunion."

"Are you trying to get us killed?" Jesper hissed at Isa. She smiled sweetly back at him.

"Perhaps."

As they approached the low-sitting building, Jesper could feel his heart sink. Part of him wanted to see her again, but part of him didn't want to know what she thought of him. Isa acted with much more confidence than he felt, striding up to the door and slipping inside. Walking through the doorway was like hitting a wall of darkness and mustiness, and Jesper fought back a cough in the lingering dust. Some things never changed.

"This place still looks as lousy as it did all those years ago," Jesper muttered under his breath to Isa as he looked around, his eyes still straining to see in the dim lighting.

"I could say the same about you."

Jesper's head snapped up at the voice of a tall figure coming down the stairs. Despite Jesper's whispers, the figure had still managed to hear him and reply in a booming voice that was unforgettable. Jesper shot her a tight grin, laced with sarcasm.

"Nice to see you, too, Clary."

"What are you doing here, little brother?"

"Don't blame me," Jesper argued. He pointed to Isa, trying to shift his sister's attention to the woman at his side. "She dragged me back into this."

Clary's big hazel eyes refused to move from Jesper. "I thought you said you were done with this life."

"Yeah, well … I guess I was wrong."

"Apparently. I'm not surprised, though."

"You're not?"

"Of course not," she laughed, coming to stand in front of the two pirates, the gold bangles on her wrists and massive golden earrings clinking with each step. Despite living in a world where being elven was taboo, Clary sure did love to adorn her ears in beautiful jewels and precious metals. "We were born into this life. It runs in our blood, Jesper. The piracy, the crime; it runs in our family. You cannot escape it, even if you tried."

"Yeah? Well, maybe this is where it runs out. You know, I'm so glad you have an unwavering faith in me. Your vote of confidence is overwhelming."

An expression of what looked like amusement passed over Clary's face before she turned to Isa and nodded in greeting. Clearly, she didn't know of what Isa had done to Jesper on that fateful day.

"What can I do for you, Miss Fielding? You have something for me, don't you?"

Isa brought forward the small sack in her arms, placing it before Clary. A grin growing on her face, Clary opened the sack and pulled out a wooden chest. She didn't even need to open the chest to know what was contained inside.

Jesper narrowed his eyes at the chest, as if gazing hard at it would allow him to see through the walls of the chest. There was something about the box that he didn't like. It looked oddly heavy for such a small thing, and the wooden sides were too pristine for how old the chest had to be. "Hold on. What is that?"

"Nothing you need to be concerned about," Clary replied nonchalantly. Jesper's frown only deepened.

"Last time you said that, you ended up getting me arrested and left me in jail for four days before breaking me out. Four days!"

"What? It was entertaining!"

"It was terrifying!" Jesper retorted. "I was *nine*!"

"Stop being such a baby. I wouldn't have left you in there if I didn't have the complete and utter belief that you would be fine. You probably could have broken out yourself if you wanted to."

"Shut up," he muttered, averting his gaze from his sister and the mysterious chest in her hands.

"You know I'm right."

"In your dreams." Clary had already moved away with the chest, clearly bored of the conversation. Jesper clenched his fists angrily, frustrated at her neglectful attitude towards him. She always did this, and it drove him crazy every time.

"Isa, what's in the chest?"

"Like Clary said, nothing that concerns you."

Jesper threw his head back and groaned loudly. "Not you too!"

"Sorry, Tiger. Not today."

"But you literally dragged me back into this business! Why are you both keeping secrets from me?" Jesper protested, making wild gestures towards Isa and in the direction of which Clary had disappeared once more.

"Because now you have moral standards," Clary called from the next room over.

"No, don't pull that on me! Only Mom was allowed to say stuff like that!"

"Perhaps, but Mom's not around anymore, is she?"

"Friendly word of advice," Isa murmured to Jesper, "Stop talking now before you dig yourself into a hole that you can't climb out of."

"I hate you both."

"So, brother, what are you doing with yourself these days?" Clary asked as she returned from the adjacent room. "I rarely hear of your notoriously idiotic adventures anymore."

"I picked up a new crew, and we've been smuggling contraband to the islands. Quietly."

Clary raised her eyebrows in surprise, a slight smile tugging at the corners of her mouth. "Quietly. I'm amazed. It doesn't seem like you to fly under the radar like that."

"Yeah, well, it's not exactly exciting, but it gets the job done. And keeps my crew safe," Jesper explained as Clary patted him on the shoulder.

"Look at you, being a responsible human being. Good for you."

"Are you mocking me?"

"Of course not!"

Clary turned her back to her two guests, busying herself with rearranging the various colored bottles on her shelf. "So, where are you two headed after this?"

"Headed?" Jesper asked. "Oh, um, I don't know."

"I believe we'll stick around the island for a bit and then make our way over towards the coast of Aerithos." Isa quickly jumped in upon Jesper's uncertainty. Both Jesper and Clary made the same face, their brows furrowing in confusion. Jesper asked,

"Aerithos? Why Aerithos?"

"You'll see when we get there."

"Why do you always have to leave me in the dark?"

"Don't worry. You'll like it," Isa reassured him, smiling gently to Jesper. Jesper couldn't help but feel his stomach twist into knots at her smile. Something seemed off about her.

"Again, I hate you."

"Oh, believe me, I know. You don't need to keep reminding me every few minutes."

"Are you two just going to stand there and bicker, or are you going to get out?" Clary quipped, still pointlessly rearranging her colored bottles. Jesper shot a glare at her as he said,

"My apologies. I wasn't aware that you wanted us to leave so soon. And I thought our family reunion was going so well."

"I hate to burst your bubble, but this little reunion is anything but 'well.'"

Jesper smiled sarcastically at Clary and then turned to Isa. "C'mon, Isa. Let's get out of here before we bother my dear sister any further."

"But, I thought –"

"You thought wrong. Let's go."

Isa made no reply as Jesper ushered her out the door. Jesper refused to look back over his shoulder at his sister, resisting the urge to show Clary his desire to rekindle the close relationship they once had in their childhood.

"Jesper!" Clary called suddenly, and Jesper stopped to look back at her. "You know you don't have to stay away forever, right?" Jesper nodded gratefully, surprised that she was actually extending some sort of warmth to him. "I made a promise to Mom that I would protect you. I'm afraid I haven't kept that promise over the years, but I want to start now. Will you give me that chance?"

"Of course. Thank you, Clary."

"Don't thank me just yet."

SIXTEEN

SOMETIMES I WISH MY LIFE WAS NORMAL

JESPER

The ocean stretched out for as far as he could see. Moonlight cast a silvery glow on the world below, the surface of the water brilliantly lit by the cloudless night sky. Millions of stars dotted the heavens, but Jesper could have sworn that he had never seen those particular constellations before. They certainly didn't exist on any map he'd ever studied. The moon, too, was abnormally small, especially considering the amount of light it was giving off. It was full and bright, but if he was a complete idiot, he could have easily mistaken the moon for just another star. Perhaps even weirder than that, though, was the stillness in the air. On the open ocean, the air always moved. But here, there was nothing at all, and yet, the ocean surface still rippled and swayed gently.

He looked down, expecting to see the familiar wood boards of his ship or the white sands of the shore. It registered in his mind that there wasn't a deck to stand on or any kind of land at all. He stood instead on the surface of the water itself. His feet refused to move, as if they were glued to the floor. Well, the ocean surface. But it wasn't panic or fear that clouded his mind; it was peace. He couldn't describe it, but it was almost as if he knew somehow that he was safe. And then he looked up again, and that's when he saw *her*.

She was like a mirage on the horizon, dancing and shimmering with an otherworldly aura. Her copper hair blew gracefully about her face, despite the unnatural tranquility of the wind, as if the entire world was holding its breath. She wore a dress that hugged her waist and draped down to her ankles, and it sparkled so brilliantly that he swore it was made entirely of minuscule diamonds. Or maybe it was stars. The luminous fabric pooled around her wrists and swished about her legs as she walked, looking blue one minute and white or silver the next.

As she came closer, her toes clinging to the tiny ripples of the ocean, his breath caught in his throat. Now he could see her face more clearly, her features illuminated by a soft glow that seemed to come from within her.

"Karyna …" he whispered, his voice almost inaudible so as not to disturb the peacefulness of the moment.

"I know who you are."

Jesper's breath caught in his throat. "You do?"

"You cannot hide a secret like that from me forever. Their blood stains your hands red."

"Kie, I'm sorry. I didn't want to –"

"What are you doing here, Jesper?"

He didn't know. But the words rolled off his tongue all the same. "I came to see you."

"You shouldn't be here. It's not safe."

"Why not?"

"You don't have much time left. They are coming for you."

"Who?" She didn't respond. "Kie, who is coming for me?"

"You must leave now, while you still can."

Jesper shook his head. His feet were still stuck to the ocean. "I can't."

"Watch your back, Jesper Kelsey. Not everything is as it seems."

"What are you talking about?"

"This is your one warning," Kie cautioned, completely ignoring Jesper's questions. "You will not get a second."

"A warning for what?"

"Now go."

"I can't," Jesper insisted. No matter how much he internally yelled at his feet to move, they didn't listen. Kie slowly sauntered over, closing the gap between the two of them. She reached out and placed a hand on Jesper's chest, and Jesper would be lying if he said he didn't secretly hope that she would pull him closer. But, much to his dismay, Kie instead pushed him gently, the gesture somehow powerful enough to send him falling backward. His body crashed into the ocean, the icy water swallowing him within seconds and stealing the air from his lungs.

Jesper shot upward, gasping for air. Once his eyes adjusted to the darkness, it struck him that he was no longer drowning in an endless sea. He was sitting by the docks, his back against a stack of crates and his legs outstretched in front of him. Isa was sitting above him on one of the crates and eyeing him with what looked to be a sort of amusement.

"Morning, sunshine."

"What happened?" Jesper asked groggily, wiping his sweaty brow with the sleeve of his jacket.

"What happened was you fell asleep when we're supposed to be on watch. You really have gone soft."

"Shut up."

"Bad dream?"

"None of your business."

"I'll take that as a yes, then."

"What do you care, anyway?" Jesper snapped.

"Oh, I'm sorry for trying to be a decent human being and be empathetic. Believe me, I won't bother you again."

"Good."

Sighing dramatically, Isa rose to her feet and proposed an idea. "Well, now that you're up, I was thinking we should go to the tavern. I'm bored."

"Fine."

"Fine."

Jesper groaned as he stood up, instantly feeling the regret of having slept on the street in the aching of his body. Isa eyed him, a smirk tugging at her lips.

"Shut up."

"I didn't say anything!"

"Let's just go, okay?"

Isa threw her hands up in surrender before throwing her bag over her shoulder and starting off down the street with Jesper at her side. Jesper did his best to push the dream to the back of his mind; he knew better than to ruminate on what it could have possibly meant. Because everyone knew that dreams were often just complete nonsense.

As they strode through the sleeping town, Jesper let his eyes wander along the windowed stores that lined the street. All just full of junk that he could only wish to afford in another life. But one item in particular caught his eye.

Jesper stopped suddenly in his tracks, staring dumbfounded at the windowfront of a clothing store. There it was; the dress Kie had been wearing in his dream. But, that had to be impossible. Right?

"Jesper? What is it?"

"Do you ever have the feeling that you've seen something before?"

"Yes, that's called deja vu, genius," Isa said, crossing her arms over her chest. "It's not that uncommon."

"No, but like, with dreams."

"Uh, no? Why?"

"And we've never walked down this street before, right?" Jesper took a moment to glance up and down the street, but nothing rang a bell. Isa furrowed her brow at him before replying,

"No, I don't think so. Jesper, what's wrong? What did you see in your dreams?"

"Nothing. It's, uh, not that important."

"You're sure you're okay? You look like you've seen a ghost or something." Isa leaned in to get a better look at his face, and something like concern seemed to cross over her features. But Jesper waved her off.

"Yeah, yeah, I'm good. Go on ahead to the tavern. I'll be right there."

"Okay …"

Isa reluctantly backed off and continued walking down the street. Jesper didn't let his eyes leave the dress in the window, studying every fold of fabric. There was something less ethereal about the dress in person, but he partially believed that was because Kie wasn't in it. Then his mind wandered to what dream Kie had told him: *You don't have much time left. They are coming for you. Watch your back, Jesper Kelsey. Not everything is as it seems.*

What was that supposed to mean? Surely there was nothing meant by it, as it was a dream. But Jesper couldn't shake the feeling away. That, perhaps, something about what Kie had said was true.

After some time had passed, Jesper finally shook himself out of the weird trance he was under. He had places to be, things to do. That didn't include staring at a dress.

"What am I doing?" he muttered, turning on his heels and striding off down the street. As much as he longed to buy that dress and give it to Kie, it wasn't exactly reasonable to assume that he would ever see her again. If Isa had her way, that was.

* * *

Jesper walked into the tavern cautiously, his eyes constantly scanning everyone in the room. He kept his hat tilted down over his face to remain relatively unidentifiable. There was no use in making a scene. Not just yet, anyway.

Isa had said she would meet him at this specific tavern once he caught up with her just before disappearing down the street. But for what purpose and why here, Jesper didn't have a clue. He could only trust that she would actually be here, and that this wasn't a trap he was walking into. It somewhat reminded him of their relationship years ago, him blindly believing Isa solely on her word and trusting that she had a plan that she was enacting in their favor. Jesper absolutely hated the idea, and it made him sick to his stomach.

The tavern was completely packed, ready to burst at the seams. Everyone was celebrating something, or perhaps drinking just for the fun of it. He knew that Isa would be doing the same, celebrating her rekindled freedom and adventurous life. After disappearing off the face of the planet for seven years, Jesper was sure that she was just itching to get back into the game. And, even though he didn't want to admit it, Jesper felt the same way.

Jesper picked his way through the crowded building, slipping between the countless drinkers that swayed merrily to the fiddle. It was like navigating a labyrinth, having to carefully pick his footing with each step to avoid getting smashed in between two careening locals. And while the tavern was an impossible jumble of human bodies, it was at the same time a target-rich environment. Perfect for stealing unprotected valuables from unsuspecting people. A bejeweled necklace here, a few coins there. All so expensive, and all so ripe for the taking.

As he slipped past one of the tables, Jesper reached out and silently grabbed the coin pouch resting on the table, pocketing it without a word and moving on. He grinned to himself, believing he had gotten away with stealing the money, until the wealthy man who owned the money stood up and yelled at Jesper.

"Hey! You stole my money!" Jesper stopped, raising his head ever so slightly but refusing to turn around to face the man. The man, realizing that he had gained Jesper's attention, continued to yell and draw the attention of everyone else around them. "Get back here and give me my money!"

And when Jesper still made no move, he could hear the pounding footsteps of the man striding up to him. The man clamped a firm hand on Jesper's shoulder, turning the pirate around to face him. But he froze when he felt the barrel of Jesper's gun pressed into his gut threateningly, horror plastered on his face. Jesper stared the man down shamelessly, willing to pull the trigger if the man so much as moved a muscle.

"You're no gentleman."

"Hurts, doesn't it?" Jesper mocked, the corners of his mouth turning upward into a smug grin. "Sit back down." The man obeyed without hesitation. "Enjoy the rest of your evening, good sir. Barman, get this man another drink, would you?"

A beat passed of complete silence, until another drink had been set on the table before the wealthy man. Then the tavern was back in full swing, the guests having forgotten entirely of the disturbance.

"That ain't a good idea, kid."

Jesper wheeled around, his fingers curling tighter around the coin purse in his hand. The mysterious man sat in the corner at a booth that was shrouded in shadow. The man that had helped save his life; the man that had been in the tavern the day Jesper met Kie. His wide-brimmed hat was tilted down over his forehead, making it impossible for Jesper to get a good look at the man's face past all the darkness. He was reclined comfortably at the booth despite the rowdiness of his surroundings, his feet perched on top of the table and his hands rested in his lap. A sly grin was spread across the man's face, revealing a row of surprisingly pearly white teeth.

Nervousness tugged at Jesper; this man had clearly been following him around. He had somehow managed to figure out just where Jesper was going to be at the exact time. But the feeling that was overwhelming Jesper wasn't the hot rage and icy horror he had felt when Isa had shown up on the deck of his ship. It was instead more of a hesitant curiosity.

Jesper took a moment to glance over his shoulder before sliding into the booth across from the man. "Who are you?"

The man laughed, the little wooden toothpick hanging from his lips. "Stupid question to ask. It don't matter who I am."

"You've been following me."

"Followin' you?" he scoffed, as if the idea of it was absurd. "Could be you who's followin' me."

Jesper gritted his teeth. Leaning over the table, he hissed, "Who are you?"

"Reckon I'm an ally."

"An ally."

"I tell you what needs doin', and you do it. All in your best interest, 'course."

"And why would I do that?"

"So I can keep you from doin' somethin' foolish again."

"I'm leaving."

"Pleasure talkin' with you, Captain Kelsey!" the man declared, tipping his hat in a gesture of farewell. And then the grin melted off his face for perhaps the first time ever. "Oh – one more thing. I wouldn't be too quick to, ah, jump ship, so to speak. Some folks are pretty skilled at tellin' lies. Best keep your distance."

"I'm sorry? What's that supposed to mean?"

The wide grin had reappeared on his face. "You do have a habit of askin' too many questions. Don't. You'll find yourself stickin' your nose in all the wrong places."

"Whatever," Jesper mumbled before turning on his heels and walking away. He was tired of trying to get any sort of answer out of that man.

Jesper continued picking his way through the crowded room, spotting Isa in the far back corner. He tossed the coin pouch to her as he approached, trying to appease her constant appetite and lust for wealth, and Isa proceeded to examine the bag's contents as soon as she had caught it.

"Really? You think a couple hundred shillings are going to give me a good time?"

"I never expected that. Besides, I thought tonight we were supposed to be laying low as we celebrate."

"Oh, come on! Who said we couldn't have a little fun?"

"Doing what exactly?"

"You know … making use of our swords perhaps, having some excitement to get the energy flowing?"

"Last I checked, most folks don't go around killing people during a celebration for fun."

"That's no fun," Isa pouted.

"Your idea of fun is very different from mine," Jesper argued before taking a drink of whatever it was that Isa had bought that was on the table. "And mildly concerning, too."

"Really? Considering our line of work?"

"No. No, don't go roping me in with you."

"You don't need to be so sour all the time. Loosen up a bit, have some fun!"

"You know I'm not going to do that."

"Why not?"

"Because you know what happens when I loosen up a bit."

"I'm sure it's not that bad," Isa insisted.

"You don't remember the night of the Countess's dinner party with Valentine Lytton and the free, bottomless drinks?"

"Fair point."

"I'm not about to let myself do that again." Shockingly, Isa nodded in understanding.

"Say, what happened to Valentine? I haven't seen him in ages."

"Who knows. He disappeared off the face of the planet, just like you did."

"He's probably dead."

"Not Val. He's probably basking in the millions of pounds he's stolen."

"True." Then she poured another glass of the mysterious drink and held it out for Jesper to take.

"Just have one more glass. We don't want all of this to go to waste."

"You paid for the drink. It's your fault for buying so much."

"That's the thing …" Isa trailed off, lowering her gaze guiltily to his coin pouch. Sighing, Jesper grabbed the coin purse that sat on the table and counted the remaining coins.

"You used my money."

"We'll get it back. Tenfold!" she insisted, but Jesper didn't care.

"You used my money!"

"Stop complaining!" Isa scolded, snatching the pouch from his hands. "You act like a child! It's a wonder you've survived this long, having the mind of a five-year-old like you do."

"Are you done insulting me now?"

"Yes, I'm done."

"Thank you." Jesper plopped down in the seat across from her.

"Have another glass," Isa commanded, sliding the drink over to him.

"I'm fine. Really."

"Just one more? Then the bottle's almost gone. I swear."

Jesper took a moment to eye Isa, noting her sly smile and glinting eyes. He couldn't tell if she was up to something or if that was just her natural look, but he supposed one more drink couldn't hurt.

A couple minutes and several drinks later, and Jesper's vision was starting to turn fuzzy. His head began pounding, and the booming liveliness of the tavern faded to a buzzing. Jesper felt somehow more lighthearted, and yet, he could hardly walk in a straight line. It was exactly what he hadn't wanted, relinquishing complete control of himself like he had.

So, when three drunks approached Jesper with knives and fists brandished, it was all too easy to tap into his unbridled rage. The three men, who towered over Jesper and trumped him in nearly every regard, knew exactly how to push Jesper's buttons. Almost too well.

"Look at this moron!" One of the men shoved Jesper in the shoulder and crowed with laughter at his attempt at a joke.

"Looks like someone decided to drink a little too much tonight! How's it feel, Half-Pint?"

"I'm not short," Jesper muttered under his breath, keeping his eyes glued to the floor. Luckily, his murmur was drowned out by the consistent hum of the tavern. The three men surrounded him, shoving him repeatedly, and when Jesper tried to slip away into the crowd, he was yanked back.

"Don't run away!"

"Who said anything about running away?" Jesper quipped.

"So the mute speaks!" the second man exclaimed. "I thought you were deaf *and* dumb."

"Honest mistake, really. Now get out of my way."

"You're the one in *my* way, scum."

The third joined in, too eager to insult the younger pirate. "Yeah, that's what you are. Pond scum."

"Lowlifes like you, with your dark skin and filthy bloodline, don't belong here." Jesper's confident demeanor faded away in an instant, and anger seeped in to fill the void. Despite the commonly-held prejudices held by most of the world against the people of his country, it had been several years at least since Jesper was last insulted for being Ra'Seharan. And it stung. Perhaps even more than it would feel if he was singled out for being elven.

He growled, "So that's what this is about."

"I don't know what you're talking about."

"Say that to my face again. I dare you."

The men didn't hold back, clearly not intimidated in the least by Jesper's anger. "Your kind is the scum of the world."

His patience would last no longer. He couldn't help it. Reaching down and grabbing his sword and pistol, Jesper's mind clouded with white rage.

The next thing he remembered, he was standing in the center of the room, his chest heaving and his fists clenched tightly around the weapons in his hands. Isa was making her way toward him, cautiously stepping over the three bodies and pools of blood that covered the floor.

"All of that blood looks good on you," she teased. "It really brings out the green in your eyes."

"What did you do?"

"Me? I didn't do anything. This one's all on you, Sparky." Isa patted his shoulder. Realization dawned on him, and his eyes widened in terror.

"How much did I have to drink?"

"You just had a little, that's all."

"How much is a little?"

"Just the rest of the bottle … plus some."

"That's a lot more than a little! I told you not to let me do that, Isa! I told you bad things would happen from drinking too much!" Jesper yelled, throwing down his pistol and sword. He completely ignored the crowds of people who looked on with horror evident on their faces and the eerie silence that hovered in the air.

"These past couple of years have made you weak, Jesper."

"Weak?"

"Seven years ago, you would have been itching to jump into battle. Now, you get sick at the sight of blood!"

"I've changed, Isa! You can't compare me to the person I was the last time you saw me!"

"Jesper, like it or not, you are a weapon, a killer. Do not make the mistake of thinking you're not."

"No," he uttered, not wanting to hear the very thing he feared most. "No, I'm not."

"Put it this way: a sword can be used as a walking stick, but that doesn't change anything. At the end of the day, it's still a sword."

"I'm not a killer!"

"Yes, you are! Even your sister acknowledges that! So why is it that you can't see it too?" Jesper shrunk back slightly, drawing back into himself upon Isa's yelling. He hated it. He hated being a monster. And he didn't want to be defined by it. "Jesper," she sighed. "I don't mean to insult you. Really, I don't. I'm just trying to help you recognize what everyone else sees in you."

"What if I don't want everyone else to see that?"

"You can't change who you are."

Jesper lowered his gaze, a wave of utter defeat sweeping over him. He had tried, desperately, to change himself for the past seven years, and now Isa was telling him that it was an impossible notion. Jesper didn't want to believe her words, and yet, they were eating away at his insides like an undeniable truth. "Let's just … let's just get out of here before the authorities arrive."

Isa didn't hesitate to grab hold of Jesper's arm and drag him out of the tavern, pushing through the throngs of gawking people. And Jesper could have sworn, out of the corner of his eyes, he saw a tall, rugged figure standing towards the doorway. Sure enough, there was that mystery man, his face not shrouded in shadow for the first time. He had a rugged handsomeness to him, and his blue eyes sparkled with a playful mischievousness, that smirk once again brightening his features. A wink, and the man slipped out the door into the night, perhaps never to be seen again. But something in Jesper believed that wouldn't be the last time he and the mystery man would cross paths.

Tugging at Jesper's arm, Isa exclaimed, "Jesper, come on! Let's go!"

Relenting, Jesper let her lead him through the crowded room, a sort of invisible force field separating them from the people. No one wanted to stand too close to a killer.

The moment they had broken away from the seemingly endless crowd, Isa let go of Jesper's arm and began running down the street. Jesper watched her for a minute, his nose crinkled in confusion. But when he realized that she wasn't stopping, he started chasing after her.

"Where are we going?" Jesper yelled, sprinting down the street after Isa. For wearing heels on cobblestone, she could run surprisingly fast.

"Where do you think?"

"I don't know! I can't read your thoughts!"

"Somewhere we can hide from the authorities until we get out of here?" She was obviously trying to hint at something without just telling him.

"I swear, if you are taking us back to my sister's place –"

"Of course that's where we're going! Clary has the perfect spot to lay low."

"Isa …" he whined, slowing his run ever so slightly.

"Stop whining and c'mon! We haven't got all night!"

"I'm coming, I'm coming!"

He sped up again to come side by side with Isa as they raced through the town together. They had such a way to go, and Jesper was already running on so little energy. But Isa wasn't going to let him stop, and there was nothing he could do but push on and keep going.

Miles later, and Clary's house appeared in the valley below them. Jesper couldn't help but breathe a sigh of relief upon finally seeing their final destination. So close.

Jesper threw the door open and rushed through, Isa hot on his heels. Clary didn't even seem fazed by the sudden entrance, and she simply glanced up at her new guests before returning to her work.

"You're back so soon."

"Surprise," Jesper announced sarcastically, dramatically throwing his arms open in greeting. When Clary didn't react, Jesper rolled his eyes at her and strode over to the bar top where she stood.

"What did you do now?"

"Nothing!"

Clary turned to Isa without hesitation, her face still just as emotionless as it always was. "What did he do, Miss Fielding?"

"Just a small argument and a few bodies; no big deal."

"I swear I didn't mean to!" Jesper insisted desperately.

"You don't need to state your case to me." Clary picked up a small crate from behind the counter and started walking to a different room. Jesper trailed after her, completely dumbfounded that his sister still wasn't reacting to the news at all.

"You're not mad at me?"

"Mad? Why should I be? This is your life. And I'm certainly not far off either."

"Well, Mom would be mad."

"I'm not Mom, am I?"

"I mean …" he muttered, shrugging slightly. Perhaps not, but being that they had been left to fend for themselves at such a young age, Clary practically *was* his mom from the day that their mother died.

"If I'm being honest, I'm surprised you didn't come back to this life sooner. But now that the word's out, there's no going back."

"What do you mean?"

"Jesper, the whole Navy is going to be after you now. You just became their number one most wanted fugitive," Clary stated matter-of-factly. "I mean, you pretty much already were … but now they're going to know where you are," she muttered. Shoving his hands into the pockets of his jacket, Jesper shifted his glare to Isa.

"And I'm sure this is what you wanted, huh?"

"One step closer to immortality."

"Immortality?" Clary asked, standing up suddenly from her crouched position on the floor with the crate. Isa bit the inside of her cheek, somewhat uncomfortable with being the target of Clary's skepticism. Despite trying to stay off the grid for the last seven years, Jesper could tell that some unspoken tension lingered between the two women.

"You heard me."

"Doesn't exist."

"That's exactly what I said!" Jesper exclaimed. Clary sighed.

"Please tell me *immortality* isn't the reason you came back."

"What?" Jesper feigned surprise. "Pff. No! I'm not *that* dumb."

Clary stalked up to Jesper, poking him firmly in the chest. "You may be a good liar, but I can see right through you."

Jesper quickly swatted her hand away, frowning deeply. He hated when his sister was right.

"You wish."

"Don't pretend you don't know the truth. I've *always* been right."

"As if. Stop sounding so much like Eirik," Jesper accused, his stomach turning slightly at the thought of his oldest brother. "It's disgusting."

"Eirik?" Clary forced out a short laugh, her way of showing how irritated she truly was. "Eirik's dead, Jesper."

"You don't know that."

"Pretending he's still alive isn't going to bring him back!"

"I know he's alive!" Jesper roared, as if to drown out Clary's protests. He refused to believe that Eirik was dead. It had been too many years to count since he had last heard from his brother, but Eirik was never one to go down without a fight. And surely Jesper would have heard if his brother died.

"How do you know?"

"I just do."

"So your magical power of belief is somehow going to keep Eirik from death?" she mocked, infuriating Jesper even further.

"He can handle himself out there, much better than we can."

"Yes, and so could Trystan. But he's gone too."

"That was a freak accident, and you know it!" Jesper roared, pointing a finger in Clary's face accusingly. "He wasn't supposed to die!"

"Freak accidents happen, Jesper."

"Not to Eirik, they don't."

"I'm sorry. Am I missing something?" Isa asked, butting into the conversation. But her interruption did not have the desired effect she was going for. Instead, both Kelsey siblings directed all their frustration to her.

"No!"

"Whatever. Don't tell me, then."

"I won't," Jesper shot back, his irritation coming out in the shortness of his replies. He could tell that Isa was holding back as she responded,

"Fine!"

"Fine."

Pinching the bridge of her nose, Clary sighed deeply. "Stop fighting, you two. You're going to give me a headache."

"We're not fighting. I don't have to tell her anything!"

"Yes, you are! Gosh! Neither of you changed! You're just as insufferable as you were all those years ago."

"You're the insufferable one," Jesper muttered, temporarily forgetting that Clary could hear everything he said.

"You need to learn to control your tongue. It's only going to start fights."

Grinning smugly, Jesper turned up the intensity of his gaze at his sister. "You have no idea how many times I've heard that."

"Then you would think you would learn something from that."

"One would think."

"I've been telling him that for years," Isa pointed out, much to the displeasure of Jesper. Her comments were beyond unnecessary, but neither of the Kelsey siblings had the energy to start another argument by trying to shut her up.

"Other than disturbing my perfectly peaceful night, is there another reason you decided to barge in?"

"We just need to lay low for a bit, until the town authorities move on."

"You're not laying low here and letting the military find out about this place, that's for sure."

Jesper furrowed his brow in confusion, and he couldn't keep the childishness out of his voice. "What? Why?"

"Oh, I don't know … maybe because what I do isn't exactly legal."

"One more favor. Please," he begged. But Clary wouldn't have it.

"No! Go find someone else's life to ruin."

"Clary …" Jesper whined.

"Get out."

"All right, all right! I'm leaving! Geez!" Jesper threw his hands up in the air, exasperated. There was no point in pushing Clary any further because she certainly wasn't going to budge. "C'mon, Isa, let's get out of this craphole."

"Where are we headed?"

"Anywhere but here," Jesper spat. Isa nodded in agreement.

"The coast of Aerithos it is."

* * *

The only problem was, getting back to the ship required crossing back through town. Which, at this point, would be flooded with soldiers and guard patrols. The odds of successfully making it to the other side of town without getting caught were pretty slim, but Jesper was never one to back down from a challenge.

So, as they walked briskly down the road back towards the town, Jesper wrapped his long jacket around him tightly to hide the sword and pistol at his sides and tilted his hat down over his face to mask his identity. It wouldn't do much, he knew that. But he was willing to do whatever it took to keep from being caught by the Navy.

"Stay close and keep your head down," Isa muttered as they entered town. Jesper scoffed at her softly.

"Like I didn't know that. Don't worry about me."

"Fine. Forget I ever said anything."

Putting a hand on Isa's back, he pushed her along. "Let's move faster."

They sped down the streets, unspeakably happy at how empty the town seemed at this dreadful hour at night. The streetlamps lit their path, the faint light flickering playfully against the night sky. A full moon hovered above their heads, brightening the sky with its warm glow. Normally, Jesper would stop to admire the moon's beauty. But there would not be time for that tonight.

Jesper and Isa hurried around a street corner, stopping dead in their tracks when they noticed a large group of soldiers stationed in front of the docks. Isa pulled Jesper down behind an empty fruit stand, Jesper's mind already racing. How were they supposed to get out of this one?

To get a better view of what he was dealing with, Jesper slowly raised himself from his crouched position. He peeked over the top of the stand, carefully analyzing the scene before him. And then, without warning, a hand grabbed his arm and yanked him back into the dark alley behind him. A hand clamped over his mouth to keep him from making any noise, and Jesper could feel the attacker's breath on his neck. Jesper tried to fight back against the mysterious attacker, but whoever it was was strong enough to hold his grasp.

"Stop fighting!" the voice hissed in his ear. "I'm not going to arrest you."

Jesper knew that voice. *Phineas.* Pushing the hand off his mouth, Jesper growled, "What's this about?"

"You were the one who murdered those three men, weren't you?"

"What makes you think it was me?"

"Because you're trying to escape town the same night that three men were mysteriously murdered in a tavern."

"What are you going to do about it?"

"Nothing. I don't have evidence to bring you in."

"So let me go." Throwing his arm down, Jesper felt the hand let go. He whirled around to see Phineas glaring back at him. "I'm guessing you're not going to help me get out of here."

"Of course not. That would make me an accomplice."

"Right. Because us stealing the brig from the Admiral never happened."

"Exactly."

Out of the corner of his eye, Jesper could see another figure jumping at them. And before he could react, Isa had Phineas pressed against the wall of the alley with her dagger at his throat.

"Isa, no. Leave him be."

"But he –"

"Leave. Him. Be." Isa glared at Jesper but obeyed and stepped away. "I know him. He's not going to arrest us."

"Then why –"

"We were just parting ways, actually."

Phineas snorted and crossed his arms over his chest. "Yeah, good luck with that."

"Excuse me?"

"You're not going to be able to get back to your ship, and you know it, too."

"And?"

"Make another deal, and I'll get you out." Jesper frowned at Phineas, but he had to at least hear him out.

"Okay …"

"You hand the girl you abducted over to me, and I'll distract the guards long enough for you to escape."

"Are you talking about Kie?"

"Yes, the aristocrat. Her parents are very powerful people, and they're rewarding us significantly if we return the girl home."

"Absolutely not," Jesper retorted, feeling the blood in his veins beginning to boil. No one was touching her. Not on his life. "She's out of the question. Besides, I didn't abduct her. She came with me."

"Yeah, right. Like she would willingly leave the city with someone like you."

"She made her choice to leave. And I'm not handing her over."

"Then no deal."

"That's fine with me. You underestimate my ability to get out of sticky situations."

"I'll leave you to it, then."

"You do that."

Jesper watched Phineas leave the alley with a cold expression on his face. Isa remained silent until Phineas was out of sight before asking, "So, how exactly *are* we going to get out of here?"

"I have absolutely no idea."

Silently gliding back over to the empty fruit stand, Isa crouched down and peered over the top at the docks. Jesper followed closely behind, studying the situation before them. It was going to be tricky to navigate, that was for sure, if they wanted to get away without causing chaos.

"You abducted a girl from the cities, huh?" Isa crooned, her curiosity piqued. Jesper sighed deeply, rubbing his temple with a slightly shaky hand.

"No. I didn't."

"It was the pretty little thing with the copper hair, right? I didn't know you fancied gingers."

"I don't," Jesper said flatly.

"Right. Very believable, Kelsey." Jesper shot her a pointed look before going quiet and turning his head back towards the docks. *I don't fancy Kie – not a girl like her.* Something like that would never even work in the first place. Besides, she had a fiancé to go back to anyway.

"Wait, Jesper, look."

"What?" He didn't have a clue where he was supposed to be looking or what he was supposed to be seeing.

"Who's that?"

"Who's who?"

"Him!" Isa hissed, pointing to a man walking up to the group of sailors standing by the docks. It didn't take but two seconds for Jesper to recognize the hat and long, tattered jacket as the mystery man he had just run into once again in the tavern.

"I know him!"

"You do?"

"Yeah! He's the guy that's been following me around."

"He's been following you? How am I just finding out about this now?"

"Relax, it's fine. He's been helping me out … kinda."

"Clearly not! He's in cohorts with the Navy! They're probably paying him off very nicely. He's talking them up like they're best friends!"

"Well …" She wasn't wrong. Jesper watched as the mystery man cracked a joke, making the sailors keel over with laughter. The man said a few more things that Jesper couldn't quite make out, clapped one of the sailors on the back heartily, tipped his hat in farewell, and walked off. "What was that about?"

"What do you mean? He totally just told them about you! And your ship that's right there! Now we're never getting off this island."

"Okay, well, there's no need for over exaggeration. You trust me, right?" Isa nodded. Jesper released a heavy sigh before muttering to himself, "But I could have sworn he was helping me out."

He slid back down onto his butt, his back pressed up against the fruit stand. Jesper's mind was already whirring, trying desperately to come up with some even slightly plausible escape route. But nothing was coming to him. Nothing at all.

Something moved to his right, and Jesper's heart practically leapt out of his chest. A man was sitting down next to him behind the stand, and at first Jesper couldn't understand for the life of him why this man was joining them. Jesper's face must have been saying exactly how he was feeling, because the man chuckled softly and drawled,

"Surely I don't look that different without the hat." *That voice.* Of course. Mentally, Jesper put the image of a wide-brimmed hat on his head and a jacket around his shoulders, and it dawned on him that this was, once again, the mystery man. Jesper internally kicked himself for not putting it together sooner.

"What … how did you …?"

"I doubled back after I left. Stashed the hat and jacket down the alley."

"Jesper, is this the guy –"

"Yeah. Isa, meet … sorry, I never did catch your name."

The permanent smirk on the man's face widened into a bright smile as he took Isa's hand and kissed it. *Charming.* "Jayme. Name's Jayme Schooner."

Jayme Schooner. The name felt vaguely familiar, like Jesper had heard it before. Perhaps in passing, or through a friend of a friend. But it felt more personal than that, like he had read the name in one of his brother's letters when he was younger. It was a name he couldn't quite place, but he somehow knew that this was a person he was supposed to recognize.

"I don't take kindly to snitches," Isa snapped as she ripped her hand away from Jayme. He didn't seem hurt by the gesture – or her words for that matter – in the slightest.

"My sailor friends over there reckon you're headed for the cove on the far side of town. They oughta be leavin' right about …" he crouched up to peer over the top of the fruit stand, "Now."

And as he spoke, the sailors parted ways and dashed down the street, leaving only one of them to guard the entrance to the dock. Jesper snorted; so he hadn't ratted them out after all. Isa, on the other hand, wasn't so easily convinced.

"What, are they just going to double back like you did?"

"They're gone, sweetheart. At least for now."

"What do you want? Money or something?"

"A 'thank you' wouldn't hurt."

"You wish," Isa spat, her fury not abated by Jayme's charisma. But nor was Jayme deterred by her unpleasantness. He simply let out a chuckle, sliding back down behind the stand and running a hand through his dirty blond hair.

"Okay, so what now?" Jesper asked, eyeing the man sitting next to him.

"What's that s'posed to mean exactly?"

"What do we do with the last guy?"

"You go through him?"

"I don't want to kill him!"

Isa, on the other hand, seemed to be completely on board with the notion. "I'll do it gladly."

"Yeah, I know you would," Jesper quipped before turning back to Jayme. "We're not killing any more people."

"We're not?" Isa put in, her voice concerningly close to a whine. Jayme just rolled his eyes.

"C'mon now. No need to be modest. I saw you kill those three guys just fine."

"That doesn't mean I want to."

"All right, then. Let your lady friend kill the guy, and y'all can get goin'."

"No!"

Jayme sighed, passing a hand over his face before scratching at the stubble along his jaw. "Why you always gotta be makin' things so difficult?"

"I'm sorry, always?"

"Stop talkin'. Let me work."

"Yeah? And what's your master plan, exactly?"

"I'm gunna tell him what to do."

"*That's* your plan? Just tell him to leave his post?" It was completely absurd. There was no way that he actually believed that just talking to the guard would work.

"Might not be in the service anymore, but he don't need to know that." He took a minute to look around, his eyes finally settling on the leather jacket Jesper was wearing. "Hand me your jacket."

"What? No! I happen to really like this jacket."

"Ain't gunna do a thing to it, I promise."

"Fine," Jesper snapped, throwing off the jacket and handing it to Jayme. He failed to see how the jacket would make much of a difference, considering that Jayme didn't look like the most put together person ever and his clothes were in pretty rough shape. But Jayme seemed to disagree.

Sliding the jacket on, he buttoned it completely closed to hide his faded blue vest and worn shirt. He ran a hand through his hair once more, trying his best to smooth down the strands that hung down in front of his face before flashing a grin at the two and stepping out from behind the fruit stand.

With the confidence that Jayme presented as he sauntered over to the dock, Jesper would have never thought twice about who he was or what he was doing there. The lieutenant that stood at the docks apparently thought the same thing, as he straightened his posture as Jayme approached. Jesper and Isa were too far away to hear the words that were exchanged, but it wasn't long before the lieutenant saluted Jayme and proceeded to walk away down the street just as his counterparts had done not too long ago.

"Let's go," Jesper hissed to Isa, the two of them bolting out from behind the stand to join Jayme on the docks. "How did you …"

"Don't sweat it, kid."

"Who *are* you?"

"A friend."

Jesper knew that Jayme's answer was going to be the best he was going to get out of the man. Jayme pulled the jacket off his shoulders and handed it back, that smug smirk still stuck to his face.

"How can I repay you for your help?"

"By stayin' alive."

Jesper chuckled, grasping Jayme's hand in a firm handshake. "I can't make any promises."

"C'mon, Tiger! We have to get out of here before we're caught." Isa motioned up the gangplank to her vessel. Jesper nodded before quickly turning back to Jayme.

"See you around?"

"Possibly."

SEVENTEEN

I COULD HAVE SWORN I WAS DRINKING AWAY THE PAIN

ARI

It felt exceedingly unnatural, just sitting around and waiting like they were doing. They should've left port days ago, but Kie was so insistent on sticking around in case Jesper came around again. But, of course, that wasn't going to happen. Ari was sure of it. But, of course, it wasn't like he had a say in anything at all. It wasn't like he was filling in as the captain in Jesper's absence.

Ari was lounging in Jesper's spacious captain's cabin, his feet propped up on the desk, when the door suddenly swung open. With a small yelp, Ari toppled backward, his chair giving way and falling back onto the floor and sending him sprawling. So that's why Jesper was so irritated every time Ari came in without knocking.

Jumping to his feet as fast as his body would allow him, Ari found Kie just standing in the middle of the room, completely dumbfounded.

"You need something?" he asked curtly, smoothing out the front of his shirt.

"Are you just going to sit there moping all the time?"

"I'm not moping."

"Fine, then. Teach me how to sword fight."

"I'm sorry?"

"I'm living on a ship with a bunch of pirates, and your lives are considerably more dangerous than you let on, so I think I should learn to protect myself."

"Kie, I don't have time for this."

"You're not doing anything else."

"No, I'm not teaching you to sword fight."

"Well, if you can't do that, then certainly you can make time to tell me all about how you and Jesper met and what his story is."

"Do you have a sword you can use, or do you need to borrow one?"

"Um, I have this." Kie pulled out a dagger from a small side bag on her left.

"Where'd you get that from?"

"Jesper bought it for me."

"He did?"

"Yeah? Is that weird?"

"Never mind," Ari muttered, waving the question off. "Anyway, you can't use that. It's too small."

"I don't think so."

"And you don't know anything about sword fighting. That's why I'm teaching you." Kie frowned but didn't say anything as Ari walked out of the cabin and out onto the main deck. Without saying a word to anyone else, he grabbed the sword from Deacon's side.

"Hey!"

"We're just practicing. You're fine." Walking back over to where Kie stood, he handed the sword to her. "Here you go. Use this. Do you know how to hold it properly?"

"I think so," Kie replied, proceeding to grab the sword handle in a completely awkward fashion. Ari sighed deeply.

"Let me help you."

As unknowledgeable as Kie was about how to use a sword, she began picking things up quite quickly. And fairly soon, a crowd had gathered on the deck around them to watch them spar. Out of the corner of his eye, Ari could see Gen watching on, her arms crossed over her chest and a look of contentment on her face. Something always stirred in Ari's chest when Gen studied him with her deep blue eyes like that, and today was no different. It was a certain kind of tightness in his chest, almost an inability to breathe. But he hated when she wasn't paying attention to him.

He broke out of whatever trance Gen had put him under as he almost missed the chance to block Kie's clumsy attack. "Good, you're getting better. Let's take a break for now."

"Okay," Kie breathed, her chest heaving with exhaustion. Wiping the sweat from his brow, Ari casually started making his way over to where Gen stood, but he was very quickly stopped by Newt, who came running up to him and Kie with the biggest grin on his face.

"That was amazing! You have to teach me, sir. Please!"

"Not now, okay? I'm tired."

"Oh, yeah, sure. That's okay." The look of disappointment that Newt gave him reminded Ari of his younger siblings whenever they didn't get what they asked for. It stung just a bit.

"Maybe some other time."

Newt's eyes lit up, a bright smile tugging at the corners of his mouth. "You mean it?"

"Yeah, sure."

"Really?"

"Don't make me regret it, okay?" Newt nodded vigorously in response. He could hardly contain his excitement; it was like he had never been given any positive attention in his life. "Don't you have chores to be doing right now?"

"Oh, yeah. The captain wanted me to organize all his maps."

"Well, you're not going to find his maps lying around out here."

Finally registering that he was no longer wanted, Newt scrambled off to Jesper's cabin to the mess of maps that was practically overflowing from the drawers. He had quite a bit of work laid out for him, that was for sure.

An amused chuckle came from over Ari's shoulder, and he turned on his heels. Gen brushed a stray hair from her face as she smiled softly at Ari.

"The cabin boy really likes you."

"You think?"

"Kids have always liked you, Cadwell. Don't act so surprised."

"Well, I suppose it's just been a minute since I was last having to take care of a kid." The faces of Ari's siblings flashed to the front of his mind. It had been much too long since he had last seen them.

"You don't need to take care of him. He's strong; he'll figure things out for himself."

Ari let out a small scoff, wiping his forehead with the rag Gen had handed him. "Yeah, and that's more than we could ever say about Jesper."

"There's only so much you can do; don't beat yourself up about it."

"It's just … I can't just sit around and do nothing. He's my best friend – actually, he's more like a brother. And sometimes, he's just – he's so *stupid*!" Ari threw his hands up in the air, exasperated. Gen cocked her head slightly at him, obviously attempting to repress the tiniest bit of amusement. She always seemed to get some level of enjoyment from Ari's outbursts. It was somewhat infuriating, if Ari was being completely honest.

"Well, I'm not saying you're wrong. But perhaps the captain doesn't realize that."

"I – I'm worried, Gen. Typically I'm able to smack a bit of sense back into him every once in a while, but this time I might be too late. He's gone."

"He'll come back around. He always does."

"I wouldn't be so sure this time." Ari rubbed his face, letting his exhaustion and irritation show. Gen was never one to judge; he knew that.

Walking over to the side of the deck, Ari sat down on top of the railing to catch his breath. He sighed heavily to himself; Jesper was really starting to get to him. Not that he hadn't been already.

"And what do we tell the crew? We can't have them thinking he left for good. That could start a mutiny."

"How about …" Gen thought for a moment, pondering the question. "How about we tell them that the captain just disappeared for a bit to draw the Navy away from us, to gather allies quietly. After all, the Admiral is more set on hunting down Jesper than he is the Fortuyna."

"You think that'll work?"

Gen shrugged. "Better than nothing." She leaned her back against the railing at Ari's side, not saying anything. She was good at that – just listening. Putting a hand on Ari's leg to comfort him, Gen hesitated a brief moment before saying, "Perhaps we go out to the town tonight. You and me, and Kie and Newt."

"Yeah?" Ari glanced over at Gen through a curtain of limp bangs. She was smiling at him again, and Ari's heart fluttered in his chest.

"Yeah. It'll be fun. And it'll get your mind off of Jesper. At least for a little bit."

"That sounds good."

Ari knew that splurging for a night wasn't going to solve any of his problems, but if Gen was right about one thing, it would at least make him feel a little better.

And she certainly didn't disappoint. Gen had the whole thing planned out, leading the four of them to a decently respectable tavern in the middle of Corsair.

*   *   *

At the tavern – with a name which Ari was too Vyenan to pronounce – they slid into a booth towards the back with a great view of the front door. Just in case any unwanted visitors came calling.

They ate well that night, more luxurious than Ari cared to admit in a long time. But, that whole time, something still felt missing. Jesper was missing.

It was perhaps close to four in the morning when they decided to call it quits. The moon had long since risen into the sky, its silvery glow streaming in through the tavern's windows. By some miracle, the night life was still going strong, the building threatening to burst at the seams for lack of any more space to hold occupants.

And just as Ari began to rise shakily to his feet to stumble out of the tavern into the crisp night air, an uncomfortably familiar figure was sitting down next to them. Phineas.

He slipped seamlessly into their booth next to Newt without saying a word, pulling out the pistol from its holster at his side and setting it down on the table. The barrel of the gun pointed right at Ari.

"Sit back down." Ari eyed the pistol that sat on the table in front of them before reluctantly obeying.

"What do you want?" Ari snapped. He internally kicked himself for somehow failing to notice Phineas entering the tavern in the first place. "Jesper isn't here."

"Oh, I'm aware. I had a run-in with your captain just a few weeks ago."

Kie's eyes immediately lit up at the mention of Jesper. "You did? Is he okay?"

"Unfortunately. Causing trouble as usual. But he always manages to escape unscathed. Actually, he was in a bit of a tight spot when I offered my assistance in exchange for one thing."

Ari frowned and crossed his arms over his chest. "And what was that?" Phineas turned his gaze on Kie as he replied,

"Taking you back home to your family. He very passionately declined."

"What do you mean?" Kie asked, her brow furrowing.

"I didn't push it, but I could tell that man was ready to fight to the death to keep you out of my hands."

"That sounds about right," Ari muttered under his breath. Next to him, Gen shifted in her seat before clearing her throat to get everyone's attention and asking,

"I'm sorry, I'm lost. Who are you supposed to be exactly?"

Ari quickly jumped in to answer the question for Phineas. He didn't need Gen thinking that the naval commander was any ounce a good man. "Gen, meet the man Jesper was with when he got shot."

"That was not my fault!" Phineas exclaimed.

"I would beg to differ."

Then Gen decided to butt in, stopping the argument between the two men from going too far. "All that aside, you never answered Ari's question: What do you want?"

"I'm here to take Miss Marfont home."

Kie's eyes flashed with unease. "What?"

"You will do no such thing," Ari snapped. Phineas smiled back, amused.

"This isn't really the situation in which you get a say in the matter. Miss Marfont is coming back with me. Admiral's orders."

Leaning over the table, Ari glared at Phineas with every ounce of hatred in his body. "Perhaps you don't know me very well, but I don't exactly take orders from people like the Admiral. Or from you. And you don't exactly scare me."

"You should be scared."

"Yeah? And why's that? You made the mistake of coming in here, completely alone, with only a pistol and a flimsy sword to defend yourself with. You have no backup; it's four to one." Of course, Ari was bluffing entirely. He had no idea if Phineas was alone or not.

"Perhaps I know something you don't."

"Or perhaps you're just stupid."

"A man doesn't get to where I am today on sheer stupidity."

Throwing back his head, Ari let out an unrestrained laugh. "Oh, I'm sure you've managed to get by. Money can get you a long way."

"Are you suggesting that I paid my way to the top?"

"I don't know, am I?"

"I'm starting to get that idea, yeah."

"Hey, you said it, not me," Ari crowed, leaning back into his seat with satisfaction. Phineas sighed deeply, pinching the bridge of his nose.

"As much as I missed our little chats, I really do have orders to fulfill. I'm not exactly joking around, here."

"Yeah, neither am I."

Phineas's bright blue eyes studied Ari intently, almost as if he was trying to decide his next move. Then he rose to his feet, grabbed his gun off the table, and motioned to Kie.

"Come on, Miss Marfont. Let's be on our way."

"No" was Kie's response. And Phineas was completely taken aback.

"I'm sorry?"

"I'm perfectly fine right where I am, thank you very much."

"If I remember correctly, you have a fiancé waiting for your return, no?" he pushed, his forehead creased with confusion.

"I highly doubt he thinks of me very much, if at all."

"Wait, wait, wait," Gen blurted out. "Hold on. You have a fiancé?"

"Yes?"

"Then what have you been doing hanging out with Jesper all this time?"

"It's not like that."

"Oh, sure it's not. And you definitely are never thinking about him. Ever. It's not like he's constantly on your mind."

"That's not true." Kie's face flushed a bright red. "And besides, how would you know anything about that?"

"You'd be surprised," Gen muttered under her breath.

"I'm sorry?"

"Look," Phineas pressed, trying to regain control of the conversation once more. "Lord Lurcock is anxious for your return back to the city. I really do insist –"

Ari and Newt could hardly control their snickering. *What in the world was a name like Lurcock?*

"Commander, my answer is no. And gladly tell my family, too. There is no need for them to wait on me. At least, not now."

"That means get out, Blondie," Ari managed through fits of giggles. Phineas huffed in defiance but shockingly obeyed and stormed off. Ari knew he was too lawful a man to get violent with some common-looking folk in a sailor-heavy town. In a tavern brimming with drunken pirates and vagrants.

The minute Phineas was out of sight, Ari and Newt absolutely burst into uncontrollable laughter. But the two ladies at the table could only frown.

"What's the big deal?" Gen asked curtly. Ari wiped the tears forming in his eyes.

"Lurcock – what kind of name is that?"

And for the first time that night, Newt spoke up. "So let me get this straight: you're engaged to a man with the name Lurcock who's waiting for you back home, and you go running off with some other random guy because …"

"Because we had a deal."

Gen frowned deeper. "What deal?"

"That Jesper would find me a ship to sail on to see the world and go on adventures, as long as I accompanied his crew to Sovi."

"But … that deal's done now," Ari said slowly. Something wasn't exactly adding up. "And yet, you're still here."

Something about what Ari said set Gen off, and she immediately whipped on him. "You knew about all of this?"

"Well … I was kind of there when it happened …"

"Why didn't you say anything?"

"You never asked!"

"How am I supposed to ask for something I don't know anything about?"

"I don't know!" Ari exclaimed, the pitch of his voice rising to an uncomfortably high level. An odd sort of silence followed suit, none of them wanting to say anything to break the awkward tension. So much for a successful night.

"So, what now?" Newt spoke softly, just barely above a whisper. Ari could only sigh.

"Let's get back to the Fortuyna. We're casting off tomorrow morning." And looking at Kie dead in the eye, Ari added, "We're not waiting around for Jesper any longer. Our cap'n's abandoned ship."

EIGHTEEN

LIFE, LOVE, AND LOOT

ISA

Jesper wasn't usually one to let loose for an hour or two, but for some reason today, he was particularly easy to convince. A day beside the waterfall was exactly what they both needed, especially after all the exhaustion of evading the Navy and traveling from the days before. It was by some miracle that they were able to escape the town that night, and it had taken everything out of them to remain out of the hands of the naval soldiers. Bags had formed under her eyes and her back ached with stress. She needed this break desperately. So there she lay, basking in the warmth of the fierce Aerithos sun and the infinite blue sky, just like things used to be. Well, almost as they used to be.

She purposefully ignored how on-edge Jesper seemed, instead focusing on the calming repetition of the falling water and the breeze rustling through the trees overhead. Taking a deep breath of the musky air, Isa let her hair blow loose in the cool breeze. The tall-reaching trees rustled and beckoned with their generous shade, and Jesper was quick to hide from the sunlight. He seemed preoccupied with his thoughts once he had found solace under the tree. Isa frowned slightly to herself. Jesper was supposed to be distracted from his worries, not stress about them even more than he already did on a day-to-day basis. But it seemed as though the shimmering waters of the waterfall weren't helping in the least.

Dipping her toes further into the frigid pool below the waterfall, she called out to him. "Hey Tiger, what are you doing over there? Come enjoy the sun and the water!"

"I'm fine."

"Jesper," she groaned, twisting to glance back at him. "Stop worrying and let loose a little! It doesn't hurt anyone to have fun every once in a while."

"I'm fine."

"Remember when we used to come here all the time? To get away from everything. And when the sun would go down in a blaze of oranges and reds, we would build a fire and break into our secret stash of booze. In fact, I'm sure the cellar is still around here somewhere. We could go find it. Though, on the other hand … I'm not sure how good the rum would be after letting it sit for so long in the heat."

Jesper didn't react for a long minute, but then he replied, "I remember."

Isa silently rolled her eyes and repressed her feelings of annoyance. Why did he have to be so terse with her? Why couldn't he just be like he was all those years ago? Then again, his temper never was ideal to work with, but his fame and wealth were always too good to pass up.

"Stop being so bothersome and get over here."

"I don't have to listen to you," he quipped. "As I recall, last time we worked together, *you* were the one obeying *my* orders. The only reason why we ever got anything done was because I was the one calling the shots."

"Please?" she asked, not wanting to pick a fight with him at that moment. They had bigger fish to fry, and she couldn't afford to lose his fame and wealth now.

Sighing deeply, Jesper relented and stood up. He silently walked over to where Isa sat on the forest floor and stared at the roaring waterfall in front of them. His gold earrings and embroidered waistcoat shone brightly in the sun, his waistcoat blending in almost perfectly with the striking turquoise water of the falls. In the sunlight, his eyes seemed to change from a hazel to a brilliant green, and his skin glowed a golden brown. Isa couldn't help but take a moment to stare at him before shaking herself out of the trance she had somehow fallen into.

Jesper seemed to contemplate sitting down next to her or standing there for quite a while, and Isa was tempted to urge him to sit. But she said nothing, and Jesper did nothing besides stand above her and stare endlessly at the beauty of the waters and the rainbow-lit mist that hovered around them.

"The waterfall's beautiful, isn't it?" Isa mused, almost to herself. Jesper grunted a reply of agreement. She sighed and attempted to continue the one-sided conversation. "Its splendor never ceases to amaze me."

There was no reply. And just like that, the conversation was dropped in favor of complete silence. He was giving her the silent treatment. If only it could be like it used to be.

The heat had really begun to kick in as midday approached, and Isa felt beads of sweat appear on her forehead. Jesper clearly felt the same, his arms and face glistening with sweat. He eagerly shed his long waistcoat and unbuttoned his linen shirt in favor of the cool breeze. But he still didn't utter a single word and he didn't move. Isa watched him for a minute, and then she stood up to walk down into the water.

"Where are you going?"

"To cool off." Isa settled on Jesper's method of short responses before heading to the pool. As soon as she stepped in, the cool waters instantly expelled the heat from her body, and she breathed a sigh of relief. She could feel Jesper's gaze pierce the back of her head, and without looking back, she called out,

"I can feel you staring at me. Are you just going to stand there and brood or come over?"

Jesper made no reply, and Isa thought he had retreated back to his haven in the shade until he appeared noiselessly at her side. He still wouldn't talk and refused to look at her, but it was nevertheless a start. All she had to do was keep pushing him, little by little. Baby steps.

Isa walked further out into the water, until it met her knees. Jesper didn't follow. "Come on," she urged. Jesper just shook his head at her. "Come on!"

Leaning down, Isa dipped her hands in the water and threw it up at Jesper. She giggled slightly at his surprised reaction, which was followed by a hesitancy when she studied his face. He clearly wasn't happy with getting splashed, but then something seemed to change in him. It was though he had desperately tried to hide his true feelings and failed as a small laugh escaped his lips. And before she knew it, they were both running around in the water and splashing each other, laughing hysterically.

"Jesper!" she cried as he wrapped his arms around her waist and tossed her into the water.

"You're asking for it!"

"Jesper, stop!"

*　*　*

Isa and Jesper collapsed on the rocks together, trying to catch their breath from all the laughing and running around in the water. Even just making eye contact sent them into fits of giggles. But once the laughter died down, the two pirates laid in silence, looking up at the clouds that rolled past the branches of the trees lazily. There was something so relaxing, so comforting, about the rumble of the waterfall and the warmth of the rocks on her back, with Jesper at her side. She could have stayed there forever if she wanted. Jesper seemed to feel the same, as he had stretched out on the rocks with his hands behind his head and his eyes closed peacefully.

Rolling on her side, Isa spent a moment studying Jesper's face as he lay on the rocks with his eyes closed. It had been too many years since she had last seen him, and it was evident that much had changed about him. Life had not been easy on him.

"The scar on your eyebrow … when did you get it?"

She immediately knew she had ruined the moment when Jesper tensed up at the question but still gave her an answer. "The day you left me for dead. Our ship crashed on the shores of Vyena in a storm, and Ari found me in the wreck. Must have bashed my head on something real good in the storm."

"You don't remember?"

"Of course not," he snapped. "I was practically dead, all thanks to you. It took me months to recover."

"And the crew?"

"All dead. And I should have died with them that day."

Isa rose to her feet and clenched her fists in anger, Jesper following suit. "If I would have wanted you dead, I would have killed you. I had every chance to do so."

"Then why didn't you?" Jesper roared. Isa's anger flared, and this time, she didn't have the decency to hold it back.

"Because I needed you!"

"What could you have possibly needed me for?"

"We were rich and famous, Jesper! We were feared! No one would dare –"

"Hold on!" Jesper put a hand up to stop her. "You mean to tell me that the reason you needed me is for *money*? You were using me this entire time!"

Isa scoffed and let her jaw drop in false disbelief. "I – I was not using you!"

"You were! And you still are! I can't believe you! After all that time, I had the stupidity to think we made a good team under my command, but clearly you couldn't handle that!"

"We were! And we still are!"

Jesper shook his head furiously at her. "I'm leaving."

"You can't!" Isa wanted to scream at him and pull him back to her; he couldn't just leave! They were just getting started, and she so desperately wanted to restore the life that they had created together.

"Yes, I can! Watch me!" Jesper roared. She watched in desperation as he turned his back to her and reached for the pile of clothes that lay heaped on the rocks. Isa needed to make him stay.

"Fine! You want to know the secret to immortality? I'll tell you, since you want to know *so* badly!"

"You have nothing to tell me. You've been bluffing the whole time."

"It's not the immortality that you think it is! It's not physically living forever. It's your name."

"My name?" Jesper questioned, glancing back at where she stood. "I'm not following."

"The story that gets told about you, the story that is passed down from generation to generation. Your legacy lives on, even after you die."

"I knew there was a catch! I knew it!"

"It's no catch! I just … didn't tell you the full truth right away …"

"Oh! Oh-ho-ho! I swear! If you weren't a girl, you'd have a fist-sized hole in your teeth right about now!" Jesper balled up his fists, and Isa could see the tension in his muscles as he attempted to restrain himself from quite literally pounding her into the ground.

"Oh, yeah? Well, don't let that stop you! C'mon, Jesper! Give me your best shot!"

"Don't tempt me! I'll do it!"

"Go on, then! I want to see you try!" But she knew that he wouldn't. She could see it in his eyes. Behind the tough and hard-hearted demeanor that he presented, Jesper was hurt, afraid, lonely. And as much as he hated it and refused to believe it, he needed her. Because she could give him everything his crew couldn't. Love, attention, excitement. A chance to run from his problems and live in the present.

"You are not worthy enough to be my opponent." Jesper dropped his fists and shook his head as if to shake off his anger.

"Stop making excuses and just admit that you can't do it."

"I can do whatever I want."

"Right," Isa scoffed, crinkling her nose in smug amusement.

"You keep mocking and insulting me, but you're the one who's running to me in the end. *You're* the one falling to your knees and begging for my help. You can't live without me. So watch your words carefully."

Isa was speechless, her mouth open but no words coming out. So Jesper turned his back to her with every intention of leaving her behind. "Fine then!" she yelled at him. "Walk away! See if I care! You'll just end up alone and miserable, a shell of your former self!"

Jesper suddenly wheeled on her, pointing a finger in her face and hissing, "I should have stayed away from you from the moment we first met."

Isa took a step backward, her anger suddenly switching to desperation. His words cut into her, and her eyes stung with the tears she held back. "You don't mean that."

"I mean every word of it." And with that, Jesper picked up his waistcoat and boots and walked away across the forest floor, leaving a trail of wet footprints behind in the soft moss.

"Wait!" she screamed after Jesper. "The reason I didn't kill you was because I loved you!"

Jesper turned on his heels upon hearing her and strode over to where she stood, coming only inches from her face. Isa resisted the urge to back away from him, instead standing her ground. His anger was practically tangible, and it hovered in the air around him suffocatingly.

"You are the biggest liar I've ever had the misfortune of coming across, Isadora Fielding. You never loved me. I know that now."

"I did. I promise."

"Don't make promises you can't keep."

"Why do you think I put up with you for so long? Or why I was willing to risk my life for you?" she cried.

"Risk your life for me? You left me for dead!"

"I was foolish! I see that now! And I'm sorry!"

"Sorry? Sorry isn't going to bring back my crew! Sorry isn't going to make me feel better!" Jesper roared at her. "There's nothing you can do to fix what you did!"

Isa knew that what he said was true. But, all the same, she didn't want it to be. She was almost paralyzed with fear, his anger towards her unbearably fierce. "Why are you so full of hatred?"

"My hatred for you is reasonable!"

"Reasonable? I said I was sorry!"

"And I said it doesn't matter!"

"It does! It matters –"

"Isa! Stop trying to win me over. It won't work. I'm done putting my life in the hands of someone who can't even give me the truth. I'm doing what I should have done years ago: I'm putting my crew first."

"Your crew," she scoffed. "Your crew never cared about you."

"You're wrong. But even if that was true, at least I can rely on them to give me their all."

"I do that!" Isa protested. But he wouldn't listen to her, no matter how much she argued with him. Jesper simply shrugged and turned away again.

"Maybe someday you'll find what you're looking for. But I'm not the solution to your problems. Goodbye, Isa. I wish you the best of luck."

III

PART THREE

NINETEEN

WHAT DID I DO TO DESERVE THIS?

JESPER

He had to have been walking for ages. There were trees for as far as the eye could see, a sea of endless green that stretched to the heavens. Jesper groaned and rubbed a hand over his face, gradually growing tired of being lost in the middle of nowhere. The intense sunlight coming through the branches beat down on him, and he silently wished for the blissful shade of his old hat. And the comfort of his own clothes. He tugged at the stiff collar of his shirt, suddenly feeling extremely claustrophobic in the dense forest. It was as if Isa was still following him, hovering over him like a devil on his shoulder. And no matter what Jesper did to try and get away, he couldn't shake her off.

He shouldn't have listened to her in the first place. He shouldn't have gone running off with the person he hated to go on a wild goose chase for something that didn't exist. Of course, that's what he should have anticipated. As much as he wanted to blame her for the situation he was now stuck in, it was really all his fault. He should have known better.

Ari would have told him the same thing. His best friend, if he was standing there right beside him, would give Jesper his best *I told you so* look before going off on some long-winded rant about how Jesper should have listened to Ari's advice from the start. And then Jesper would tell Ari to shut up and leave him alone, because Jesper hated it when Ari was right about something. Which happened more often than Jesper was willing to admit.

"Gosh, I'm such an idiot," he muttered, squeezing his temples with a tense hand. Chasing after immortality with his enemy; how much more stupid could he get? But, really, should he have expected any less? Coming from a retired world-class killer with little family and commitment issues?

Jesper paused a moment to scan the horizon around him, hoping that something – anything – would give him any sense of direction. Life was really giving him a good slap in the face, and he was only helping out by making stupid decision after stupid decision. Of course he had to go running off away from the familiar path that would take him home.

Nothing around him had changed, so he continued forward, stumbling over upturned roots and loose stones in the dirt beneath his feet. *Stupid dirt, stupid sun, stupid trees.* He kicked frustratedly at the dirt, stuffing his fists into the pockets of his pants and wishing for a miracle to save him from his self-inflicted torture. Of course, that miracle wouldn't come until hours later, but it didn't hurt to have at least a little sliver of hope.

Jesper fingered the compass that hung from his neck in boredom, stopping every once in a while to pull it out and stare at the arrow spinning wildly in all directions. The old thing freaked out whenever he came to this coast; something in the area was no doubt throwing the compass off. It was times like this that Jesper silently wished for the compass to work, to actually be his guide when he was lost. And he was going to be lost without a guide once again, left to fend for himself and stumble forward blindly.

As he continued to trudge among the trees, a bright flash of light eventually caught his eye, shining brilliantly through the tightly packed trees and brush of the forest. The crashing of waves grew louder and the musk in the air began to fade the closer Jesper came to the light. Even the ground beneath him started to change, the soft moss disappearing to be replaced with a rocky beach.

* * *

Coming out of the seemingly endless forest, Jesper could see the ocean go on for miles in every direction ahead of him. The air was much cleaner by the water, and Jesper inhaled a deep breath gratefully. He had been hiking in the forest for hours on end, and he could have sworn he was going in circles for quite some time. There was a good reason why he stuck to the oceans and not the land. Navigation only got him so far, and, being directionally challenged, he relied heavily on the sun and stars to light his path. *If it wasn't for the stupid trees in my way, I would have been fine.*

As relief flooded him, the ever-growing pit in his stomach dissipated and the tension in his body subsided. The dread of Isa's presence was gone, and with the relief came a sort of wobbly instability in his legs that Jesper couldn't control.

His legs collapsed from underneath him, and Jesper crashed to the rocks. It was as if his body was refusing to let him leave the country, refusing to put the past behind him. So, he obeyed.

He found himself staring at the shoreline in front of him, the water crashing upon the rocks. The water surged toward him and then retreated, only to be replaced with a new wave a second later. There was something so peaceful about the repetitive rumble of the ocean. It was familiar, it was home. Or, it had been home for almost as long as Jesper could remember.

Reaching out, Jesper absentmindedly fingered the delicate petals of the violet flower that danced in the ocean breeze in front of him. He was trying to take it all in one last time, remember every inch of this place down to the wildflowers that grew up between the rocks. Because, deep down, Jesper knew that he probably would never come to these shores ever again. It would be too painful to come back and relive these awful memories.

Jesper was torn about what to do next, the conflict in his mind thundering like a storm behind his eyes. One part of him longed to stay there on the coast of that country for the rest of his days, to live alone in peace until his dying days. He deserved it, especially after everything he had been through. But the other part of him wanted to sail the seas again, to see the beaming smile of Ari and wrap Kie in an embrace once more. And he knew that there was no way to have both.

Slowly, Jesper rose to his feet and let his head fall back to gaze at the infinite blue sky. He was going to do it. He was going to leave. This was his last goodbye.

Jesper took one more moment to close his eyes and take everything in, the sounds of the waves and gulls calling overheard, the smell of the salty ocean, the feel of the wind in his hair. Goodbyes were too hard. And boy, was Jesper exceptionally bad at saying goodbye.

"You really are quite predictable. You know that, right?" Snapping out of his trance, Jesper unsheathed his sword and spun around to face Isa. She didn't flinch as the blade came only inches from her neck, instead smirking at Jesper with an artificial confidence. "I knew you wouldn't leave. You couldn't leave me behind. Not really."

"What do you want with me?"

"I want you to stay, of course!"

"If you value your life, you walk away right now," Jesper growled, not lowering his sword. "No tricks, no silver tongue."

"No tricks." Isa nodded in agreement, signaling surrender by raising her empty hands. Jesper narrowed his eyes at her, hoping to read her and predict her next move. She had to have a trick up her sleeve. She always did.

"Now's your chance to walk away. I'm not going to warn you again."

"You see, I would; believe me. But it's just that my ride back to my brig is right there behind you." Isa pointed behind him to the dinghy that sat on the rocks of the shoreline.

"Oh, my apologies," Jesper muttered sarcastically. "I was under the impression that that dinghy was *my* ticket out of here."

"Sorry to burst your bubble."

"Yeah, well, I'm getting off this coast."

Isa cocked her head at him mockingly, her pale hair falling over her smug face. "Since when are you so eager to leave?"

"I was just giving myself a minute, that's all."

"*Right.*"

"Yes," Jesper snapped. "So I'm leaving. Without you. And you aren't going to stop me."

"Is that so?"

Jesper watched Isa's eyes flick to the dinghy, then back to him. Her muscles tensed to leap into action, and Jesper knew that she would bolt for the dinghy as if it was happening in slow motion. Just as he predicted, she darted around Jesper toward her only escape. But Jesper was ready. He had seen it coming. Jesper sprinted after her, roaring as he raised his sword to strike. Unfortunately, Isa was just as fast, spinning around and bringing her own sword to shield herself against Jesper's attack.

Then she suddenly lunged back at him, cutting the air between them. He barely had time to dodge the sword, the blade flying so close to him that he could feel the tip of the blade graze the skin on his cheek. In an instance, his brain switched to fight mode, and he relinquished control of his body. It moved on autopilot, reacting to Isa's attacks with a speed that Jesper could never tell himself to do. He began to memorize her movements until each attack was predictable, expected.

The fight rushed by in a blur of blood and sweat, the clanging of the swords ringing deafeningly in his ears. Isa wasn't holding back, and she was certainly fighting dirty with each opportunity she had. Every movement was a chance to throw a punch to the gut or an elbow to the nose. It wasn't long before his ribs were throbbing fiercely, forcing his breathing to be shallow and torturous.

As much as he hated it, Jesper had no choice but to fight dirty back. He used his surroundings to get back at Isa, slamming her unrestrainedly in the leg with a stone to give himself a break to catch his breath. Both of their chests heaved with exhaustion and sweat poured down their faces.

Gasping for breath, Jesper watched Isa closely as she clutched her leg. She grunted in pain between clenched teeth before shooting a hateful glare at him.

And then, jumping up, Isa lunged at him and slammed her blade against his, knocking the sword from his hand. It clamored on the rocks, close enough to beckon his attention but too far away to grab quickly. There was now nothing to stop Isa from finishing the fight. And that's when Jesper decided to make his move.

He waited until she swung the sword at him once more in a wide arc, her defense suddenly dropped. Ducking, Jesper dodged the swift blade and kicked Isa in the stomach, sending her tumbling to the rocky ground. She crashed to her hands and knees, her back dangerously facing Jesper. It didn't take her long to regain her balance, quickly rising to her feet and clutching her sword in her hand.

She spun on her heels and then stopped as if frozen in time. Her eyes were locked on the pistol in Jesper's hand. Jesper had undeniably won the fight. Isa's gaze betrayed a deadly fury, yet at the same time shock and sadness.

"I should have figured."

"Well, I can't take any chances when it comes to you," Jesper said, shrugging and tilting his head in a mocking manner. Out of anyone, surely Isa should know what would happen when a gun was brought to a knife fight. He cocked the gun, the clicking sound making Isa flinch ever so slightly. The movement of fear didn't escape Jesper's gaze in the slightest. "I'm sure you can understand."

She seemed to hesitate, as if she was unsure of what to do next. Continue to fight and risk being shot or surrender? Jesper knew better than to assume the latter. Isa was like him in that way: she would never go down without a fight. But this time seemed different. For what reason Jesper couldn't quite put his finger on.

"Do it then. Finish the fight." The sword fell from her hand, and she dropped to her knees in front of Jesper. He couldn't believe it. It was almost as if his eyes were betraying him. She was surrendering. Jesper had never thought it possible, but she was giving up. After all these years, it was going to be over.

Dropping his aim at Isa, Jesper retrieved his sword and pressed the tip of the blade into Isa's chest. Isa watched him with an unnerving stare, waiting for death to meet her. She muttered, "Maybe I was wrong about you, Jesper Kelsey. Maybe you do have the strength and ruthlessness of a pirate after all."

Jesper looked into her eyes, and for the first time in years, he saw a genuine person. An imperfect person who was scared to die. Everything she had done; it was all to protect herself. She was desperate for security and attention and love, but she had gone too far to receive those things. She had made mistakes; she was human. Who was he to decide whether she lived or died?

Raising the sword above his head, he felt himself hesitate. Her words echoed in his head, and he couldn't silence them. *Maybe you do have the strength and ruthlessness of a pirate after all.*

Jesper let out a roar, for a brief moment picturing what it would be like to plunge his sword into the heart of his enemy. But she needed to be proved wrong. He wasn't like Isa at all; he was determined to show her that. He wasn't a manipulator; he wasn't going to be a killer or a deserter or a backstabber anymore.

And then he threw the sword down, wedging the blade in between the rocks in front of Isa's bowed figure. She flinched once more as the blade came down, expecting it to be the instrument that would cut her life short. But when she opened her eyes and glanced up, all she could see was a sword rammed in the ground and Jesper looking at her as he tried to blink back furious tears.

"I've made mistakes, but I'm not that person anymore. I'm not like you."

When Isa had no response, Jesper picked up his sword and walked away without another word or even so much as a glance at her. There was closure in that moment, the grand finale of a seven-year-long battle. It wasn't the ending Jesper had imagined or hoped for, but it was satisfying. It was comforting … in an odd sort of way. He hated the thought that she would live to see another sun, but part of him hoped that she would change with the second chance she was given. Because he couldn't bring himself to kill her, not after what he had seen in her eyes as she yielded to his punishment. Not after she had claimed he was just like her, that he was just as heartless as she was. He couldn't accept that; he *wouldn't.* At any rate, Jesper knew he would sleep at least a little easier at night.

One battle was ending, and another one was just beginning.

TWENTY

IF KARMA DOESN'T, I WILL

ARI

"Ari! What's going on?" Jesper asked, barging into Ari's tiny living quarters. Besides the bed and a small dresser, there wasn't much in the room. That, of course, was discounting the numerous piles of junk that crowded the floors. And Ari sat in the middle of it all, scrambling around in the piles, looking for something, *anything* that could be used to solve his problem. His glaring, impossibly hard problem.

He jumped to his feet as soon as Jesper came through the door, fury written all over his face. "Where have you been?"

"I asked you first."

"I've been trying to captain your ship for like half a year!" Ari exploded. "And it was going fine enough at first until we pulled out of the port and started getting chased by the Navy again! Turns out, they were just waiting for us to leave. Chased us all the way to the Chain Islands and then disappeared as soon as we docked here. Who knows what they're planning now, and I have to figure out what to do because *I'm* the cap'n!"

Jesper frowned to himself. Both pirates knew that it wasn't like the Navy to just suddenly give up on a chase, especially when it came to Jesper's crew. They were planning something big, all right. "That can't be good."

"You put me in this position! And now I have absolutely no idea what to do! How am I supposed to know how to deal with the Navy like this?"

"I obviously didn't mean to do this to you!"

"You still haven't answered my question," Ari said shortly, crossing his arms over his chest. "Where have you been?"

"Oh, you know, around."

"Around?"

"All over Sovi, Aerithos, a bit of the Chain Islands … around."

"Doing what exactly?"

"Nothing that would be of any interest to you. It doesn't really matter, either." Ari took that vague explanation with a grain of salt. He had no doubt that Jesper had resorted back to his old lifestyle, which included various activities of absolutely no moral value. And while Ari certainly couldn't be one to judge, given his own occupation, he knew that this lifestyle Jesper so happily engaged in consisted of a great deal of killing. Not in self-defense, but for the fun of it.

"I can't believe you, Jesper! You killed more people, didn't you?"

"It was an accident, I swear!"

"How …?" But before Jesper could respond, Ari held up a hand to stop him. "You know what? Don't answer that question. I don't even want to know what happened."

"Yeah, well, now that's behind us, and I'm here to help however I can."

"Behind us? You think that stabbing me in the back and betraying me is behind us? It doesn't work that way, Jesper."

"I'm sorry, okay?" Jesper protested, but Ari shook his head.

"No, you're not. You're not sorry at all."

"What are you talking about? Yes, I am."

"I've known you long enough to know when you're not being honest. I know you enjoyed your little killing spree, or whatever you want to call it, probably a lot more than you should have."

"I was not out on a killing spree!"

"Oh, yeah? Then what were you doing? And don't say nothing!"

Jesper struggled to come up with a good response. "Not … killing people."

"It really hurts to know that the person I used to call my closest friend willingly left the life we had built together for seven years to kill some people and run around like a maniac."

"I promised I would come back, and I did!"

"It's been six months, Jesper!" Ari exclaimed, his voice rising. His ability to control his rage was wearing thin. Real thin. "Months since you left, with no guarantee that you would come back! I didn't think you were coming back! Ever!"

"But I did!"

"And left me to fend for the crew all by myself in the meantime! Do you know how hard that is when you've always been the glue that keeps this crew together and then you just leave? I'm just the temporary replacement, and I'm not you!"

"I'm sorry, Ari! That was never my intention!"

Jesper should have come to him crawling on his knees, begging for mercy at Ari's feet. That's how it should have been. But Jesper had no shame. Clearly none at all. Because he didn't come to Ari on his hands and knees. He wasn't begging for forgiveness.

"You slimy, backstabbing, lily-livered … hedonistic liar! You're just as bad as all of the stories I've heard of Isa! In fact, you're probably worse!" Ari screamed, shoving Jesper hard in the chest. Unprepared, Jesper lost his balance and stumbled backward before recovering to shoot the aggression right back.

"How dare you –"

"Get out of my room right now! Or I'll shoot you! I swear I'll do it!"

"Ari, let's just talk." Jesper didn't believe that Ari was telling the truth; that much was clear.

"You've had your warning!"

Wheeling around on his heels, Ari turned to the piles on his floor, his eyes scanning for any sign of his gun. The search left him fruitless, and frowning, he dropped to his knees to dig through the clutter. Jesper watched on quietly from the center of the small room, every once in a while shifting on his feet and sighing.

"I'll find it. It's here somewhere."

"It might be easier to find if you didn't have such a hoarding disorder."

"I don't have a hoarding disorder; people just say that."

"I can't imagine why," Jesper replied sarcastically, watching as Ari rummaged around in his tiny room. Ari could feel Jesper's eyes penetrating the back of his head, and he had little doubt that Jesper was scanning the masses of clutter that lined the floor of his room just as rapidly to get to the gun first.

"I swear, everything has a place and a purpose."

"What purpose? To take up space?"

"Ha-ha, you're real funny."

"I try my best." Jesper mustered out a small laugh, but his smile faded when Ari said shortly,

"It's not working."

"I'm sorry?"

"Your jokes. They're not going to work," he snapped. "You're not going to distract me from being furious with you."

"Okay, look. Before you kill me, I wanted to explain myself."

"Well, at least we're on the same page there."

"Ari, I know I screwed up –"

"Really? I hadn't noticed," Ari muttered, interrupting Jesper.

"– and I wanted to say that I'm sorry. I was only trying to protect you."

"Protect me? From what exactly?"

"Myself." The silence in the room was deafening. Ari couldn't find a response for the life of him. "But I've changed now, and –"

"You've changed? Huh. You know, funny thing, I've heard that one before. From you. The day you told me your story and swore on the lives of your dead parents that you were a changed man!" he roared, jumping to his feet to confront Jesper. "Now, I might not be the smartest guy out there, but I don't exactly see how doing the same thing you swore you would never do again is being changed!"

"I know I've made mistakes –"

"Oh, really? You're just noticing this just now?"

"Isa said she knew the secret to immortality!"

"Since when has trusting Isa been a rational idea?" Ari exclaimed, wildly throwing his hands into the air. "You've always known her deals come with strings attached!"

"But she was serious this time!"

"Yeah? And where did that get you?" Jesper opened his mouth to reply, but not a sound came out. He had no excuse, nothing he could use to defend himself with. "That's what I thought."

Ari went back to rummaging through his various piles, uttering a small exclamation of joy when he finally found his gun. Drawing the pistol from its holster, Ari slammed the weapon down on the top of his dresser. He could feel Jesper's eyes boring into the back of his head once more.

"You're not immortal, you know. It doesn't exist. No matter what lies Isa tries to tell you. You're not a god."

"Yeah? You want to pull the trigger and find out?"

Ari didn't know how to respond to that one either. Surely Jesper couldn't be serious. He had to know that what he was saying was ridiculous, absurd. Furrowing his brow but still refusing to turn around to face Jesper, Ari asked, "Who in their right mind would even consider putting faith in Isadora Fielding?"

"Well, that's a dumb question, because the answer is obviously me."

"Jesper, she left you for dead!" Ari protested, wheeling around to stare incredulously at the captain.

"I know! But I thought –"

"No! That's just it! You weren't thinking!"

"It wasn't supposed to go this far, Ari! I swear!" Jesper's voice began to rise and his eyes glinted with forming tears. "You know for a fact that this wasn't supposed to happen!"

"And yet it did."

"What more do you want from me?"

"I want you to get out of my life!" Ari suddenly shouted, releasing all his pent-up anger. Jesper seemed to shrink back at the demand, and Ari could swear that he had never seen Jesper look so small and timid in his entire life. When Jesper spoke, even his voice was meek.

"Really? That's how this is?"

"Yes! It is! That's why you left, right? So it's what we both want!"

"You can't just get rid of me that easily! You can't just push me away!"

"Yes, I can!"

"Yeah, well, like it or not, you need me!" The rash confidence had resurfaced, this time stronger than ever. "If you haven't noticed already, the Navy's on our tail again. And this time, they're not going to leave any survivors. So, I'll make you a deal. You let me captain this ship one last time, and once we win, you can drop me off at Citadelle, and you'll never have to see me again. The crew, the ship, it's all yours."

Something about the deal seemed off to Ari. He couldn't quite place a finger on it, but he didn't like it. Was it even possible that Jesper was willingly giving everything he owned to Ari? "Why do you want to do this?"

"I just want to make sure everyone makes it out of this alive. I screwed up once, and I let you down, and I'm not going to do that again. And I'm certainly not losing another crew. So, do we have a deal?"

"Fine."

Jesper stretched out a hand to his friend, and Ari reluctantly sealed the deal with a handshake. If they were going to have a falling out, he figured he might as well get something out of it. Even if that meant robbing Jesper of all his possessions.

And, of course, they weren't even going to mention the fact that this deal entailed making it out of the coming conflict alive. Fighting the Navy and surviving. Now that was a feat that could be accomplished by only a few people. Jesper was a good captain and a great warrior, there was no doubt about it, but Ari was worried that maybe he wasn't good enough. Sure, he had made promises to keep everyone alive, but when was the last time he actually kept a promise?

"So, what now?"

Ari could see such weariness in Jesper's eyes, such sadness, despite the smile that Jesper managed to put on. "Now," Jesper sighed, "I rally the crew, come up with a plan, and hope for the best."

"And then we go our separate ways." Jesper nodded in agreement, lowering his gaze to the floor. The sharpness in Ari's stare faded ever so slightly when he noticed Jesper's pain, but he kept his mouth shut and tried to ignore it. Now was not the time for pity or regrets. Not in a time of war. He could only push the emotions away and save them for a different day, a day hopefully far in the distant future.

He refused to acknowledge the intense pain that was ripping a hole through his chest, or the undying desire to wrap Jesper in a hug and forget everything that had happened. But he couldn't forget. Not when Jesper had abandoned the crew and their friendship to pursue a blatant lie with the one person who had left his life in ruins years before.

"We might as well get to it, then. Let's hope you know what you're doing, Cap'n."

"I really hope so, too." Jesper paused, his eyes intently studying Ari's worry-creased forehead and tired eyes. Ari internally wished that Jesper wouldn't say anything and just move on, but then he rubbed the back of his neck and said, "Hey, I have a good feeling about this, okay? Everything's going to be fine."

"You say that every time, and it never works out."

"This time is going to be different. I'll make sure of that."

"I don't know whether to be comforted or terrified by your confidence."

"I'm trying to be more optimistic about the situation, okay?"

"Never mind," Ari replied quickly. His pent-up anger made his chest tight, and he suddenly became desperate for fresh air and sunlight. He had to get out of that room. "Just forget I said anything. We've got a war to prepare for, anyway."

"Ari, wait –"

But Ari was already striding out the door, and he wasn't going to look back. What was the purpose of looking back if not for regret?

TWENTY ONE

I'M NOT CRYING, YOU'RE CRYING

JESPER

Knocking lightly, Jesper turned the handle and swung the door open. He could see the silhouette of Kie sitting at the table in the dim light of his cabin, seemingly unmoving. She hardly acknowledged his presence, until Jesper came up behind her and placed a hand on her shoulder. It was then that Kie gasped and lifted her head, her sorrowful eyes meeting his. Jesper smiled weakly back at her before pulling up a chair and sitting across from her. He held her hand in his gently, trying his best to show his regret without speaking a word. Kie couldn't look up at him, instead watching his thumb trace circles on her knuckles. A single tear slipped down her cheek, and Jesper brushed it away gently. They remained huddled together in the dim cabin, relishing in the silence until Kie worked up the courage to whisper,

"Why did you leave?"

"I'm sorry, Kie. I really am."

"But you promised to protect me and that no harm would come to me. You promised that everything would be okay."

"I know."

"Why did you lie?"

He was at a loss for words. How could he possibly make her understand? With a small groan, Jesper leaned back into his chair as Kie watched him with a keen eye. He could tell that some of the trust that she used to have in him had faded away, and he couldn't help but feel slightly saddened and angry at himself for doing that to her. She deserved an explanation, a reason for all the stupid decisions he had made. Perhaps that was the only way to give her an answer, to put her mind at rest.

"I should probably explain myself, shouldn't I?"

"I don't think you could possibly come up with an answer good enough to excuse what you did. But I want to see you try."

"Where do I begin?" Jesper sighed, thinking back to the beginning of his story. The extremely painful beginning. It made his stomach drop with nerves; never had he even dared to tell about his life before to anyone, not even the likes of Ari. But for Kie, he told himself that it was worth it. In order for her to trust him, she had to know the truth. All of it.

"Growing up, I lived with my parents and my older siblings in Ra'Sehara. Eirik was the oldest, then Trystan and Clary. We were extremely poor, couldn't make ends meet, but we were happy, you know? We had a small farm in the hills, where we grew our own food and provided for ourselves.

"Then we moved to the cities near the northern border for my father to take up work at the port as a dockhand because we were going to starve to death unless he could find a job. I was probably about four at the time. That's how I learned to love the sea. My brothers and I would accompany my father to his job every day, work on building and patching up the vessels, and explore the area. The people my father worked with loved me, and they would take me out on joyrides on their ships. It was one of the happiest times of my life."

Jesper took a minute to himself, smiling as he recalled the warm face of his father and the shimmering waters of the port's bay. If only he could travel back in time, relive that one moment over and over.

"Then what happened?" Kie prompted.

"Well, it was the happiest time of my life, until my brothers left to join the Navy. We had no way of getting a hold of them, so we couldn't tell them that our father died when I was six. Then we got the news that Trystan had been killed in battle. My mother followed suit not long after from the smallpox virus that was spreading like wildfire around the city, leaving my sister to take care of me by herself. As two young kids, we couldn't make money to survive by moral means, so we got roped into the smuggling business in the inner Citadelle area. It started off as small jobs, like pickpocketing and things like that, but we got good. Like, really good. Best in the business.

"When I got older, I quickly picked up a crew, and we traveled around together, smuggling and stealing money where we could. And then I got a little carried away. Obviously, I didn't mean to, but when you grow up with nothing, it feels awfully good to have the world in the palm of your hand. So I kept pushing for more. And more. I lost sight of who I was in favor of obtaining as much wealth and power that I could get my hands on. Even if that meant killing people for it. I killed so many people, Kie. And I regret all of it." He could feel himself curling inward, his palms going cold and clammy. Jesper squeezed his eyes shut for a moment, regretting it instantly when the faces of his past victims flooded his mind – every last one of them. He couldn't unsee it.

"I'm sure you do."

She urged him on, placing a hand on his arm. Jesper took a deep breath to steel himself before continuing his story.

"During the peak of my … career, I met Isa on a job. She was ambitious, and brilliant, and just as power hungry as I was. We bonded instantly, and we ran our crew so smoothly and flawlessly. That's when I became the Hellburner of Sovi."

"Wait. You …"

"I know. It's a title that I'm not exactly proud to bear. Though I definitely used to."

"You were the scourge of the Seven Seas, the story that parents told their kids to get them to behave! You terrorized sailors for nearly a decade."

"I did."

"You killed tens of thousands of people and stole even more than that in riches."

"Indeed."

"You're supposed to be dead!"

"I'm sorry?" Jesper responded, confused.

"Well, I didn't mean it like that," Kie said quickly, realizing her mistake. She pressed her lips together, going quiet.

"Uh, where was I?"

"Something about being the Hellburner of Sovi?"

"Oh, right. Yes, uh, Isa and I, we were practically untouchable in our line of work. Our friendship grew so strong that we were both willing to do anything for each other. We were even willing to die for each other, if it came to that. And then it became more."

"More?"

"I loved her," Jesper admitted, perhaps for the first time ever, the words leaving a bitter taste in his mouth, "and I thought she loved me. But I was wrong. I was so wrong. She was using me the entire time to gain more wealth for herself. The intimidation that we brandished so stupidly was what she most craved, I suppose because it gave her a sense of identity and recognition. So, Isa continued to persuade me to kill and loot and create destruction with the lie that she genuinely loved me. I fell for it, too, until the day that she decided she'd had enough. I remember the day like it was just yesterday."

Jesper hesitated, the story cut short. He didn't want to recall that awful memory. But Kie was curious, and he had promised his story. "We were transporting some of our most expensive possessions to a secure location off the coast of Aerithos after finishing another job. I guess someone had tipped the Navy that we were in the area, so they came after us. I still cannot figure out who did it, though. Isa saw that the Navy was coming after us before any of the rest of us did, so she secretly moved all the goods we were transporting to the ship's dinghy, managed to handcuff me to the table in my cabin, and took off. She completely disappeared off the face of the planet, so I thought she was dead until she just reappeared now.

"The Navy attacked us without any warning and destroyed the ship with their long-range cannons, killing everyone in the crew except me. Believing they had finished the job, the Navy vessels moved on. I was left completely alone, somehow still chained to the table and a huge wreck from the ship being blasted to pieces around me. The ship crashed on the shores of Vyena in a huge thunderstorm, where Ari happened to find me in the wreck a couple days later. He brought me back to his family's place and nursed me back to health, and we've been close friends ever since."

Jesper paused, studying Kie's reactions for a moment. Her face was void of emotion, almost as if she had gone numb. Kie was in pain, and it was all his fault. Jesper wanted to comfort her, wrap her in a hug. But he wasn't good at that sort of thing. And he knew that no matter how much he tried to explain himself or how much he tried to apologize, he couldn't gain back the trust that had been lost.

"No one knows this – no one knows who I am – so you cannot tell a single soul, you understand? Not even Ari knows everything that happened. My crew respects me and trusts me, and I can't let that change. You have to understand."

"What are you so afraid of?"

He didn't want to answer that question. He couldn't. His eyes traced the lines of Kie's face, glowing in the candlelight. In the silence, Jesper began to count the freckles on her cheeks. He got to thirty-three before she spoke again.

"The crew loves you and respects you for who you are, Jesper. Not for your past self, not for your mistakes. You don't need to fear them. They trust you. I wish I still could trust you."

"You can," Jesper insisted. He wanted to make her understand, make her see that he was changed.

"Trust doesn't work like that. Once it's broken, it's incredibly hard to get it back. Apologizing isn't going to fix it."

"What do you want me to do?"

Kie sat still in silence for a moment, deeply pondering the question. "I wish … I wish we could just go back in time and erase what happened."

"But we can't."

"So then you earn back my trust."

"You make it sound so easy."

"I never said it was easy. I just said that's what you have to do."

"Okay, I will. I promise."

"Stop making promises, Jesper. It always ends badly."

"This time it won't."

"You say that every time."

"Yeah," he whispered. "I know." A beat passed, and Jesper's mind returned to the past life he had disclosed for the first time ever. Kie hadn't shied away from him, so that had to mean something. Right?

Blinking back tears, Jesper whispered, "Are you … scared of me?"

"Why should I be? My trust might have been hurt, but I don't fear you."

"Because I'm a murderer."

"But you've changed. Believe me, when I look at you, I don't see a murderer."

"That's what makes murderers so good at what they do. They're good at blending in."

"Jesper, I've been with you long enough to know that you're not going to suddenly snap and kill me, or your crew. In fact, you'd rather give up your life than let your crew die. A murderer wouldn't do that."

"You have no idea how much that means to me to hear that," Jesper muttered, his heart lightening ever so slightly.

"I'm guessing people don't tell you that very often?"

"Not really. I would imagine most people would be absolutely terrified of me and would run away in fear."

"You would imagine?"

"Well, it's not like I go around telling people who I am. I don't really talk to that many people in the first place, now that I think about it. I don't like getting close to people."

"Why is that?"

"Because I hurt people, Kie. It's what I do best."

Jesper's eyes suddenly shifted to the table, finding the grain pattern in the wood oddly interesting. The silence that followed made him squirm with discomfort, and he found himself returning to his old habit of tapping the table with his knuckles like he did in poker.

She wasn't disagreeing with him. Not even Kie could deny that, when it came down to it, all Jesper could manage to do was hurt the people he loved the most. It had happened with Isa, with his sister, with Ari, and it had inevitably happened to Kie.

"What happened to your oldest brother?"

"Eirik? I have no idea," Jesper admitted. "I haven't heard anything about him in years. For all I know, he could very well be dead."

"Do you want to know?"

"Honestly … not really. Either way, I think I'd be let down, you know?"

"That's fair enough."

He paused for a minute and frowned before saying, "I think he's still alive, though."

"You think so?"

"Yeah. I just have this gut feeling, you know, that he's out there somewhere. And I'm going to find him."

"I'll help you."

"What about going home? You've got a family, a fiancé. What was his name again?"

Kie chuckled at the odd question before replying, "Eugene Lurcock."

Jesper whistled and raised his eyebrows, eternally grateful that he wasn't the one with such an unfortunate name. "You really dodged a bullet there."

"Don't be cruel!" Kie gasped, playfully shoving Jesper in the arm.

"How did you manage to come across such a pleasant person?"

"It was arranged, for your information."

Jesper paused, his smile fading ever so slightly. "Are you going to return to him?"

"I don't know."

"Were you happy together?"

"I suppose that depends on how you define happiness."

"How would you define it?"

"I'm … not really sure."

"Well, were you happy?"

"You know, the more I think about it … I don't think so," Kie said slowly, thinking long and hard between each word. "I never truly loved Eugene, not as I should have, anyway. I was just pretending I was in love with him to please my family."

"Are you pretending now?" Jesper could barely muster up the courage to ask that question, part of him too scared to hear her answer.

"I'm sorry?"

"Are you pretending? To be happy now?"

"I'm not, Jesper. I really am happy here." He could tell that Kie wasn't lying, and she wasn't pretending. Jesper felt the corners of his mouth turn upward into a glowing smile. She wasn't lying. A sudden wave of relief flooded Jesper, and a huge weight was lifted from his shoulders. Isa had been lying to him and manipulating him the entire time, but Kie didn't lie once. The realization shocked him to the core, and the feeling was so incredible that Jesper wanted to just bask in it for a good long minute.

"Ari still hates me, doesn't he?" Jesper asked quietly, turning the conversation over in his head.

"He'll get over it. Just give him some time."

"I really screwed up, huh?" He was so frustrated with himself that he let out a small chuckle. Kie raised her eyebrows at him, and Jesper knew that she couldn't disagree with him.

"You're not wrong. But I'm sure it'll all come together in the end."

"How are you so optimistic all the time?"

"What do you mean?"

"Well, you can always see the good in every situation. How do you do it?"

"I don't know," she replied, shrugging. "I guess that's just how I was raised."

"Yeah? Well, you're lucky, that's for sure."

"I am?"

He leaned forward in his chair as Kie's eyes widened in curiosity, silently demanding an explanation. "I'm sure life's a lot better when everything looks great. At least, it's got to be better than how I look at it. All I do is focus on the pain of my past. And it sucks."

"Then let go."

Those three words were so simple, but so profound. *Let go.* But how? He didn't even have the slightest idea of where to start. His past, his mistakes, they were the very essence of who he was. So how was it even possible to let go of something so fundamental to his identity?

"I don't know how."

"Maybe start by focusing on the present. Are you content with the life you're living right now?"

"I guess."

"You should be. You have so many friends, and you're not scrambling for scraps to survive, and you've got me. In my opinion, that's all you really need in life."

Jesper smiled gently, biting back a laugh. "You're smart, you know that? A lot wiser than me, anyway."

"Don't sell yourself short."

"Shut up and just take the compliment," Jesper laughed.

"All right. My apologies."

He pressed his lips together and rubbed the back of his neck before saying, "I just wish that I was smart enough to recognize and be content with the life I had before I completely destroyed it."

"It's not too late to fix it."

"I'm afraid it is. Ari wants me out of his life, I'm going to be left without a ship or a crew when this is all over, and I'm sure my sister won't be of much help."

"Jesper, it's *never* too late to mend what is broken," Kie insisted, squeezing Jesper's hand tighter.

"I wish I could believe you."

"Don't be so hard on yourself all the time. At least you have one pirate to start your new crew."

"And who might that be?"

"Me."

"You?" Jesper raised his eyebrows in shock. "I thought you'd said that you would pass on the whole pirate thing."

"Yeah, well, now I'm kinda retracting that statement."

"Is that so?" Jesper chuckled. Kie smiled and nodded back at him, her cheeks matching the color of her hair.

"I'll let you pick the tattoo design and everything."

"Oh, wonderful. I feel so honored."

"You should be."

"A pirate needs to trust her captain, though."

"We'll worry about that when the time comes. For now, just focus on getting out of our situation with the Navy alive."

"Yes, ma'am," Jesper replied politely, bowing his head in genuine respect for her. With his gaze leaving Kie, he didn't notice the warm smile that quickly crossed her face.

"Are you scared?"

"Me?" he scoffed, raising his head to smirk at her. "Scared? Never."

"Right. Of course."

"Of course." Jesper grinned cheekily at Kie for the first time since he had returned. He took a moment to sit in the peaceful silence, letting her process everything she had just been told. She seemed to take it surprisingly well, considering the bombshell of information he had just thrown at her.

"Look, I know this might be really bad timing on my part, but do you know what today is?"

"No? Should I?"

"Well, I don't know. You studied it in your classes," Jesper teasingly hinted. After a moment, a spark of realization lit up Kie's face.

"It's St. Elyor's."

TWENTY TWO

THE DAY THE STARS WENT SWIMMING

KARYNA

Her heart pounding in her chest for a spectacular phenomenon she only knew on the pages of her father's books, Karyna let Jesper guide her out of the cabin and onto the Fortuyna's main deck. Other members of the crew had already congregated on the deck, waiting in anticipation for something to happen. Once Karyna and Jesper joined them, a few men began going around and extinguishing the lanterns that provided light to the main area, until the deck was completely shrouded in darkness. The disappointment at the lack of … *anything* was almost immediate, but Karyna pushed the feeling aside and continued staring intently into the night sky. Waiting for something. Anything to happen.

"Just wait," Jesper muttered beside her, his eyes also fixed on the heavens. At a painfully slow pace, a small bright star – the one Karyna recalled Jesper calling Shéaspar – inched its way towards the star Catarуna. Then the two touched, and the whole sky erupted in a flash of silver light.

The billions of stars, once hung delicately in the night sky, began to fall, creating streaks of silver and white against the void of darkness. As they fell, the stars let off a faint whistling sound, almost as if they were singing to her.

"The stars," Karyna breathed, not wanting to disturb the magic of the moment. "They're singing."

"Not a thousand words in a thousand books could describe this majesty."

"What are they saying?"

Jesper smiled gently. "Well, it's a dead language, but some say that the stars are declaring the praises of their Maker, or perhaps that they are singing the accomplishments of the Lightweavers that learned to understand them."

"Of St. Elyor?"

"Yes, of him and those that first discovered the language of the stars and learned to chart their paths across the heavens. They're also hailing in the new year, and people say that if you can manage to catch one, you get to make a wish."

"It's beautiful." *That* was an understatement. Karyna couldn't find the words to describe just how incredible the stars were. Such a word surely didn't exist.

"Just wait," Jesper repeated once again. "There's more."

Karyna laughed, bringing a light to Jesper's eyes. "It couldn't possibly get more incredible than this."

"You have no idea." And just as he said it, something more *did* happen.

Some of the stars started falling down towards the world instead of streaking across the sky, creating a momentary chaos as they hurled themselves full force into the ocean. Up close, the stars were so bright that they simply looked like miniature suns, glowing so brilliantly that they threatened to blind Karyna.

As they crashed into the surface of the water, they illuminated the ocean in vibrant silvers and blues and greens, almost as if the water itself was glowing. Where the stars crashed into the sea, beacons of starlight shot upwards back to the heavens. The horizon, for as far as Karyna could see, was littered with pillars of starlight and glowing waves of shimmering blue.

Seized by a surge of excitement, Karyna rushed to the edge of the deck and leaned over the railing, unreservedly gawking at the view.

She could hear Jesper chuckling at her from behind, but she didn't care in the least.

"You impressed?"

"You could say that."

"Happy St. Elyor's Day, Karyna."

"To you as well." Karyna peeled her eyes from the waters to gaze at Jesper. The expression on his face threw Karyna off momentarily, his eyes soft in a way that she had never seen from him before.

"Will you dance with me?"

Her breath caught in her throat, her mind trying to comprehend what she had just been asked. "What?"

"It's tradition," Jesper explained quickly, almost like he was embarrassed. "For the host to ask the most beautiful woman at the party to dance. I know this is less than acceptable; I don't have any music for us to dance to or a big feast or –"

"I'd love to dance with you."

Bowing deeply, Jesper outstretched his hand for her. Karyna tried in vain to repress the redness spreading across her face, dipping into a curtsey before taking Jesper's hand. Her hand slid almost too perfectly into his, the palm of his hand rough with calluses.

Guiding her to the center of the deck, Jesper slipped a hand around her waist and pulled her closer to himself, and Karyna couldn't help but gasp slightly as the butterflies flew into uproar in her stomach. He immediately backed off, the regret painted into his features.

"I'm sorry. I didn't mean to …"

"No, you're okay. This is good."

"Yeah?"

"I promise." She didn't need to tell him twice. Jesper pulled her in again, and this time Karyna was prepared. Once they were both situated, Jesper began to lead her in a simple waltz, her feet falling in step next to his. They danced silently to the delicate music of the falling stars, but it wasn't the magnificence of the stars that had captured Karyna's breath and sent her heart racing.

There was something so different about him, but she couldn't tell if it was reality or her eyes just playing tricks on her. Jesper seemed gentler, almost more careful, with her, as if he was holding a fragile valuable in his hands. Yet, at the same time, he was still confident and sure of himself. His presence wasn't small, wasn't meek. But it wasn't cocky either. Jesper had changed.

Karyna couldn't put into words the emotions she was feeling. She felt as though she could cry, and laugh, and melt into a puddle on the floor, and ascend into the heavens all at the same time. No one had ever looked at her like that before. Not her family, certainly not Eugene. But an outlaw, a criminal, a man who had terrified her just a year ago was looking at her like she was his entire world. Like she was the stars falling from the sky and painting the ocean with their heavenly glow.

No one had ever looked at her like that.

She must have been staring back, because Jesper smirked amusedly and asked, "What?"

"What do you mean, 'what?'"

"I don't know. You just have this look on your face. You look like you want to tell me something."

Karyna shook her head. "We don't always have to talk. Sometimes the silence is nice."

"Sorry," Jesper smiled softly. "I'll stop talking, then."

The two of them fell quiet, swaying gently from side to side in a dance that was supposed to resemble a waltz of sorts. In the cool of the night, Jesper's body felt comfortingly warm next to her's. But she didn't even feel the chilling breeze that danced along; there was a weird warmth that had spread from the core of her being to the tips of her fingers, a fuzzy kind of feeling. And her mind wasn't racing, wasn't reeling like she thought it would. It was silent, dead calm.

Jesper's gaze was still locked on her, his hands still cradling her. No one had ever looked at her like that. No one but Jesper.

* * *

It was as if her brain was lagging, but his hand had slipped out from hers and come up to the side of her face, and they had stopped dancing. His mouth stopped smirking, and his eyes no longer held their mischievously playful glint. She hadn't even noticed.

As gently as humanly possible, Jesper pulled her closer at her waist, closing the small distance between them. Karyna's heart seemed to stop beating entirely, and time came to halt, the whole world holding its breath. He was so close.

Karyna felt a magnetic pull towards Jesper, a sudden urge for a sense of closeness like that day they had hid from the navy sailors in that miserably small wardrobe. She had never experienced anything like this with Eugene before; Karyna couldn't help but wonder if this was what she was supposed to feel.

Eugene.

What was she doing? She was engaged to a different man, and here she was … What *was* she doing?

"Wait, Jesper …" Karyna put a hand on Jesper's chest to stop him, and for a moment, she swore she could feel his heart pounding. Immediately, he stopped leaning in, worry painted on his face.

"What's wrong?"

"I – I just … I don't know if –"

"If you should be doing this. Since you have a fiancé."

"Well, it's just –"

"No, Kie, it's okay. I understand." His hands dropped to his side, and he dejectedly took a step backward.

"Jesper –"

"I'm sorry," he shot back quickly. "I shouldn't have assumed …"

"Assumed what?" She wanted him to say it. To finish the sentence. But Jesper just shook his head furiously.

"No, never mind." He took one more moment to look at her, his gaze still soft and calm, but now filled with sadness. And perhaps regret? Then he bowed his head cordially and slipped away without another word, the door to his quarters closing behind him.

It had all happened so fast. Had she been dreaming? She stood alone on the deck of the Fortuyna; the rest of the crew had long since gone to sleep. The stars continued to fall from the sky, their silvery streaks the only light against the dark void of night.

And the thoughts had returned. There had been something about Jesper's presence that had silenced the roaring of her mind. But now they were raging even louder than before. And they were all yelling at her.

She had messed it up. When the moment finally came, she hesitated. And ruined everything. It was all her fault.

Karyna couldn't tell what the right thing to do was anymore. She had accepted long ago that she was leaving her old life behind and starting new with Jesper's crew, but there was still a small part of her that was stuck in her old life. Her life with Eugene. They were still engaged, technically speaking. She still wore the ring on her finger to prove it.

Glancing down, Karyna fidgeted with the ring, twisting it around her finger. Then she took it off, letting it sit in the palm of her hand, its jewels sparkling in the starlight. The ring was a promise, a commitment. A promise she no longer wished to keep.

Feeling the weight of it in her hand one last time, Karyna let the urge overtake her and threw the ring overboard as far as she could. There wasn't even a small splash to confirm to her that the ring was gone. The only sign of its absence was the tiniest of tan lines on her finger where the ring had once sat.

No more hesitating. No more messing things up. No more Eugene.

TWENTY THREE

SORRY NOT SORRY

KARYNA

From the bow of the Fortuyna, Kie quietly watched the sun falling towards the horizon after another day of waiting. Just sitting around, waiting for the Navy to inevitably catch up to them. Jesper kept her company in silence, but the quiet wasn't uncomfortable. He didn't even seem to contemplate bringing the awkwardness of the previous night into the space, almost like it had never happened at all. The silence, rather, was relaxing, peaceful. A moment to rest and breathe. "Do you think mermaids are real?"

"Mermaids?" Jesper raised his eyebrows at her and chuckled, seemingly amused.

"Yeah, well, there's all these stories I was told growing up of sailors falling in love with mermaids and being dragged to the depths of the ocean."

"I hate to break it to you, but those stories are made up. They're not real."

"How do you know for sure?"

"Kie, I've been on the ocean for almost as long as I can remember. Never once have I seen a mermaid."

"Perhaps you just don't have the right person on board."

"And now I do?" he guessed. Kie smiled at him and shrugged.

"Perhaps."

"Kie, the mermaid whisperer."

Holding back a laugh, Kie felt the corners of her mouth tug upward. "I never said I was a mermaid whisperer."

"No, but I did."

"It does have quite the ring to it." Kie couldn't look at Jesper without bursting into laughter. So she instead settled on letting the wind blow through her hair as she watched the waves play on the horizon. Risking a glance at Jesper, she couldn't help but notice the worry lines appearing on his face.

To cheer him up, she playfully nudged him in the shoulder, jolting him from his deep thoughts. He let a short laugh escape his lips before bumping her back, harder this time. It quickly became a game of who could push harder and who could be the last to fall backward, both of them laughing uncontrollably.

And then his arms suddenly wrapped around her and pulled her in, and Kie's shoulders tensed up. But once she realized that he was hugging her, she let her body relax and melt into the embrace. Jesper spoke softly. "I know you're scared. I can see past your walls. Trust me, I am too. But, this time, I *promise* I'm going to protect you."

"You promise?"

"I do. And I'm going to keep that promise."

Kie hesitated, but then glanced up at Jesper and asked, "You could tell I was scared?"

"Maybe …"

"I mean, you're not wrong, though," she chuckled. Jesper smirked back at her.

"Of course I'm not."

"Shut up!" Kie laughed, pulling away and pushing Jesper in the chest. The laugh was surprisingly not forced, coming from someone who was petrified. In any other circumstance, Kie would be putting on a fake smile and trying to drown out her endless worries. But there was something about Jesper that comforted her. Something that just felt right.

"You're staring."

Snapping back to reality, Kie's eyes came into focus to find Jesper watching her with a playfully quizzical look on his face. "I'm sorry?"

"You're staring at me. Is there something on your mind?"

"Oh, sorry. No, I'm fine."

"You sure? You look concerned about something."

"Concerned?"

"You know, tense shoulders, that worry line on your forehead, a little pale-looking."

"I always look pale standing next to you."

"True," he chuckled, nodding in agreement as he glanced away. He seemed to do a quick scan of the horizon as he said, "But you know what I mean."

"I'm fine. Really. I just came to the realization that I'm going to die surrounded by idiots," she half-lied. It wasn't what was on her mind, but it concerned her all the same.

"Hey! At least we're hot." Kie snorted in amusement, making Jesper smile proudly. "Besides, you're not going to die."

"You don't know that."

"Oh, I do. Because I'm not going to let it happen."

"If you say so." And just like that, the conversation was dropped. Silently, Kie was grateful that he chose not to push her because she didn't know if she would be able to explain the emotions she felt. "Thank you."

Jesper glanced at her in shocked confusion. "For what?"

"For everything, really. I'm glad I'm here."

"Despite the fact that we're about to go into battle with the Navy?"

"Yes, despite that."

"And despite the fact that you refused to leave port with pirates just months ago?"

"That too," Kie laughed, prompting a smile from Jesper. It was as if he felt obligated to say something kind back to her, as he somewhat awkwardly said,

"Well … I don't mind that you're here, either."

"Don't mind?"

"You're tolerable," Jesper joked, and Kie feigned indignation as she gasped dramatically.

"Hey!"

But, just as every moment Kie treasured ended, the conversation was cut short when Jesper's helmsman ascended the steps to where Kie stood with Jesper. "Captain! The crew is awaiting orders."

"Thank you, Ozias. I'll be right there." Jesper studied Kie fondly for a minute before smoothing out his shirt and standing up straight. "Well, looks like I've got a job to do."

"Don't sound so disappointed. I know you love what you do."

"Sailing? Definitely. Waging war? Not at all."

"Stop making excuses and buying time for yourself and go lead your men. They need you."

"They don't need me," Jesper whined. Kie realized that he was enjoying the moment they were having together, like it was a temporary escape from the real world. And, as much as she shared the same sentiment as he, she knew that there were bigger things at hand than her feelings.

"Go."

"Yes, ma'am. How do I look?"

He tugged his shirt once more and slipped on his gloves as he sighed deeply. Reaching up, Kie fixed the collar of his jacket that had been blown up by the wind and ran a hand down the front of his shirt. But she quickly took her hand off once she realized that it had been resting on his chest, her cheeks immediately heating up.

"You look great. Now go."

He obeyed respectfully, glancing back at Kie one more time before leaving her to stand by herself at the bow. She watched him walk away with a warm smile tugging at the corners of her mouth, giving herself a minute to tie her long hair back with a leather cord and collect her thoughts before going to join Jesper at the helm.

By the time she had made it to the helm, a large crowd of pirates had gathered around Jesper, who was beginning to address his men to boost morale.

"My brothers, my friends!" Kie looked up over the heads of the men to see Jesper standing at the helm above his crew, the red bandanna around his head blowing in the wind like a battle flag. All of his crew turned their heads toward him as well, an eerie hush falling over the crowd of men as they waited to hear what their beloved captain had to tell them.

"Now is the time to stand and fight for the rights that are so desperately owed to us! Fill your hearts with courage and your veins with righteous fury as the enemy closes in! We should not be kicked to the curb simply because we are trying to find our place in this world! We deserve our place at the table, not picking up scraps off the floor!"

A cheer rose up from the masses of men, fists punching the air in high spirits. Kie took a moment to step back and observe the scene before her, admiring the power that Jesper held over his men. With just one word from his lips, he could rally all the men to his side and storm the world in a whirlwind of thunder. The crew trusted their captain wholeheartedly, and Jesper didn't even need to do anything to produce such an air of respect and charm.

"This is the hour when you decide where you stand, to decide what price you are willing to pay for freedom. The Navy is fast approaching; even now, you see their ships on the horizon. And believe me, when they reach us, they will show you no mercy! To them, to show mercy is to be weak! So choose your place, my friends! Stay with me and fight, or run and hide from the dangers of battle. The choice is yours; you won't be condemned either way. But, if you choose to remain at my side, have no fear or doubt in your hearts as we face the enemy! For in our courage, victory is ours!"

And as Jesper spoke, he walked over to the main mast and yanked on the line to raise the ship's flag. The beautiful colors of crimson, black, and gold soared over the white sails, boldly proclaiming the freedoms that Jesper boasted. Despite the inevitable destruction and death that was drawing closer by the minute, Kie couldn't help but feel hopeful at the comradery that banded the pirates together. It was somewhat of a supernatural sensation, seeing the men in such high spirits. Rarely did she ever see such an air hovering over a group of men like what held the crew captive.

"So, who will stand their ground and fight with me?"

Another thundering cheer rose up from the crowd, each and every man willing to fight for the rights that they deserved. But, as soon as the enthusiasm of the crew had filled Kie with so much hope, a sharp pain shot through her as she realized that not every one of these men would make it out alive. Some of these men, who had families at home that loved them dearly, wouldn't last the night. And there was nothing Kie could do to prevent this tragedy.

She watched as Deacon strode over to where Jesper stood at the mast, both of them grinning boldly at each other. They reached out and grasped each other's forearms in comradery.

"My place is by your side, Captain," Deacon proclaimed. "I fight with you."

"Thank you, my friend. Your valor will not go unnoticed."

"Do you have a plan? You'd better come up with something quick; this will not be easy by any means."

"Do you trust me?"

"You know I do."

"Then believe me when I say that every man will walk away from this alive."

Kie chose this moment to approach the two pirates, coming to stand on Deacon's left. "What *is* the plan?"

"Let me think for a minute," Jesper replied. Deacon frowned and shot back,

"I don't think we have a minute."

"Well, if you keep *distracting* me, I'll take longer!" Then Gen walked up to them, her face contorted in tense worry. She didn't hesitate to interrupt and interject herself into the conversation.

"What's going on? What's taking you guys so long?"

"Jesper's thinking," Deacon teased, playfully bumping Gen in the shoulder. "Can't you smell the smoke?"

"Ha-ha, very funny. But seriously, what are our orders? I've been waiting in the hold for instructions to give to the men."

"Well, why don't you ask the big man himself?"

"Because I prefer to keep my head, thank you very much."

"Dramatic much?" Deacon scoffed. Kie shrugged and said,

"I think she's being quite reasonable."

A light suddenly seemed to go off in Jesper's mind, and his face lit up with some insane idea he had no doubt invented. "Okay, I think I've figured it out."

"All right. Let's hear it," Deacon said, folding his arms over his chest.

"Well, I don't have it completely figured out –"

"How much of a plan do you have here?"

"What do you mean?"

"How much of your plan do you have figured out?"

"I don't know, Deacon! Not a lot. I'm not a genius."

"You don't have a plan at all, do you?"

"I have part of one!"

"Let's just hear him out, Deacon," Kie insisted calmly, trying her best to stop the argument that was starting to form. Jesper nodded in gratitude to Kie before continuing. After he had finished explaining his idea, Kie frowned to herself. Deacon was certainly right. Jesper didn't have much of a plan at all. But, she supposed, if anyone could make it work, Jesper could. So, as the crew began to move into their positions and the navy ship closed the distance between itself and the

Fortuyna, Kie tried to control her nerves by closing her eyes and breathing deeply. They could do this. They had to do this.

* * *

It didn't take long for the navy ship to come up right along the Fortuyna and connect the two ships with ropes and a gangplank. And it certainly didn't take long for the sailors to begin boarding their ship.

"Hold! Hold! Don't attack until I say so!" Jesper hissed to the men around him, crouching next to Kie at the helm. Kie took a deep breath in an attempt to calm her racing heart, her knuckles white from gripping her gun too hard. She had never fought in a battle before, much less even considered taking another man's life. The thought that she might have to do so twisted her insides into knots, and she struggled to justify killing with the argument of self-defense. If she was killing to save her own life, or the lives of her friends, then it was okay … right?

"Hey, it's going to be okay. Just stay close to me, all right? I promise nothing's going to happen to you."

"I'm scared, Jesper," Kie whispered, trying desperately to relax the firm grip she had on the gun. The fire in Jesper's eyes seemed to die out a little as he saw the terror that Kie felt.

"I know. And I wish there was something I could do to fix that, but I can't. All I can do is make you promises and hope that I can keep them."

"I know you'll keep them. I trust you. Everyone on this ship trusts you."

"And that's what scares *me*. What if I can't keep my promises, and I let you all down? What does that make me?"

"That makes you human," Kie insisted, placing a hand on his shoulder to comfort him. "No one expects you to be perfect."

"But, that's not good enough, is it?"

"You're carrying too much on your shoulders, Jesper. Making yourself responsible for all of the lives on this ship is unreasonable, because deep down, even you know that it's impossible to protect every single one. It's not like you can shield every person you've ever cared about from death."

The fiery courage returned to Jesper's eyes, and he squared his shoulders in determination. "I can try."

Jesper's head suddenly shot up at the sound of the commander's voice below them on the deck. He clearly recognized the booming voice, and he *clearly* wasn't happy about it. She watched as he clenched his jaw in frustration and tightened his grip on his pistol. Kie admired his unwavering courage in the face of death, and she silently wished that she could have a part of that. The fact that Jesper's dominating emotion was, at the moment, anger and not fear baffled her. How could he be so bold, so fearless at a time like this?

Kie attempted to shift on her feet, her legs aching from holding herself in a crouched position for so long. Jesper shot her a quick glare as the wooden planks beneath her feet creaked and strained. So she stopped moving, mouthing a silent apology before returning her attention back to the boarding sailors. Their bright blue coats littered the deck below her, slowly growing in number. Kie's impatience was becoming too much to bear, but she scolded herself for wanting to jump the gun.

Her eyes darted to the pistol in Jesper's hand as he adjusted the grip on the handle, his index finger sliding to the trigger. He shifted his feet under him, somehow not disturbing the boards beneath him. Kie could tell that he was anticipating his next move, his cocked position reminding her of a cat ready to pounce. It was like he was waiting for something, or someone, his gaze not moving from the gangplank. Kie released a slow breath, her eyes constantly bouncing between Jesper and the sailors on the deck.

The anticipation was killing her, and she had to remind herself to breathe. With each passing minute, the ranks of sailors were increasing, along with her heart rate. They had to fight back now, before it was too late.

As if he was reading her mind, Jesper suddenly jumped up and fired his pistol at one of the sailors below, the bullet piercing the sailor's chest and sending him flying to the ground. With furious screams and battle cries, Jesper's men launched themselves into the fight, mercilessly attacking the intruders. Kie barely had time to blink before bullets were whizzing past her head and death was already everywhere. She clung to the crate she hid behind with everything in her power, her fear paralyzing her. Kie wanted to help, wanted to fight for the Fortuyna, but her body wouldn't listen to her demands.

She crouched even closer to the floor as a massive roar rattled the ship, the heat wave hitting her just seconds later. *There are bombs now?*

And just when she thought things couldn't get worse, one of the navy sailors sprinted up the stairs to the helm and skidded to a stop as he made eye contact with her. Kie held her breath as the sailor aimed his gun at her head, her own gun hanging limp at her side. This was it. This was the end.

She squeezed her eyes shut, preparing for death to come. When the ear-splitting fire of the gun sounded, she flinched and squeezed her eyes closed even tighter. But no pain came. Perhaps that's what death felt like. An absence of pain, the seamless blackness hanging like a thick cloud. Was this death?

Kie stayed completely still, refusing to breath, until she felt a rough hand grasp her arm. Opening her eyes, she saw a rougher-than-normal naval sailor pulling her up. The sailor that was going to kill her was dead in front of her, a bullet hole in his chest. Her eyes flicked between the dead sailor and the one holding her upright, an overwhelming confusion clouding her thoughts. The sailor that held her up wasn't clean shaven like was customary of naval soldiers, and the shirt that peeked out from underneath his blue uniform jacket was crumpled and dirty. But his eyes were kinder.

"I asked, you okay? You hurt?" The ringing in her ears had died down enough that she could hear him talking to her. His voice was soothing, not cold and rigid like the other sailors. It was really familiar; she had heard it somewhere before.

"I'm okay," she managed to whisper, her entire body shaking uncontrollably with terror and adrenaline. Then another figure came bounding up the stairs, and Kie immediately recognized it as Jesper. He was quite a sight to see, covered from head to toe in bright red blood, and his gun smoking from the barrel. She had never been so happy to see someone in her entire life.

Jesper grabbed the fistful of the sailor's bright jacket, turning the sailor to face him and sending his fist flying into the man's cheek. The sailor stumbled backward, cradling the side of his face before straightening up again.

"You got a mean arm, kid. I'll give you that."

"Jayme?" Jesper exclaimed in complete shock. So Jesper knew who this guy was? Suddenly Jesper burst out laughing, pulling Jayme into a hug. "I can't believe this! What are you doing here? How did you get here?"

"You'd be surprised how much goes over sailors' heads. Not the sharpest bunch, most of 'em."

"You saved Kie's life," Jesper said gratefully, putting a hand at the small of Kie's back. "I can't thank you enough."

"Survive this, and we'll settle it up later."

"Yeah, of course."

Jayme threw the uniform hat and jacket off to reveal a tattered blue vest and dirty shirt underneath. The belt around his waist sagged with the weight of his various blades and pistols, not counting the gun already in his hand. It was then that Kie recognized him. The random man that had saved Jesper's life, that had bought the rooms for them at the inn. *Of course.* Why hadn't she seen it sooner?

Jayme grinned widely; "Let's get movin'. I promised a friend I'd keep you in one piece, but that don't mean I can't have a good time."

"Wait, who? What friend?" Jesper called after him, but Jayme had disappeared into the mass of gunpowder smoke and bodies. Jesper's hand still wrapped around Kie, and she was secretly glad that he wasn't letting go. His hold on her kept her grounded, kept her from losing control.

"Do you have the gun I gave you? And your dagger?" She could only nod. "You know how to use the gun?" Again, she nodded. But the confusion was still gnawing at her insides.

"Who is he?"

"Who?"

"That guy!"

"Honestly, not entirely sure. He's a friend." But he didn't seem to want to talk about Jayme much. "Now, listen to me carefully, Kie. I have to go help Deacon, so you go into my cabin and lock the door behind you. I'll try my best to keep everyone out, but if someone comes in, don't be afraid to use the gun. You understand?"

"Yeah, okay."

Kie let Jesper guide her down the stairs and towards the cabin, half in a daze. But then she saw Newt. A boy no older than fourteen, fighting grown men with more bravery and tenacity than all the crew members combined. Watching Newt in battle jolted Kie awake, and she suddenly wanted nothing more than to fight by Jesper's side. Surely, if a young boy had the guts to fight an army, she could too.

"Wait, Jesper. Wait." She pulled her arm from his grasp, not peeling her eyes away from Newt.

"There's no time to wait! Kie, c'mon! We have to go!"

"I want to stay."

"You want to what?" he yelled, his desperation and confusion evident in his voice.

"I want to stay and fight."

Jesper strode over to her, placing his hand back in its place on her arm. "Kie, I can't let you die. I wouldn't be able to live with myself if something happened to you."

"You're letting Newt stay!"

"He's different!"

"Different how?"

He struggled to come up with an explanation, every defense not good enough. "It just is!"

"That's no excuse!"

"I'm not making excuses!"

"Yes, you are! Now stop grumbling and let me fight!" Kie began to walk past Jesper, her argument made against him. She didn't want to deal with him anymore; her patience was exhausted. But, apparently, Jesper thought otherwise.

"Okay, Kie! Okay! The real reason I'm making excuses is because I'm scared! I'm scared that you're going to be taken away from me, just like everything else in my life! So please, for my sake and for yours, go hide in the cabin."

Kie could feel a pang of guilt and pity strike her heart as she looked at Jesper. She saw the pain in his eyes, the vulnerability. He was being honest in what he said, and Kie understood that without a shadow of a doubt. But, despite the guilt that she felt, she couldn't let Jesper hold her back. Not now.

"I'm done hiding, Jesper. I realize that now. And I'm not going to sit back and let everyone else do everything for me when I can go fight my own wars. So let me stay. You know that this is the whole reason I left everything behind."

"Kie, I'm begging you."

It didn't matter, though. No matter how much he begged with her, she wasn't going to back down. She had tuned him out, and instead of listening to his plea, she raised her gun in one hand and her ruby-handled dagger in the other and charged full speed into the fray. If she was being completely honest, she had absolutely no idea what she was doing. By no means had she ever fought in a war before, so to her, there was no method to the madness. Simply survive, or, if she were to die, at least she would take down a few sailors with her.

Because she knew that deep down, obeying Jesper and hiding from her problems would put her right back where she started. That's all she had ever done back in the city. Stay by Eugene's side, and stay silent. Pretend all of the world's problems don't exist, and if you ignore them long enough, then they don't exist at all. But, of course, that wasn't how it worked. She couldn't just pretend that everything was okay. Because it wasn't. Eugene had wanted to hide that truth from her for so long, hoping that her ignorance would keep her from leaving him behind. And, for a time, his plan succeeded. Until Kie finally decided to really look at the world and question everything. It was at that point that she fully realized what her heart desired most. Adventure. Reality. She wanted to experience the world in full, all of the struggles and obstacles included.

Kie was torn from her thoughts when she heard a familiar voice calling her name amidst the chaos of the fight.

"Kie!"

She wheeled around to see Jesper running up beside her, the long coattails of his jacket and his bandanna billowing in the wind. "What are you doing?"

"I can't stop you, so I might as well help you out!"

"Who said I needed any help?" she said smugly before blocking a sailor's sword with her own and stabbing him in the gut with her dagger. Jesper seemed impressed but refused to answer her question.

"Just shut up and thank me later!"

Kie obeyed, averting her gaze from the handsome pirate beside her to the battle around her. She commanded herself to focus on the situation at hand instead of Jesper. Kie had to sort out her priorities.

"Watch out!" Jesper cried out, shoving Kie to the side. She couldn't understand why he had pushed her, until she noticed a small knife on the deck and Jesper shielding the both of them with his sword.

"What did you shove me for?"

"You always have to keep your eyes open for danger! You could have just been killed by that throwing knife!"

"I didn't see it coming!" she protested, but Jesper shot back at her.

"Exactly! That's the point!"

"I'm sorry!"

"Get down." Jesper pushed her down by her shoulder to stab a naval soldier in the chest with his sword. Then he lifted her back up, his gloved hand gripping her arm. "You were saying?"

"I'm sorry, okay?"

"Yeah, yeah, I get it. You're sorry. Let's move on."

And the small talk was dropped. They continued to fight in silence, Kie sustaining very few injuries under Jesper's watchful eye. She would never admit it, but she was happy that Jesper was there fighting beside her. He was the only thing she needed to get her through the battle.

TWENTY FOUR

ALL IS FAIR IN LOVE AND WAR

JESPER

This is what he had been missing. *This* was what he had been longing for all this time. And it felt incredible. The adrenaline coursing through his veins, the instincts that kicked in just when he needed them, the roar of battle surrounding him. He could somehow see clearer, fight with a speed he would have thought impossible, and hear a pin drop in the very center of the battle. His body moved on autopilot, a sensation like flying among the clouds. It was an intricate dance that Jesper had learned to master over the years. Slide one foot forward, bring the sword up to parry, twist and follow through. The nature of battle was buried deep in his soul, his identity and his entire being. He was a fighter, a warrior.

Years ago, Jesper wouldn't have thought twice about the lives he was taking. Now, things were different. He recognized the immense power that he wielded by his sword and gun, the power he held in his hands to control life and death, but there was no room in battle for regret. In reality, as a pirate, there was no room for regret anywhere. That was just how life was. Take lives and learn to deal with the guilt another day. Save yourself and worry about no one else.

But then there was the flip side. Jesper knew that if any of his crew members were to have a hair singed on their head, no doubt, there would be no holding back. He wouldn't even attempt to restrain himself, and there would be no survivors left after Jesper was done.

Because he couldn't. Simply the thought of his friends getting hurt made him furious.

He had been separated from his friends, instead being surrounded by faces he didn't recognize. The faces of his enemies. Kie had disappeared into the sea of sailors, and Ari was nowhere to be found. With the desperation of needing to protect his friends lodged deep in his gut, Jesper began to frantically scan the heads around him. Surely they were still standing. Surely they were still all right.

"Kie?" His call yielded no results, so Jesper settled for trying again. "Ari?"

"Jesper!" Ari's response was faint and far away, but it was there nonetheless. And that meant that Ari had to be okay.

"Ari!"

The call and response method was useful for some time, and Ari seemed to be getting closer as they continued. He couldn't have been more than fifteen feet from where Jesper stood when Jesper's focus was quickly redirected. A swift blade came into Jesper's view from out of nowhere, and he barely managed to jump out of the way just in time to avoid being cut in half. The sword belonged to none other than the traitor Nyssa Lovelle, one of the few people of whom Jesper despised with his whole being.

Jesper yelled, "Get out of my way!"

"I have a duty to fulfill! And I'm certainly not letting you stop me!"

She brought her sword down on his, the ringing vibrations traveling up through his arm. The attack threw him off guard slightly, and he stumbled backward slightly before recovering and returning Nyssa's act of aggression. Their anger penetrated the air around them, each of them looking for the opportunity to land a hit but neither able to strike the other. Jesper and Nyssa danced around each other, their glares doing more damage than their swords.

"You're a traitor!" Jesper growled. "And a liar!"

"Since when do you think I've cared? My loyalties lie with the Admiral and the Navy, certainly not you!"

"Perhaps you don't, but do you know what pirates do with traitors? We feed them to the fish."

"Yeah? That means you have to get to me first! Good luck with that."

Again she launched herself at Jesper, a cloud of blackness surrounding her. Her shadow seemed to move on its own accord, grabbing at Jesper's feet and pinning them to the floorboards. Jesper barely managed to dodge the blade as it came swinging for his head, a cold sensation at his feet throwing off his concentration. The shadows were crawling up his legs, carrying with them a cold and stiffening feeling. He couldn't move his legs.

Absolutely basking in having the upper hand, Nyssa charged once more, Jesper wildly flailing his sword around in an attempt to protect himself. There was a cry of pain, and suddenly the cold sensation vanished from his legs. Looking over his shoulder, Jesper's heart leapt in his chest. Nyssa was clutching her left arm, blood seeping out from between her fingers. He had hit her.

When Nyssa had mustered up enough strength to go again at Jesper, he was ready. Something was different in her demeanor, a change of strength and speed. And then she motioned forward again to fling the shadows at Jesper, but nothing happened. The shadows would not obey her commands.

Of course. She knew it at the same moment that he did, the realization slamming into them like a wave.

With her left arm hanging limp at her side – unable to use both hands – she was completely useless. Reduced to merely flesh and bone, just like everyone else.

Her fury flared when Jesper calmly swatted her blade away. Every time she attacked, her movements were easily countered by her opponent. Her skill couldn't even rival Jesper's. To him, it felt like dealing with a five-year-old having a tantrum. All he needed to do was let the tantrum blow over before making his move.

"You done yet?"

"I'm never done. Not until your body is lying at my feet!"

"You can't win this fight, Nyssa."

"Watch me."

Sighing, Jesper waited until Nyssa chose to attack once more, sidestepping and smacking her in the back with the broad side of his sword as she passed by. She stumbled forward before catching herself and wheeling around to face Jesper, her aggressive movements almost animal in nature. But Jesper was already moving away. He was done pretending to care about her. Jesper had come to realize that there were some people in this world who just couldn't leave others be, couldn't let go of the past. *She* was one of those people. But there were more important things to do than get back at someone who was just doing their duty to the Navy.

"Hey! Don't turn your back to me! How dare you walk away from me, you coward!"

Jesper didn't respond. Anyone could just simply turn their back and walk away. But truly letting go demanded a kind of courage that Jesper didn't know if he had. And he had made a promise to Kie. He had promised to protect her, and he wasn't going to be able to do that if he was busy having a playground fight with Nyssa Lovelle.

With his back to Nyssa, he began to resume his search for his friends. But Nyssa wasn't done with him. Not yet. In a last ditch effort to end the fight, Nyssa launched one more attack at Jesper, roaring as she raised her sword above her head to strike.

Instinctually, upon hearing the battle cry of Nyssa's fury from behind him, Jesper ducked the swing of the sword by dropping to his knees and whirled around to face her. He brought his sword out to defend himself, the blade ramming into Nyssa between her ribs. Nyssa gasped in shock and pain, her eyes quickly glossing over. Standing up, Jesper reluctantly pulled the blade from Nyssa's rib cage and watched as she crumpled to the ground. There was nothing he could do now but move on.

Jesper clenched his jaw in guilt, muttering an apology to the dead sailor. "I'm so sorry."

He couldn't shake the image in his mind of the officer that would be doomed to knock on the door of Nyssa's family and tell them that she wasn't coming home. How terrible would it be to be the bearer of bad news, the person who would ultimately ruin the lives of the family? How unbearably difficult would it be to know that no matter how delicately you tell them what happened, the family would be weeping on the floor uncontrollably?

Jesper squeezed his eyes shut for a moment, trying to desperately push away the thoughts. Maybe Isa was right. Maybe he *was* really turning soft. It was only a few years ago that Jesper would have jumped at the chance to fight to the death. But now, things were different. Now, it was like he had gained a piece of himself back that was lost in his youth. A piece of himself that had disappeared the minute his family died.

And putting that piece back into place was painful. Dreadfully painful. It felt like a million tiny needles stabbing his heart, like a heaviness that anchored his feet to the floor. But perhaps it was worth the pain in the end.

"Jesper!" The desperate cry shook Jesper from his thoughts, and his eyes shot open again. A mad scramble from amongst the chaos ahead drew Jesper's attention, and not a minute later Deacon emerged, his breath coming in heavy gasps and his usually smooth hair in a mass of tangled knots. His eyes were wide with fear as he took a moment to regain his breath before yelling, "We have to get out of here! We're all going to die!"

"Be more optimistic!"

Throwing his hands up in the air dramatically, Deacon exclaimed, "Yay! We're going to die! Woo-hoo!"

"You'll be fine!"

"Easy for you to say!"

"Just trust me," Jesper insisted to the older pirate. But Deacon wasn't having it.

"Last time you said that, you made me go to the Admiral's dinner party and set the house on fire! While I was inside!"

"You didn't die! Besides, they served venison and chocolate. Chocolate!"

"Oh, shut up! That's beside the point!"

Glancing over Deacon's shoulder, Jesper noticed a sailor rushing up behind them, his sword lofted above his head to strike. "Behind you!"

Deacon twisted his body to the side as Jesper thrust his sword forward, the blade easily meeting its target and the sailor falling to the floorboards. Nodding nervously, Deacon turned back to Jesper.

"Thanks. I owe you one."

"No, you don't. I'm just doing my duty."

"You saved my life," Deacon protested. Throwing his arms up, Jesper shrugged off the gratitude.

"Okay. You're welcome." Jesper knew that accepting the gratitude was the only way to get Deacon to shut up. "Have you seen Kie or Ari anywhere? I'm worried about them."

"No, I haven't. I'm sure they're fine, though. They both should fare well in battle. Kie did a bit of training under Ari when you took your leave."

"Good, good." Jesper sighed, running a hand over his face. He could feel the sticky warmth of blood running from his temple, and brought his hand down to see the bright red liquid smeared on his fingers. "Oh. I'm bleeding."

"Yeah. Are you okay?"

"I'm fine. I didn't even notice."

"We'll just make sure to get you patched up after this is all over."

"Right," he chuckled. "If I'm not already dead."

Deacon frowned but didn't protest. He chose instead to give Jesper a look of disappointment before nudging him and suggesting, "Go find Ari. And stick with him. He's your best bet at staying alive."

"And what about you?"

"I'm going to find the others and get them to the dinghy. It's the only way we're going to make it out of here alive. But don't worry about me. I've been friends with you long enough to know how to defend myself."

"Ha-ha, very funny."

And just like that, Deacon was gone and Jesper was all alone once again. Well, alone in a sea of skilled soldiers who were completely capable and willing to kill him. Deacon was right. He needed Ari at his side, no matter how mad Ari was with him. It was the only way they were going to stay alive.

"Ari!"

A moment passed before he heard the response. "Jes! I'm over here!"

"Start coming towards the sound of my voice!"

"I'm a little bit busy at the moment, Jes!"

"All right, then stay there! I'm coming to you!"

The lack of response scared Jesper. Ari could have at least made some sort of noise of acknowledgment, but there was nothing. Jesper automatically assumed the worst, that something had happened to Ari. His throat seemed to close at the thought, and his breath was expelled from his lungs. It was as if he was suffocating in his own panic.

"Ari! Where are you?" Again, nothing. "Ari, hold on! I'm coming!"

Jesper shoved his way through the sailors, throwing elbows to faces and knees to stomachs when necessary. It was a wild blur of pain and panic, and Jesper's body had resorted to a numb tingling. He moved slower than he normally did, as if his brain suddenly couldn't tell the rest of him what to do. In every sense of the word, Jesper was screwed. And that was before he came face to face with the biggest guy Jesper had ever seen.

The navy sailor was utterly terrifying as he towered over Jesper with the darkest scowl written all over his face. His fist alone was the size of Jesper's head, and his unnaturally black eyes seemed to stare straight into Jesper's soul. The sailor that stood before Jesper was the literal embodiment of evil, and Jesper wanted to just melt into the floorboards beneath his feet. So when the sailor began to charge at the pirate captain, Jesper felt his legs go to jelly and his heart stop.

And as he brought up his sword to defend himself, he saw a small blur from the corner of his eye jump out in front of him. "Jesper! Get out of here! Go!"

It was Gen, fighting with all the strength in her against the giant, her small frame trembling under the weight of the sailor's sword crushing down on her. The metal of the sailor's blade against hers seemed to shudder violently from the inside out, the sailor pressing down with everything in him but the sword almost not wanting to obey. It was like Gen was trying to control the sword.

"You're a Metalbender!" Jesper blurted out. He couldn't believe that the thought had never occurred to him before.

"Jesper, go!"

She'd saved his life, and Jesper would be forever in her debt for it. Gen always had a way of outclassing Jesper in every way that mattered, but now she was paying the price for it. Still, Jesper couldn't help but be somewhat proud of her heroics and recklessness; perhaps he was rubbing off on her a bit.

"What about you?"

"Go find the others! I'll be fine!" Jesper hesitated but obliged when Gen glared at him from over her shoulder. She wasn't asking him to go, she was demanding it. And he had no choice but to listen to her command, because she wasn't going to let him do anything else. Jesper could only hope that she would be all right.

So, once more, he stumbled back into the fight. Ari couldn't have been far away at this point, and he could only hope that he wasn't too late. Because, more often than not, Jesper had the unfortunate tendency not to arrive until it was too late and there was nothing that could be done. This time couldn't be like that.

The battle around him raged on, with such intensity that Jesper could have sworn that it was all a dream. A dream – no, a nightmare – that Jesper was cursed to relive over and over again. No matter what he did, he couldn't change the fact that he was bound to mess everything up and get his entire crew killed in the process. This was no different.

His feet pressed forward, his body being pushed as if by some invisible hand. The mass of bloody sailors seemed to part before him as if the sea was splitting by some miracle, and Jesper didn't hesitate to follow where the path was leading. And then the throngs of people shifted again, and over all the chaos, there was Ari.

Jesper breathed a sigh of relief; perhaps his people's god was watching over him after all. From a distance, it looked as though Ari was standing relatively unhurt. That in itself was all Jesper needed to see to start thinking clearly again. The thought crossed his mind that he had absolutely no idea what Ari was "a bit busy" doing; he didn't seem to be doing anything. Jesper wanted to call out to Ari, to grab his attention. But Ari was intently focused on something – or rather, someone – ahead of him, so Jesper followed his friend's gaze. And his blood froze.

TWENTY FIVE

WILL BOMBS STOP GOING OFF NEAR ME?

JESPER

The shiny blond hair. The piercing blue eyes. The rigid stance of a soldier so ingrained with the gentleman's traditions of proper warfare that he looked out of place on the battlefield. *Phineas.*

Jesper had hoped that after stealing the navy brig for the young commander, they would never have to cross paths again. Clearly, he couldn't have been further from the truth.

What worried Jesper the most wasn't Ari being beaten in combat by Phineas. That outcome was completely impossible. Ari was a better swordsman in almost every regard. No, that wasn't what terrified Jesper. But the circumstance that made Jesper's legs tremble and his heart race was the possibility that Ari would underestimate his opponent. Phineas was weaker, he was less skilled. But that didn't mean he was incompetent. One wrong move, miscalculation, or distraction, even overconfidence, and Ari was done for.

So Jesper kept his distance, protecting himself from other sailors attacking him while still keeping a hawk eye on Ari and Phineas. The tension between the two sailors continued to escalate and their blows at each other were becoming more aggressive, but Ari seemed to be winning as the fight progressed. Jesper's worries were fading, until Ari's confidence got the better of him.

Ari had just slammed Phineas's blade away with his own with a fancy flourish, a move that Jesper had taught Ari years ago. Phineas took the blow hard, stumbling backward with the momentum of the sword, barely recovering before he was slammed again by Ari. Seeing that moment of weakness, Ari lowered his guard. And Jesper was too far away to be able to save his best friend.

"Ari!" he screamed as the sword pierced Ari's gut. The world seemed to slow to a halt, the look of fear and pain frozen on Ari's face. This wasn't supposed to happen. If anything, it should have been Jesper taking the blade, not his best friend. He didn't deserve this. Looking around him, Jesper realized that none of his friends deserved any of this. He couldn't let them die, all because of the mistakes he had made years ago.

"Kie! Gen! Get everyone out of here! Go!"

Frantically, Jesper pushed his way through the mass of soldiers towards his friend. Red lined his vision and the noises of death dimmed to a faint buzz.

There were too many people pushing at him from every direction, and too many people wanting him dead. Jesper's feet froze beneath him, his head spinning with panic. His eyes darted left and right, trying to determine which way to go. And then, almost miraculously, the crowds parted. There was Ari, lying motionlessly on the deck, a small pool of blood spreading from under his body.

"Ari!" Jesper screamed, sprinting as fast as his legs could carry him over to his friend. "Hey, hey. You're going to be okay. This isn't the first time you've been stabbed, right?"

"Yeah, right," Ari grunted, clutching Jesper's hand tightly. "Does it look bad?"

"No, not at all," Jesper lied. "Look, I'm going to get you out of here, and we're going to get you all patched up, all right?"

"Okay, okay."

"Up on three, okay? One, two, three!" Jesper firmly and slowly pulled Ari up by his arm, but he stopped when Ari let out a cry of pain.

"Set me down. I just – I just need to catch my breath for a minute."

"Okay. You catch your breath."

"Jes?" Ari squeezed Jesper's hand to get his attention.

"Yeah?"

"Promise me something?"

"Anything for you."

"I want to be with my family." At first, Jesper didn't understand what Ari was talking about. "Remember that hill that overlooked my house? The place where I found you, where the sunlight danced through the branches of the oak tree in the afternoon breeze. My – my family … they're buried there."

"Ari, no. Don't say things like that. You're going to be fine. We're going to get through this together, like we always do. You're all I've got left. We –"

"Jesper. Promise me."

"… Okay," he whispered, tears threatening to blur his vision. "I promise."

"I knew you would." Ari smiled despite the pain and the tears. "You've always had my back, brother."

"Of course. And I always will."

"And one more thing."

"What is it?"

"I forgive you, Jesper."

Ari's firm grip on Jesper's hand loosened as his whole body went limp. Jesper stared in horror as the light in Ari's eyes faded away, as if his spirit had floated away to join the hosts of heaven. He had fought the good fight, and he had lost.

"Ari? Hey, hey, Ari! No, don't do this to me! Please … you can't leave me. Please …" Jesper whispered, giving in to the pain and letting the hot tears fall down his face. "You promised you wouldn't leave me …"

Around him, the world collapsed into a cacophony of smoke and blood and death. Each man was caught up in their own fight, struggling to stay alive in a ruthless and desperate scramble for power.

No one saw Jesper kneeling there. And in the madness, he saw none of it either.

He covered his mouth with a bloody hand to try and repress his sobs, his eyes squeezed shut as if to block out the universe itself. Jesper felt tense, each muscle in his body coursing with ice and fire. But just as quickly as he locked up, the intensity disappeared, and Jesper wilted into a shaking, sobbing heap. His arms draped loosely around Ari's body, and his shoulders heaved with every gasp.

The pain was ripping a hole in his chest. And that void was filled with a numbness. A cruel, cold numbness that overwhelmed him. How could someone describe such pain? How could someone go about living in a world that now seemed dull and colorless in the absence of one person? He wanted to scream; he wanted to mourn in silence. He wanted to tear everyone to pieces, and yet, he wanted to just lay down and cry. His best friend, the one person who could make his day that much brighter, was gone. And he was never coming back. There was nothing Jesper could do to make Ari stand before him once again. And how Jesper craved Ari's radiant smile and jubilant laughter more than ever before.

What an odd thing it was, to lose someone so close. It was a whirlwind of everything, and nothing. Jesper felt so numb, so void, and yet he was angrier than he had ever been in his entire life. Why was it that Ari had to die? Why not the millions of people that roamed the planet, whose lives meant nothing to Jesper? Why not *himself*?

The questions spiraled around his mind in a giant frenzy, gaining momentum like a stone rolling down a steep hill. They grew louder and louder, the same question repeated over and over again until it found a voice. His voice.

"Why not me?" he whispered, the bitter question lingering on his lips. Then he found the courage to say it louder, to scream it. "Why not me, huh? Why didn't you take me instead? This was my fate, not his! Take me!"

"Death was never your fate." A calm voice spoke from behind Jesper, and he glanced over his shoulder to see Phineas standing before him, his perfectly manicured hair hanging loosely in gold strands in front of his eyes. Ari's killer. "You were always too good for Death. You were the only one who could look Death in the eye and resist him."

Jumping to his feet, Jesper practically launched himself at Phineas. "You took *everything* from me!"

"I'm sorry, Jesper."

"You are not sorry, Phineas!" Jesper spat, lashing out at the commander. He couldn't even stand to look at Phineas's face any longer. "You are happy! You took everything from me and left me standing alone in the destruction that you caused! I have nothing left!"

"I would never wish this on my worst enemy."

"I am your worst enemy, aren't I? So that's what this is all about, huh? You think that killing everyone I ever loved is going to bring me down, have me bowing at your feet? Well, guess what? That's not going to work!"

Phineas reached out a hand towards Jesper's shoulder to comfort him. "You're not –"

"Move that hand one inch closer to me, and I'll tear you apart limb from limb."

The commander instantly retracted his hand, his arm falling back to his side. There was so much pity and guilt in his eyes, but Jesper couldn't understand it. What right did Phineas have to feel bad for Jesper, when he was the one who had ruined Jesper's life in the first place?

"I'm sorry, Jesper."

Jesper noticed the ominous glint of the shackles in Phineas's hand, but he didn't care. There was no way he was going to let some high and mighty jerk take him in. Not after Phineas had just killed his best friend.

"You're going to arrest me? Your dishonor knows no bounds, does it?"

"I have a job to do, Jesper."

"Yeah, I'm sure you do. But I don't care," Jesper spat, reaching to his hip and pulling out his pistol. He didn't hesitate to aim it at Phineas, his finger resting on the trigger.

"You're not going to shoot me."

"Watch me."

The look of genuine fear paled Phineas's face as he recognized the truth in Jesper's words, and he jumped into action to avoid being shot. Ducking down, Phineas plowed straight into Jesper, wrapping his arms around Jesper's torso and sending them both to the ground just as Jesper pulled the trigger. In a tangle of limbs, the two sailors fumbled around on the deck, throwing as many punches as they could muster. Phineas was easily overpowered by his opponent in almost every aspect; Phineas's close-combat training could never even come close to rivaling Jesper's. It was easily a winning battle for Jesper, and he knew it. Phineas seemed to know it, too, as he scrambled away from Jesper as fast as his legs would allow. Jesper barely had the time to register that Phineas had his own pistol aimed at Jesper before the shot was fired.

With everything he had in him, Jesper flung himself out of the way, feeling the bullet just graze his arm. Another crack of the pistol went off, but Jesper was already up and running. That was two shots fired. Meaning that Phineas only had two bullets left before he was forced to reload the pistol. And *that's* when Jesper would make his move.

Out of the corner of his eye, Jesper noticed a stack of water barrels by the deck's railing, shockingly untouched by the war ensuing around them. He didn't even stop to weigh his options before diving behind the barrels, pressing his back up against the rounded wood. And just barely over the deafening roar, he heard the voice of Phineas screaming his name. It was piercing and fiery, sending a wave of chills down Jesper's spine.

"Come out, you coward!"

"And give you an open target? I'm not that stupid!"

The whizzing of another bullet, and Jesper covered his head as the barrel at his back cracked. *Just one left.*

"You can't hide from me forever, Kelsey! The world is getting smaller, and your kind is dying out!"

"Oh, c'mon, even you know that's a lie! We're like cock-roaches; you can never fully get rid of us!" Jesper yelled back, daring to turn around and peer over the top of the barrel. He hardly had the time to see where Phineas was standing before the fourth and final bullet struck the top of the barrel. Phineas's aim was almost dead on; Jesper had to give him that.

And now was his chance. Grabbing a small knife from his belt, Jesper launched himself from over the top of the barrel at Phineas. But as his feet hit the ground, his eyes locked onto the pistol being pointed straight at him. And before Jesper could even react, the bullet had made contact with his left shoulder, piercing through the soft tissue just below the shoulder cap. Crying out, Jesper recoiled and clutched his injured shoulder, the fiery pain immediately spreading down his arm and chest.

Had he miscalculated? Had he somehow counted wrong and forgot about one bullet? In his mind, Jesper was scrambling for how he could have screwed it up that bad. But he couldn't have.

His knees turning to jelly, Jesper sank to the floor as Phineas just stared at him, motionless. There was a new glint in Phineas's eyes, something almost wild. Almost animal.

"What are you waiting for?" Jesper hissed through gritted teeth. Slowly, the barrel of the pistol lowered and the fiery glee that shone in the commander's eyes faded.

"I told you, Kelsey, I'm not killing you."

"And yet, you're willing to fire openly at me?"

"The idea was to slow you down."

"Congratulations." The intensity of the pain was stealing the air from his lungs, and the warm, sticky liquid was seeping through his fingers.

No. This wasn't how it was supposed to happen. The last place Jesper would go was a cage. With every fibre in his body, Jesper willed himself back up to his feet. Pushing through the pain, he held Phineas's gaze and growled, "You killed my brother. You hurt my crew. You had five chances to kill me, but you failed. And now you're going to sorely regret that."

Phineas chuckled under his breath. "I'd like to see that."

Without a second thought, Jesper charged full speed at Phineas, sending them both to the floor. He let his fists fly, the rage inside him growing stronger with each punch he threw. Jesper could barely even register the punches slamming into his own sides. With Phineas under him, Jesper was only concerned about fighting until he couldn't anymore.

And then he stopped.

His chest heaving and his fist raised over his head, Jesper stared down at Phineas, the commander's face covered in his own blood. And his eyes. Phineas looked terrified, his eyes shining with a fear that Jesper had only come across once before. In the eyes of the Admiral's wife. Right before Jesper killed her.

Perhaps his morals had made him weak just as Isa had said, but Jesper knew that he couldn't kill Phineas in cold blood. He couldn't do the same thing to Phineas that he had done to Phineas's mother. It made him sick just thinking about the fact that Phineas would continue to walk the earth, unharmed, while Ari lay rotting away in the ground, but he couldn't do it.

Horrified at himself, Jesper jumped off of Phineas and stumbled backward, his eyes not leaving Phineas's. *What am I thinking?*

*   *   *

If he was being completely honest, Jesper couldn't remember the minutes that followed. It was all a numb blur, gunpowder smoke coating his lungs and his clothes sticking to his skin with blood. Not until he was standing alone in the middle of the deck with no one attacking him did Jesper's focus come back to him.

Out of the corner of his eye, Jesper could see something flying in the air towards him. It looked like some sort of glass ball that sparked and hissed. Time seemed to gradually slow down as Jesper tried to identify the glass object, and just as the realization dawned on him that it was a bomb, the glass ball hit the deck and exploded.

A flash of brilliant light, and the ear-splitting sound of an explosion, and Jesper was laying on the deck. His body couldn't move, too shocked and too painful to function properly. And this time, he accepted it. There was no getting back up this time, no recovering from the blast. Because he didn't want to. What was the point, anyway? He thought back to the conversation he had had with Kie before retrieving his compass.

None of it matters … I'm not the hero! I'm not some knight in shining armor! I don't get a happy ending!

But what if, for one moment in time, Jesper was the hero. What if he could still save Kie? She deserved to live just as much as Ari did. The only difference was that she still had a chance.

Then, as if it were a sign, the heavens opened up and the rain poured down, washing away the blood that covered Jesper from head to toe and the tears that lingered on his cheeks. It was a new start, a chance to make things right.

His whole world threatened to fade to black, and Jesper was tempted to give in to the darkness. But he couldn't. He wouldn't give up. Because Kie needed him. Jesper had made a promise to his crew and to Kie. A promise that he wouldn't abandon them. And he wasn't about to break that promise now.

So, Jesper staggered to his feet, every bone in him screaming in pain. His legs shook with the effort, a singular cry escaping his lips before he forced his mouth shut. Jesper's feet felt like lead beneath him, and he could barely take one step before collapsing again. But he ignored the pain, instead focusing on his growing determination and anger. It fueled him, pushed him to keep going when all he wanted to do was quit. He felt as if he had just been hit head on by a thousand ton ship and then been given Clary's strongest drug. Everything in him was in so much pain that he didn't want to move, but the adrenaline and energy he felt made it impossible to sit still.

He scanned the heads of all the men still standing on the deck, trying to spot the striking red head of Kie. But he couldn't find her, not anywhere. His eyes instead stopped on a head of shining brunette hair that was tied back into a loose plait. Gen. And surely Kie was with her. Without letting his eyes leave Gen, he frantically made his way through the ongoing war, doing his very best to avoid getting shot or stabbed. Of course, that was nearly impossible, and he had gained a few new sword wounds by the time he reached Gen on the other side of the deck.

Gen was herding what was left of Jesper's crew onto the ship's dinghy and stopping any other sailors from boarding, looking remarkably unharmed by battle. She immediately stopped when Jesper approached her, her face betraying her shock. Jesper didn't doubt that he looked like quite a mess.

"Jesper! Are you okay?"

"Ari's dead."

"What?" she whispered, almost too stunned to even speak.

"I couldn't … I couldn't save him."

It took a moment for the realization to hit her, Gen furiously blinking back the forming tears. And then she let out the most gut-wrenching cry Jesper had ever heard, collapsing into Jesper's arms. Jesper grimaced in pain, a shudder running through his body as the bullet wound pulled in protest, but he kept his mouth shut. Gen needed him. She buried her face into Jesper's chest, her body wracked with sobs. And the only thing Jesper could do was hold her and try in vain to comfort her. Gen had loved Ari; that much was obvious.

"I'm so sorry, Gen …" Jesper murmured, squeezing her tighter. But at his voice, Gen seemed to come back to reality. She tore herself out of Jesper's arms, wiping her soaking cheeks.

"We need to get everyone else out of here. Hurry up and get on." She pointed down to the crowded dinghy.

"No. You get down there. I'll watch your back and make sure the rest of the crew is safe first. There are still men out there that need my help."

"Jesper –"

"I'm the captain, Gen. I have to stay with the ship."

"Fine." She moved to climb down the ladder on the side of the ship, but Jesper grabbed her arm.

"Where's Kie?"

"I don't know. I thought she was with you."

"Crap," he muttered. That meant that Kie was still somewhere in the middle of the battle, and *that* meant that Jesper would have to go back in to find her. "I'll be right back."

"Captain!"

"Yeah?" He turned around as Gen called for him.

"Be careful, okay? I can't lose you, too."

"I will. I promise."

Another promise to keep. But he didn't intend on breaking it … well, maybe a little bit. There was no such thing as being careful in war. That didn't mean he couldn't take risks *and* survive at the same time.

Jumping back into the fight meant reentering a world of chaos and death, but Jesper knew what he was doing. After all, seven years ago, that was all his life was. Death and destruction. It was second nature to him. And while Jesper had tried to rid himself of those instincts, he supposed that it didn't hurt to bring out the fire one more time. For Kie.

His eyes scanned the deck, searching for a familiar face. And then he saw them. Kie was surrounded by sailors, but she was surprisingly faring quite well defending herself. Newt, on the other hand, was not doing so well. He stood on the exact opposite side of the ship's deck, cowering in fear and trying not to get killed. There was only enough time to help one of them. In Jesper's mind, the obvious answer was going to Kie's aid. But Newt needed more help, no matter how much Jesper wanted to ignore it.

Crinkling his nose in frustration, Jesper groaned and turned to Newt. He limped over to where Newt cowered, rushing up behind the sailor that stood with his gun aimed at Newt. Jesper tapped the sailor on the shoulder politely.

"Excuse me, sir."

As soon as the sailor turned, Jesper quickly grabbed the barrel of the gun and shoved it down while punching his opponent in the jaw with the other hand. The sailor stumbled back in shock and pain, loosening his grip on his gun just enough for Jesper to yank it out of his hand. Newt flinched as the trigger was pulled, the bullet piercing the navy sailor in the chest. Jesper's opponent was dead before he hit the deck.

"Get up. C'mon," Jesper grunted, pulling the trembling boy up by his arm.

"You saved my life."

"Thank me later. Let's go."

Newt obeyed silently, and Jesper was internally grateful that Newt chose not to push his emotions on the captain. If there was one thing that Jesper dreaded, it was talking about emotions. It was a concept that he had never been able to understand, so it was always easier to just avoid the subject than make himself extremely uncomfortable. Besides, there wasn't time for that sappy nonsense anyway. Kie still needed his help.

"Head straight for where Gen is at the dinghy," Jesper instructed. "I'll meet you there."

"Where are you going?"

"To help Kie. And before you ask, no, you can't come with. Go get on the dinghy."

"But –"

"No! I don't need another one of my men dying today. I already saved your life once, now you repay me by keeping yourself alive."

"Yes, sir."

"Newt …"

Realizing his mistake, Newt's eyes widened in fear. "Captain! Sorry, Captain."

"Much better." Jesper allowed himself to smile at the boy before clapping him on the back and gently pushing him towards Gen. Newt hesitated slightly, as if he was scared to leave Jesper's protective presence. Jesper nudged him once more, and Newt begrudgingly started towards Gen. Satisfied, Jesper nodded and moved away before stopping and taking a moment to watch Newt. Something about the boy, maybe it was the way he walked, seemed off to Jesper. Something that shouldn't have been off.

"Newt!"

The cabin boy turned around, surprise evident on his face. He almost seemed relieved as Jesper rushed up to him. "Yes, sir?"

"Are you hurt?"

"No."

"Don't lie to me. Where are you injured?" When Newt didn't reply, Jesper intensified his glare and demanded, "C'mon, show me. I don't have time for this."

"It's just a scratch," Newt insisted. "I'm fine. Really."

"Duck."

"Sorry?"

"Duck! Now!" Newt obeyed, and Jesper managed to get a shot at an oncoming soldier with his pistol before they were attacked. The soldier's partner was, on the other hand, much too close for the pistol. One slash with his sword down the sailor's body was all Jesper needed. And with his chest heaving, Jesper returned his attention to Newt.

"Show me."

Reluctantly, and somewhat shakily, Newt pulled up his dress-like shirt front to reveal a deep gash across his thigh. "See? It's nothing bad."

"You're losing a lot of blood. That's a deep wound."

"Your wounds are worse."

"Don't compare yourself to me. I've been at this for far longer than you have." Reaching down, Jesper grabbed the blue sash around his waist and began tearing the fabric apart. "Here. Stand still."

"What are you …?"

Newt trailed off as he watched Jesper, his eyes following the captain as Jesper reached for his thigh. Jesper began to wrap the torn fabric around the gash, tying it tightly with a sudden yank. Newt yelped and clutched his injured leg, whimpering as Jesper rose from his crouched position.

"There. That should slow the bleeding for a bit. Gen will be of better help to you once you're safely on the dinghy."

"Thank you, Captain."

"Don't thank me yet. Thank me once we both get out of here alive."

"Yes, sir."

"Go on. Get out of here."

Then Jesper sprinted over to where Kie stood, his feet pounding the deck in time with his racing heart. They were lucky to have made it this far in the middle of a war with the Navy, but Jesper didn't want to push his luck much further.

He slipped in beside Kie, moving to cover her unprotected back. Automatically, she pulled away and began to turn to see who was behind her but turned back when she noticed the familiar tattoo on his arm peeking through the ripped fabric of his sleeve.

"It's you! You freaked me out there for a second!"

"C'mon, Kie, let's get out of here!"

"You're asking me to run from a fight? Never!" With his back to hers, Jesper couldn't see the expression on her face. But he had no doubt that her face was contorted into a look of utter disgust and re-sentment.

"We're leaving now! Before you get yourself killed!"

"Fine!"

"When I say so, you run for the dinghy and don't look back! Don't worry, I'll be right behind you!" Jesper heaved one last thrust at the sailor in front of him, his blade hitting its mark dead on. "Now!"

From the corner of his eye, Jesper could see Kie dart out and around the remaining sailors in her way. She was in the last stretch, home free. He could feel his feet pound the wooden deck as he raced after her, each thud in time with her bouncing hair. A light, airy hope began to well up and fill the dark void of his heart. They were going to make it. And then Jesper felt hands grasp at his arms and torso, gripping hard and pulling him backward.

TWENTY SIX

A GOOD DAY TO DIE

JESPER

Jesper was yanked backward forcefully, his world going black for a moment before his vision came back to him. Large, rough hands held him firmly, and he could feel the cold steel of a barrel jammed into the back of his skull. He found himself bent at the waist, pushed down at the shoulders with his arms restrained behind him.

"Jesper!"

Kie. Kie was screaming his name, but her voice wasn't getting any closer. Had they gotten her, too? Panic welled up inside him, the fear that they would hurt her. He wanted to run to her, to protect her from the brutally heartless soldiers. Jesper strained to look up, only to stare into the sickly blue jacket of a naval officer. Kie was somewhere behind the officer, out of sight. Then he heard Gen.

"We have to go! Kie!"

"No!" Kie shrieked. "I'm not leaving him behind!"

"We don't have a choice!"

More yelling and protests from Kie followed, accompanied by the scuffling of various sailors, and then silence. It was like a lull between waves. Complete silence and no movement besides the falling rain.

Another yanking motion practically gave Jesper a heart attack, turning him from his current position and walking him some ten paces across the deck. He was kicked in the back, pitching forward to meet the ground beneath him as a sharp pain shot down his spine and through his shoulder where the bullet had pierced him. A pair of unnaturally spotless boots stood before him, and Jesper didn't need to look up to know who the wearer was.

"Make it quick, then. Just do it."

"I'm not going to kill you," Phineas scoffed, clearly amused with such an absurd request. "You don't deserve death just yet."

"Please." Jesper practically begged, but Phineas would not listen to his plea. Phineas may have been many things, but he certainly wasn't a traitor. Not to the law, or his father, anyway.

"I can't do that. You know I can't."

"So what, then? You're going to haul me back to the city and throw me before the judges to stand trial so I can die there instead?"

"Exactly."

"One of the greatest wishes of a pirate is to die a glorious and honorable death. From one sailor to another, Phineas, please grant me that one wish, if nothing else."

"I have orders I must follow. I am not given the liberty to rule over myself as you are."

"You've done it once before, with the Admiral's vessel. So, for my sake, do it one more time."

"I'm sorry, Jesper. You cannot convince me otherwise. Get on your feet. We have a long journey ahead of us."

Grabbing Jesper by his arm, Phineas hauled the pirate to his feet and turned him around. The feeling of the shackles around his wrists and the clanking sound they made when they were locked on filled Jesper with dread. It was all too familiar, sending waves of nausea through his body. But this time, there would be no promise. There would be no assurances that he would go free again.

"Don't fight me, and nothing will happen to you," Phineas whispered as he secured the shackles. "Your friends are safe – they got away – I made sure of it. They took your friend's body, too."

Jesper fought the urge to react, his rage flaring again in his chest. Who was he, to talk about Ari so carelessly like that? It wasn't fair. Ari deserved to be the one standing at Jesper's side, not Prescott. And did Phineas somehow think that by helping Jesper's crew escape, he was pardoning himself? The thought was foolish. But then again, Jesper liked to think Phineas was, too.

As if in a haze, Jesper stumbled forward, being led down to the cells by his captors. He gave up on fighting; it was useless to try. His eyes glazed, emotionless, from underneath the dripping cover of his layered hair, a bleary demeanor that he couldn't shake.

The shackles that bound his hands behind his back rubbed his wrists raw with each movement that Jesper made, but he ignored the chafing and the searing pain in his left shoulder. He forced himself to. There was no room for physical pain right now, as bad as it was, not when his emotional pain was so great that he felt like he couldn't function. He had no doubt that he looked like an absolute wreck, blood staining his clothes and hair and sopping wet from the pouring rain. But it didn't matter. None of it mattered. Not when Ari was dead, and certainly not when there was nothing Jesper could do to bring him back or fill the void that dominated Jesper's heart. And despite the numbness that he felt, Jesper knew that he couldn't just sit on his butt and wait around for a miracle to happen. It would be up to him to avenge Ari's death. And that meant escaping first.

He highly doubted that he would have the patience to wait for Phineas to slip up. Phineas was slow, methodical, cautious. Jesper didn't have the time or the patience for that. But, at the same time, something told him to wait, to stop and breathe for a quick minute. It was likely that using Phineas would be his only chance of escape, whether he liked it or not. And then afterward, Jesper could turn on Phineas. Make him wish he had never crossed Jesper. He would never see it coming until it was too late. Just the thought of Jesper getting his revenge made him giddy with excitement. He was going to keep his promises this time, and then he could go find Kie again and life would be perfect. *Surely Kie will come for me.* But what if she didn't have the guts to break him out? *What about Deacon, or Gen, or Ari* – Jesper cut himself off. No, Ari couldn't save him this time.

It was an odd sensation, having the dreaded realization that he couldn't rely on Ari any longer. So many years had passed that Jesper had Ari by his side as his second in command, his crutch to lean on in hard times. Who would he turn to now?

The cell door slammed shut behind him, making his stomach drop and his skin tingle with anxiety. It was going to be a long journey back to the city, and Jesper was already skittish and on edge. Every little noise sounded like an explosion in his ears, and every voice seemed to be threatening to kill him. Jesper's eyes darted from side to side, constantly scanning the hallway in front of him. He was partially convinced that something was coming for him. Something … or perhaps someone.

In a desperate frenzy, Jesper slipped his cuffed hands underneath his legs to bring them in front, giving him a little more control if something were to happen. His injured shoulder screamed in protest at the straining movement, and he took a moment to press a hand to the gunshot wound to staunch the bleeding. Jesper was going to need to find medical attention soon. *Maybe I can sneak into the surgeon's quarters and steal some supplies once I get out of this cell.* Which, again, meant escaping. He tried in vain to make his hands small enough to twist through the shackles, only injuring his throbbing wrists more.

"You're not going to be able to worm your way out of this one."

Jesper's head shot up to see Phineas strolling down the hallway towards him. He stopped twisting his hands to let his gaze follow Phineas's movements, cocking his head slightly and managing a smug grin.

"You could have loosened the shackles to make it a little easier on me."

"And make the others think I'm your ally?" Phineas hissed. Raising an eyebrow, Jesper walked up as close as he could to the bars of his cell. "I have a reputation to uphold here."

"Why'd you let my crew go, then?"

"I've always been after you, Kelsey, not your crew. They won't be any threat to me if I turn them loose. And I have what I came for, don't I?"

"What do you want, a round of applause?"

"Save it. I don't need you mocking me." Phineas waited for Jesper's spiteful clapping to die down, a tight frown tugging at the corners of his mouth. "Once we get you back to the Citadelle courts, you're going to testify that you were the one who killed my mother, stole my father's ship, and was responsible for the deaths of most of my men. Understood?"

"Do I have a choice?"

"Not really."

"Right." Jesper snorted and turned his attention back to the shackles on his wrists. Phineas simply watched Jesper work, sighing deeply when Jesper winced in pain.

"Stop doing that. It's not going to work."

"Yeah? Watch me."

"I'm watching," Phineas insisted, sighing in defeat. "There's not much happening. Other than you hurting yourself."

"I've gotten out of them before. I can do it again."

"How do I get you to stop being so stupid?"

"I'm not stupid. I'm getting out."

"Not without me you're not."

Jesper paused for a moment to glare at the commander before resuming his work. "Stop telling me what I can and can't do."

"It's called being realistic. But you have to stop fighting, Jesper. This is a battle you cannot win."

Jesper refused to believe that. There was always a way to win, even if he couldn't see the victory in that given moment. "Never in the history of my entire life have I lost a battle. And I'm certainly not about to start now."

"Jesper, stop. There's no use. It's over!"

"It isn't over until I say it's over!"

"No. I know people like you. You will never say that it's over. You would keep running and fighting until you dropped dead if you had the choice rather than lose a fight."

"Don't pretend to know me! You know nothing about me!" Jesper yelled, abruptly stopping his attempted escape from his bonds. He didn't want to admit that what Phineas said was true. Completely true. "And since when was having the guts to stand up for myself and for my crew against tyranny a criminal offense?"

"Oh, so we're tyrants now?"

"Yes! All you do is prance around in your fancy blue uniforms, keeping everyone in a neat little line. Well, guess what? Some of us don't have a choice! Some of us break the law because we have to!"

"You always have a choice!"

"Every day, I have to break the law to protect and support the lives of my crew. You think I would choose this life, always having to run and hide and look over my shoulder? You think I want this?" Jesper roared, his anger bursting.

"I get it," Phineas said, his voice soft as if to sympathize with Jesper. "You're selfless, you have a servant's heart. I too –"

"Don't even start down that road! It will only end with a blade through your heart. And don't go thinking that I have the decency not to do it."

"You're about one insult from starting a war. I'd be careful if I were you," Phineas threatened. Jesper wasn't even fazed in the slightest.

"Yeah, right. You're not like me. You could never do such a thing."

"What's that supposed to mean?"

"I thought you just warned me to watch my mouth."

Phineas seemed to hesitate, and Jesper could practically see the gears turning in his head. But the desperate scramble for a comeback was fruitless, and he settled instead on, "Stop talking."

"Did you come visit me just to argue, or is there actually a reason you're here?"

"I have to make my rounds. I had to come down here to make sure you weren't escaping …" Phineas trailed off to stare at Jesper squirming in his shackles again, "… which you are very much doing."

"And? What are you going to do about it?"

"Nothing. But you do that in front of anyone else and you're screwed, you understand?"

"Yeah, yeah, everybody here wants to murder me, I get it." Jesper snorted and casually shoved off Phineas's advice. It wasn't what he wanted to hear, so he refused to hear it. He could tell that Phineas wanted to argue with him, but the weariness Jesper saw in Phineas's eyes won out.

"Not what I said … okay."

"Did you at least bring bandages or something? If you want to put me on trial, you kind of need me alive."

Phineas took a moment to study the wound at Jesper's shoulder, the blood soaking his once-white sleeve. He sighed, passing a hand over his face before turning to leave. Jesper frowned as he watched the commander leave, the realization dawning on him that Phineas wasn't going to come back. "Wait! Where are you going?"

"I could find someone to clean and bandage the wound, but I'm not getting you out. What would I do? Even if you did manage to get out, where would you go? You're stuck on this vessel in the middle of the ocean. You're not going anywhere."

"I am not stepping one foot into a prison," Jesper hissed, launching the entire force of his glare at Phineas.

"I'm sure we can arrange something."

"Yeah? Well, for your sake, you'd better hope you can."

"Is that a threat?" Phineas's demeanor suddenly shifted, his calm and stoic expression changing to one of anger and authority. Jesper chose to remain unfazed, instead forcing a smug grin on his face.

"Maybe."

"Watch your mouth. Don't mistake my patience for friendship. And that certainly doesn't give you the right to threaten me. I can always walk away for good, and you'll be dead before the week is up."

"I don't need your help," Jesper scoffed. "Like I said, I've escaped prison before, and I can do it again."

Phineas didn't need to be told twice to resume walking away down the hallway. "Then I wish you the best of luck, Captain Kelsey. Try not to bleed out before morning."

Jesper glared holes into the back of Phineas's gold-haired head, the pit in his stomach growing with each step the commander took. He *needed* help if he even wanted a shot at escaping captivity and fulfilling the promise he had made to Ari.

"All right, all right!" There was a pause as Phineas stopped. He was waiting for Jesper's response, and Jesper didn't want to say it. "I suppose … I could use some bandages."

"That's not the same as asking for help."

"*Fine,*" Jesper spat. "I … need help stopping the bleeding."

Admitting that he needed help almost tasted bitter on his tongue. It wasn't a sensation that Jesper was used to experiencing, and he absolutely hated it. Even more so, he hated that Phineas was just fishing for such a confession. But it was the only way to stay on Phineas's good side.

"So … are you going to help me, then?"

"That was always the plan," Phineas confessed. "I'm not letting you die on my watch. I just wanted to hear you admit that you needed my help."

"Yeah, yeah, whatever. Just don't let it get to your head. We don't need to boost your ego anymore."

"Boost my ego? You're one to talk."

"Shut up." Jesper let his eyes fall to the floor, his shoulders sagging with the visible weariness he felt internally. "So, what happened to my crew?"

"I watched them leave on the dinghy, albeit shot at. But none of them looked hit, I don't think. Your lady friend didn't seem too thrilled to leave without you, but they all made it safely off the vessel."

"Don't call her that," Jesper growled, his anger tangible in the air around them. Phineas did his best to remain calm, instead taking on an attitude of amusement.

"Oh? She's not your lady friend? And what would you prefer me to call her?"

"She is part of my crew, nothing more."

"Right."

"You doubt me."

"I never said I did."

"Your face says it all."

"I'm sorry?"

Jesper opened his mouth to reply, a snarky comeback on his tongue. But his focus shifted as he heard a pair of boots coming down the stairs. Someone was coming down to check on them, and if this someone found Phineas and Jesper talking on somewhat friendly terms, they would both be in a great deal of trouble. Phineas seemed to quickly come to the same conclusion at exactly the same time, and to avoid getting caught, he slammed his fist against the cell bars and began yelling at Jesper.

"You lousy piece of filth! Utter one more word and you're dead, you hear me?"

"Is everything all right down here, sir? What seems to be the problem?"

"Problem?" Phineas perked up, turning on his heels to face the officer and pasting a smile across his face. "There is no problem at all, officer. Just making sure our prisoner knows his place. He was mouthing off to me, nothing more."

"Of course. Your presence is requested on the deck, sir."

"All right. Let's head up, then, shall we?"

The officer nodded agreeably, and the two sailors began to head up to the deck together. But just before Phineas disappeared up the stairs, he glanced back over his shoulder at Jesper. They made eye contact for a split second, that one moment filled with a million different emotions. And then he was gone, and Jesper was left all alone in the damp confines of his cell.

* * *

Minutes felt like hours, and hours felt like an eternity. Loneliness quickly became Jesper's best friend, and the only faces he ever saw were the surgeon who visited occasionally to check the dressings he had wrapped around Jesper's shoulder the other day, the guard who came by every once in a while to make sure Jesper hadn't escaped, and the cook who brought him moldy bread one time each day. Phineas avoided the cell block completely, and Jesper couldn't help but hope that Phineas was doing anything to not face the guilt of killing Ari. Jesper wanted nothing more than for Phineas to feel an inescapable sense of dread every time he saw Jesper's face. The dread that retribution was coming for him.

Jesper was sitting on the floor of his cell with his back to the wall, staring at the ceiling, when he heard the booming thud of boots on the stairs. Frowning, he moved his head to stare at the stairs. It wasn't the right time for the guard to come check on him, and he had already received his rations for the day. This time, it was someone new.

"Come on. We're going." Phineas. Jesper jumped to his feet, almost too eager to get out of the confines of his cell. He had spent too much time in there; how much time that had passed exactly Jesper didn't have the slightest clue.

"Going where?"

"We're here."

"Already?"

"What do you mean 'already?'" Phineas questioned as he unlocked the cell door. Grabbing Jesper by his shackles, Phineas dragged him out of the cell and towards the stairs. "Just come on."

Stepping onto the deck for the first time in what felt like ages, Jesper couldn't help but breathe deeply in the fresh air. Overhead, a flock of white gulls called and welcomed him, the wind pushing at his back. His hair danced playfully in the wind, drying away the rain and blood from the battle. Below him, the water was as silver in the afternoon sun. And as they neared the docks, Jesper felt an odd sense of peace. It was all going to work out. It had to.

The sailor took a deep breath as he walked down the gangplank, a smug grin on his face as he observed the place he thought he'd never see again.

EPILOGUE

JESPER

The bright sunlight flitted in through the metal bars on the window, dancing playfully on the crumpled, dirty paper in his hands. He scribbled frantically on the page, trying to finish before the guards came back through their rounds like they did every hour. The handmade pencil he used didn't work nearly as well as he would have liked, but he wasn't going to complain. It was a miracle that Jayme had managed to find him once again and was able to slip him scrap food and writing materials through his tiny cell window in the first place. That man certainly had dedication, Jesper had to give him that. For what reason, though, Jesper didn't have the slightest clue.

He had to keep reminding himself to be grateful and appreciate the little things in life, and while it certainly didn't come easy to him, he was learning. Slowly but surely.

His chicken scratch handwriting on the paper was hardly legible, but he knew that she would be able to read it. That wasn't what he was worried about in that given moment. The only glaring problem he could see was Jayme actually being able to find Kie to deliver the letter. But perhaps Jayme was better at finding people than Jesper thought. After all, he had been able to find Jesper several times. And that was a problem for another time. His brother Eirik had always told him to take things one step at a time, to focus on the next thing ahead and nothing more. So that's just what he was going to do, and he would remember to thank his older brother for it one day, if Eirik was still somehow alive.

He paused for a moment as his hand cramped up from writing so frantically. Taking a deep breath to calm himself, he quickly ran a hand through his hair to push back the strands that had fallen in his eyes before picking up his pencil once more.

I'm not supposed to be here. Groaning in frustration, he threw his pencil at the ground and put his head in his hands. He wanted desperately to rip the bars off his cell and burn this place to the ground. His breath was heavy and hot against the palms of his hands. But then he heard the sound of the guards' boots thudding on the concrete and felt the unsettling booming in his chest.

Scrambling to grab the pencil that lay on the other side of his cell, he frantically wrote down his final thoughts in a last ditch effort to reach his crew. Or what was left of it. He wanted to write down what he would need to hear, the advice that should have been given to him long ago but took him years to discover for himself. The words that she deserved to hear before it was too late.

* * *

Endings are hard. And they're messy. Nothing ever really gets tied up with a nice little bow, and the story never ends the way it's supposed to or the way you want it to. There are always loopholes, always parts of the story left untold. And there is always someone who isn't satisfied with how it all turned out. But maybe that's the whole point. Maybe, just maybe, endings aren't supposed to be a happy ever after. And maybe they're not supposed to be complete. Because endings are really just new beginnings.

A chance to start again, a chance to introduce new characters and get rid of old ones. A chance to wipe the slate clean. Friendships are broken, and family ties are strengthened. And it might be painful, almost unbearably so, but after every storm comes the sunlight. Trust me, I know from years of experience.

Keep the promises you make to others, and they will do the same for you in return. And always rely on your friends. They are the ones that are going to be there for you, through thick and through thin. They may not be your blood, but they are family. And family always looks out for each other. Even if they're separated. So don't lose hope, ever. A new tomorrow will come, even if it means that this day has to end.

Endings are hard. But they're part of the story. That's just how it goes. They are part of who we are, and that's what makes us human. And sometimes, you'll find that you end up right where you originally started, with the perfect opportunity staring you straight in the face. All you have to do is have the faith to dive in headfirst and trust that you aren't alone in this fight. Because you are never alone. I'll always be there for you, right by your side. I promise.

— J.K.

ABOUT THE AUTHOR

R. E. VAN ROSSUM is a writer and artist with a passion for character-driven storytelling and mythical worldbuilding. Originally from Illinois, she writes out of Minnesota and studies journalism and political science. When she's not writing, her favorite hobbies include collecting '80's hard rock vinyls, yelling at Formula 1 cars on the TV at 4 a.m., and exploring new cultures and foods around the world. *The Hellburner of Sovi* is her first novel. For more information, please visit revanrossum.com.

www.ingramcontent.com/pod-product-compliance
Ingram Content Group UK Ltd.
Pitfield, Milton Keynes, MK11 3LW, UK
UKHW041632190726
13854UKWH00006B/2445

9 798218 928926